THE RISING

Robert Ovies

THE RISING

A Novel

IGNATIUS PRESS   SAN FRANCISCO

Cover photograph from iStockphoto.com

Cover design by John Herreid

© 2014 by Ignatius Press, San Francisco
All rights reserved
ISBN 978-1-58617-851-2
Library of Congress Control Number 2013917063
Printed in the United States of America ∞

One

It was, as wake services go, unremarkable. Marion Klein had been a faithful wife for twenty-one years, a gracious mother for seventeen, and a genuinely loved member of the St. Veronica parish staff for nearly six. She had more than what some might consider the usual number of close friends, due both to her highly visible position as parish secretary and her natural affinity for smiling one of those smiles that surges up easily and often to signal a deep and contagious appreciation of life.

Her easy disposition was a joy not only to her husband, Ryan, but also to her children, Truman and Dawn, both teens and both the only children of a St. Veronica parish staff member not named after a Roman Catholic saint—a meaningless aside that Father Mark Cleary had rolled his eyes over in mock dismay on more than one occasion during the half-dozen good years that he and Marion worked so closely together.

Since it had been her nature to find reason to smile in what others knew must be difficult circumstances, everyone wondered how Marion would handle the spreading cancer that her doctor whispered upon her exactly three years ago this month. But as everyone who came to the MacInnes Funeral Home agreed, she handled it as well as anyone could. She fought it with chemistry and good humor until a few days into June when she finally lay too weak to walk and too toxic to pretend and let Father Mark—her pastor, employer, and friend—anoint her with the oil of a sad and quiet blessing for what Father Mark said was her peace and healing but for what Marion knew was, in fact, her death.

Now, with a thin, gray Tuesday rain sprinkling the beginnings of another humid Michigan summer and 124 friends and relatives gathered to visit and cry and smile and say good-bye to a dear friend and companion, Father Mark recalled Marion's cheerfulness and offered a prayer that she now, at last, would be completely and finally healed in God, the One in whom, for all of eternity, "Marion's joy will be complete."

He felt the loss of her company personally, and everyone knew it. It was appreciated. Then he invited others to share some memory and a number of them did, including Marion's sixteen-year-old son, who told about having to eat tomato soup and bacon at his mom's insistence every time he broke a fever, "to get salt back into my system", and how his mother's jokes had helped him through so many hard times of his own, even though he was only a teenager, and that he would really, really miss her. His thirteen-year-old sister talked briefly about carnivals and how her mom had always laughed a lot, and how that is the way she would like to be, and she would be, even though she was crying now. Others cried with her. Her dad chose to avoid speaking, not for lack of memories but from the weight of too many, too quickly passed. Ryan and Marion had been married in college, and this was a hard, hard night.

After fifteen minutes of memories, which passed quickly, Father Mark prayed his final blessing, and the service quietly ended. He shook hands with Ryan and Marion's brother, Kerry, who lived on the west side of the state but seldom visited. Dawn hugged the priest briefly and then her dad, long and hard. Nearly a hundred people came slowly up to the casket, some in pairs, to kneel beside Marion's body and make a quick sign of the cross, a few to touch her rigid hand, some hovering very near for a long moment of reflection or discomfort or both, some nodding quickly and moving on. One leaned over and seemed about to kiss her, but didn't, whispering several words instead. Most stood at a safe distance and simply stared, perhaps thinking of Marion's death, perhaps thinking of their own.

Good-nights were exchanged. Doors opened. Umbrellas were raised. Giles MacInnes and his two assistants, Dave Harmon and Giles' own daughter, Melissa, still in college and still in training, stood in black and thanked everyone for coming. They smiled, but not too much.

The mourners filed into the night carefully, as though afraid something else in their life might break. Ryan Klein finally cried, barely, and Dawn and Truman did, too. They spoke briefly to Father Mark and to Giles about the next day's service. Then it was time to close.

Melissa went to the office to note the evening's service for her files. Dave Harmon quickly straightened the chairs that had been rearranged during the service, then checked the restrooms for lost articles. He found nothing. He slipped on his coat, said good-night to Giles, and walked with Melissa to the parking lot, locking the front door behind them. Giles, by his own choice, was also responsible for final lockup. He glanced quickly around the now-silent viewing room. He had an efficient eye. The room was in generally good order. It always was. He would leave the red-padded folding chairs in place, probably too many for the morning, but better too many than too few. A black silk scarf had slipped to the floor next to the couch. His assistant hadn't noticed it. There was always something. Giles picked the scarf up with a casual sweep of his hand and placed it on the coatrack by the door, where someone would certainly see and retrieve it if they made their way back for the morning service. If not, no matter.

With that, he straightened two more chairs, glanced briefly at his watch, and turned just in time to see Marion Klein's crystal rosary slide with a terrible grace, like the world coming to an end in sickening slow motion, over the back of her rising left hand and across her trembling, rose-polished fingernails to drop with a click as tiny as death on her slowly stirring chest.

It was still raining when Father Mark got back to his rectory at St. Veronica's. He considered the old house "his" in more ways than one. He and the rectory had arrived on earth in the same year. Now they were both fifty-one, and, in their own ways, starting to show it.

He was an athlete out of training, a trim man of average build and average physical skills who spent more time reading mysteries over the past few years than he spent playing hockey, his once-favorite pastime, and who dismissed serious thought about the way his knee sometimes ached or how noticeably his short, black hair was giving way along the sides to signs of gray. In moments of doubt, he would compare himself to the rectory, with its leaking pipes and loose bricks and relentless squeaks and rattles, and at those times he would decide that he was still doing pretty well.

His parish, like his house, was small. It once had twenty-six hundred registered families, now it was down to fourteen hundred. Royal Oak's south-end commercial expansion had knocked down a lot of nearby homes. But still, fourteen hundred was a lot to handle for the young priest and his only associate, the very young Father Steve Kennedy.

He eased his dark-blue sedan into his garage and clicked the remote control clipped to his sun visor. The garage door groaned as it moved— another thing he didn't do. He made his way out of the garage into the dark drizzle and jogged across the shimmering concrete patio to the back door of the house, smiling on the way, thinking about how desperate he must have become to try and compare himself favorably to a fifty-one-year-old garage.

The kitchen phone was ringing in the dark as he unlocked the back door—an uneasy sound for some reason, a phone ringing in the pitch black of an empty room, but he didn't bother to hurry. The answering machine would handle it if Father Steve wasn't home, and he probably wasn't. Father Steve was a helpful young priest—tall, red-haired, athletic, and better-looking than anyone has a right to be, and, partly for all of those reasons, very good at working with the parish's teens and younger kids. But he wasn't around the rectory much in the evenings. If he wasn't at necessary meetings he'd be with friends or his nearby family.

Father Mark reached for the light switch just inside the kitchen door as his own voice told a caller that no one was home. Weird feeling, his own voice in the dark, saying to him and to someone else far away, "We'll be happy to get back to you as soon as possible."

He clicked on the light. No dirty dishes; thank you, Steve.

He unbuttoned his raincoat and had started toward the phone when the answering machine beeped once and the voice that he would hear every day for the rest of his life, the woman's voice, high-pitched and brittle and pleading, said, "Father! Oh Jesus! It's Helen MacInnes!"

He stopped, his hand frozen on his coat's top button, his eyes locked on the phone.

"Giles' wife from the funeral home!" Her voice was even louder now, and shaking. "I need ... please go back to the funeral home right away when you come in! Giles is in so much trouble! But the lady *can't* still be alive because he knows when someone's *dead*, for God's sake!"

Father Mark still didn't move. He would wonder, in the days to come, why he froze, whether it was because he didn't want to interrupt her message, or because he was so tired and didn't want to deal with a hysterical call after such a long day, or whether it was because the edge of terror in the words "but the lady *can't* still be alive ..." made him afraid, even then.

The caller was crying. "He's ... I don't know if he's gone crazy or what! But, oh good Lord!"

Now his mind was racing, trying to find a picture of Giles MacInnes' wife. He had met her at least twice, but only briefly. He remembered her as being thin and very tall, like her husband, only with sandy hair. And neat. And very quiet.

But she wasn't quiet now.

"I know it's impossible," she was crying, "but Giles just called me, Father, from the funeral home ..." She dropped her voice suddenly, now whispering, as though her secret was too terrible to let escape. "... and he said that Marion Klein is alive! And Giles is the one who found her!"

He was holding his breath and startled into a strange kind of detachment, like he might be dreaming or listening to a TV show left on in a distant room. But the voice that he didn't want to talk with was very near and very real, and it had just said that Giles MacInnes had found

Marion Klein alive, just now, after the service, after he had left the funeral home. But he knew that was not true, of course, because he knew that Marion Klein was dead.

The voice agreed, talking faster. "He's serious, Father, but she *can't* be alive. Only she is, he says, and he swears to God! The poor man's beside himself, and I'm going to go over there myself as soon as I can, but he's called 911, and I know you were just there, too, so I told him I was going to call you because he's calling his father in Florida, and he's crying!"

She was still crying, too, now harder than before.

The call wasn't a prank; that was the next thing he realized. Rule out kids trying to be funny. But what could possibly be going on?

"Please come back if you can", the voice begged. "Even if you get this late. Giles trusts you, and he knows that *you* know that the woman is dead. Or *was* dead." A pause, and then, "Oh God, I'm sick. I've got to get a sitter. I don't know. Please hurry, Father!"

There was a click, a pause, a double beep, and the answering machine whirred in rewind and clicked again, its red light still flashing on and off, telling the priest that someone else had called, requesting attention.

He took in a deep breath and exhaled hard. Was it really Helen Mac-Innes? On hallucinogens, maybe? Or broken down; gone crazy? He shook his head and pushed Replay.

The machine clicked and beeped, and another woman's voice spoke to him, this one soft and apologetic. "Hi, Father Mark. I hate to bother you but thought I'd better call. It's Kathy Draner, and I'm sorry, but I'm not going to be able to make the Mother's Club lunch deal tomorrow. Kid stuff . . ."

He deleted it. His heart was racing; he hadn't noticed that before. Russian roulette flashed into his mind. How many messages would he go through before Giles' wife was back?

He didn't wait long. He had to listen again.

"Father! Oh Jesus! It's Helen MacInnes! . . ."

He heard the whole message again, and then a third time. He listened to her say, "Marion Klein is alive", and, "Giles is the one who found her", and he listened to her beg him again to "please hurry, Father." He wondered for a second if the call had actually come in before the wake service took place, but realized just as suddenly that he'd just walked in on her as she was talking, just two minutes ago.

He spread his left hand over his face and rubbed his eyes. He'd have to think more clearly than that.

First of all, he knew that Marion was dead. That was that. He'd even touched the skin of her hand, and it was cold and hard, and he knew that feeling. But it was a live call, just happening, and not just kids messing around, but an older woman, someone very serious.

He snapped open the parish file next to the phone, found "MacInnes Funeral Home", and punched in the number. The line was busy. He tried a second time. Still busy. He wished Steve would come back. He pulled out the city phone book. He pictured Helen MacInnes again, staying off to the side at the funeral home those few times he'd met her, everything about her very neat, standing straight as a rope. A tightly wired lady. But if it was her, and if she was at home and hysterical, was she just flipping out or was she on drugs? Or, most likely at all, was it Giles who had taken something, after the service, when everyone had left, Giles doing some drug or other and then hallucinating and calling his wife to pass along his chemical nightmare?

MacAllister. MacBaine. MacInnes, Giles, Troy.

He punched in their home number. It was busy, too.

It was 8:56. The call had been placed just short of 8:45.

He remembered how the voice said Giles was calling his dad in Florida to tell him that a dead woman was alive again. After the wake service. After the embalming. He thought of that phone call, and he fought against a smile. *That* would be some conversation!

He tried both numbers one more time, but got busy signals again and faced it; he'd have to go back and see for himself. However he cut it, somebody needed serious help, maybe quickly, and they had called him to ask for it.

Another picture flashed through his mind: Helen MacInnes calling back in five minutes and saying in a very perky voice, "Hi, Father. Helen MacInnes here. Oh, never mind."

He tried to smile at that image, but couldn't make it happen. The voice had been too serious. Too much in pain. And what it said had been too disturbing.

He drove north on Hilton—his windshield wipers slapping in a steady rhythm, his mind tumbling through new possibilities and new questions.

Giles MacInnes was a man he'd known for a long time, and Father Mark doubted very much that the man took drugs. Which left a nervous collapse as a strong possibility. But he had seemed so calm and satisfied just a half hour ago. Which left his wife, if it was his wife on the phone; what would her history be with drugs, or booze, or nerves, or schizophrenia, or something?

If nothing else, he thought, it would make a good priest story, the next time he and his friends got together. He pictured himself in his occasional racquetball game with Ed Prus from Guardian Angels, saying: " 'And she's alive', this voice said."

He felt very nervous and wished that he didn't, and for the first time he let his mind drift toward the bizarre thought: what if Marion hadn't really been dead, hadn't been embalmed or anything, and what if she had just regained consciousness, or even climbed out of her casket and walked away? Impossible, he knew, but he wondered, what would it be like to wake up in a casket? And then he thought, I'd rather be dead than have them think I was, and wake up in a casket with cancer all through me again.

He drove through an amber light at Twelve Mile Road, the point at which Hilton changes into Campbell Lane for its trip through the pricier northern suburbs. Still light traffic, still steady rain. He turned left on Normandy toward Crooks Road, where Giles MacInnes' funeral home lay a half mile north of Normandy.

He wondered what would happen with the law if a person like that would really turn out to be alive. The coroner would have a field day, is what would happen. Somebody signed a death certificate. Fremont Hospital would be involved. She had probably been put in a morgue, where he knew the temperature was kept about forty degrees. But that would probably kill her in itself, he thought, keeping her like that over-night, which they did.

Or at least they said they did.

The light turned red at Crooks. He slowed, saw no traffic nearby, and turned right. "Lord," he whispered, "let me know how to deal with this when I get there." And that simple prayer caught his attention. It was the first time he thought to say a prayer about what he was in for, and he found himself wishing he thought about praying sooner when he or somebody else needed help. He wished it would come more naturally.

It was at times like this, just in the quick, fly-by moments when traces of what he saw as his spiritual inadequacies snapped their heads up and grinned at him, that he found himself wondering what happened to his priesthood the way he had envisioned it would be way back when he was first ordained. Back when he was still playing hockey.

Crooks Road. No traffic coming by in front of him. He paused at the red light, breathed a deep breath, the funeral home was coming up soon.

He could already see the red and blue emergency lights a quarter of a mile north, on the right-hand side. He could see the outline of the funeral home lit up red and blue, and he could see the lights bouncing across the wet, black pavement and into some bushes and up the sides of the rain-slicked trees, shaking the night with their red-and-blue worry, and he heard himself whisper a tight, "God!"

Someone had taken whatever had happened seriously enough to call for help. Not just messing around, not just calling the rectory and letting it go at that.

He gripped the steering wheel tighter. It's just somebody gone over the edge, he said to himself. I'm a priest. I've seen this before.

There was an empty red-and-white Advanced Life Support vehicle and a single, empty, gunmetal blue Royal Oak police cruiser near the side entrance to the building, all of their lights still flashing. As he turned into the parking lot a radio in the cruiser squawked at him, and then fell silent again.

He pulled past the vehicles, swung to the building edge of the parking lot, and turned off his engine. Then, clutching his unbuttoned coat tightly against his chest to protect himself against whatever was about to happen, he splashed through the falling red and blue splinters of rain toward the silent funeral home where he had prayed, not even sixty minutes before, that Marion Klein would not really die, but would live forever.

There was no motion in the foyer, and no sound. There was only Giles MacInnes, sitting on the edge of the couch behind a shining brown table with a crystal dish filled full of red and white candies in its center.

He was facing the door. He did not acknowledge Father Mark's entrance. He just stared straight ahead, like a portrait of a man dying from the inside out. He looked like he had been waiting on that same couch forever. He looked like he would never move again.

Father Mark approached the undertaker slowly, without speaking. He wondered why he didn't see the emergency medical technicians and the police. Then he stopped.

From the visitation chapel up the stairs and down the hallway to his right, from the place where he knew that the body of Marion Klein still lay, voices could be heard, and the clinking and scraping of metal on metal. And in that surrealistic moment of distant sounds, he realized that the medical technicians and the police were in the chapel with Marion Klein's body, and that they were using their life support equipment and they were not scoffing, laughing, and were not coming out quickly.

He put his hand against the wall for support. This time he whispered, "Jesus." This time he was asking for help.

Giles tilted his head at the sound of the priest's voice. He noticed him and thought about what his presence meant, and then he whispered very slowly, as though to someone else, far away, "I had to open her mouth."

Father Mark felt his legs weaken.

Right now, he decided, before his heart pounded any harder, before it became any harder for him to take a deep breath, before he had to sit down himself, he had to go and see what was causing the clinking of the metal and the murmur of the voices that came from the visitation chapel up the stairs and down the hall to the right.

He turned and moved on unsteady legs down the hallway.

And then he was there.

He saw two blue-uniformed paramedics, a Royal Oak policeman, and a stretcher in front of Marion's casket. He saw the policeman craning his neck to study the face of the lady who had been moved from the casket to the stretcher. He saw an IV stand that stood as tall as the tallest of the men, and for the second time he heard himself breathe a sharp "Jesus!"

The policeman heard the sound and glanced at the pale-looking priest. That was all. The paramedics never looked up.

Even from the back of the room he could see the clear drops of fluid dripping into the line, telling him that Marion was on an open IV, and he knew that an open IV was for a living person, not for a corpse, and he knew that it was true. Marion was really alive, or at least they thought she was alive, these men who knew how to tell. He felt a wave of weakness rush over him. He reached instinctively to hold onto the back of the nearest chair.

She's unconscious, he thought, but she's alive. It was really true, and he didn't know what to do. He didn't know what to think.

His friend was really alive. She was covered to her neck with a sheet and surrounded by equipment, all of it saying that she was alive. She was attached to oxygen and breathing it in, and to three lines of an EKG monitor, and to the IV that was dripping.

He started toward her, his mind racing, willing his body forward. Then he became aware of a voice at the front of the room saying important things: one of the paramedics talking to someone by radio, saying softly, "That's *if* she comes to."

He continued slowly, now practically shaking with questions. He wondered how she could have been declared dead in the first place. He wondered why she hadn't been embalmed, getting all the way here, to a funeral service. He wondered how he could have missed it. He wondered why she and her family had to go through all this terror only to have her wake up, and now to die from cancer all over again in another day or week, or two weeks or three. He wondered how Ryan and the kids would take this news, and realized that they almost certainly didn't even know it yet. The police and the hospital call the family when somebody dies, but would any of them think to call Ryan because Marion was still alive?

He'd have to call the family himself, he thought, just to make sure. But not yet. He reached from chair to chair and row to row, steadying himself as he went, making sure, moving closer.

And then he could see her face. She had an oxygen tube hooked to her nostrils. Her eyes were closed, but her mouth was hanging open. Mark saw two brass wires jutting out from between her lips—two twisted brass wires curving up toward the overhead lights, one from inside her upper lip, the other from inside her lower lip; two yellow wires, looking like two living things, like two blades of metal grass growing horribly from inside Marion's gums.

He remembered Giles saying that he had to "open her mouth". He felt nauseated. He felt faint. The wires had been attached inside Marion's mouth, then probably twisted together, but to do what? To keep her mouth closed? But now Giles had separated them and opened her mouth, and they looked like they were alive and growing toward the ceiling because Marion Klein was still alive.

He heard a sharp voice saying, "Yeah, 125 over 70, honest to God."

He felt like he had to sit down and did it suddenly and awkwardly, falling into the nearest chair just five rows from where the world didn't make any sense anymore.

The paramedic with the radio transmitter assured the Emergency Care physician one more time that all of Marion's indications were stable and they were bringing her in. Just ten minutes, he said.

Father Mark thought, don't let her wake up here. And not on the way to the hospital. That would be so awful!

The second paramedic and the officer gathered up medical bags and the transmitter and hurried out the door. The paramedic who remained looked grim. He nodded to the priest, finally, without words, and quickly folded a light-green blanket over Marion's body. Then he double-checked her IV and the small oxygen monitor that was still on her fingertip.

Father Mark wondered when the police officer would be phoning in his incident report, and wondered what he would say.

The technician and officer were back in a matter of seconds, moving quickly. Then the three men were on familiar ground, packing up to leave, every movement quick and professional.

Just for a quick prayer, a blessing, something, Father Mark wanted to get to Marion's side before she was taken away. It was what a priest should do, and what a friend should do. But when he tried to stand again his head was so light that he thought he might pass out, so he held onto the chair in front of him and sat down again, closing his eyes to try and pray silently.

One of the paramedics said with finality, "That's it."

They had covered her tightly with the green blanket to protect her against the rain and the night and against being caught up again in her own death. They were already wheeling her past the priest and up the aisle to the door. He did not get to touch her. He reached out with his left hand as the stretcher rushed by him and said, weakly, "God bless you, Marion", and she was gone.

Then he heard another voice cry out from down the hall, a high-pitched woman's voice that he recognized, shouting, "Giles!"

Helen MacInnes had burst in from the parking lot and come face-to-face with the medical team rushing with the stretcher toward the front door. She cried for her husband and reeled backward, hurling herself away and to one side, trying desperately to escape whatever it was that was happening to this woman and to her husband, and to her children and to her world. Her face was white and ghastly.

There was a sharp, "Excuse us, ma'am!" as the two paramedics rushed Marion passed the reeling woman and out the door.

Giles rose in front of the couch, focusing on Helen but hopelessly unsure about what he should do.

Helen began to sag at the knees, and the police officer jumped aside to support her. He held her steady by her upper arms and shot a hard glance at Giles, silently demanding help. He would not wait long.

Helen saw Giles looking at her and spun toward him, twisting free from the officer's grip, her knees firm again, her right hand reaching out, begging support.

The officer saw his chance and escaped as the whoop of a siren sounded outside.

Doors slammed. Another siren joined the first in uneven screams as the Life Support Unit and the police cruiser with their reds and blues and living but unconscious Marion Klein left to spread their high-speed panic south on Crooks Road, all the way to Fremont Hospital.

The phone in the office was ringing. It was a distant office, down the hall to the left, and with the office door shut it was a distant ring. No one moved to answer it. Enough was enough.

Helen held Giles, and they sat down together slowly on the couch like a single, heavy, aged figure. Both were crying. They were holding hands. The phone in the office kept ringing.

Helen began to rock in slow, emotional waves—slight at first, then more pronounced—and she began to cry. She gathered herself up suddenly, trying to be a strong companion to her struggling husband; then she sagged into tears again, simply rocking at her husband's side, back and forth—the helpless wife, unable to bear so much pain and confusion.

In fact, Father Mark thought, she *was* the helpless wife. And in fact, Giles was the helpless husband. And in fact, he was the helpless priest. Marion Klein had grown toxic with a raging cancer. She had stopped breathing, been examined at Fremont Hospital by competent doctors, and declared legally dead. She had been kept in a morgue at forty degrees for nearly twenty-four hours and delivered to a funeral home. She had been wired with brass wires and dressed for burial and prayed over and mourned and God only knew what else; he was afraid to think what else.

But her breathing was now regular. Her color looked normal. Her flesh was soft enough for insertion of an IV. Her blood was flowing, and she was alive.

He realized that he was crying, too.

Two

The phone call came in to Channel 3 TV from a ham radio operator in Grosse Pointe. The caller said he had monitored an emergency call from a paramedic to Fremont Emergency. He told him he had the last half of the conversation on audio and wanted to play "the hottest thirty seconds of it" for Adam Mitten, the station production intern who took the call.

Adam listened, stood up at his desk, got the man's name and phone number, and hailed George Willie, the assignment editor of Channel 3's "Action News at Eleven", as he walked away from the coffee machine, signaling him with a shout and exaggerated hand signals to get back to his office and pick up a phone call, quick.

"Adam's peein' his corduroys", George remarked to his secretary as he moved into his office. The phone was already ringing.

"Just for the fun of it?" she smiled.

The caller's name was Leon Brock. He told George he monitored high-frequency police, fire, and emergency medical calls as a hobby, and, yes, he heard one tonight that "you gotta hear to believe."

Adam showed up grinning after his jog across the newsroom. George waved him in and motioned for him to shut the door behind him.

"Turns out a funeral home in Royal Oak had a body all set to bury", Brock said. "Got all through the wake service and everything when this lady wakes up alive! Honest to God!"

George sat down and grabbed a pen. He drew a question mark on his pad, then held it up to Adam, eyebrows raised. He was smiling. "And this supposedly happened where?"

"Royal Oak. Honest to God. And the paramedic guy said the funeral home had a death certificate signed by her doc at Fremont Hospital."

Adam was pleading in an animated whisper, "Play the audio! He has the medics on audio!"

"You have an audio of all this, Mr. Brock?"

"Oh yeah, I have an audio. But I just got the last half of their call."

A secretary from Editorial knocked on the door and handed Adam a note. Brock's name and number checked out. So far so good.

"Can you play that for me now?"

"Yeah, but you gotta understand, what they said first off, before I got the recording going, was about this lady, and she was breathing through her nose, which wasn't plugged up with cotton, but they couldn't get her mouth open because it was sealed shut, like an embalmed person's, not only with the glue, but they were talking about twisting the wires the guy said were pinned into her gums, for God's sake, only she wasn't even dead!"

"I'd sure like to hear that audio", George said, sitting up straighter, now pounding the nails of his left hand rapidly on his desk. He was not smiling anymore. He glanced at his watch. If there was any story at all in this, there was still plenty of time for the eleven o'clock broadcast.

"Trying ...", Brock muttered suddenly. "Give me a second here ..."

"What's up?" George asked. He thought maybe the guy had to pour another drink.

"Just a sec", Brock mumbled without further explanation.

"What funeral home in Royal Oak?" George asked. "Did they say?"

"MacInnes. Somewhere around Fremont. Said it takes ten minutes to drive."

"Did they say the name of the lady?" He was writing "MacInnes funeral h/Fremont".

"Ready to go here", Brock announced. "Here they are."

The audio began to play. George let his last question go unanswered. He was listening hard, trying to pick out signs of authenticity.

"Any bleeding?" a voice asked. Hard to tell if that was supposed to be the paramedic or the doctor at the hospital. Impossible to tell if it was authentic. "From the pins or otherwise?" Same voice.

That could be a doctor, the one asking questions, George thought. "Just a drop from the pins", the first voice answered. "Nothing to choke her or anything. And no bleeding now."

George handed the "MacInnes" note to Adam. "Call them!" he breathed. "If no answer, find the owner at home. Get somebody to run down a police report, too. And verify a 911."

Adam was nodding as he grabbed the note and ran out.

The second voice again: "Mouth? Nasal passage?"

"Nothing. The wires and what they had in her eyes is all. She's breathing easy."

Guys are way uptight, George thought. Trying to act cool, but not feeling it at all.

Brock interrupted, talking over the audio. "She's totally unconscious. That's what they're worried about now. Can't get a response from her."

George made a note.

The first voice was saying, "Funeral guy here is really scared, I'll tell you that."

"He won't be the only one. Keep dealing with what we got."

"Right."

The voices kept talking. Numbers now. Vital signs. Pressures. Oxygen level. A running checklist, quickly covered.

George was hooked. It had that ring about it. Something had happened, and it was weird, and it was bad. He scratched staff names and directions on his pad as he listened to the maybe doctor and maybe paramedic finish their checklists and then he hit the Call button on his phone to alert his secretary. He wanted two camera vans ready just in case, the note said, one of them ready to broadcast live from Fremont, and he wanted the hospital contacted, to see what they had to say.

Adam came back. He spoke in rapid-fire whispers. MacInnes' was in Royal Oak. Nobody answering phones. They'd keep trying. He handed George the funeral director's name. "Giles MacInnes: Troy." They had tried his home, too. Babysitter wouldn't say a word, sounded scared, hung up on them. Schatner was checking out any 911 call and trying for a police report. The whole office was buzzing. What now?

"If there's a 911 on it, get the juniors with a camera and a release for this guy to sign and head them over toward Grosse Pointe now!" George whispered. "We'll get to them in the car with directions to the guy's address. Get that audio, tell 'em. Interview the guy, but keep it short. Promise him airtime. He'll give it to us if it's real. Guy can't wait."

Adam nodded and disappeared into the hall again, slamming the door behind him. "She has the Narcan", the first voice was saying. George wrote it out phonetically: nar-can.

The second voice: "You ready to come in?"

"Wrapping up."

George's secretary came back; 911 checked out. A Giles MacInnes called at 8:49 P.M. "Medical emergency" was all he said. He wouldn't say more, but he sounded like he couldn't breathe. Sounded hysterical. They still hadn't pried loose a police report, but they did respond to the 911; they had to. Fremont PR doesn't know anything about it—they say.

"Just hope you make it before she regains consciousness", the second voice was saying. "If she ever does."

George gave the secretary his "nar-can" note and waved her out. She nodded. He breathed another order just before she hustled away: "Dennis Plansker, my 11 P.M. producer; get him."

"Still stable, Doctor. We're ten minutes away."

George nodded twice, hard. It was the first time either of them had used the word "doctor".

"Can't wait", the doctor said.

Then it was Brock, back again and booming with pride. "Well?" He knew he had a hit.

George got directions to his house and told him he'd like to air at least parts of the audio "if everything checks out". Brock happily agreed he would pull them a duplicate right away. He didn't even want money for it, he said, just a mention on the news. George told him somebody would be there momentarily for just that reason. As he hung up, his secretary came back in. Narcan was a drug antagonist, often administered to offset the effects of an overdose of morphine. Which, George thought, could mean the lady was drugged, then done up to look like she was embalmed and laid out for a wake service. Which meant they might have actually intended to bury her. Which would mean, what? Insanity? Cults? Murder in the first, totally blown? "Detroit", he muttered through a sharp grin, "have we got news for you!"

Father Mark watched Giles and Helen without speaking. He was trying to sift through his experience for something appropriate to say, but he came up empty. When in doubt, he thought, fall back on the truth. "I don't know what to offer you", he said. His voice was close to a whisper. "I'll listen if you want to talk—if that'll help."

Helen's lips stretched tightly, an attempted smile. She managed a whispered "Thank you." Her wide eyes were ringed red with fear.

He decided he had to go to the heart of it. Some questions had to be put on the table. "Giles," he said, "did you ... prepare Mrs. Klein for burial?"

The word "embalm" wouldn't come out.

"No", Giles whispered, staring at the candy dish. "Dave Harmon did."

"And did Dave actually ..." Now he said it: "... *embalm* her? With embalming fluid and everything?"

"Oh Giles", Helen moaned, already exhausted.

Giles nodded but didn't speak.

Helen dropped her head on her husband's shoulder and wrapped her arm slowly around his waist.

Their pastor and friend took another deep breath and tried to think of the possible loopholes. "Giles, I have to ask you. Did you see Dave do it? Personally? Or did he do it all by himself?"

Giles understood what was happening. The priest was questioning the fact of the embalming, suggesting that Dave didn't really do what he said, just put the body out with facial prep and nothing more. He not only resented the question; he was badly frightened by it.

"She was embalmed, Father!" he insisted. He waited for a response but there was none, so he continued, talking fast. "He and I do all the embalming, but not together, and then my daughter, Melissa, helps dress if she's around, and she almost always handles cosmetics, but ..." His lips curled. He was suddenly silent again, trying not to cry.

Helen tried to force a supportive smile but just drew her lips tight once again. More tears formed in her still-startled eyes. She was stroking her husband's back.

"Do you know if Melissa saw the procedure?" Father Mark asked.

Giles turned to stare at the priest. He didn't answer.

"Because if she didn't, nobody else would have actually witnessed it. Just Dave, there by himself. Is that correct?"

"*You* saw her!" Giles shouted. He suddenly jumped to his feet.

Helen cried out lightly and covered her mouth with both hands.

"At the service!" Giles yelled. "*You* saw her! *You* can tell, can't you?"

Mark had gone too far, too fast. He tried to backtrack quickly enough to soften the edges. He was straining to keep his voice calm. "Yes, of course I did. And I know she looked embalmed to me. And I'll say that to anybody. But these are the questions people will ask, don't you think?"

"You don't take a needle injector to somebody unless they're dead!" Giles shouted, still on his feet, his arms suddenly waving. "For God's sake, Father! There are incisions to make! She'd bleed! You'd see her bleed! Do you think we're all insane?"

The shaken priest shook his head no, but he was thinking that they'd only see bleeding if Dave had actually made an incision—which was exactly the point behind his questions.

Giles was storming in half circles around the table with red and white candies—left to right, right to left. Helen was motioning desperately to him from the couch, begging him to sit down again, embarrassed by his tantrum in front of the priest, frightened by so many things.

"You'd say, 'Why is this lady bleeding?'" Giles shouted. He took even longer strides. The half circles widened. "You'd say, 'Oh look, this woman—we just scissored her carotid artery in half, but she's still alive!' You think Harmon saw her bleed and then ... what are you suggesting? He covered it up so we'd just go ahead and bury her anyway? Bury her alive? For the love of God, Father!"

Helen was sobbing, moaning, terrified. "Oh Giles. Please. Please. Please."

Giles wheeled as though he wanted desperately to move away but had nowhere else to go. He was tall and thin and rounded at the shoulders, but he looked strong now, rising up like a sword, his eyes blazing. "She had eye caps on, for God's sake!" he cried. "Her mouth was wired shut!" He wagged his finger in the priest's face and began to cry. "She'll have a trocar button in her side, too! You look and see!"

Helen jumped to her feet, then spun to face Father Mark. She grabbed his sleeve and tugged at it hard, pulling him sideways. She was sobbing.

"Oh Father!" she wailed. "Don't you believe in miracles?"

Fremont Hospital's director of Public Relations had been called at home by the director of the hospital staff, who had been called at his home by the Emergency Care director, who could recognize the difference between a curious screwup and a five-alarm medical and PR disaster any day of the week. In fact, everyone that would be most shaken by the evening's events had been contacted, including the physician and nurse who had declared and confirmed Marion's death to the medical chief of staff, Marion's own physician, her attending oncologist, the chief hospital chaplain, one of the assistants to the hospital's chief legal counsel, and the chairman of the Fremont Hospital Corporation Board of Directors.

The attending staff was as ready as it could be on ten minutes' notice. They were forced to immediate decision by a simple lack of alternatives. For the moment, they would try to focus on Marion as another incoming medical emergency—a woman with advanced malignancy and a traumatic immediate history, but who, despite normal vital signs, was unconscious and not responding to either voice or touch. She would be received as a Code Blue, level 4—a patient absent any conscious response. And that had to be their immediate concern—not the ripples of whispers and astonished "oh my God's" that were already sounding through the physician rooms and nursing stations; not the signed death certificate; not what did or did not happen in her hospital room three and a half days ago, or in the hospital morgue, or at the funeral home; not the phone calls that were even now coming in from at least one TV station, knowing what was going on and asking for permission to interview inside the hospital itself; not the size of the potential lawsuits that everyone knew would land on them if what the paramedic reported was true; not the public relations implosion this would certainly generate; not even the fact that before long the Oakland County Medical

Examiner's Office, and quite possibly the Oakland County Prosecutor's Office, would be clamoring for answers of their own.

The charge the staff members were given was this: Focus. Do not speculate. Assess the patient's immediate condition. Determine the reasons for her level condition. Ease her back to full consciousness as quickly and with as little risk as possible.

With that charge in mind, two Emergency Care Unit physicians, two nurses, Marion's oncologist, the hospital's medical chief of staff, and the director of Public Relations watched the dark-blue police cruiser and the red-and-white Life Support vehicle and their pulsing red and blue lights turn onto Emergency Drive and close in on the people who had certified Marion Klein's death, and on all the hard questions that would now have to be answered.

Giles and Helen were holding each other like orphans in a cemetery.

"I better call Marion's family", Father Mark said. He stood in front of them, sounding uncertain. He said, "Did anyone else call them yet, do you know?"

It took a couple of seconds, but Giles eventually lifted his head. "The policeman did", he said slowly. "He told the others he would. He went into my office."

The priest tried to imagine what would have been said to Marion's husband but shook it quickly from his mind. "Reporters will be coming soon", he said.

Giles didn't respond. His eyes were as flat as dimes.

Helen looked newly terrified.

"Marion's at the hospital by now, and there'll be reporters", Father Mark said again. "Five, ten minutes, maybe. I have to go to the hospital myself."

Giles nodded and returned his gaze. He was trying to focus. He whispered a weak, "Yes."

Father Mark felt sick for him. He was thinking, if a priest finds it all but impossible to accept a miraculous resurrection in Hometown, USA, how could this guy expect reporters to go for it, not to mention the lawyers that Marion's husband would be sending in with a bloodlust all their own? The guy will be roadkill. Marion Klein may not be dead, he thought, but this guy's future in the funeral home business sure is.

"You may want to lock the door behind me, is all", he said. "You can call me tomorrow if I can help or anything, but you may want to get ready now for how you're going to handle reporters. You may want to leave and go home before they come."

As he pulled away from the funeral home and headed south toward Thirteen Mile Road, Father Mark wondered what he could really do for Marion's husband, Ryan, when he got to the hospital, and the kids, of course. But what could anybody do, other than be there? What could anybody say?

The question floated through his mind slowly, without finding an answer, and then, right behind it, as though the two were strung together, Helen's darker and much more insistent question came back to mind. And this time it stayed there, without distractions, with nowhere for him to hide as he turned left in front of a slow-moving minivan on Thirteen Mile Road and began the two-mile run to Fremont Hospital. The question: "Don't you believe in miracles?"

Only it wasn't Helen that was demanding an answer now. Did he believe in miracles or not? Did he believe in real, honest-to-goodness miracles, or just in the good turns of events that the faithful thank God for and others call coincidence, which allowed everyone to stay cozy in their own beliefs because no one was ever sure?

Did he believe that Lazarus was brought back from the dead by a spoken word or didn't he? And if he did, why wouldn't he believe it could happen today? Or would handling an embalming be a lot bigger hurdle for God than handling a man that was already decomposing, like Lazarus?

He thought of all the times that he had prayed for miracles to happen, and all the pain and all the grief that went into those prayers that were never answered, not once that he could really tell, not in anything he could call a miraculous way—all the people sick and dying, the little kids, his own family members, his dad, especially, in the long good-bye of his lung cancer, and his praying and asking and begging. He thought of all the hopes gone by and a thick sadness rose up inside.

Was it that he didn't believe anymore in miracles? Or was it that he no longer believed very much in himself, and his own significant place in God's plan for things?

He was just a hundred yards east of Woodward Avenue, the last intersection before Fremont Hospital would rise up on his left like a city, when he saw the white-and-blue television station's camera van approach and hurdle past him, heading in the opposite direction. It had "Action News 3" stenciled in massive blue, red, and black letters on its side and a microwave TV communication mast on its roof. In the rear-view mirror it suddenly became two red lights shrinking into the center of a cloud of mist churned up from a rain-soaked road.

It was moving fast.

Ruth Cosgrove had anchored Channel 3's "Mid-Day Action News" at noon as well as the station's "Early Action News" at 6:00 P.M. That was enough action news for her, even if there was not much news to it. She left the station at 7:15, had dinner with friends in Southfield, and arrived back at her Bloomfield Village apartment, just two miles northwest of Fremont Hospital at 9:20.

George Willie had called her cell phone from the station at 9:35.

"Ruth, you're gonna be glad I caught you!" He didn't have to identify himself.

"Promises, promises", she said, smiling.

"How soon can you be at Fremont?"

"What have you got?"

"Can you be in the car in sixty seconds and talk to me on the way? Call me on 06."

"What have you got?" she asked again.

"I'm going to say this one time and then I need you in the car and driving, ready for a newsbreak ASAP, and ready to go live at eleven from the hospital. We just now confirmed it with Royal Oak's finest that a wife and mom laid out at a funeral home, her mouth and eyes sealed up, the whole embalming shot. They have the wake; then they find her still alive in her casket. That's what they're saying, honest to God. Last thing we heard, she's still alive, so get in your car!"

"Good God!"

"God's a good angle, yes. We can play with some raising the dead language, but the other side's the real story: major negligence, possible attempted murder, the whole nine yards. In the meantime, Roper's on the road with Alex, on their way to get the director of the funeral home on audio—if they can still catch him there. Maybe not. We'll see what he says. But you'll go live for the break and the eleven o'clock. And guess what? We're not only exclusive, as far as we know right now, but we actually got an audio of the radio call from the paramedics at the funeral home and the docs in Fremont, the medics asking what should they do, describing the whole thing!"

"Oh George, my God!" She was already moving, grabbing her attaché case, and rushing to retrieve her raincoat from the closet.

"So call me back on 06. Now go, go, go!"

"Who's the Lazarus lady?"

"Don't know, but I love 'Lazarus Lady'. Now go!"

"I'm going!" She was struggling to get her coat on and hold the phone at the same time. "Which funeral home?"

"C'mon, Ruth!"

"C'mon to where? The name!"

"MacInnes. Crooks Road, Royal Oak. Call me on o6!" He hung up before she could ask anything more.

She shuddered as she grabbed her keys from the table near her front door. MacInnes, she thought, on Crooks Road. How many people might have been buried out of there that they *didn't* find in time?

It was cool in the countryside seven miles north of Westhaven, New York, and dark in the room of fifteen-year-old Anthony Cross Jr. A single 20-watt bulb burned in the dark mahogany-paneled hallway immediately outside his bedroom door, which was never shut. A single night-light was lit beside his bed.

Like Marion Klein, young Tony slept with an IV. Unlike Marion Klein, his cancer was leukemia, now in its final stages.

The room was too big to be a young man's bedroom, and too darkly appointed, with mahogany everywhere. It had been designed as the study in the original plans for the Cross mansion, and in fact had been the study for nearly twenty-five years. But because the room faced west and overlooked both the lake on the grounds and the beauty of the rolling New York hills beyond, Tony's widowed father, sixty-nine-year-old Anthony Sr., had moved his son's bed and medical equipment into the room in early January.

Now the room was as well-equipped as most hospitals. Tony's three nurses rotated a twenty-four-hour watch. There were daily visits from Mr. Cross' personal physician, as well as periodic visits from a senior oncologist at the highly respected Long Island Jewish Hospital. Mr. Cross had spared no expense to keep his only child comfortable, and to keep them both together for as long as possible.

They were together tonight, but Tony didn't know it. While the boy slept, his father stood in front of the middle of three windows, staring out at the dark lake, turning occasionally to make sure that the nurse was still awake and that his son was still comfortable. Despite his age, Anthony Cross was thick with muscles just now turning soft. Despite his six years of virtual retirement, he still dressed every day in a dark, $1300 suit and a silk tie, usually blue. Despite losing his young wife to lung cancer six years before, he still refused to believe that medical science had done all that could be done to keep his son, Tony, from leaving him, too.

He had known power for most of his life, and he had used it freely. But now, facing this unthinkably early death of the last person left on earth that he really loved, he found, for the second time in six short years, that his utter powerlessness was very nearly more than he could bear.

He had been standing in the same spot for forty minutes when his friend, attorney, and associate in much of his life's work, which today involved holding vast sums of money in well-hidden compartments somewhere in cyberspace, came in to join him.

Torrie Kruger was the more efficient of the two. He was younger by fourteen years and crudely handsome—lean, with long, hard features and straight, short black hair parted neatly on the left side. His eyes gave the impression, not entirely inaccurate, of a person who seldom smiles. Torrie was a man uniquely capable of managing even the smallest details of time, properties, and power, but right now he was here simply to be a friend and support to his long-time employer. He had never married. He had no children of his own and no living relatives. Mr. Cross and Tony were as close as he would ever get to caring about other people as family.

"Can I get you something?" Kruger asked, knowing the answer would be no. He had visited Mr. Cross here before, by the same window, in the same, sad watch. The answer was always no.

The man with the dying son and sad eyes shook his head in the low light without speaking. They both stood side by side in silence, as they had often these last thirty days.

"It's so backwards is the thing", Cross said, finally. Kruger did not respond. He was in the habit of listening. "All backwards. That's the thing." Cross was speaking more to himself than to Kruger. Another minute of silence, then he said, "How's it get so crazy-backwards?"

The father sighed and turned toward Tony. His eyes were accustomed to the dark, and he could see his son lying thin and quiet in his white field of bedding.

They stood still for five more silent minutes; then Cross shook his head slowly and moved to the side of Tony's bed, carrying all his pain with him. It made his steps slow and heavy. The nurse sat still and waited. Cross leaned over and kissed his son on the lips. "My boy", he whispered.

Tony didn't move.

Cross straightened very slowly. "Good-night, Mrs. Hummel", he said softly to the nurse. "I'll be back sometime during the night. You'll be awake, won't you?"

"Yes, Mr. Cross." She knew he wasn't really asking. He was telling, making sure of what he could still control, just like he did every night.

"Thank you", he said.

He bent down and kissed his son again; then the two men walked slowly out of the room together, leaving the door open, and moved down the hall to the next door on the right—Cross' bedroom. Neither spoke.

Cross paused. "It should never be the son first", he whispered. His voice was thick and bitter. His head shook once with ineffective protest. He entered the dark room slowly and alone and began to swing the door closed without turning on the light. Just before the thick mahogany took him away, he whispered one more time, very softly, "I would give *anything* ...!"

Three

Seventy-three hours after she was declared dead at Fremont Hospital, Marion Klein returned. She was wearing what had been her favorite blue evening dress, now cut from just under her left arm and down her left side to just above her waist. She was connected to an IV and a pulse oximeter. She had two brass wires protruding from her mouth. She was unconscious. She was not responding to voice or touch.

Dr. Roger Jankowski's emergency assessment team consisted of himself as Emergency Care director and two other physicians—Dr. Kevin Deem, the hospital's chief trauma surgeon, who had been called from his home, and Dr. Paine Meininger, the senior cardiologist on duty. Marion's personal physician and her oncologist had also been notified and were in transit. Dr. Harold Taube, Fremont's chief medical officer, signaled Marion's dramatic status by joining the team with two attending nurses as they rushed down the hall and into room E16 through gawks and whispers uncommon to the seasoned Fremont EC Unit.

Marion's intrusion gave rise to more than professional curiosity in the growing cluster of physicians, nurses, aides, and hospital administrators who stretched to full height and squirmed for vantage point as much as professional demeanor would allow. Everyone who watched the Code Blue emergency knew that this woman would mean nothing good for any of them. She would embarrass some and break others and make life very hard for everyone in between.

The door to E16 was closed behind her. A full blood screen, EEG, another EKG and catheter would be required. X-rays; full-body CAT scan; head, chest, and abdominal MRIs; arteriography; a spinal tap; and bone scan were also readied, to be orchestrated by the attending ECU physicians.

The immediate suspicion was that Marion was still unconscious due to some combination of drug-induced toxicity, hemorrhaging, or infection. The immediate medical priority was that she not slip away from them again.

The senior nurse drew blood. Dr. Meininger prepared the EKG, Dr. Deem the EEG, and Dr. Jankowski reviewed Marion's vital signs. Her pulse was regular. Breathing: shallow but regular. Oxygen: normal. Her exposed skin was warm and dry, with no discoloration, no signs of bruise, puncture, or swelling. Temperature: 98.4. Blood pressure: 125/85.

The team relaxed a little. There was no immediate deterioration.

Dr. Taube moved in to examine the metal pins securing the brass wires in Marion's supper and lower gumlines. "What the hell was going on here?" he mumbled, expecting no answer.

The nurse took scissors to cut away the dress and underclothing and to insert the catheter. She cut the dress from her waist down and peeled it back, then stopped abruptly. "Doctors", she said softly.

"Oh my God." It was Dr. Taube again.

"What the hell's going on?" This time it was Dr. Jankowski who said it, his voice louder and even more angry than Dr. Taube had sounded.

Marion wore the oversized, white plastic bloomers with tightly closed elastic cuffs that undertakers put on their cadavers. The nurse was scissoring through them with no further comment, but Dr. Taube had already moved, holding his breath, to Marion's left side, and was staring now at the flat, orange, half-inch plastic circle embedded in her flesh approximately two inches to the left and two inches above her naval.

"Trocar button", he whispered sharply, reaching out and touching the nurse's arm. He sounded out of breath. The nurse stopped scissoring. The others stopped as well, rigid and staring.

Dr. Taube's right hand reached toward the orange circle as though he was waiting for permission to touch it, to prove that it was real, to confirm that it was actually screwed into her abdomen and not just lying there as a grim prop. It was a trocar button to plug the hole left by the undertaker's metal suction tube used to drain internal organs and body cavities, including the lungs and heart.

Dr. Taube was pale and suddenly moist with perspiration. No one spoke. The doctor's fingers probed the plastic plug. It was clearly embedded. His left hand took hold of the nurse's wrist, making sure that she didn't begin cutting away any more clothing. His eyes went slowly from the trocar button to Dr. Jankowski.

Dr. Jankowski was staring at the button and slowly shaking his head, his lips curled in a silent protest. His mind, far from wandering, was rifling through experiential data, searching frantically for answers. Suddenly he turned with a look of puzzlement and slowly pulled the collar down and away from Marion's collarbone. He had moved it exactly four inches when he froze.

A gasp sounded behind him.

"What in God's name ...?" he whispered.

The nurse drew back, her eyes wide and disbelieving. Dr. Taube was just staring, not moving. Dr. Deem stared with his mouth hanging open. The second nurse whispered, "I don't understand", and for the first time, Dr. Meininger spoke, uttering a single, softly breathed and strangely out-of-place word. He said, "Wow."

His face was ashen.

The scar they saw marked the site of a five-inch incision that had been made directly under and parallel with Marion's right collarbone. It was an uneven cut, and the wound had been sutured without concern for appearance and without normal suturing thread. Instead, her skin had been sewn together with regular no. 10 household string. It had not even been drawn tightly together, but rose up looking to the doctors to be loosely secured; it was reckless and awful.

"I don't believe this", Dr. Taube muttered.

"Do you think they actually went in?" Dr. Meininger asked.

"Making it look one hundred percent in case anybody checks her out", Deem whispered.

"Arteriography", Dr. Taube whispered. "Move the arteriography up."

Dr. Jankowski asked him, "How long ago, Harold, would you say this incision was made, as far as the level of healing goes?" Then he nodded toward Marion's abdomen. "This and the trocar button. How long have they been in there?"

Dr. Taube studied the degree of healing along the suture, then ran his finger around the skin that was already pushing up and over the edges of the orange plug in Marion's abdomen, claiming the plastic button as its own. "Four months", he whispered. "Something like that, the way they're healed over. What would you say?" He looked at Dr. Meininger, then at the others.

Jankowski was nodding his head. "Long time", he said. "But she was here, as our patient, during the last few months. Did any of you see her? Is this stuff in her records?"

"What in the hell ...?" Dr. Meininger whispered. "What ... in the bloody hell?"

To a reporter as competitive as Ruth Cosgrove, it was news heaven. She had covered "mega stories" before, but nothing close to this—whatever this really was.

The broadcast plan was simple. She would take a full thirty-second newsbreak at 9:55, five minutes before her competition's Channel 20 "First News" broke at 10:00. That would establish Channel 3's exclusive position. Then she'd be back with three more fifteen-second teasers in the next hour before she gave it both barrels at 11:00 P.M.

In a perfect world, she thought, everything would have happened an hour later and they would have broken with an exclusive full coverage story at 11:00, but three other Detroit channels were already setting up positions around her, as well as several radio stations. The rest would be here in minutes. But while they all had word about the 911 call and the Life Support radio conversation by this time, as well as access to the police report, none of them had the actual paramedic/doctor call on audio like Channel 3 did; Ruth felt certain of that. Put that audio together with what she was gathering from the paramedics and medical and support staff members here at the hospital, and Ruth would have enough exclusive grit to curl the average Detroiter's socks.

The time in news heaven was 9:53, two minutes to Ruth's first news-breaker alert, and she was already in place, feeling the rush. They would intro for five seconds, then cut to her live. Her name would be super-imposed, along with "Fremont Hospital, Royal Oak". A graphic would show viewers the blinking "Channel 3 Newsbreak Exclusive" visual, while Ken Brooks, back at the station, would introduce her.

One minute to go. Her hair was fine. No other cameras looked ready around the other news vans, the ones that had just gotten there, with everyone still hustling like mad. Their camera operators and reporters saw Ruth ready to go on now, wondering how much she had, knowing she had the jump, wishing they were her. It was the greatest feeling a reporter could have, and she was drinking it in. Adrenaline pumping. Ready to go.

Thirty seconds. She took a deep breath and cleared her throat and rehearsed her first few words out loud. "'Action News 3' has learned exclusively ... exclusively ..." Another clearing of her throat. "'Action News' ... 'Action News 3' ..." The lights went on. Counting down: 4 ... 3 ... 2 ...

Her in-ear receiver picked up the station announcer's lead-in. "And now, from Ruth Cosgrove, live at Royal Oak's Fremont Hospital, this exclusive 'Channel 3 Action Newsbreaker Alert'!"

Suddenly she was everywhere in southeastern Michigan and southern Ontario, Canada, talking fast and loud: "'Action News 3' has learned exclusively that a local woman declared dead at Royal Oak's Fremont Hospital on Saturday evening, and reportedly *embalmed* yesterday at a Royal Oak funeral home, was found *alive in her casket* just one hour ago! Some are calling this 'Lazarus Lady' a miracle of biblical proportions, but others call her the victim of probable criminal negligence or much worse. As prosecutors, medical examiners, and police investigate, the rest of us are left to ask, how can we can be sure that the same thing hasn't happened to any of *our* loved ones ... without being discovered in time? Hear the actual voices of the Life Support Unit as they make their shocking discovery ... *only* on 'Action News 3' at eleven!"

C.J. Walker, whose name was Christopher Joseph but who never heard himself called "Christopher", let alone "Christopher Joseph", although his dad called him "Ceej" sometimes, was nine years old and alone with the TV in his living room in south Royal Oak. His mother, Lynn, was upstairs, putting laundry away. His father lived somewhere else. His mom and dad had gotten divorced, he told his friends, when he was just a little kid. It had already been over two years, but he could remember it, easy.

When he saw Ruth's announcement, the boy knew that she was talking about Mrs. Klein. He knew Mrs. Klein was a friend of his mom's from church. He knew her kids, too, because he was in the fourth grade at St. Veronica's school and he had seen them around St. Veronica's High, which was right across the street from the grade school. He even knew who the dad was, Mr. Klein, because C.J. had just seen him and the kids crying at the funeral home, where his mom took him right after supper so she could say good-bye to her dead friend and tell Mr. Klein and the kids that she was sorry and that she really loved Mrs. Klein, too.

Ruth's face disappeared into a commercial for Detroit-area Ford dealers, but C.J. stared after her. He had heard Father Mark pray for Mrs. Klein at the funeral home. He had seen the visitors cry and Mrs. Klein dead in a blue dress in her casket under a picture of her family that showed when she was younger and the kids were about as old as C.J. was right now. He wasn't scared when he saw her because he saw both his grandmothers when they were dead, and Steve Luccini, who drowned last winter in the pond at the golf course, and seeing dead people didn't scare him. He had even leaned over and whispered to Mrs. Klein while his mom was talking to her husband at the other end of the casket, but now he wished he hadn't. Now he was scared.

An old announcer with a red tie was telling him that he had a friend at Frankheart Furniture.

C.J. picked up the remote and switched off the TV. He put the remote on the table in front of the couch, pulled his knees up to his chin, wrapped his arms around his legs, and stared at the dark monitor with wide eyes, not moving.

He sat like that for nearly fifteen minutes, until his mom came down the stairs and into the living room, humming.

Lynn Walker was thin and athletic, with short-cropped, dark-brown hair, and wide, brown eyes and a full lower lip that, as at least a few of the men she had casually dated over the last several years had remarked, made her look French. Although she wasn't. She was English and Irish. And right now, she was curious. She had come downstairs to tell C.J. it was time to hit the sack and found him staring at a dead TV, then turning to stare at her.

She knew the look. He looked guilty. And it wasn't because he had his feet on the couch.

"Is that a good show, the screen blank like that?" she tilted her head and gave him a smile. She added, "What'cha been doing, hon?"

C.J. didn't answer. His eyes went back to the dark TV.

She sat down beside him. Her son's large, dark eyes, which Lynn had once described to Nancy Gould, her best friend and look-alike, as being "incredibly capable", were not looking capable now. In fact, she realized, he looked more than guilty. He looked scared.

A tremor of concern ran through her. C.J. had been in too much trouble over the last few years, ever since she and her ex-husband, Joe, separated. Nothing malicious or criminal, really, but angry things. Fights with the other kids. Arguing with teachers. Letting his language run away with him in ways he knew was wrong. Not often, but it was there—the hurt under the surface that would not go away, the hurt and the anger.

"What's the matter, babe?" she asked. "Tell me." She reached to turn his head toward hers, then rubbed her hand lightly through his short brown hair. "Something happened. Was it something on TV? Tell me what's wrong."

Suddenly the phone on the coffee table beside the couch rang, making Lynn jump. "Jeez!" she exclaimed, trying to lighten the moment. "Scare me much?" She was still smiling as she snatched the receiver, but her eyes never left C.J., who hadn't seemed startled and was not smiling at all.

"Hello?"

Nancy Gould bypassed the usual, second "hello" to shout, "Lynn, can you believe this? Oh sweet Jesus!"

"Believe what?" Lynn asked, suddenly sitting upright.

"Oh my Lord, Lynn! Didn't you just see Channel 3, and then the ten o'clock news on 20? Oh my Lord, girl! Burr, get the audio ready; they'll have more at eleven!"

Her friend was actually crying, Lynn realized, crying and then laughing, not knowing which to settle on.

"What, Nancy?" Lynn asked sharply, suddenly knowing that Nancy and C.J. had seen the same thing, only it had scared C.J.

"Lynn, it's on TV! Somebody's alive at a Royal Oak funeral home and Channel 20 just said it was Marion!"

Lynn leapt off the couch. Her color drained. Her mouth dropped open. She wheeled to look at C.J. and saw tears gathering in his eyes, so she sat down beside him and reached awkwardly to grab his hand. She mouthed, "It's okay", not letting go of C.J., not taking her eyes off his eyes.

Over the next few minutes, Nancy poured out her precious few details with a string of "Praise God's" and other exclamations bordering on hysteria.

When she hung up, Lynn was trembling.

C.J. sat watching her, still not speaking, still afraid, only now Lynn knew why. And now C.J. wasn't the only one who was afraid.

Lynn wanted to speak but she couldn't. Questions tumbled through her mind. What did they do to Marion? Why did they think she was dead? Wasn't she, the way she looked at the funeral home? Did she feel anything when she woke up? Was she feeling anything now? Was she really going to be okay? Isn't she still going to die from cancer anyway? Do they make this kind of mistake all the time?

"Is that what you saw on TV, honey?" she finally asked in a heavy whisper, her left hand reaching out to gently hold her son's left shoulder, her right still holding his hand. "Were they saying things about the funeral home?"

She realized that her voice was still shaking, even at a whisper. She knew C.J. could hear it, too.

C.J. nodded slowly, and Lynn's heart broke the way only a mother's can. The poor kid had been so afraid and was even afraid to tell her, and she felt so bad about it. She slid her hand from his shoulder and eased it around his back, pulling him closer.

"And now they're saying that Mrs. Klein isn't really dead, after all, huh?" she said. She didn't want to show tears in front of him, but hearing herself say the words out loud made it happen. She couldn't help it. It was all so insane, and it was so close to home.

C.J. watched her begin to cry. He still didn't speak. He still didn't move.

"Why didn't you tell me they said that, honey?" Lynn asked.

No word. No gesture. No change of expression.

She thought, God help him; the kid's really traumatized.

She whispered, "Oh C.J., honey. Come on, now." Her voice sounded a little more steady, so she tried it again. "It's okay, whatever happened." She paused and forced a light smile; no more crying. She said, "Wow. It really is incredible, though, don't you think?" Then she put her other arm around him, and, moving even nearer to him, hugged him. She didn't really know whether hugging was still okay, or whether this boy that wanted to be a man would rather shake hands now, or get a punch in the arm, but C.J. let it happen. He didn't raise his arms to hug her back, but he let it happen.

"It's like a movie, isn't it?" she said, easing away from him once again, lowering her head, looking into his eyes, her hands back on his shoulders, resting easy. "It's *scary*, too, isn't it? I mean exciting scary. But is it scary for you, too?"

C.J. shifted slightly.

The phone rang again. This time, C.J.'s eyes shot open wider and he stiffened.

"I think it's scary for me", Lynn added quickly, reaching for the receiver one more time. "I think it's kind of scary for all of us."

A man's voice answered her, sounding high and excited: "Tell me you heard about Marion Klein!"

It was Joe, the man she'd divorced after she caught him for the second time with a gushy little note in his pocket signed by someone he was enjoying on the side. She had worried for months that the affair had really been her own fault somehow, even telling herself that Joe had kept the note so she'd find it and rescue him. Then one day, for no apparent reason, she was absolutely certain that it wasn't her fault, that he got the action on the side because he liked the excitement of the hunt more than he loved her and C.J., that he kept the note because at heart he was a cavalier jerk who never grew up and just didn't think about throwing the note away, and that even if she did rescue him he'd go find somebody else the first chance he got, because Joe didn't really want to be married.

Just like that, she was certain. And just like that, Joe was gone.

Still, they kept in regular touch, largely for C.J.'s sake. And, in fact, there were things about him that she was still at home with. Not enough to make a new life together even close to possible, but some things.

"Yeah, I did hear", she said. "I'm not sure I believe it, though."

"Tell me that doesn't blow you away!" he laughed. "God, they're gonna shred that undertaker." Another laugh. "And the hospital. Did you go to the funeral home?"

"Yeah. But there didn't seem to be anything unusual. I mean, it's so creepy, because she looked dead. You know how they always look?"

"This is so unbelievable!"

"But whatever happened, happened after we left, Joe." She noticed C.J. perk up at his dad's name. "So I don't know what to tell you. But C.J. and I are pretty upset, if you know what I mean. And he's right here."

"What are you saying, Lynn? You took C.J. to the funeral home with you?"

There was a sudden edge in his voice and she didn't like it. She'd heard it before, his getting protective about C.J., now from three miles away.

"I don't think you want to get into that", she said.

"The Kleins are nothing to C.J., Lynn", he said sharply. "And nine-year-olds are okay to leave home for an hour, you know?"

"I told you, nothing happened. But we're both really thrown by the news, if you're listening to what I'm saying for a change. C.J. is right here, and we're both pretty upset."

"Well, what the hell's going on with her, do you think?" Joe wanted to get back to his own subject.

"You know more than I do, Joe," she said, suddenly sounding bright and forceful, "but yeah, C.J.'s right here and he'd like to talk to you, too. 'Cause we're really having a rough time with this, him and me. Did I tell you that? So here he is now."

She handed the phone to C.J. and pressed her jaw tight and hoped.

C.J. took it without expression. He listened. He said, "Mm hmmm." Several seconds went by. He said it again, softer: "Mm hmmm." Five seconds more, and then a soft, "I know."

Lynn was relieved. At least Joe was talking to him, saying *something*. She rubbed C.J.'s back and waited. Another ten seconds went by.

"I know", the boy whispered again. Then he raised his arm slowly, gave her the phone, and looked at her with dark eyes that were still afraid.

She paused with the phone at her chin for several seconds, wondering whether to probe the conversation that just took place. She decided against it. She just said, "I better go."

"He's really in space, isn't he?" Joe asked. "I'll have to deal with it. I'll get in touch tomorrow, okay? Or call me if you hear anything in the meantime, would you?"

"Yeah, I'll call if there's even more you can do to help", she said, then hung up.

At 10:25 P.M., Fremont's director of Public Relations, Ms. Diane Whitney-Smith, invited the patient's husband and two children, as well as their pastor, Father Mark Cleary, to move from ECU's conference room number 3, where they had been waiting, into the more comfortable physician's lounge on 4 East, directly around the corner from the Intensive Care Unit. She apologized that they could not see Mrs. Klein just yet, but assured them that she was stable, although still unconscious, and that her initial evaluations would be concluded soon. At that time, they expected to move her into ICU, where the family could not only see her but stay with her as long as they liked.

At 11:00 P.M., huddled in the conference room, the small group watched the anchor of Detroit's Channel 8 late-night news fairly shout the entire story. He was followed by a short list of station-picked "experts" who weighed in with ethical, medical, and legal opinions. One of them, a short, gray-bearded Jesuit priest from the University of Detroit, reminded viewers of the reality of miracles. Two others, a representative from the Oakland County Medical Examiner's Office and an assistant prosecutor from the Oakland County Prosecutor's Office, hinted at much darker possibilities and promised what they agreed would be "an immediate and unrelenting investigation".

The group did not hear the intercepted audio that Ruth was playing on Channel 3.

At 11:25, Dr. Jankowski, who had spoken to Ryan and the kids earlier, came in to introduce the hospital's chief medical officer, Dr. Taube, who extended his large hand and smiled at them with tired eyes.

"What we've come in to tell you is good news", Dr. Taube said. "It will be made public within the hour."

The family braced themselves.

Dr. Taube inhaled, smiled broadly, although somehow mechanically, and said, "The fact is, while Mrs. Klein is still unconscious—and that condition is still a matter of critical concern, we don't want you to doubt that—but at this time we can find no evidence of drugs, infection, or internal bleeding, cerebral or otherwise."

Ryan whispered, "Thank God."

"Beyond that," the doctor said, looking grave, "I'm here to tell you that we find no evidence, at least not to this point, of her malignancy. Blood, liver, nothing yet. At this point, we can't find it."

Dawn let out a soft, "Wow!" and rose to her feet. Truman was stunned, sitting motionless. Ryan's eyes filled with tears. He whispered, "No sign of her cancer?"

Both doctors shook their heads. No sign of her cancer. "She's in remission," Dr. Taube said, "and it appears to be complete."

Ryan's lips twisted as he reached to grab his daughter's hand and looked helplessly at his son, whose lips were also twisted by the sudden, silent shock of a promise too deep for words.

Father Mark rose to his feet slowly, his heart racing. "Was she really dead?" he breathed.

No one heard him.

He said it louder, this time looking at the doctors. "Was she really dead?" But Ryan had thrown his arms around the doctor and was laughing loudly, letting out all of his tension and grief and shock in a sudden, giddy outburst—his head thrown back, his eyes wide and filled with tears. Beside him, Dawn and Truman were jumping and clapping and crying and laughing out loud, too.

Lynn Walker didn't hear C.J. sneak into her bed shortly after 3:15 A.M., but she did hear him breathe several deep sniffles ten minutes later. She heard him the first time from very far away, it seemed, and although the sound was small and strangely mixed into a dream about a fat man who was applauding, for some reason, near a graveyard that Lynn remembered being near the railroad tracks when she was a young girl in Columbus, Ohio, the repeated sound of C.J.'s sniffle was so familiar to her that she not only recognized it but realized that it was coming from just a few inches away from her ear.

The graveyard faded. She opened her eyes and turned to find her son nestled close to her side, something he had not done for a long time.

She turned her head to glance bleary-eyed at the clock, then moved to inch her arm across the boy's waist in a lazy and gentle embrace. "Let's just go to sleep together, honey," she whispered softly into the dark, not knowing if he was awake or asleep, "and tomorrow it will be better; I promise."

No answer.

"I'm glad you came in, though", she whispered.

C.J. still didn't respond, but he felt warm to Lynn in the dark, with her arm snuggled close around him in a way that he seldom allowed her to snuggle anymore. He felt so warm and good to her that in a matter of seconds she felt her deep sleep returning softly to steal her vision and carry her away in the dark.

C.J. waited. He heard his mom breathing more deeply and more slowly. Then he turned his face toward her in the dark and lay very still for a long time, very still and very close, staring at the familiar eyes and lips and the hair that was traced by moonlight in such soft lines on the pillow beside him.

Once, nearly thirty minutes later, he felt Lynn stir. It surprised him and he held his breath, not wanting to wake her up. But she was still asleep.

Clouds drifted over the face of the moon, sealing the room in darkness for what felt to C.J. like a very long time. Then they drifted away again, and he watched the soft moonlight reach through the venetian blinds like fingers. The fingers drew lines that glowed across the foot of his mom's bed and across the floor all the way to her dresser. He watched the lines, and he thought again about Marion Klein and about what the announcer on TV had said—especially about the criminal part, and the police.

Then, in the darkness, in the middle of the night, to the woman who slept beside him and to whatever else might be there, listening in the dark, C.J. Walker whispered, "*It was me!*"

Four

Dennis Henry, chairman of the Fremont Board of Directors, sat at the head of the conference room's twenty-four-seat cherry wood table and informed his three associates that their 6:30 emergency meeting would, indeed, begin on time. A former automotive executive, the sixty-year-old Dennis prided himself on his full head of still-thick brown hair, his administrative efficiency, and his full range of life experiences. He had bragged to hospital staff members on more than one occasion that he had, in his forty-one professional years, "seen and done it all". He was about to learn that he hadn't.

On his right was Harvey Bailey, one of three associate legal counsels for the Fremont Health Care Corporation. Harvey was a trim forty years old, impeccably dressed and impeccably prepared.

On Harvey's right was the weary, but willing Diane Whitney-Smith, dressed in a dark-brown, pin-striped suit. She had been too keyed up to get any sleep the night before, but she was ready.

Across the table from Diane was Dr. Harold Taube, a formidable presence in any meeting, but dominating in a meeting as compact and medically driven as this one. The doctor had come in armed with three hours of sleep plus a quarter-inch pile of notes, records, and photographs stuffed into a single manila folder. He looked dark with questions. He didn't drink coffee. He didn't care for small talk. He wanted to begin.

So they did.

"Thank you for rolling out early on this one", Dennis said, repeating what he'd already said to each of them individually. "We're going to cut right to the chase." The others nodded. "Mrs. Klein is still unconscious, it seems." He glanced at Dr. Taube, who signaled agreement by simply closing and opening his eyes. "And the TV news, I'm sure you're aware, has dubbed our patient 'the Lazarus Lady'." With that, the chairman stopped. He stared at his own notes, then tapped the eraser end of his pencil on the table several times—a muted gavel. "So, Harold", he said sharply, glaring at Dr. Taube, "What exactly do we have here?"

The doctor took a measured breath as his large hand peeled open the folder on the table in front of him. "Medically speaking", he said, "we have a remarkable situation. The questions still up in the air are remarkable, too, and I'm afraid we're a long way from having all the answers."

Dennis leaned back into his chair, his hands settling into his lap. Not what he wanted to hear.

"Mrs. Klein is still unconscious, as you say, Dennis, although she's now showing distinct response to both touch and voice, as of 5:00 A.M. That's one reason I'll move through what we have quickly and be on my way."

"That's the other new tack the media's taking", Diane injected. "The city's on a vigil. Everybody wants to hear what the Lazarus Lady will say when she wakes up."

"Her lawyers will be first in line", Harvey remarked quietly.

"What I'm going to make you aware of now is in strict confidence", Dr. Taube said. "And I emphasize 'strict'. We don't need any more hysteria."

The hint that there might be new reason for even more hysteria shot a nervous pulse around the table.

"I assume you've heard that the patient is experiencing what appears to be a dramatic remission", the doctor began. "It's already leaked to the news, and we'll be confirming the fact of it, if not the detail, in some way at this morning's news conference. From what we see, her tumors are gone, enzymes normal, toxicity negative, the whole nine yards. Apparently a complete and immediate remission. We don't say 'miracle', but we do say 'remarkable'. No doubt about that, not with this lady."

Dennis had been alerted about Marion's remission, but it still struck him hard to hear the doctor make it so official. He stared, wide-eyed.

"That's number one."

The three reacted again with slight movements, tense and uncomfortable. Dr. Taube withdrew eight Polaroid photographs from his folder and fanned them out like playing cards on the table in front of them. Everyone leaned forward for a closer look.

The first two photos were close-ups of Marion's incision, string-sutured through a five-inch scar just below her collarbone. The next three were close-ups of the late-night procedure to remove the string. Next was a close-up of the orange "trocar button" she arrived with, virtually screwed into her abdomen. And the last two: their procedure to remove the bright plastic plug.

"This is how we found her", the doctor said. "The incision here, with the string pulling it together, this is what an undertaker does. You may or may not be familiar with it."

Harvey sounded their common confusion. "You mean an undertaker actually *did* cut this woman?"

"As though it would be an actual embalming, yes. It looks crude to us, and it is crude, but no one sees it, is the whole thing, not with a real embalming. Just the undertaker and whoever dresses her. They make the incision you see across here; four, five inches, and then they go down through the muscle into the jugular vein and common carotid artery. Some go into the femoral artery, too, but this is standard, right here. They tie-off the artery and the jugular. They sever them three-quarters of the way through so they can put a tube in and drain the blood out; then they use the same incision to inject their embalming fluids."

Dennis snatched up the first photo. "Are you saying this woman was or was not actually embalmed?"

"She obviously couldn't have been embalmed", the doctor answered, still hurrying his words. "Embalming fluid is 'sclerosing', which means it destroys the circulatory system, plugs everything up, nothing flows anymore. So I think we can agree that no living patient has actually been embalmed."

Dennis sat down again, agitated and impatient. He stared at the picture of the surgical procedure and the string, and he saw lawsuits and doctors' resignations, forced or otherwise, and a great hospital's reputation cracking and perhaps even sinking, with himself alone at the downward helm.

"What's the orange thing?" he asked.

"It's called a trocar button. In an actual embalming, a thin metal tube is used to drain the internal organs and cavities, including the lungs, heart, stomach, intestines, and so on. Not pleasant to think about, but it's inserted through the abdomen to poke into everything and drain it, and then, and when the procedure's done, this plug is put into place to seal the opening. Usually the 'button', as they call it, is yellow; sometimes it's orange."

Dennis stared at the doctor, his words failing.

Dr. Taube moved slowly to take the photo from Dennis' hand. "Some other things to point out, other questions. The scar you see here under her collarbone? Look at it again, the level of healing. That kind of healing takes at least three to four months is our guess. That's been healed on her for a long time."

"But it's still got the strings in it", Diane said.

"But it's still got the strings in it", Dr. Taube repeated. "If you ask what's happening here, I really don't know. Her skin has healed over the trocar button, too. Look there, at the edges, where the flesh has already closed over the rim. It's healed there."

He stopped and began biting his lip and staring at the photos as though he hadn't really studied them before. One more time, he felt the level of their alarm being raised.

"Not only is the scar healed over, but no one claims to have seen it before last night", he said, not wanting to go too fast for either himself or his colleagues. "Not while she was here at the hospital over the past few weeks. Not the past few months. Not even as recently as a day or two ago." He paused, giving the situation time to sink in. "What can we say? Doctors. Nurses. We asked everybody who dealt with her. Candy-stripers. Aides. Her X-ray techs. Her own husband says he never saw this before. But it's been there healing for months and months. It had to have been."

His hand reached out again, this time slowly, finding the photo of the trocar button. "Same with this", he said. "No one's seen this plug before; they swear it. Right there in her side. And it had to be healing around it for three, four months at least."

The silence pressed on them thick with tension for a full ten seconds.

"Are we talking miracle here?" Dennis finally whispered.

Dr. Taube said, "We're talking facts, I hope; being members of the Fremont Hospital rather than the Fremont Metaphysical Center. And those are just some of the facts." He paused to pick up and study another of his sheets of paper, then said, "I have more."

The chairman began to drum his pencil. "Just go from A to Z for us, Harold, for Pete's sake. Everything that's left, one top-to-bottom run. Please."

The doctor nodded. "Just three more points. For now."

"For now", the chairman muttered.

"Number one, we have arteriography on this lady, taken last night, and her carotid artery actually does appear to have been severed. Although, again, it was some time ago. Healed now, but scarred from whatever, whenever ... we don't know."

Dennis shook his head and looked sharply away. They heard him mutter, "Holy God!"

Diane shook her head slowly.

Harvey said it softly, sounding awestruck. "And the hits keep on a'comin'."

"Number two, we performed an endoscopy and colonoscopy last night. Dr. Chapman was called in. The fact is, there are multiple puncture wounds in the woman's stomach. They're distinct. And, again, guess what? They look to be old. They're well healed. Two to four months, we both agreed, and they appear to have been puncture wounds from

44

something about as big around as your little finger. A dozen of them in the stomach alone."

Three mouths opened without speaking. It was like a horror movie, getting more terrible with every scene.

"MRI shows similar wounds in her heart, her lungs, kidneys, bladder, all through her abdomen. All of them healed over. Maybe eighty, all told. And that's just what we could find."

Harvey and Dennis said it together. "Eighty?"

"A lot of them."

"The trocar rod?" Diane asked.

"At least consistent with a trocar rod. We can say that. We don't know it as a fact, though—yet."

"And consistent with the trocar", Harvey whispered.

Dennis said, "Get to the third thing."

Dr. Taube seemed to be studying the first picture of the trocar button. He spoke very slowly, even distantly, as if the outrageousness of what he had just said was sliding him into a kind of daze. "We have to keep this woman here", he said. "We have to keep her until she or her family lets us explore her surgically."

"Get to it, Harold. For God's sake."

"About the trocar rod, and knowing it for a fact. We targeted the second round of MRIs, and it looks like there may be metal tracings, microscopic stuff, but tracings at a number of these puncture points. Listen to me now. They'd very likely be recent, if the scan can pick them up that way."

"And?" Dennis asked.

"And if we scrape them, and if we can analyze them, and if they prove to be identical to the metal in an undertaker's trocar rod ... well ..."

"Do you realize what you're messing with?" Diane asked breathlessly.

"We have to keep her here", the doctor said.

"Are you, then, are we ... talking a miracle?" Dennis asked.

The doctor let his sheet of paper float to the table. He said, "Then, Dennis, we are talking all hell breaks loose."

Father Mark had crawled into bed exhausted, shaken, exhilarated, and bewildered at nearly 4:00 A.M. He did not think to reset his alarm. It went off, as usual, at 6:30, just in time to get him up for his turn at 7:00 Mass. He slept through it.

At 6:40, his young associate, Father Steve Kennedy, came in to shake him. Steve looked even younger than his early twenties, like a tall college sophomore, and very Irish with his fair skin and light-red hair and thick eyebrows raised over dark eyes that laughed easily but were now wide with questions and the thrill of a new and sensational hunt.

"Mark?"

One eye opened. The room was already light from the sunrise, but the eye stared at nothing and shut again.

A slightly harder shake this time. "Mark? Do you want me to take the seven o'clock Mass for you? I can do that. But you've got people waiting for you, man. I'm sorry."

Both eyes opened. Father Mark squirmed. "Is she conscious yet?"

"Not that they're saying. You awake?"

"Is she still alive?"

"That's what they're saying. You want me to get a coffee up here?"

"What time is it?" He was too tired to roll over and look at the clock at his bedside.

"Almost seven. I'll take the Mass, but you've got one phone call you may have to answer." As if on cue, the phone rang downstairs. "That's about call number ninety-two."

"What else on Marion? Anything at all?"

"You know more than I do. They're saying on the news this morning her cancer is gone. You hear anything about that? Their news conference isn't for another hour, and they'll tell what they know then."

"That's what they told Ryan last night."

"*Major* stuff. That's fantastic."

"It gets your attention."

"You gotta tell me about it, okay? At least, tell me the deal on 'was she dead?' And the embalming and all?"

"That'd be good, if you'd take the Mass", Mark said as he swung his legs over the side of the bed and sat upright in his T-shirt and boxers. He noticed his pants and shirt crumpled on the floor. He still had his black socks on. "I'll come down for the coffee. I've got to take a shower and get back there."

"Was she was really dead, though?"

"I can't say for sure. I really can't. Who's the call I've got to return?"

"Monsignor Tennett, calling for the boss. Wants you to call him back right away. Actually, he told me to wake you up so you could call his room at the seminary before he leaves. Can't imagine why, right? But I better go now."

Father Mark nodded. Monsignor Tennett was director of the archdiocesan Curia, which meant he was the diocese's head priest, after Cardinal David Schaenner. As such, he was Cardinal Schaenner's eyes and ears and mouthpiece, especially where things both public and controversial might be concerned.

Father Steve was halfway through the doorway when he stopped and looked back. "Mark?"

"Yeah?"

"Please. About, was she really dead? I understand you can't say for certain, but just, what do you think? You, personally? Did she really rise from dead, do you think?"

Father Mark stared at the young priest for a long time, surprised by his own need to remain undecided. Here he was, a fifty-one-year-old man sitting in his underwear and socks and having to go to the bathroom and having less than three hours of sleep and somebody had just asked him if he thought a woman that he had prayed for not twelve hours ago had literally been resurrected from the dead, and the word "no" wouldn't even come out.

After nearly ten seconds, the bewildered associate breathed a very soft, "Wow", turned slowly, and, with one more wide-eyed glance back at his fellow priest, started quietly down the stairs.

Lynn Walker's eyelids quivered against the early morning light. She made another effort. They quivered again and opened halfway, slowly. It was too early. The alarm hadn't even gone off, but it had stopped raining sometime during the night and the sun would be out today. Her mind was struggling to clear.

When it did, she remembered the night before. Her eyes popped open. Her heart raced. Her head snapped several inches off the pillow to face the terrifying questions that shot up suddenly before her, looming like towers. Was Marion Klein still alive? Had she regained consciousness? Had she really been dead in the first place? What really had happened last night, anyway?

She realized she'd have to turn on the TV right away and maybe call Nancy Gould before she went to work, to see if anything happened during the night. Then she remembered that C.J. had come into her bed.

She turned over carefully, feeling his arm against hers as she did, knowing that he was still there, trying now to be very quiet so she wouldn't wake him up. But she saw that his eyes were wide open, too, waiting to meet hers, and it startled her.

"Oh honey", she whispered. She was smiling, but C.J. just stared at her with his wide child eyes still filled with fear, and her heart sank. She remembered it all. He had gone to bed scared to death by the whole Marion Klein thing, and he was still scared.

She nestled all the way over onto her right side, settling close. "I'm glad you came in last night. Did you sleep okay once you were here?"

He looked exhausted.

Oh, no, she thought. If he didn't sleep, the poor kid would be a mess all day.

She moved to take his cheek in her open left hand, holding his attention while her right hand wrestled its way gently under his head. "You were awake a lot last night, weren't you?"

He shrugged his shoulders slightly and nodded. Just once.

She tried to read his eyes. What did he want her to do? What should she be saying?

"You know, we still have a few minutes till the alarm goes off, if you want to talk. Or do you want to just lie here quiet for a while?"

C.J.'s lips suddenly shuddered. He pressed them together hard, as though he didn't want to look afraid in front of her, as though he could feel something to be very much afraid of crawling into his expression against his will to threaten his mouth with twisting and his eyes with fresh tears.

It broke Lynn's heart, but she didn't say anything.

And then, very cautiously, like someone slowly rolling on thin ice, C.J. twisted and leaned over, coming very close to Lynn. He cupped his small right hand around her ear, and he leaned forward again. And then, as soft as a baby's breath, he began to whisper. He whispered it in tight to her cheek, where she couldn't see that his lips were still fighting the tightening threads that come with fear. He whispered it all—what he had said to Mrs. Klein, and how he had said it, and what had happened to her as a result, and what the announcer on TV had said about the police coming to find the person who did it. He whispered it as carefully and quietly as he could, as though he was terrified that someone else might be listening to his secret, too, someone that he didn't want to hear him, someone in hiding—maybe even God.

Father Mark remembered the time five or six years ago when a pizza delivery man in Royal Oak said he saw the Virgin Mary's face on the farmers' market building over on Rochester Road. Hundreds of people gathered on the lawn of the market every day for nearly three weeks straight, a lot of them staying there all night. They stayed and waited and prayed and wished heavenly company through good weather and bad with nothing to satisfy them but shadows from a spotlight on the building's white aluminum siding and dreams that they, too, might be visited, even in the most obscure way, with some hint of the real presence of God.

He wondered now, as he came down the stairs to glance carefully out the front window of the rectory, how many people would be gathered to pray and wait and wish on his own front lawn. He wondered, too, if some of those same people from the farmers' market vigil would be among them, here to set up a brand new vigil, insisting by the sheer doggedness of their presence that they be rewarded with sightings of a resurrection from the dead.

What he saw, when he carefully pulled back the curtain of the front window, was seventy to eighty people waiting along his sidewalk and squeezing onto his lawn to wait for an interview or a look or a touch.

He turned away. He didn't see their vigil as faith. He saw it as madness. He remembered something he heard somewhere: It isn't really God that people want. What people want is miracles.

He felt like hiding.

He turned on the small TV on the kitchen counter and poured a cup of coffee. The news was repeating what Father Steve had said: Marion was alive; "authoritative sources" said her cancer was in full remission; there'd be a news conference at 8:00 A.M. There was also a chilling sixty-second playback from something that he hadn't heard before: the full audio of the two-way conversation he'd heard just one side of when the Life Support tech at the funeral home talked to somebody at the hospital.

He shook his head. It was so incredible, like he was caught in a movie. He turned off the TV and made the one phone call he felt obligated to make.

Monsignor John Tennett was still a young man for a person with so much clout, still in his midforties. He was sharp-minded, efficient, and direct. "Hey, Mark" were his first two words. "What in God's name is going on?" were his next seven.

It took less than five minutes for Mark to go through it. He didn't hurry and he didn't omit details. He told everything he knew, in order of appearance, with just one interruption by the Monsignor, asking if Father Mark thought that there was "any way on God's green earth" that Marion Klein had really been dead.

"I'll have to say this a million times, but it's all I've got, John. I don't know. I thought so at the time, but what's that good for? You expect it. She looked like it. But I don't know."

"You watching for the news conference? On TV?"

"No. I want to get back there."

"It's not just local. CNN's got it. Like blood soup to sharks."

49

"Just what we need."

"Mark?"

"That means it's international."

"I know. Mark?"

"I'm going to go back and see her, John. I'll just keep you posted, okay?"

"Go slow on any public pronouncements though. One way or the other. You know that."

"I don't have any pronouncements to make. Tell the boss not to worry."

"All he knows is, this means a whole wide world of attention. He's going to want to set up a time when you'll come down to his place and talk about it."

Father Mark sighed. He pictured the Cardinal, who was so calm and quietly professional in the affairs of the diocese but who was so thin-skinned about his own and his archdiocese's public image. With CNN on the case, he thought, the guy would want to be involved up to his Roman collar. "CNN means the Vatican's already hearing about it", he said, sounding discouraged.

"Yes they are."

"And he's in Rome now, isn't he? For that Peace and Justice Symposium?"

"He's called me already", Monsignor Tennett said. "Nobody in Rome will believe it, of course. But they'll all be aware of how he handles it."

"The mind boggles", Father Mark said. He heard the Monsignor laugh lightly.

"Does he want to talk with me now?"

"He wants you and me to stay close; make sure the cradle doesn't rock. He'll be back sometime in the middle of the night on Friday. His Saturday is wall-to-wall, I know that. He's asking about three in the afternoon on Sunday. First chance he's got."

"Three'd be okay." He jotted it down: Cardinal, Sunday, 3:00. "Just so he realizes I won't be able to tell him anything he won't have already heard."

"I'll pick you up", the Monsignor said. "Two thirty." Suddenly he made an abrupt sound, like a sharp, "Whoa!"

"What?"

"Your TV's not on, you said?"

"No. What happened?"

"Get going. Your lady woke up. At the hospital, just a few minutes ago."

CNN had been the first international service to broadcast excerpts from the audio that Channel 3 had received, and the first to broadcast Marion's return to consciousness, but the other services were quick to follow suit, including the tabloids.

In fact, the morning was a time not just for news, but for rumors, which ranged from stories of heavenly visions to sightings of hell's fire, and which, from a media standpoint, were pure gold. The Lazarus Lady promised to hold the public's attention for as long as the media could dig the story just a little bit deeper or string it out just a little bit further.

Predictably, Giles MacInnes was back on the news, flying in the face of heated investigations by heralding Marion Klein's continued health as proof positive of his own integrity and of the miraculous presence of God in his Royal Oak funeral home, which, he insisted, "is really now more like a shrine than a funeral home".

The news community, however, like the legal community, remained universally skeptical, if not openly derisive. Within hours of Marion's regaining consciousness, the media were busy making her the latest symbol of John and Jane Q, the public's pathetic vulnerability in the face of commercial exploitation—the kind of exploitation that was now being exposed so blatantly, through the abuse of Marion Klein, even in that one extreme of human life that none of us can avoid.

Anger at possible criminal exploitation within the "national business of dying" was mounting fast. But so was the interest from within the entertainment industry.

By 9:00 A.M. eastern standard time, TV programming executives across the country were busy setting up lunch meetings in New York and breakfast meetings in California to discuss potential "resurrection projects". The hottest possibilities included cutting deals for Marion's personal story, developing feature films or TV miniseries hinged on all the possible extremes that death and resurrections might involve, both heartening and horrifying, and specials or miniseries to expose in detail the potentials for abuse in that final corner of human buying and selling known as the funeral business.

But for all the news and all the spin and all the deal making, most people around the nation, and many around the world, were starting their day by wondering. And what they were wondering, in terms so dark for some that the question was practically suffocating, was, What about my mom and dad? Or my sister or grandmother? Or my friends, that the doctors said had died? When they were being kept and finally buried, what was really happening to them?

Joe Walker saw the news about Marion Klein's being cancer-free as he was getting ready for work. He didn't call Lynn again, knowing that she'd be leaving for work herself, but he made a note to call her at her real estate office first thing, as soon as he settled in himself. He heard about Marion's waking up again from one of the bubbling agent-pool secretaries as he walked in the door of the Waldon Insurance Group in Ferndale—he and his morning coffee from McDonald's. She chirped details of the latest TV reports as Joe sat down at his desk, and he chirped back that he not only knew the Lazarus Lady personally, but that his ex-wife and son were at the funeral home looking at her dead body just a few minutes before "it" happened the night before.

When his phone rang, the secretary answered it. "Your ex on one!" she announced; her green-brushed eyes were as wide as quarters. "God, it's serendipity! Or is that clairvoyance?"

Joe picked up the phone. He didn't begin with "hello". He began with, "Hey, I just heard about the waking up deal, but what'd she say? I didn't get any feedback on that."

Lynn said, "I don't know. They're not saying. But we have a problem."

"What kind of problem? And you heard that her cancer is supposed to be gone, too, right? I heard that before I left the apartment." Joe was waving three other curious insurance agents and another secretary away from his desk, shaking his head no to signal that Lynn didn't have any more news about the Lazarus Lady, sorry.

"C.J.'s having some trouble", Lynn said. "And, yes, I heard about the cancer. The whole thing's too much to even take in. I'm already tired thinking about it."

"It's bizarre, is what it is. What kind of trouble is C.J. into now?"

She told him, not the whole thing, but most of it, all in one stream: how C.J. was scared, how he came in to sleep in her bed, and then wouldn't get out of bed, and wouldn't talk, and looked all shaken up, and how hard it was for her to force him to get dressed and to go to school, and how now, just a minute ago, the secretary from school called and said that C.J. wouldn't talk or look at his teachers or anything, or even answer questions, and how they wanted to know what it was all about.

"So what's going on?" was all that Joe said, and that in a whisper, not really asking for an answer.

"I told them I didn't know what it was about, either," Lynn said, "so the school people asked me to pick C.J. up at the school office as soon as possible and take him home and 'work with him', saying that if he didn't show signs of bouncing back by tomorrow morning I should consider seeing the school counselor for advice on what could be some level of juvenile traumatic reaction."

"I don't get it", Joe said.

"They're sure it has something to do with Marion", she said. "I'm not thrilled with it, either, and I can handle him later on, after noon, sometime, but they've got him waiting to be picked up right now, and I can't do it because we've got clients coming in from Gary, Indiana, in twenty minutes from now, and I have to handle a presentation on a commercial tract in Oxford."

"Do I have to say anything else about why you don't take nine-year-olds to funeral homes?" Joe asked. He sounded mad.

"You're his dad," Lynn said, lowering her voice, "and I'm calling you, and I'm willing to put up with your Mickey Mouse potshots, that I knew would be coming, rather than calling Nancy Gould or somebody that would really want to help, because I think it might be very important for C.J. to be with you or me right now. That's the one and only reason." She could feel her temper rising and struggled to keep it under control. She hated realizing that his criticisms could still intimidate her that way, but she knew it was true. "If you could keep him just till twelve thirty, when I'll have a chance to get home, then I can take over. Because I can get out of the lunch part of the deal with the Gary people, for sure."

"I still don't get it", Joe said, with a mild response again. You never could tell with Joe. "I mean, I'd 've guessed he and his buddies would wear this sucker like a badge instead of getting thrown by it. 'Hey, C.J. Walker was there!' you know? Kids eat that stuff up. And just skip the school counselor. Are you kidding me?"

"He won't need actual counseling."

"Everybody wants to make his job seem important."

She paused. Then she hit him with the rest of it, but quickly; shooting through it without stopping, as if saying it fast enough might allow it to be accepted without really being noticed. "Well, don't laugh, Joe, because it's really not funny, but this morning he told me, which is the real reason he's all in a shell at school and all, although I'm sure he didn't tell them about it, but he honest to God told me that he's the one who made Marion come back to life again, and I think he really believes it."

It was noticed. "He what?"

"It's not a joke with C.J.", she said again. "Or to me. He's got it in his head that he made this happen to Marion. That's what's got him so shook up, that, and the police investigating and all. He told me all of it this morning, but I'm pretty sure he didn't tell them that at school, or

I'd have heard about it. One advantage to not talking. But he was like a zombie this morning, honest to goodness. And if it was any other day, I'd get him myself."

There was another pause; then Joe laughed, loudly, and with sharp edges. He had succeeded long ago in developing the art of laughter as criticism. Now it was a weapon.

"I'm calling for a serious yes or no, Joe, not a little laugh-fest at C.J.'s expense", Lynn said. "Will you get your son or not?" She waited for an answer, but Joe was quiet. She decided to go on. "Kids that age think they cause things, you know—that whatever happens, they caused it. That's how they think."

"Like their folks getting a divorce?" Joe said in a low voice. No more laughing.

Lynn steadied herself. She didn't want to get pulled off the track—not back onto that one, certainly: Joe still mad that she'd kicked him out of their home. Right now Joe could help. That is what it was all about, nothing else. "It's fantasy and we know that," she continued, "but it's not fantasy to him. He was all teary-eyed and staring and not talking, and if you want to help, then you can be there for him. I don't know, maybe you can even help him to come around."

It was a hook and she knew it. Challenge Joe with it. Give him the chance to do what she hadn't done. She threw it out and waited. She didn't have to wait long.

"Did he cure her cancer, too?" The grin was back in his voice.

"If that's a serious question, I doubt very much that he knows about her cancer or anything else. At least he hadn't heard about it when he left the house."

"So what the hell'd he do? Whack her and bring down the power on her?" Again, the grin in his voice.

Lynn glanced at her watch. She knew he was going to do it now, knew that he was avoiding his answer on purpose, knew that he was grinning, knew, most of all, that he was enjoying the fact that she had to call him and ask him for something. The stupid little games they played. It had been part of their problem all along.

She said, "He touched her arm and said something like, 'Be well, Mrs. Klein.' He'll tell you himself. Will you get him or not?"

"For a kid with enough imagination to cook this story up, he didn't bother making up much of a ceremony, did he?"

She thought about it. "No, I guess not."

"Sounds like something he heard on Star Trek. Be well and prosper, all that."

"Can you get him or not? I gotta go."

"And they don't know about this at school? Nobody asked him, 'How'd you spend your Tuesday night, there, Christopher?' and he said, 'Oh, I raised this dead lady to life and watched some TV'?"

"He wouldn't talk about it to teachers, I'm sure. So we agree I'll call them and tell them you're coming, and you go and get him right away. Yes or no? Have him home by twelve thirty."

He paused, but this time not for long. "Call 'em. I can leave in five minutes. And fifty bucks I have him out of orbit by twelve thirty."

"It'd be worth fifty bucks."

"Them that can't, teach. Them that can, do."

"Twelve thirty for sure."

"Teachers don't know as much as they get credit for."

They both hung up.

Anthony Cross paused over his slight breakfast of a soft-boiled egg, an English muffin, and cranberry juice, and watched CNN's latest report on the Lazarus Lady in silence. Unlike most viewers, he was hearing past the speculation about life and death and embalming and resurrection. He had heard the reports of a supposed resurrection when he woke up shortly after 6:00 A.M., and had been hearing the rest for the last several hours. By 8:00 he had heard the words "cancer" and "complete and immediate remission" all used together, and he had just heard the words "regained consciousness". And while the reports didn't broadcast the name of the priest who had prayed for this mysterious lady at the funeral home that held her as a dead woman the night before, they did give the name of his parish: St. Veronica's, in Royal Oak, Michigan.

He would remember. And he would ask Torrie Kruger what he thought about it, although he wasn't sure it would mean anything at all. The old man had seen too many scams touted on national news as being genuine events to be easily impressed. He'd not only seen them; when it had suited his overriding purpose of gaining and holding the advantages of power, he'd arranged some of the most costly scams himself.

Still, he sat silently, without motion, staring at the television, thinking.

When the report ended, his eyes dropped heavily to the yellow smear of his morning egg and his still-untouched English muffin. He was deep in thought: St. Veronica's. Royal Oak, Michigan. The lady awake again. And no more cancer. He would ask Torrie about it. He would remember.

Joe had always considered himself to be, in his own street-wise way, somewhere between smart and brilliant. He wasn't the most dedicated insurance agent in the world because he didn't really care a lot about other people's lives or about insurance, but he did really care about making money, so he hung in and regularly dazzled clients with his seeming passion for their families' now and future well-being. Nor had he, when he had the chance, been the most dedicated husband in the world, or father or friend or anything else. Dedication, he knew, was not his forte.

But he was a very good "reader", and he made the most of that—not a reader of books, a reader of people. He could read, sometimes in a heartbeat and with what he was convinced was a rare talent, what a person was really like, where his priorities lay, what games they were playing in order to achieve those priorities, and, in the long run, how to get the best of them virtually every time.

True, he hadn't read Lynn with one hundred percent accuracy. She turned out to be hypersensitive and a lot more unreasonable than he'd thought. And while he still kind of wanted to be with her, he'd resented her shortsightedness and puppy dog rigidity.

He also didn't take a lot of time to try to "read" himself, although, as he was quick to admit with a laugh to any close friend or easy conquest, his talent for accurately "reading people" was probably tied to his being devious himself. But who cared? For whatever reason, he could smell someone trying to con him downwind and a mile away.

Especially if it was his own kid, who was, after all, just a nine-year-old.

So C.J. was serious; Joe knew that in three minutes. His son touched the Klein woman and said, "Get well, Mrs. Klein", and she, no kidding, sat up alive and kicking, and in the kid's mind it was all because of him—all because of little C.J. Walker and that knack he suddenly developed in the fourth grade for raising people who were stone-cold dead and already embalmed. Comical, actually—to Joe, not to C.J.

While it was one problem for C.J., it was another for Joe. Yes, Joe missed his son when he didn't get to see him, and he loved to be with him, doing anything at all. And yes, the kid was messed up and hurting by this nutso fantasy. But hey, this was kiddy stuff, and C.J. would look up all of a sudden any time now, or wake up tomorrow morning or the next day, maybe sooner, maybe later, and it would all be over. Bang! Just like that. Joe was certain of it.

But Joe needed it to be sooner, not later. In fact, he needed it before 12:30, because what he really wanted out of this little side trip was to show Lynn that he was the parent with the magic touch, and that he was, in this way and in others, even better with C.J. than she was.

So he got to St. Veronica's Elementary School a little before 10:00. He walked into the principal's office and C.J. was there, so he "father-talked" for sixty seconds with Brigg's secretary, and then he left with his son.

Joe was sure that somewhere there was the right button for C.J., and he would be the one to find it, and he would find it, well before 12:30.

Their first stop was a video store, where Joe tried with some success to get C.J. to talk about video games, anything to open him up. He even encouraged C.J. to pick one out that he really wanted, and he did: *Earth Dawgs II.* Joe realized that Lynn would complain. She didn't like games in which a lot of things died bloody, even if they were mud lumps from Middle-earth. But there were a lot of fun things Lynn didn't like.

He gave the game to C.J. with the understanding that he wouldn't go home and play it for a couple of hours. He wanted C.J. feeling grateful, but he didn't want him disappearing into a video game right now, or into a movie or anything else that resembled one more fantasy. Joe knew how to focus on a challenge.

From Video Valley they drove straight up to the Woodward Coney-Shack, where they ordered chili dogs, root beer, and coffee, even though it was only 10:40.

Halfway through the first chili dog, C.J. confirmed to Joe, with shrugs and nods and a few reluctant words, that when he touched Mrs. Klein and said the words, he "just knew" that she was going to be okay. And yes, he could do it again, another thing he "just knew". He said it all tentatively, slipping it out as a series of feelers dangled in front of the father who had left him and his mom for another lady, and who might believe him but probably wouldn't, any more than his mom or anybody else.

In fact, Joe would have laughed out loud if he had more time, but he nodded seriously and thought about how he could best move on from here. It was 10:50 and ticking.

He sat silently, studying the boy who was showing his own capacity to brood over not being believed by people close to him, much as Joe himself still brooded over Lynn's decision to throw him out because of one or two completely meaningless nights with somebody else.

He and C.J. shared a lot physically, too, and that made Joe feel good. In addition to wide and deep-set, charcoal-brown eyes, which were Joe's most striking feature, C.J. shared Joe's fair skin, his brown hair, his sharp and angular features, and his broad, no-holds-barred way of smiling. At just nine young years, C.J. was also slimming down to show the lean, athletic build that Joe so much admired about himself, and still took special pains to keep in shape. They even had the same noticeable quirk, what Joe called "messing with his lip". But while Joe's habit was pulling his lower lip in and running the tip of his tongue over it when he was thinking hard about something important, C.J.'s most noticeable habit was biting his lip—always the lower lip, always the left side— nibbling at it when he worried.

But, Joe wondered, what about inside C.J.'s head, where the kid was feeling so withdrawn? If Joe was nine years old and believed this kind of thing about himself, and was scared by it, what would be scaring him most of all? What would he want to have happen most of all? What could anyone say or do to get through to him?

He circled the idea of maybe pinning C.J. down, asking him why he thought God or whatever had picked him out of the all the people in world and made him able to raise people from the dead. But that would just be covering the same ground that Lynn must have already tried, obviously without success. And while Joe was sure he could pursue it smarter than Lynn, he knew that wasn't the answer. Argument would just drive C.J. further back into himself, alone—which is where he already was. He was all alone with this.

Joe thought about that, about how that's always the scariest way to be: all alone.

He took a quick sip of root beer. He could feel an idea coming to life, something happening, an instinct. C.J. was scared, Joe was sure, but not just about the unknown, or about why this happened with Mrs. Klein, or about if the police would arrest him or anything like that. It was more than that, at least that's the way it would be if Joe was nine years old.

It would be that you had this thing happening, and you were all alone with it.

He shifted in his seat. Getting close. Staring. His lower lip tucked in, the tip of his tongue sliding over it, left to right, right to left.

He watched C.J. take another small bite of his now-cold chili dog and he thought, which is scarier to a nine-year-old kid? Thinking you had the power to do magical things with dead people or thinking you were suddenly all alone with the power?

"Did you ever try that mustard that isn't bright yellow?" he asked. It was time to plug in, to get some lines of communication open. "They have stuff that's got like little dark stuff in it. You ever taste that kind?"

C.J. thought for a minute and shook his head no.

"I don't like it, actually", Joe continued, acting casual, knowing there was a button to be pushed, knowing he was closing in. "It's okay, but I like what this is, the bright yellow stuff."

Joe watched C.J. nod his head and take another sip of his soda, and all of a sudden, he knew C.J. had to try it again. It was obvious:

58

instant therapy. He'd try it, he'd get embarrassed that it wasn't him, he'd make an excuse or two, and he'd be fine—all before noon, the only way.

He couldn't try it with another corpse, though. Joe couldn't pull that off. At the other end of things, a dead moth from a light fixture or something would be easy, but that wouldn't do it. C.J. would just say it wasn't the same thing at all. And it wouldn't be. Joe wouldn't buy that, either, if he was C.J.

"I think it's possible, Ceej", he said matter-of-factly, still thinking.

C.J. looked up. It was a gesture that was, in itself, an answer. C.J. was listening, and he was asking for more.

"Anything is possible", Joe said. "Just because somebody's a kid, people think they can't have awesome things happen. But I think it's possible."

C.J. stared in silence. He was biting his lower lip, left side.

"It might be scary, too, though", Joe said. "It's scared you, hasn't it, pal?"

His son shrugged, staring, his lip still caught carefully between his teeth. Then he said, "Would it be against the law?"

Joe laughed. "Hell no, not against the law. They don't make laws for what never happens, you know? Why do you say that?"

Another shrug. "That's what they said. They said the prosecutor was there, and the police, and it was criminal."

Joe shook his head, half-amused, half-sympathetic. A nine-year-old kid, and thinking he raised the dead, and if that wasn't enough, he's got to worry about the police arresting him.

"Forget that, C.J.", he said. "Honest to God. The police that are there, all that talk about criminal stuff, I heard that, too. That's just saying they want to know if the undertaker's robbing the people, like taking their money but not doing what he said he was doing. That's all they want to know."

C.J. stared. His eyes had slightly narrowed.

"See, they don't think she was dead. They think the undertaker just made her look that way."

C.J.'s lower lip again just held there, between his teeth.

Joe smiled. "Okay?"

A nod. Another sip of soda. Big eyes, waiting.

"But even so, it must be hard not having anybody else believe what happened, isn't it? Like you're alone with it, right? The biggest secret in the world, but that's where you are in a way, isn't it? All alone with it. Except for me."

C.J.'s lips parted, and he had tilted his head so slightly that Joe only noticed because it was something he did himself. When he tilted his head he was listening hard.

He smiled again at his son. "I got an idea", he said. And he did. "Want to hear it?"

C.J. nodded and sipped again on the soda.

"The thing is, you don't have to feel all alone with this thing, like nobody knows what happened but you. 'Cause I can be there with you—as soon as I know a little better what happens, I mean. And then we can convince Mom easy, and it will really be cool. I mean, it's an amazing thing to be able to do, right?" He tried a light laugh.

C.J. said, "I thought it was so great at first, but I was still scared. But I would've told Mom right away. But then they were shouting about it and about the police and all . . ." His voice trailed off.

Joe was still smiling. "Yeah, well, here's what we do, pal. It's easy. You did it once, and you didn't do anything wrong at all, believe me. You helped some lady big-time, right? So, you do it again."

C.J.'s eyes narrowed into a question, but Joe went ahead nonstop. "Not at a funeral home, though."

C.J. tilted his head.

"I don't mean another dead person", Joe continued, still smiling. "I'm thinking instead, we can get a dead bird, maybe, or a dead dog."

C.J.'s eyes widened. He leaned forward and sipped his drink hard and loud, draining it. He didn't take his eyes off his dad.

"Uh-oh", Joe muttered, showing sudden concern. "Do you think it would work, though? On a bird or a dog? What do you think?"

C.J. hadn't thought about it. He looked across the table and said, so seriously that Joe wanted, again, to laugh, "I bet it would."

"Well, then, that's great!"

For the first time, C.J. looked animated. "Where do we get a dead bird, though?"

"Yeah. Problem. I don't know." Joe looked down, rubbing his chin.

"We can't kill one", C.J. said, half-grinning. Nervous.

Joe laughed. "Probably couldn't catch one to kill it, anyway."

"I was thinking that." C.J. grinned and nodded his head. He paused to think. "Maybe the dog pound could find a dead dog?"

Joe frowned again. "Naw. They get rid of them right away. Besides," he said, making sure he looked very serious, "I'm thinking dogs and people, maybe things not working the same way."

C.J. nodded again. "It might be different."

"I don't know, man", Joe said. "I'm thinking of something better."

The waitress came over to see if they were still happy. Joe asked for two fresh root beers. She smiled and agreed.

Joe beamed again at C.J. "This is it," he said, "and it's perfect. If you can do something like that for *dead* people, it will work on *sick* people, right?" He gave it just a second's pause, then added, "Of course, it will!"

C.J. nodded thoughtfully. Of course it would.

"So we can do something that will help somebody, which is something Mom will really be proud of, and me, too, and we can show people that it's really you at the same time. And you'll be showing me, too, you know?" He paused. "'Cause I'll have to see it so I can tell people about it with you, right?" Another pause. Still okay. "'Cause I wasn't there last night, right?"

C.J. nodded. "Right."

"And I know the perfect person you can help", Joe said, slapping his open palm lightly on the table and leaning nearer.

"Who?" C.J. asked.

"I work with a guy, and we're really good friends. His name is Ed Welz. And his mom is the nicest lady, C.J., but really old, and she's really sick with cancer. As a matter of fact ..." He paused, looking happily surprised at his latest great thought, "... that's just what Mrs. Klein had. Both of them, the same thing. So this will work for sure, right?"

C.J. smiled and squirted up straighter in his chair. "Uh-huh." He even double-checked the name. "Welz?"

"Like where they put a bucket down and bring up some water. Only a 'z' at the end instead of an 's'. But you still say it, 'Wells'."

"Where's she at?"

"She's at the hospital, but that's okay. That's not a problem. I just ask when we go in; they tell us which room." Joe noticed a nine-year-old's reluctance cloud C.J.'s expression, but he wasn't worried. C.J. would try his best and go home a sadder, but wiser kid. And he'd be over it, not because somebody argued him out of it or because some counselor took notes for six weeks, but because the kid would know it firsthand. Experience, the great teacher.

Hey, he thought, Ed's mom would even be better off for it. She would be happy because this guy and his kid visited her for a minute or two. Not only that: she would tell Ed about it; he would tell everybody at the office; they would all think Joe was Mr. Nice, going and seeing the guy's mom like that. And taking his kid with him, they'd say; how could a guy be nicer than that?

"Man to man now, Ceej", Joe said, closing the deal. "This is our chance. It's you and me. If you don't want to, I'll take you home, and

I'll still try and stick by you, but I won't really know anything, and I don't even live there anymore, you know? And Mom's not going to care what I say. This way, you help a wonderful old lady. Just a 'Get well, Mrs. Welz ...'"

He heard a soft "And touch her" from across the table.

"And touch her", Joe grinned. "Right."

Five

One floor directly below the Fremont Hospital Intensive Care Unit where Marion Klein's family and pastor and attending doctors and nurses huddled around her bed to hold her hand and listen to her whisper about what, to them, were disappointingly sketchy memories of sickness and lights and nothing more, in a double-bed room where the last prayers offered had been filled more with worry than with celebration, eighty-seven-year-old Mrs. Arlene Welz was hooked to a single plastic tube by the back of her hand while she ever so slowly died near a window overlooking a parking lot.

The woman in the bed next to hers, who was also dying, was asleep.

A pale green curtain half circled her bed like a shroud, hiding her last great journey from the eyes of everyone but the very interested.

Mrs. Welz was also asleep and had been for more than an hour. She couldn't see the door of her room swinging open like a secret whispered in the dark. She couldn't hear the man and the boy who came in so quietly, closing the door behind them.

Joe moved quietly to check the nameplate on the wall behind the woman in the first bed, just making sure; C.J. stood behind him, holding back. The woman had a long name ending in "ski". Polish. The one by the window, Joe realized, had to be Welz.

Since it was going to be so easy, he wondered why he felt nervous. He could feel his heart beating: bam, bam, bam.

C.J. stopped at the foot of the first bed; he was staring at the Polish lady, and when Joe looked at her closer he could see why. The woman was a lot older than Lynn, but she resembled her, plain as anything. The same brown hair, but with a lot of gray, and the high cheekbones, and the same kind of mouth with the full bottom lip. Lady was probably great-looking when she was young, Joe thought. But she looked yellow now, and a lot older than Lynn; she had to be sixty-nine or seventy, and not pretty anymore with the cancer, even bloated a little. Worst of all, she had one of those tubes taped into her nose. Stomach, lung, Joe didn't know and didn't want to find out. He avoided looking at the bag that would be near the floor at the other end of the tube. He didn't think C.J. would enjoy it, either.

He moved to the second bed and eased back the green curtain, being as quiet as he could, and there she was. "Welz", it said, right over her head. Like wells in the desert.

She was older than the other woman by a long shot, not bloated, either, nor yellowish, the way they got, only really thin—sick-thin, skin and bones. And she just had an IV, no nose tubes or bags of blood or urine or anything disgusting. That would make it easier for C.J. to get close.

Joe turned and motioned him forward, but it couldn't have been worse, the timing of it. All of a sudden they were there, charging into the room; Joe couldn't believe it. What was going on now?

He should have grabbed C.J. and pulled him right over to the Welz lady's bed as soon as they opened the door. He should have had the kid say his thing and touch the old lady before she woke up, right then, quick. Or even if she woke up, he should have said, "My name is Joe Walker and this is my son, who wants to wish you his best", and C.J. could have touched her and whispered to her and bang, it would have been done. But he missed his chance, and now they were there, sweeping past C.J. and over to Joe and the old lady at just the wrong time.

The big nurse was first, the gigantic one in white, lumbering in like a field general. Joe wanted to shout, "Now, C.J.!", but the general was in the way so fast it was like somebody dropped a safe from the ceiling. Wham! And then she was saying, "Sorrrry! Have to ask you folks to say byyye!" and the whole plan was in the toilet, that fast.

It got worse.

Two more white uniforms came in right behind her—a smaller, quieter nurse with a sympathetic smile and a male nurse with sad eyes and strong everything else. Joe thought he looked like a bouncer he had seen, but he had the wrong eyes.

"Gonna have your picture taken!" the big one beamed, tapping the old lady's IV.

Joe thought, she stretches her words on purpose because she thinks it's cute. He hated that.

Mrs. Welz was awake. She asked the question lightly, trying to sound unconcerned, but there was pain in her voice and Joe felt sorry for her. She said, "Downstairs?" and she looked at the huge nurse, then at Joe. The question was still in her eyes.

"Mmmmm hmmmm!" the field general said singsongy.

"I'm Joe Walker, Mrs. Welz, a friend of Eddie's." Joe glanced over his shoulder, trying to nod C.J. into getting up there quick, but the boy had moved backward instead of forward, closer to the door, his eyes saying, "Please, Dad, let's get out of here."

"I work with Ed at the insurance company, and we're good friends, and this is my son, Christopher, over there. C'mon over here, Chris."

Mrs. Welz smiled.

The nurses pressed closer, wanting to get going.

C.J. didn't move. There were too many people, all in uniforms, and they'd all be watching. And when he didn't move, the general closed in, filling the breach in the visitors' lines.

"Sorrrry", she droned again. "We'll have her back in not tooooo long, though."

"Oh my goodness", Mrs. Welz was saying softly. She was trying to see C.J., trying to put off the doctors' need-to-know. But the general wouldn't stop pressing. "You and Dad come back later, okaaaay?" she called to C.J.

He stared back at her, not sure if he was supposed to answer.

The smaller nurse said to Joe, "We should have her back in forty-five minutes, maybe an hour. I hope you and your son can come back. Maybe go down to the cafeteria?"

Joe sighed and nodded and turned to smile at the dying old lady that he already liked and that he felt sorry for all over again. He assured her with as much warmth as he could that it was okay and that, yes, they would drop back sometime if they could. They were just here visiting someone else and had a few minutes, but they would see. Then he glanced around at C.J. and even felt a little sorry for him. He looked so out of his element, thrown in here and scared stiff.

He also felt sorry for himself. He didn't dwell on it, but the thought flitted through his head and he recognized it. His whole life, he thought, was one long series of things going wrong at the last minute that weren't his fault. And here it was again. Sixty seconds more, he would have pulled it off.

As he crossed the room toward C.J., shrugging his shoulders and smiling and acting easy come, easy go, he noticed the Polish lady, who looked a little like Lynn watching him with dull eyes, so he tried to smile at her, too. But not much happened.

He really didn't feel like smiling.

On the way down the elevator, he wondered if there wasn't someone else they could see, but no one came to mind. Besides, it was getting too close to noon already, with their being twenty minutes from Lynn's place. Sixty seconds more, all he would have needed.

"Don't tell Mom about the hospital", he said to C.J.

"Would she be mad?"

"No. But why bring it up? Nothing happened."

"Will she be mad about *Earth Dawgs*?"

"Nope."

The elevator door opened, and they stepped into the lobby.

C.J. was thinking about something hard, the way he did, the lip thing again, and Joe was wondering what he was thinking. The kid's mind going, all the time.

When they reached the east exit, C.J. said, "She will *too* be."

Well, Joe thought, who cares?

Joe had dropped C.J. at home at 12:25, as promised. He hadn't waited around to talk. Lynn's car was there, and the front door of the house was open, and C.J. went inside, and that was it. Joe waved from the car and went to get a hamburger and then went back to the office.

Lynn didn't call to thank him, and she didn't call to complain. C.J. still believed what he believed, so what was there to say?

He had heard, though, on his way back to work, that Marion didn't have a lot to say about what she had experienced—no Jesus, no angels, no dead relatives in white fields all loving her and whatever, at least nothing news sharks could get hold of. He wondered, though, what she was telling Ryan and the doctors in secret. Most of all, he wondered how much they would pay her when she wrote a book about the whole experience. He thought, she'll knock out a book and say it all there and end up having more money than India. She'll make a jillion dollars for dying, and I'll still be out here hustling insurance, begging some dead-beat to part with another hundred bucks. The way things happen to me all the time is a crock!

He found trying to get any work done at his office to be hopeless. His head was still at the hospital. So he made a few fruitless calls, moved some paperwork in circles, and left early.

Back at his apartment, he turned on the TV to catch the late-afternoon news, then went into the kitchen to get a beer and think out a plan for the night. Something fun for a change, he decided. Nothing about dead people or sick people or any more of that.

He heard the Channel 3 lady, Ruth Cosgrove, the blond, interviewing somebody in his living room as he opened his refrigerator door. It was a guy from Wayne State University, they said, sounding political, the guy saying something in a high voice about how pervasive the public's vulnerability is, and how we're at the mercy of often inadequately trained medical personnel.

Joe rolled his eyes and reached for the cheese. He should have left the TV off, and just put on some music. Talk about inadequately trained: the college teacher trying to pretend he was a heavy-duty TV commentator.

As he came back in from the kitchen with a slab of jalapeño cheese and a box of crackers in one hand and his cold beer in the other, he thought the blond news anchor was talking again about Marion, the way she mentioned "cancer" and was saying those same words again: "complete remission" and "instantaneous". But as he moved to his round-cushioned couch, he realized that there were different words being said now along with the others, words that shouldn't be there.

"Stomach cancer" struck him. Where did that come from?

He took a swig of his beer and sat down, paying attention now, nervous about something, not knowing why.

"In what may or may not be a coincidence," Ruth was saying, "Mrs. Koyievski is in the room *right next door* to the room recently occupied by the hospital's other celebrated case of apparent remission of advanced malignancy, Mrs. Marion Klein, better known to Channel 3 viewers as the 'Lazarus Lady'."

Joe didn't move. He barely breathed. His mind was racing, trying to get hold of what the woman was saying, his heart suddenly racing, too. What was this? What else had they been saying while he was getting his beer?

He saw Ruth turn with a perky smile to her coanchor. He heard her say, "Roger, what do you think? Is there something about that Fremont Hospital oncology wing, things happening that have to do with the hospital itself, or what?"

There had been another one, Joe thought, and nothing to do with C.J.

He rose slowly to his feet. Somebody say if there had been another one!

"I don't know, Ruth, but it's nice to see good news bumping the bad news out of the headlines these days. And whatever it is ...", the thin anchorman smiled broadly, swinging to face the camera, "... you can be sure we'll continue to be your eyes and ears as this brand-new story develops right here on 'Action News 3'."

There had been another one. The guy said "brand-new story".

"Absolutely", Ruth said. Then she shifted abruptly in her seat. The camera angle changed; she found the prompter and began again, no longer smiling. "In world news today ..."

Joe was staring without seeing. Listening without hearing. In his mind's eye he was back at the hospital. He was in the room with Mrs.

Welz, his heart pounding again. He was moving in to look for the first time behind her green curtain. He was looking around the curtain again at the sick lady that he liked and that was dying with C.J. standing behind him. But not really behind him. He was seeing C.J. standing at the foot of the bed of the lady that looked like Lynn grown old and dying; C.J. staring at her and looking sad the whole time Joe was talking with the fat nurse; C.J. staring at the tube in the lady's nose and the blood that ran into a bag and feeling sorry for her because she looked so much like his mom. And the woman had a name, on the wall, just above her bed. Polish, ending in "ski".

His beer bottle slipped out of his hand and crashed to the hardwood floor at his feet.

C.J. was playing *Earth Dawgs II* with Burr Gould in the living room when Joe rang the bell, then rang it again.

Lynn half-smiled when she saw that it was Joe. After all, C.J. was actually getting social again, the crisis seemed to be passing if not completely out of sight, and she was surprised to see that Joe would come back to see how things were going. She had expected less.

She swung the door open and was about to say, "Hi", when Joe pushed past her without a word, looking like a man running from something.

"Joe, what happened?"

He turned and started to speak, but heard the sounds of *Earth Dawgs* being killed by laser cannons in the living room and said, "C.J.!" and charged toward his boy. Lynn was close at his heels, saying it again, this time insisting, "Joe, what happened?"

C.J. looked up when he saw his dad and grinned, but Joe wasn't grinning. He took the controller out of C.J.'s hand, tugged him to his feet and started to lead him back toward the front door. "I got to talk with you" is all that he said.

Burr sat with his mouth open, hoping he wasn't in trouble again, too.

Lynn followed them. She said it for the third time, this time clearly alarmed, "What happened, Joe?"

Joe ignored her. He called over his shoulder, "We'll be back, Burr", and hustled C.J. out the door to the long, wooden front porch.

Lynn was pressing right behind, still not knowing what was going on and now getting mad about it. "Joe! I want to know!"

Joe held C.J. by the shoulders and abruptly squatted down on one knee, his face six inches from his son's. No screwing around. "What did you say to the lady in the other bed?" He asked the question and held his breath.

C.J. stared at him, his dark eyes wide.

Lynn, still demanding answers that weren't coming, asked, "The lady in the *what?*"

"I knew it!" C.J. said softly. His expression was triumphant.

Behind them, Burr paused *Earth Dawgs* and tiptoed toward the door to listen.

"What lady in *whose* bed, Joe? Talk to me!"

"Did you say the words, C.J.? Did you touch her? Tell me yes or no."

Joe's voice was so sharp, it caught Lynn by surprise. But it wasn't just his tone that startled her; it was the words themselves. She grabbed him by the arm and pulled hard. "Joe! What did you guys do? I want to know!"

C.J. didn't even look at his mother. He stared at Joe with his grin and his deep eyes, and then he nodded yes and whispered it again. "I knew it!"

Joe let his hands slide from his son's shoulders. His mouth hung open. "Lynn", he said quietly. "Can I talk with you, honey? Please?"

They sat on the top of the picnic table in the backyard, their feet on the bench. The yard was enclosed by a chain-link fence, gated across the driveway, that they had installed when C.J. was five years old in anticipation of the swimming pool Joe had dreamed about since he was a kid himself. But the pool was never started. Another casualty of their divorce.

Joe started with the second lady. Koyievski. The Polish name.

Yes, Lynn had heard the news.

Joe glanced at the screened-in back porch that ran half the length of the back of the house and noticed C.J. and Burr, both of them peeking out the kitchen door, C.J. looking like he knew exactly what was going on, Burr asking questions, Joe thought, asking what C.J.'s dad was so excited about.

He turned again to Lynn, took a deep breath, and began.

He said he thought that some people were thinking Father Mark had brought Marion back to life, but the priest couldn't have had anything to do with the second lady; he had never even met her, as far as anyone knew. Joe had even called the rectory to check. The lady wasn't a parishioner. No one in the office had ever heard of her.

Lynn let him talk, her expression drawn tight, first with bewilderment, then with something closer to alarm.

"These things both happened," he said, "Marion and this new lady, but Lynn, it's not the priest. And it's not the hospital, either; some people saying on TV they had a Magnetic Imaging Unit on the floor below this lady's room, and Marion's, too. Did you hear that part, that they were in rooms right next door to each other, this lady and Marion?"

She'd heard. Her mouth had opened slightly. She stared without moving.

"So they were wondering about energy emissions and stuff. But it's not Father, and it's not energy fields, either."

Lynn whispered, "Oh God", with barely enough force to ease the words past her lips. Then she held her breath.

Joe felt so swamped by the importance of what he was about to say that he felt tears beginning to well up, something he had never let Lynn see before, not even once in all their time together. He looked aside quickly and muttered, "Oh man", and rubbed his eyes. But when he turned and looked at her again, he had himself under complete control. So he said it. "Lynn, there's only one connection between Marion and the Polish lady. And you know who it is."

He said it and he gave it time. He felt it was tumbling toward her like an explosion in slow motion. He imagined every incredible piece of it hitting her with absolute clarity, just the way they had hit him: C.J. and Marion at the funeral home, Joe and C.J. going off together for the morning, C.J. and the "lady in the other bed" at the hospital, the news about the second lady being healed, Joe's asking C.J., "Did you say the words?" and "Did you touch her?"

She came off the table like he had slapped her. "You took my son to the hospital? You took him to a dying person when you knew what he was thinking?"

"Lynn ..."

Her eyes were flooded with tears. She began to pace. "My God, Joe!", she whispered. "You're as bad as he is! You stupid ... oh God!"

Joe twisted to face her, but he didn't stand up. "Why is Marion alive again, Lynn?"

"And I will *never* trust you with him again."

"Why's the second lady well again, all of a sudden, with C.J. the only connection between them?"

"Oh God, Joe", she sighed. "Don't you realize what you two are saying here? Are you ...? What the hell's *happened* to you?"

Joe nodded and began again, speaking softly. He felt like this was the most important thing he had ever talked about, ever, in his whole life, so he tried to spell it out exactly as it had happened, the truth this time, step by step, from wanting to prove he could make C.J. better to Mrs. Welz, to the nurse who talked so slow—everything.

"We can look all around the block for a way out of it", he said, finally, speaking softly. "But every time I think I've got one, I have to say, 'Yeah, but short of ten minutes after C.J. touches her and says what he says, Marion is alive and she doesn't have cancer anymore. And ten minutes after C.J. touches the Polish lady and says the same thing, she's walking around the halls healthy, with no more cancer in her, either.' And with no other connection; that's what has me hooked. No priest or anything at the hospital—unless you're going to buy magic rays hummin' through the walls. But I'm thinking it can't be that, or it would've happened a thousand times before."

He watched her as he spoke. He watched her mouth, still drawn tight. He watched the thin line of anger still crawling around her lips. He watched her arms, coiled across her waist, keeping herself safe. And when he quit talking, he watched her eyes.

After nearly ten seconds of silence, she whispered, "You push your away around every place you go, you know that, Joe?" Surprisingly to Joe, she sounded more exhausted than angry. "You push like you know everything there is to know."

He rubbed his face slowly with both hands. What did that have to do with anything?

"This time, though, you're pushing with my son", Lynn said, still whispering. "And I'm not going to let you do that."

"Ten minutes after we left, Lynn. The new one was found at ten after twelve, they said, walking out in the hall, grinning and asking for her doctor. From nine-tenths dead to clean as a whistle."

Lynn wiped her eyes and sighed, looking at the sky. The clouds were mostly white, but dark at the edges, and moving slowly, northwest to southeast, typical for southern Michigan in the early summer.

"He's nine years old", she said.

"I almost had a stroke, Lynn; I heard that second woman's name. I thought, my God, I'm shakin' inside. So I check it out. Was it Father Mark? Nope. Any other priest? Anybody else that could have been at the funeral home with Marion, too? Nope. Only one connection, Lynn."

"Don't say that anymore, Joe", she said softly. She was shaking her head. She glanced at the house. "I'm going in now."

"I wasn't trying to be a smart-ass, Lynn, I swear; or push him or anything. I was just trying to help him see he was wrong."

She took several steps toward the house. C.J. and Burr disappeared from the kitchen door. She said, "Don't come around this weekend. I mean it. I want this over with."

"You're not going to be able to sleep tonight, though; you know that? If you don't find out."

She didn't answer. She continued to walk away.

"Or tomorrow night. Nothin' but wondering."

She shook her head. "I want you to go now, Joe."

"The second lady will be out of that room tonight", he said, speaking louder. He still hadn't moved. "They'll have her someplace they can test her; let the crowds come in and see her. They won't have anybody in there with Mrs. Welz until tomorrow."

"No!"

Joe's voice remained calm. It just kept coming. "She isn't sick to look at, either. Nothing ugly there. And he's already seen her."

Lynn stopped at the door of the screened-in porch and turned. "I want you to leave."

Joe slid from the table and walked toward her. The most important conversation he would ever have in his life, still in play. "We can be in and out of there again in one minute, Lynn. Sixty seconds, I swear it. And it's the only way. It's gotta happen because you've gotta know. And *he* knows. He'll never change his mind now, not for all his life. Unless he tries it again and nothing happens."

She swung the door open. "Go out through the gate. Not through my house."

"Think about it after I go", he said.

The screen door slammed.

"Ten minutes and ten minutes, Lynn, both times!" he called after her. "You can't hide from that."

She had stopped in the kitchen doorway. She wasn't facing him; she was just standing there, now easing into the kitchen, but slowly, and still listening. Maybe crying, he thought. Maybe still really mad. "You think about that", he said loudly. "Call me and I'll get you, but we have to make it before eight if any of us is gonna get to sleep tonight."

He still saw her shadowed movements through the glass as the kitchen door closed.

He shouted, "But tomorrow morning they'll have somebody else in there with her!"

By the time he hit Eleven Mile Road, Joe had a pretty good idea of how it would go. Lynn would think about it; she couldn't help doing that. And she'll talk with C.J. Then she'd get mad again. But, yeah, he thought, she'll do it. She'll go crazy if she doesn't, and she won't wait; that's not Lynn. She'll figure she's got to fix C.J. up right away. She'll look at the kid, worry about what he's thinking, try to talk herself into doing nothing, then she'll say to herself, Let's settle this mess right now.

"Seven o'clock", he whispered. She would call him just about the time he got home and tell him to turn around and pick them up at 7:30. And don't talk about it, is what she'd say. She'd say, "Let's just get this over with."

As it turned out, she didn't call him until 7:35.

"We see her and we get out", she said, "If anybody else is there, or if another patient is in there, we forget it. That's it. Either way, we don't wait." Her voice seemed flat and hard and far away. "And all the way there, Joe, and all the way back, I mean it, don't talk about it."

C.J. asked Lynn just one thing. He asked it from the backseat of Joe's car as they crossed Woodward Avenue just a quarter mile from the hospital. It was the first thing he had said during the whole ride. He asked her if "for absolutely positive" she wouldn't get mad at him if he made the third lady well. He asked it quietly and seriously.

Her eyes glazed with the beginnings of tears, and she loved him and said softly, "I won't get mad at you. You're my boy."

And then they were there.

The sixth-floor hall was empty. They bypassed the nurses' station, and they found the door to room 6110 standing open. No TV going inside. No visitors. No big nurse with a singsongy voice.

They went in slowly; Joe was first, then C.J., then Lynn, hanging back.

Joe was right about the Polish lady being moved out. Mrs. Welz was alone this time, her green curtain pulled a few feet along the side of her bed. They could see her hands as they entered the room—just her hands and her lower arms limp at her side, like she was asleep.

They heard loud voices from far down the hall, and Joe felt a sudden wave of apprehension. His heart was pounding. He guessed C.J.'s and Lynn's must be pounding, too, but the voices subsided almost instantly; it was somebody going from one room to another, that was all.

But this had to be quick.

He glanced at Lynn, who had stayed just inside the open door. She wasn't coming closer.

He put his hand on his son's shoulder and eased him toward the bed. "Just step up and do it", he whispered.

He wondered, suddenly, what would happen if C.J. got the name wrong. Would someone else be healed in some other place, but not Mrs. Welz?

"It's pronounced *Welz*", he whispered quickly. "Remember the wells in a desert."

"Hurry, honey." It was Lynn, whispering from far behind them, speaking so weakly that Joe looked around to see if she was okay.

C.J. was already moving. He stepped closer to the bed and saw the dying woman breathing hard, her face long and very still, her eyes closed, her mouth hanging open. He stared at the veins in her arms, and then at the covers raised over the points of her toes.

Voices again from down the hall. The nurses' station. Maybe closer. Maybe moving.

"*Hurry*, hon", Joe said, speaking louder this time, telling him, not asking him.

C.J. reached out his right hand. He touched the blanket that covered the woman's left toes with his index and middle fingers, very lightly. It was his only contact. Then Joe and Lynn heard him say it. It was the first time they'd heard it said.

"Be well, Mrs. Welz." Just that.

The boy withdrew his fingers. It was over.

Joe let out a breath and tried to smile, a single hush of relief. It was over and no one had come to interrupt them, and Mrs. Welz was still asleep, and it was over, but his heart wouldn't stop pounding.

Lynn wrapped her arms across her waist and pressed hard, her head bowed, her eyes raised and staring, still locked on C.J.

C.J. turned to look at Joe; then he saw his mom suddenly reach out toward him with her open hand, urging him to come away from this place with her. He walked past Joe to take her hand.

Her fingers wrapped tightly around his and she turned away, leading him silently out the door. She didn't look back at Joe. She didn't speak on the way to the car. She didn't speak on the way home. None of them spoke for a long time.

Joe kept turning to her, though, as they wound their way back to Eleven Mile and over to Hilton, trying to catch her eye. He wanted to tell her he'd like to go inside and wait for the news with her and C.J. Have something to drink, maybe, or share a bite to eat—just be there with her while she had that look that she got when she was worried but too proud to ask for any help, with her hair hanging down soft around the edges of her face. Old feelings coming back. Maybe because they just went through something important together. He thought about that. Old feelings, still warm.

"Lynn?"

She turned her head. Her eyes were half-closed and dull.

"What are you going to do now? You gonna wait for the news on TV?"

Lynn shrugged her shoulders and looked back out the window. "I don't even want there to be news", she said quietly. "I can't believe what we just did."

They both heard it. From the backseat. Just the tiniest whisper. "You'll see."

The young nurse looked up from her station on 6 North and froze.

One of her patients was standing quietly outside of her room halfway down the white-tiled hall, staring back at her. It was Mrs. Welz, who was very sick in room 6110. Her IV cord still hung from the back of her wrinkled hand. Her IV stand gleamed at her side. She was standing motionless and without support—her sleeping gown hanging loosely from her shoulders, her arms at her sides, her head tilted slightly forward, her eyes wide and unblinking.

She looked as if she had been waiting a long time to be discovered.

She looked as if she was amused.

Six

Lynn called Joe at 2:10 A.M. He wasn't sleeping, either; she knew that—not after the news about Mrs. Welz hit the air, not after they'd argued about what to do and what not do, going back and forth and getting nowhere, until nearly midnight.

"I'm going to see Father Mark at church in the morning", she told him. "I just wanted you to know." She said she had already told C.J. to stay home from school, and to sleep as long as he wanted in the morning since she might be out for a while when he woke up; she told him to just eat and play video games until she got back. She was hoping he would not gravitate toward the news—as though that would make any difference.

"Why do you want to see him?" Joe said. "We didn't do anything wrong. We don't need a priest."

"He's more than a priest; he's a friend—at least to me and C.J."

The fact was, she trusted Father Mark more than she would ever trust Joe again. She'd not only gotten to know the priest when she and Joe were going through their premarriage prep at the church, but he had been there for her all during her decision to get the divorce, there for her to talk with and pray with and even cry in front of. She knew he'd be there again, now that she needed a whole new kind of support.

They had, in fact, become close enough over the years that they'd been encouraged to simply call him "Mark".

"I'm going to go see him, Joe", she said. "I didn't call to talk it over. I just thought you had a right to know."

Joe knew her well enough to know when she was locked into doing something she would do it, so he just said he would like to go with her. Pick her up, in fact. She would not have to drive.

Father Mark peered out of the rectory door, saw Joe and Lynn on the porch and let out a soft "Oh, my gosh." He opened the door with a smile, glancing only briefly at the cluster of the several dozen of the

76

curious and the faithful who called out to him and pressed closer, moving up his front walk in hopes of joining the Walkers' early-morning audience.

He reached to shake Joe's hand. "Great to see you again, Joe", he grinned. "Lynn? How are you guys? Surprised to see you, I gotta say. Come on in."

"We're sorry it's so early, Mark," Lynn said, speaking quickly, "but it's really important that we talk with you. It's really important."

She said it twice, Joe noticed: "It's really important", said twice, and quickly.

He gestured, inviting them toward the rectory living room, the same room where he had met with them many years ago, when they were still practically kids and still in love and still wanting to be married to one another, and when he was still young himself. He said, "If you're here, I know it's important." He paused and added, "If you're together, I know it's important."

"We're not together that way", Lynn said.

Joe watched her with quiet eyes.

"Oh. Well. Have a seat. Can I get you a coffee or anything?"

"No, thanks."

"We were going to come to the morning Mass", Joe lied as he sat down. "I got a late start. My fault."

Lynn glanced at him sharply, saying nothing.

"A lot of people at Mass today", Mark said. "More than usual."

"We heard that", Joe said.

"Pretty incredible", Lynn whispered.

Joe sat at the left end of the couch, looking relaxed, his left arm stretched across the back of the tan cushions, his left ankle resting over his right knee. Lynn sat at the other end, out of Joe's reach. And then, with no buildup at all, there it was: Joe, uncrossing his leg suddenly and leaning forward, launched into it without any preliminaries, giving the priest both barrels. "We know what happened to Marion Klein, Mark. And we know what happened to those other two ladies, and that's the God's truth." Bang. That straightforward.

The priest blinked. He eased back in his chair. He folded his hands in his lap and stared at Joe, straight-faced.

"It's not a hospital energy field or anything like that, either", Joe said. "Not magic X-rays and stuff, like some of the reporters are talking about. There wasn't any energy field at the funeral home, was there, like there might be at a hospital? And that's where it happened with Marion, so it can't be that techno mystery stuff. Anybody'd know that, if they'd stop for two seconds and think about it. But we know how it happened, honest to God."

"We aren't sure", Lynn protested. She squirmed and crossed her arms.

"We know because we set up the second and third one ourselves", Joe said sharply. He didn't take his eyes off the priest. "So Lynn wanted to come and tell you about it, and I did, too, just to let you know and all, and see if you want to suggest anything we should do about it." He spread his hands and added, almost as an afterthought, "Of course, you may not want to get involved, and that's fine."

Then he stopped. He wanted to give the now wide-eyed priest a second to take in what he just had said, and to respond if he wanted to. And he wanted to measure whether he was going to be taken seriously, or laughed off the stage first thing, or what.

"We aren't even sure *what* we know", Lynn said. Then her voice trailed off, as though what began as firm determination was suddenly trying to find a place to hide. Her face was flushed. "We just think we might know something about it, is all, even though we don't understand it."

Mark shifted in his chair. His hands spread slowly. He took hold of the armrests. He said quietly, "I'm listening, Lynn."

Lynn nodded and cleared her throat. She uncrossed her arms, her hands squeezed together in her lap. "Well," she said, "let me begin with when C.J. and I went to Marion's wake service."

Joe settled back in the couch. So the priest was cool these days, he thought, thinking he's got two crazy people on his hands, but keeping his cool. Which meant all Joe could do was wait. Let Lynn do her thing. See how it plays out, but be ready to respond with whatever it would take to keep himself at the center of things—not the priest.

"C.J. wasn't thrilled to be there", Lynn continued. Her gaze shifted from to the rug and back again. "He wasn't scared, though, I don't think. I'm pretty sure."

She was rubbing her left thumbnail with her right thumb—kneading it with soft, even strokes.

"C.J.'s been at funerals before," Lynn said, "but I just thought that since he knew Marion from church, and knew her kids from school . . ."

Joe studied the priest like a cat, waiting to see if an eyebrow quivered or if some tell-tale instinct raced through the priest's eyes—anything to tell him if the priest was catching on that their secret about the miracles was really a secret about C.J.

So far, nothing.

Lynn was talking about how she and C.J. came back home after the wake, how she saw C.J. sitting on the couch and looking funny, like he was afraid. That was when Joe's mind started to wander. He began to think about other, more important things as Lynn's voice faded into the background.

He began to think about how C.J. was actually the most powerful person in the world. And he was the most valuable person, too, because, how much would people give to raise their dead? How about presidents and kings, or corporation heads? How much to bring your wife back, pal, or your dead baby? How much to bring *you* back? Would ten million dollars a week be too much to expect, he wondered, once they got started? Would ten million dollars a day?

Lynn was saying things about the school, telling how C.J. wouldn't respond to the teachers, and Joe pulled himself back momentarily, measuring the priest's reaction one more time. He should have put two and two together by now, he thought, with Lynn saying C.J. this and C.J. that, but still, no change in the guy's expression.

Father Cool or Father Dumb, he thought; which was it?

And that is when it hit Joe: the most incredible possibility of all, coming right out of the blue, hitting him so hard he almost let out an "Oh my God!" right on the spot. He thought, if Marion Klein came back after three days, how about bringing somebody back who'd been dead for ten days? Or thirty? How about getting somebody back who had been dead for more than a year?

He was suddenly on his feet, starting to pace. He motioned to Lynn to keep on talking, that he was okay, that he just wanted to get up and move around a little.

How about bringing Einstein back? How much would that be worth? How about Marilyn Monroe or Elvis or John Wayne? Pick your star. How about Princess Di or JFK? Skip JFK, how about Abraham Lincoln?

"Joe, what's the matter?" It was Lynn, looking concerned.

"Huh?"

"You look like something happened. What's going on?"

"Sure you don't want me to get you something from the kitchen?" Mark asked. "I've got cold juice, too, not just coffee."

Joe shook his head hard with two quick gestures and motioned the priest to stay put. "I'm fine", he insisted.

He sat down, as though demonstrating how fine he was, and he said it again, this time heavy with inflection. "I'm really fine. I didn't mean to look funny. I'm fine."

Lynn studied him, but Joe just smiled and nodded and waited.

"Well," Lynn said, shooting one more glance to her side, checking on Joe, "when Joe was talking about taking him to see Mrs. Welz ..."

A surprise to Joe. She had already been up to the hospital visit part, and he hadn't even noticed.

"... I knew it seemed insane," Lynn was saying, "and I said no at first, for sure." She looked serious, focusing hard, trying not to leave out anything that might be important. "But I finally thought, if the woman wouldn't know what we were doing, and if we could just do it and get that crazy idea out of C.J.'s head once and for all ..."

Joe's imagination, already primed, was breaking out again. Another unexpected idea, brand-new, only this time not promising at all. This time, a threat.

What if this wasn't really something God was doing at all—not like Almighty God was sitting there and planning it all, but if God was there and really did care, what if he was just letting it happen, like rocks falling or grass growing? He thought, there's about ten million what-ifs to this thing. Like, just coming to mind, so many people kept saying "miracle" and he did, too, like there was some gigantic plan behind it, but what if C.J. had just tapped into some kind of energy pool or something, and it was more like an accident? And what if there was just so much power in this energy pool, and then there wouldn't be any more left? Or what if one dead person, like Marion, who was actually dead, used up a whole lot of the energy or whatever it was, and then maybe a cancer patient who was just sick used up less, but still a lot, so every time C.J. tapped into it, the pool drained and got smaller?

He had crossed his arms, now he crossed his legs. He was staring at Lynn but was completely oblivious to what she was saying. What if the energy was draining out of C.J. on its own, right then, while C.J. was sitting around at home doing nothing, just eating Cheerios or playing video games and waiting for his mom to come back? Or worse yet, what if there was a time limit to it, like the kid had somehow warped into this thing, but he was going to warp out of it again at some specific time, two or three days, a week, ten days, and then it would all be gone forever? How could Joe know? The biggest thing in any of their lives by light-years, but how could anybody know?

And here they were just talking about it and doing nothing, just wasting the whole morning.

Lynn finished with how she heard the news report about the Welz lady and was sitting quietly, her hands folded in her lap, staring, waiting for advice.

Joe waited, too—waited for his chance to finish the thing up and get out of there.

Mark stared at the floor. He was leaning forward in his chair, his fingertips poised at his lips. He finally raised his eyes, looking first at Joe, then at Lynn. When he spoke, it was with a tone that was both sympathetic and confidential. "I can only tell you this", he said. "This is the fourth time parishioners have come to me with some conviction that they had somehow caused this to happen. From a lady who thought she had a vision to a pair who had fasted for a really long time, and prayed that Marion would make it. Absolutely sincere, all of them; sincere and convinced. Because they wanted to be convinced." He smiled. "I want to admit something to you. I even wondered for a little while about it myself, especially the other night. I mean, me thinking that maybe I even had something to do with it, because I led the prayers and all, you know? All of a sudden it's there in your mind and you say, 'Wow, could that really be?' But the answer is 'no'. The answer is 'no', folks. But still, it seems to be a natural place for people to let their imaginations wander. It happens. And it's more than natural, I'll bet, for a kid to go there. So several of us have gone there, really. But honest to goodness ..."

"All three women, Father", Joe said sharply. He wanted to get up and pace again. He wanted to get out of there. "Just a few minutes after C.J. touches them. Did all these other people who said they did it actually touch all three of these women like C.J. did?"

The priest thought for a moment, then asked, "Has C.J. ever imagined anything in the past that might be similar to this?"

Joe set his jaw.

"He's nine", Lynn said. "There's a lot of imagination, but there's never been anything like this."

Mark nodded, pausing for another long moment. "Hasn't it occurred to you that this whole idea on C.J.'s part has brought you two back together again, and that's what he wants, probably more than anything in the world? To have you come together again. At least for a little while? With both of you focused on him again? Don't you see how there really could be something else going on with him? Some other agenda that's a lot more personal to him, and a lot more important to him, than what happened or didn't happen to Marion Klein?"

"You don't think it's possible, do you?" Joe asked.

"I know he's a little kid, and he wants you and Lynn back together, Joe."

"So you think no way, shape, or form he can do this, correct?"

"I don't think any of these things happened because of C.J., no. And I don't think you're surprised to hear that. But I'd be glad to talk with C.J. if you'd like."

"Is it because he's just a kid?" Joe snapped.

Lynn cleared her throat and stared hard at Joe.

Mark stared at him, too, like he wasn't sure about the question.

"I'm just wondering", Joe continued, "if it was a priest or a cardinal or the Pope or somebody else high up in the Church, and they touched all three of these women and prayed they'd be okay, whatever words they used, and if all three of them got up miraculously healed, five, ten minutes later ... I'm just wondering, would you still sluff it off as being totally impossible?"

Lynn glared. "Cool it, Joe", she muttered.

"I said I'd be glad to talk to C.J. Then maybe you and Lynn and I could get together and talk again. I think that's the thing to do. If you don't want to do that ..."

Lynn was on her feet. "Thanks. That sounds good", she said quickly but softly. She moved toward the door. "I think C.J. would be glad to talk with you. He really likes you."

Joe stood up, too, but slowly, his mind racing to figure out how he could cut off more useless conversations. They'd talk about it for a month and a half, he was sure of that; a year and a half, for all he knew. They'd waste the whole thing and then look back and say it never happened—the most mind-bending thing ever, in all of history. Either that or, if the power didn't really run out but just kept being there, the priest would be so close to Lynn and C.J. by that time he'd want to take it over, for sure. He'd want Joe right out of things, make himself the one planning everything, himself or someone higher in the Church so he got the credit. That'd be the way it would go, for sure.

He followed Lynn to the door, leaving it to her and her priest to set a date when they'd waste time bringing in C.J. to talk.

All he knew was, he had to be the one to get the thing on the move again. He had to jump-start it with C.J. He had to risk wasting some of it, make it happen again, only this time with a dead person, and this time with Lynn watching from start to finish, because she still didn't have a clue.

He had to be the one, he decided, so he would be the one. And he'd do it right away, before the power had a chance to run out.

It was a sunny morning in midstate New York—bright, clear skies, temperature in the midseventies. A.W. Cross had just said good-bye to several Long Island associates who had stopped in early for a short and somber visit. Nothing relating to business—just a few minutes of close talk and a moment together at young Tony's bedside, an affectionate show of support for an old comrade-in-arms who was about to lose his only son.

The old man watched his visitors' car pull away and turned toward the house in silence, his hands limp at his sides. Torrie Kruger was with him. Their feet crunched softly in the crushed stone of the entrance circle as they approached the six steps leading to the front door.

Cross stopped. He turned to Torrie; his brow wrinkled under the weight of too many questions without answers. What he really wanted to know was why other people with cancer were getting better while his own son was still dying, but what he asked was, "These ladies in Michigan, Torrie, three of them now, all with cancer. You saw on the news; all from the same hospital. What's happening there, do you think?"

Torrie looked at his boss and shrugged. "Something's in the building, a few of them said", he answered. "It's a stretch, though. They really don't know what's happening, sounds to me. Or like the lady being dead; how could that even be legitimate?"

Cross was staring west across the estate's lake toward the line of maples standing thick with spring buds on the horizon. His eyes were narrowed. He might have been trying to see all the way to Michigan. He said, "Dead or not dead, the lady gets up—no more cancer. Two more dying ladies get up—no more cancer. First woman's room was right next door to the room where the other two ladies were. What does that mean?"

Torrie shifted his weight, looking uncomfortable. He said, "They don't talk about the other hundred people that probably died there yesterday. You know what I'm saying?"

A long pause.

Two blackbirds swooped past the hedge near the driveway, one chattering loudly.

"No", Cross sighed, still staring into the distance. He raised his right thumb and slowly rubbed his right eye, then his left. "All those others that died, maybe it was a hundred of them, but they weren't in those same two rooms, were they? They weren't right next to each other in those same two rooms."

"I guess that's right."

When he lowered his hand, Cross spoke in a soft and measured tone that Kruger recognized. "I want you to go there for me, Torrie. Would you do that? I want you to take whoever you want with you. Leave tomorrow morning, maybe. That would be good." He paused. "If it's the priest that's on the news doing it, I want the priest. If it's the hospital room, I want Tony in that room. Or the room and the priest both, I don't care." His eyes were dark and heavy and suddenly growing moist. "What I want, Torrie, is for the next person that gets well to be my boy."

Seven

Joe had never met Giles MacInnes, just seen him on TV over the past couple of days. But judging from the slump of the thin shoulders and the weak, rounded eyes of the man who approached the glass door of the funeral home to let him in, Joe knew that MacInnes had not only been fragile going into this storm, but he was melting down in the middle of it. Too much talk about criminal charges, he thought; too much talk about the man's incompetence or his lying; too much embarrassment for his family; too little proof to clear the guy's name.

"Mr. Walker?" MacInnes said, pulling open the door. Even his voice sounded thin.

"Call me Joe, please. Thanks for seeing me, Mr. MacInnes."

Joe had left the message at MacInnes' funeral home less than twenty minutes before. The message said that Joe was a good friend of Father Mark Cleary's at St. Veronica's Church, and that he knew with certainty what had happened to Marion Klein. Not only that, but it was all good news for Giles and for his business, and Joe was ready to prove it beyond any shadow of a doubt.

It took Giles just one minute to call him back and invite him for a meeting.

Now the undertaker led him back to his office so cautiously that Joe actually felt sorry for him. The poor guy kept looking back over his shoulder at Joe like he was afraid that any second Joe might reach out and bash him from behind.

In the relative safety of his office, Giles settled nervously behind his desk and gestured for Joe to sit facing him. An uncertain "please" seemed built into his gesture.

Joe scanned the desktop with a glance—ads; pens; four green candy mints in a clear glass bowl next to the phone, treats from a happier time; framed photos, too, 4×5s, all family shots, a half dozen of them. Half a dozen of the reasons, Joe thought, why MacInnes had been anxious to see what kind of proof Joe was talking about as soon as he could.

"I'm afraid I don't have coffee made, or much to offer you", Giles said.

Joe smiled. "Actually, we can offer something to one another, Mr. MacInnes." Then he leaned forward. He loved that, leaning forward to nail down a deal. "I can offer you something", he said, "because, since this country's legal system can't accept the reality of miracles in a court of law, folks are going to have to find you guilty of some pretty serious charges. All of them untrue, I know. But they'll close up your business, for sure. Ruin a fine family reputation."

"They've issued a restraining order", Giles admitted. He looked like he was going to cry.

Joe raised his hand, protesting the very thought. "I don't have to tell you that the real crime here is that we've got a legal system that bends over backwards today to legislate God right out of existence. You know what I mean? So how are they going to let you defend yourself by telling them that a miracle happened here, am I right?"

The color had drained from Giles' face, what little color there had been to begin with. "You said you have proof", he whispered.

Joe grinned. He leaned forward even farther, now laying his right hand facedown on Giles' desk, as if the desk was his Bible and everything he said from now on would be under oath. "Dramatic times call for dramatic measures, Mr. MacInnes", he said solemnly. "You see, you're the one who can supply the proof, or who can make it possible for me to supply it, anyway. And when you do, I swear it, I'll save your business, I'll save your reputation, I'll save your family's peace of mind, and the way things are going, sir, I just might well save your life."

Joe didn't know for sure. It was either God, or fate, or maybe just positive thinking and dumb luck, but a call came in to MacInnes just as Joe finished laying out the whole proposition—just as he had MacInnes thinking about it and maybe even leaning toward it. Although the man was still momentarily frozen, kind of, Joe could tell, about the legal end of things.

And then the call came in.

He could see MacInnes' eyes as he answered the call and started to talk with whomever it was, his eyes surprised and excited and afraid all at the same time, the man wrestling with what he should or shouldn't do—but not mentioning the restraining order, Joe noticed that, especially. Somebody had a body ready to go, that was obvious from MacInnes' questions and answers. There was a body at somebody's home. Life Support and the police had just left. So should MacInnes break the restraining order and take the biggest leap of his life or shouldn't he? Joe knew that's what was going through his mind. A really scary time for Mr. Thin if he took the chance, breaking the rules that way, hanging his neck out to embalm a guy after they told him to shut down his operations. But it was a certain, stone-cold disaster for him if he didn't take the chance because he'd never be able to prove that a miracle had really happened any other way.

In the end, Joe knew, taking a chance to rescue yourself despite a certain amount of risk was always better than just standing on the tracks and letting yourself get run over by a train.

He nodded at Giles and whispered, "Dramatic times, dramatic measures, Mr. MacInnes."

Less than fifteen seconds later he saw MacInnes' jaw set and his eyes go thin and hard, and he knew he had a done deal.

On his way back to the St. Veronica's rectory to get the priest on board, Joe was thinking about how it was all really a matter of buttons, the whole selling thing. Buttons and timing. Push the right buttons at the right time and you can make anything happen.

And everybody had his button.

For MacInnes, it was saving his family business and reputation. Three generations, all at the same place, his whole family involved. Press that one and he'd follow you anywhere.

For Lynn, it was C.J. No doubt about it. What's best for C.J., all the way.

For the priest, Joe was pretty sure, it would be the guy's responsibility to the Church. Not letting the Church get shut out. Or maybe his responsibility to God mixed in there, feeling like God would be expecting him to keep his bosses downtown front and center, because that was a priest's whole training. Like the Marines, the Corps came first.

But he had to be right about the priest, because the priest had to be first. If he could get the priest to go along with him, then he'd get Lynn on board, and Lynn was still the only way he could get to C.J. It was that simple. No priest, no Lynn—not a chance. No Lynn, no C.J. No C.J., or no C.J. real soon, and Lynn would have Mr. Clergy trying to inch his way into C.J.'s little psyche with heart-to-hearts over cookies and milk at the guy's rectory from now until Joe's whole once-in-a-lifetime chance was right down the toilet.

He pulled up two houses down from the rectory, not wanting to park where the crowd was gathered, and smiled again at the way MacInnes had folded. It was all going his way. MacInnes, the priest, Lynn, C.J.: come to Papa.

Then how about a party to celebrate the next resurrection from the dead? How about getting Elvis back for it, with maybe Jimi Hendrix to kick things off?

It was nearly three o'clock when Father Mark returned to his rectory.

Joe called to him over the back fence as the priest crossed his patio. He knew he was just one more face in the crowd at that point, but he was the only one telling the priest that something "climactic", the word he used, had just developed. Something "climactic" about C.J. He figured that would do it. At least get him five minutes inside the house.

In fact, the priest was cordial about it. He not only invited Joe in, but even asked if he wanted to take a seat in the living room, like before. And, again, he offered him a coffee or something else to drink.

Must have had a good meeting with Marion, Joe thought. The lady must have seen angels and saints and talked with God. Or said she did.

He made a mental note to ask about that, but not then.

In fact, he declined the offer to sit down and get comfortable. He wanted to get right into it, standing right there in the back hallway.

"Father, Lynn and I do want C.J. to talk with you", he began. "And thanks again for that. But at the same time, we decided we really do have to confirm for ourselves and for C.J., one way or the other, whether or not he can really do what we were talking about. And that's really, like, the top order of business, you know? We don't think that can wait, 'cause that'll drive all the conversations and everything else, if he proves he can really do it."

The priest was nodding but looking concerned.

Joe drew a breath. "So, we've made other plans, in addition to wanting C.J. to get together with you and talk. And we think your first reaction to this may be hesitant, but hear me out, OK? The open mind everybody talks about. 'Cause what we did was, we went and saw Giles MacInnes over at his place on Crooks."

His words were tumbling forward now, even quicker than before.

"The thing is, MacInnes is actually under certain mild restrictions, although the legal edges of everything are kind of blurred right now. But he's under public indictment, either way, and that's what's crushing him. And, of course, it'll be some kind of legal move real quick. He knows that. Today they criticize him; tomorrow they're going to take that guy that works for him, who supposedly did the embalming, and they're going to nail him upside down to the wall. And the next day, or whenever it is, but soon, they'll come after MacInnes and his business and his whole family. Be on him like white on a duck. He knows that, too. Everybody knows it."

He pressed closer. Close enough that the priest stepped back, keeping a distance.

"But you see, Father, MacInnes also knows what *you* know: that Marion Klein was ice-cold dead and one hundred percent embalmed the other day. So what I'm saying is, from his standpoint, what are the man's options? Heck of a spot. And then a guy comes in, which happens to be me, and I say to MacInnes, just sitting there nice and quiet and talking, I say, 'I know who did this to Marion Klein. And to the other women, too.'" Joe smiled.

He was the only one.

"You think that doesn't get his attention?" Joe said, losing the grin. "Remember now, he knows it's a miracle with Marion, 'cause he knows she's embalmed. And so I say, 'I know who did this.' Well, the man's eyes light up the sky. I say, 'You have a miracle here, and I know who did this.' So you tell me, Father? What's he going to say?"

No answer.

Joe shrugged his shoulders. "The man's going to say, 'Well, how can we *prove* that this person, whoever it is you're talking about, really has this power, enough to raise the dead?' And you know the answer to that?" His eyes were wide and innocent. "The answer is, at eleven thirty tomorrow morning . . ."

"Don't even say it, Joe."

". . . at eleven thirty, C. J., me, Lynn, and MacInnes are going to stand next to an embalmed guy in the funeral home, just a private meeting, just us and God, no TV or anything, and we're going to see with our own eyes what is or is not happening with our son. And we all hope you'll be there, too."

"No!"

"At least, we wanted to invite you."

He said it again. "No! Don't do this to your son, Joe. He can't raise the dead. Do you know how crazy you sound? Don't do this to him!"

"Not to him, Father. To a seventy-five-year-old man. Bringing him back to life."

"For God's sake, don't do this to C. J.!"

"Maybe you ought to give God more credit. God has already decided to 'do this to C.J.', as you put it. That's our whole point, mine and Lynn's. God's already decided this; we didn't, and C.J. didn't. So the only question for you is, in respect to your position, do you want the Church to get on board or not? Because you're the only way to get that done. It's you or nobody, as far as we're concerned."

Mark was shaking his head. He stepped back and turned as though he was going to go up into the kitchen, but then he swung again to face Joe. "This is really sick, Joe. This is obscene, and you can't do it."

"Why don't you just look at it like a healing, only more of it? Because that's what it is, is a miraculous healing. Or don't you believe in miracles?"

If he had been watching carefully, Joe would have noticed a wince, showing itself ever so lightly.

"This is way beyond healing. You know it."

"A healing is when cells that are dead come back to life again, right? So that's all it is. Enough cells come back to life and the whole body's alive. Maybe if C.J. turned colors or something, or if his finger glowed red like E.T., or maybe if he levitated a few inches off the ground, would that make it easier for you to believe it?"

"It's abusive, Joe. You can't talk your way around that."

"Nobody gets hurt", Joe said. "Think about it. If nothing happens, we go home. No harm, no foul. C.J.'s embarrassed, but so what? He'll be okay. But if it does happen, then, you see, the Church should be there. Which seems right to us. Not necessary, but it seems right to us. It's up to you, though, is what I'm saying."

"And you don't want me to talk with C.J. first?"

"After. We're on this tomorrow morning, like I said."

"And Lynn wants this, too?"

Joe lied with a nod. "We both know it's gotta be done, Father. She doesn't really *want* it, I guess I'd have to say, but yeah, she does want it in the sense that we agree it has to be done. And she'd like you to be there. You know that, for sure."

"And the family of the dead person?"

"Won't even know about it." A broad smile. "Unless the man comes to life, of course, and then they'll thank God to high heaven. Everything to gain, nothing to lose; that's one of the best parts."

"And you're talking about a body that's been embalmed?"

"As we speak. Just like Marion Klein was."

"Well, I can't and won't be there. I'm just trying to decide whether to call the police or MacInnes to stop the whole thing right now."

"If it isn't done there, Father, tomorrow morning, it'll just be some-where else the next day", Joe said calmly. "The only difference is, the Church won't be invited next time."

He stared at the priest and smiled.

Mark let a full ten seconds slip by, then he answered with deliberate calm, "You get one chance here, Joe. You're working hard to get me there, and you're talking 'the Church this' and the 'Church that', but we both know you don't really care that much about what happens to the Church. If that's wrong, I'm sorry. But I'm thinking that you want me there for yourself, for your own reasons, and I'm asking you to tell me what those reasons are. Without blowing smoke at me."

Joe stared, then nodded. "Yeah, we do want you there", he said. "And the reason, to tell you the whole truth, is because we, and maybe MacInnes, especially, we'll need credibility this time. And you're the most credible witness that we can think of. That's how simple it is. Straight up."

"A dead man walking should be credibility enough".

"Marion Klein isn't credible to most people, is she? Same thing. They ask, 'Was she embalmed?' MacInnes says, 'Yes.' They say, 'Oh yeah, well, guess what? You're shut down, probably going to jail.' If they don't believe him about Marion, they'll cut his throat if he tries to claim number two. Unless they have a better reason to believe him this time. So if you're there, then you'd be able to tell them with absolute honesty, 'Here's exactly what I saw.' That's it. That's all he'd want you to do, but to him, it means everything. He certainly wouldn't ask you to lie."

Mark was shaking his head no again, but more slowly this time, and with less conviction.

"It's your decision, obviously", Joe said, turning toward the door. "Like I said, we'll be seeing what happens either way at eleven thirty tomorrow, at the funeral home. We have to know, and tomorrow's the day. In the meantime, we're hoping you'll think long and hard about Marion Klein, and about how you know she was really embalmed. And remember, too, you've got nothing to lose by coming. On the other hand, if you *don't* show up, and C.J. *can* bring the guy back, well ...", he shrugged and opened the door. "You can think it over. And no need to call or anything; we'll be there."

He stepped onto the porch, then turned and cocked his head. "By the way. Marion Klein. Did she see angels and stuff?"

Mark had to think "No", he said in a subdued voice. "No angels; no."

"Nothing?"

"It was bright. She was happy. It might just as easily have been impressions as she was starting to wake up. Hard to tell." He let it go at that.

"Not what you were hoping for, huh?" Joe said.

"A lot of things happening today aren't what I'd be hoping for."

Eight

Lynn wished that she had called Father Mark herself, right after Joe told her that the priest wanted to meet them at the funeral home at eleven thirty. She wished she had argued it out with the priest, told him that if anything bad happened to C.J. because of this she would sue the diocese or something, and the parish, too. But as close as she came to doing that, the craziness with C.J. always came out the same in her own mind: the thing had taken on a life of its own, and it had to be exposed and ended quickly. It could not be left to linger and grow in the kid like a plant. It had grown too strong already, not only in C.J. but now in Joe, and maybe even, to some degree, in her. And at this stage, with both C.J. and Joe believing that C.J. really had supernatural powers, and with her no longer being sure one way or the other, going to the funeral home, even with it feeling so sickening to her, might be exactly what it would take.

If it was, she finally decided, let's have at it.

Now she waited. Joe would pick them up soon. Get them there five or ten minutes after eleven thirty, the time they agreed on, so that everything would be sure to be ready. They could just walk in then and have C.J. say his words, and walk out. Or at least get away from the body.

Lynn heard C.J. flush the toilet upstairs. As he started down the stairs she shuddered and held tightly to the edge of her front door.

Mark had told himself as he woke and dressed that if he showed up at the funeral home it would be for C.J. Walker's sake. The boy would almost certainly need extra support when he tried to raise the corpse. His dad had a big appetite and big ambitions, and would not be a happy man when nothing happened.

He had also told himself that he'd show up for Lynn's sake—her being in such a hard place, not wanting to believe what she was being told but feeling caught up in the suction of Joe's expectations. He liked her and felt sorry for her.

He had convinced himself, finally, that it would be good to be there in order to keep the Cardinal better informed. True, this couldn't be a resurrection, but it would be an example, at least, of what the fevered edges might be doing in response to the Marion Klein mystery, in other places as well as here. That's what he had told himself.

He had not been able to admit that he wanted to come, when all was said and done, because Marion Klein was alive again, and perfectly well, and because there were two more women in Fremont Hospital now whose cancer had cleared up instantaneously, and because, as irrational as it might seem, he really did want to see for himself if the nine-year-old named C. J. Walker might actually have been given the power to break the hold of death with four quiet words and the simple touch of his hand.

Now he felt hot, as though the temperature in the room was much too high and the air, already stale with embalming fluid that smelled as strong as syrup, was getting too thick to breathe.

He moved closer reluctantly.

The light was soft on Mr. Galvin Turner, who looked and felt, indeed, embalmed.

His body, dressed in what had been his favorite dark-blue pin-striped suit, looked as if it had made it easily into old age and been generally healthy along the way. His skin was clear; his hair thick and only slightly receded, dark gray, not white; and he was a healthy-looking thin, even in death. His lips, especially, were thin, the way they were glued together and pressed flat, much like the lids of his eyes.

Mark felt the back of the dead man's hand. It was cold, a thin covering of loose skin over hard cold. He wondered if the man's gums had metal pins in them and if the gash that would be under his freshly pressed white shirt was sewn together uglily with kitchen string, the way Marion's had been. But Galvin Turner's eyes and lips were pasted shut, and his shirt was buttoned tight under his neat, red tie, so he didn't go looking for scars. Besides, he didn't have to see the scars. He knew.

He suddenly wanted to turn and walk away from the madness these people were pressing upon him, but he didn't. He felt the skin on the back of the old man's hand again, pressing it hard with his fingertips; then he pressed into the cold, hard cheeks. A thin wrapping over hard cold all the way around, and all of it smelling of embalming fluid. He held his fingers over the corpse's open nostrils. There was no need for the man to breathe.

Galvin Turner was dead. He was dead, and, yes, he was embalmed. And that was that.

Giles stood close to his priest, but said nothing. Only his eyes moved, still frightened.

"How did he die?" the priest asked quietly.

"Watching television. His wife didn't even know it until he was cold. She thought he was asleep. He had a heart attack. Two heart attacks in the past six months, and then this one."

"EMS certified him dead?"

"They certified it at the hospital." He picked up the record and handed it to the priest, who looked at it and gave it back.

"His wife called you?"

"Yes", Giles answered.

"You got the body from the house?"

"His wife asked me to."

"So you got it right from his house?"

"From his chair, in front of the TV."

"Who embalmed him?"

"I did. No one else was here."

Father Mark had not taken his eyes off the body. Now he pressed his fingertips again into the dead man's cheek.

"I need the records", he said. "Copies of the records. Everything. The ambulance. Who was involved. Time of death. Who signed off on it. Your records, the embalming and everything."

At this, Giles smiled faintly and retrieved a manila envelope from the table behind them. He handed it to the priest, saying, "All the records. All the verifications. All the signatures, and more. Sixteen photos of the embalming process, and a video recording, so there can't be any questions."

Father Mark whispered a breathless, "Good Lord!" and opened the package.

"I can cut into him again if you like. If you need that."

"Please be quiet, okay?"

After one quick glance at the report, he continued, "I'll take all of this when I leave", and returned the envelope to the table.

He realized that he never wanted anything more than to leave that room and never come back. But he didn't leave. He was trapped.

He touched the man's skin one more time, the thin layer over the hard cold. He wondered for a second what would happen if he tried to bring Mr. Turner back to life himself, without C.J. But he didn't try it. He knew perfectly well what would happen, just as he knew perfectly well what was about to happen if and when the Walkers brought their son here and set him on this grisly stage so that the father, who wanted his son to be famous, could drag the boy into a spotlight and say, "Tell the dead man to get well, C.J., like Dad taught you."

He could not only imagine the dreadful performance; he could feel it coming.

He drew a deep breath and turned away. He was sweating. He could smell the embalming fluid and was still finding it hard to get a deep enough breath. His back was to the casket, though, facing away from the body that used to be someone's husband. He visualized the rows of red-seated chairs and the dark-carpeted aisle upstairs, and imagined C.J. and his parents as they would come through the white splash of light shining through the doorway from the front lobby. He saw them in his mind's eye coming down the aisle, moving without a sound to witness this unthinkable experiment—a man, a woman, and a very, very young boy.

The pilot and copilot saw the familiar dark-gray Mercedes sedan ease around the corner of the Rockwell International hangar and sweep toward them from the east. They had been alerted nearly six hours before, and the Learjet 31A was ready for takeoff for three passengers to Detroit City Airport, ASAP.

In the front passenger seat of the approaching Mercedes, a thin, middle-aged man, sitting rigidly, studied the waiting plane without expression. Behind him was a heavy set and hard-looking attorney, looking comfortable. Nothing to worry about. Next to him, directly behind the driver, was a younger man, blond and not so comfortable. He looked like a man who was physically hard, but who still had not entirely settled into the dangers of his chosen profession.

The sedan came to an easy stop. The driver jumped out, moved quickly to the open trunk, handed two carry-on bags to the plane's copilot, then carried a third bag toward the plane himself. The young blond man stepped out of the car and handed the plane's pilot a brushed-leather attaché case. The ex-FBI agent stepped out and stood beside the blond man, waiting.

The thin man in the front seat waited until the pilot had joined the copilot and driver at the plane; then he swung his door slowly and stepped out to join the others.

"Okay, gentlemen", Torrie Kruger said calmly. "Let's go get us a miracle."

Incredibly, nothing was said when C.J. and his parents showed up. No introductions. No instructions.

Father Mark drifted backward, staring at the boy. A good kid. One of the kids that he really liked. He had baptized him and seen him so many times since; on the school playground, in the Christmas pageant, in church next to his mom, always on the left side, always about ten pews back. He had seen him the other night, too, in this same room, this same young boy with his brown hair and dark, serious eyes and features that were still young but already sharp, but he couldn't remember seeing him close to Marion's body.

He thought, so much happens while we're looking the other way.

Giles had drifted away from the casket, which was positioned in the usual viewing spot and was opened, showing the dead man—plastic skin in a nice, clean suit. He walked up the aisle to greet the Walkers halfway. He nodded to Lynn, and then to C.J. he said, "Hi, C.J.", while the boy looked at the floor without answering. He extended his hand toward Joe, who took it without gripping it tightly and asked, "Everything's set to go?"

"I guess", Giles said.

Lynn and C.J. moved past the two men, ignored Giles' forced smile and his muttered welcome, and approached the body in the casket. Only the body in the casket. All the rest of them were window dressing to her now. Now there was only C.J., and the body of this old man lying dead in a casket.

C.J. looked serious and worried. Very serious and very worried.

Lynn looked at the man's face without color in her own, and without expression, angry now and realizing it, that she'd ever agreed to this. But yes, it had to be settled.

"Let's get it over with", she said, without taking her eyes off the nameless dead man.

Mark stood at the foot of the casket, noticing that there were tears in Lynn's eyes. And they weren't, he sensed, tears from anxiety, or tears from fear, but really from sadness. A sadness for C.J., he believed. A grieving in advance. It was like watching a Pietà.

And it was then, as he watched Lynn and tried to imagine what was going on inside of her, that he wondered for the first time what the people who ran the world would do with C.J. Walker if this old man really did wake up.

But Lynn and C.J. had taken their positions. Every other movement had stopped.

Giles was six feet to the left, on Lynn's left side, looking rigid. Mark was four feet to C.J.'s right and back just a step, where he could still watch the boy's lips, because he wanted to see him say the words and watch him touch the body. Joe stood behind Lynn and his son.

The silence was stunning.

Lynn's hand slipped slowly out of C.J.'s grasp and moved to the middle of the boy's back. She patted him twice, softly; once, then again, as easily as that. And then it was time.

C.J. pressed closer to the body, his lips tight, eyes unblinking, getting ready.

Mark wondered, if he really felt sure that nothing could happen, why his heart was pounding so wildly? He glanced quickly at Giles, just a split-second glance, not wanting to miss anything, and saw an expression carved so deeply in fear that it looked grotesque.

But C.J.'s fingertips had already reached the old man's hand. His fingers were already on the man's skin itself—a nine-year-old boy touching an old man's skin, staring at the old man's closed eyes.

Joe had pressed forward, holding his breath.

Lynn's hand moved slowly to cover her mouth, ready to keep a scream from escaping, or a cry for help, or maybe her own life's breath.

Giles was swaying slightly, his expression now looking as vague as a trance.

And then it was there. Just a whisper, but it seemed to fill the room. C.J. moved his lips, his fingers still touching the back of Mr. Turner's hand, and he breathed a soft, "Be well, Mr. Turner." Four words. No more. And he withdrew his hand.

Mark blinked and looked again at the others, quickly. Lynn's eyes were shut. Joe was staring wide-eyed at the corpse, holding his breath. Giles looked white and drained and shocked, like a man who had died with his eyes wide open and watching his killer. The dead man's eyes stayed shut.

C.J. turned, wondering what he should do next, but a smile was seeping into his dark eyes and inching its way across his lips.

"Oh my God", Lynn whispered. She looked sharply at Mark, still looking sad, but now desperately so. Then she reached out to C.J. and took his hand, then turned in the aisle and started to move quickly toward the door, pulling C.J. beside her.

"Mom, wait", C.J. insisted softly. He tugged in her grip, hoping to twist away from her.

"We aren't leaving, honey, okay?" she said. "We're going to wait in the lobby, but not in here." Her voice was shaking.

"No, Mom. You gotta see!"

She paused and pressed her eyes closed, then squatted down in front of C.J., her back to the casket. She was holding her son's arms with both hands and looking hard into his eyes. "C.J.," she said, "I'm asking you to wait with me in the lobby, honey. Do this for me!" Tears again, now obvious, moving down her cheeks. "I'm not going to wait in here. I'm willing to wait, but I have to wait in the lobby. Please do this for me, honey; please, please, please!"

C.J. turned and looked past his dad and Father Mark. He looked again at the man named Mr. Turner. "But he's alive, Mom", he said softly. Then he looked again at his mother, saw the tears again, saw her quivering lips and how hard she was trying not to cry even more, and, holding her by the hand, began to lead her slowly back to the lobby, with neither of them looking back.

Mark was exhausted. He looked at the face of the old man who was still dead, and he moved to slump in a chair in the front row. He was back to wishing that he wasn't there. Nothing would happen, and he felt like such a fool.

Joe sat down, too, front-row center, staring blankly at the casket.

Giles was staring at the body in the casket, still. Giles had never looked away.

Five minutes passed.

The old man, Joe, Father Mark, and Giles—no one was close enough to touch another or be touched by another. No one was speaking. No one knew what the other was thinking. The old man was still dead.

Ten minutes.

And then, like a quiet splitting of the earth, Mr. Galvin Turner wasn't dead anymore.

Father Mark noticed it first. He thought he must have imagined it, so he came to his feet slowly, his heart thundering. He stared at the old man's hand. Crazy, but did he see it? Just one finger, shifting up into sight, just an inch, two inches maybe, but moving, visible from the front row.

Giles and Joe saw the priest get up, and they were suddenly on their feet, too, not knowing what was going on but seeing the look of astonishment in the priest's eyes and knowing that the priest thought he had seen something.

Joe practically shouted to Lynn, making her name sound like a question. "Lynn?"

The three men moved closer to the old man that might not be dead after all, their eyes fixed on his face, not knowing but wondering, standing close enough now to touch him, standing close enough to be touched.

Lynn and C.J. moved into the doorway at the back of the room. They just stood there, far away, not coming closer.

Then, there it was there again. The hand twitched, only this time they all saw it.

Giles sucked in his breath and let out a sharp cry, like an "Aw." Joe whispered, "Jesus", so fast that the name was barely pronounced. Father Mark turned away from the hand that seemed to twitch and looked desperately for orientation, just needing to make sure that he was still there in a real place and that he was really awake. He saw Lynn. He saw C.J. Then he looked back at the old man, and it was there again, just a little, but it was there. A twitch. The man's finger was moving. His index finger was rising from its place on his chest, rising a half inch in the air, then an inch in the air, then his whole hand rising with it, with Giles breathing a sound like "Aw" again and rocking back and forth and Joe saying, "Jesus", over and over and not moving at all.

The priest staggered, his legs shaking. Turner's hand rose more, now to the right, pulling away from his other hand.

My God, he thought, this is really happening! He felt his eyes flooding with tears and the whole room flooding with prophets from all the ancient ages—prophets and angels and saints. What was happening in this place? A man is being raised from the dead!

Prophets and angels and saints—with all of their old chants and praises ringing higher and higher, with all of the them seeing this time and this place and this group gathered now in the power of God to make this room a tabernacle, to transform this building into a cathedral. A man is being raised from the dead!

Turner's hand was poised now in midair, as though waiting, as they all heard the priest's voice whispering loudly and with desperate certainty, over and over again, "This is really happening! This is really happening! This is really happening!"

They had agreed that Giles would call 911 as soon as the Walkers left. They had also agreed that Father Mark would stay to verify Giles' account of what had happened to Mr. Galvin Turner. Finally, they had agreed that C.J., Lynn, and Joe would remain unidentified until Lynn okayed a release of the information, giving them time to plan their next steps in secrecy. That process, Joe estimated, would only take a few days, tops. Then the full story could come out. But not until they were ready; 911 was called at 12:15.

"If he dies again before they get here," Giles asked Father Mark, "then what?" One more thing the pastor admitted that he didn't know.

The emergency medical team arrived at 12:23, better time than they had made on Tuesday evening. Mr. Turner, still unconscious, was breathing normally. His condition appeared identical to the immediate condition of Marion Klein.

By 12:40, fourteen reporters were on the scene, representing not only local and national news but several tabloids. Most had come in a fast-moving caravan directly from Fremont Hospital, where the combination of two new healings, Marion Klein's return to consciousness, and the new buzz about magnetic fields was still generating major interest. Others came from their local offices in the area, alerted through heightened private and public monitoring of medical and police frequencies, as well as hurried calls between the growing army of media spotters in and around Fremont Hospital and the Royal Oak area in general.

This time, Father Mark had to wait and speak with them.

It was only 9:00 P.M., but Joe was home again and feeling exhausted. It was too much tension, even for him, watching an actual dead man come back to life again. But he didn't care how tired he felt or how long he'd lay awake; he was having too good a time seeing everybody go nuts on the news.

He had been news watching all afternoon and evening, most of the time with News Radio 970 providing background from the clock radio in his bedroom. He'd watched Giles MacInnes bobbing and flapping on four different channels like a grinning, grounded bird, telling reporters everything but "who". He'd watched the priest tiptoe through his clerically correct minefield, talking about what he saw without ever drawing conclusions that could come back to haunt him, or haunt anyone above him.

He wasn't surprised by either performance. What he was both surprised and amused by was the fever pitch of the public when they heard the news.

He had expected more cynicism. So a priest says, "I saw this and that." So what? But the public's doubt wasn't nearly as strong as Joe had expected. It was like the people being interviewed in bars and shopping malls and restaurants and hospitals were rushing past their usual cynicism to hold on, instead, to something they wanted so much to believe that they chose to believe it no matter what any of the "experts" said.

So the coverage was getting huge. One of the network affiliate station managers even gave a commentary about the dangers of the media setting off a "resurrection wildfire".

Joe loved that idea: a wall-to-wall resurrection wildfire.

He opened another beer and wondered about what other people would do in his shoes. Other ways of looking at where he should take it next. He had a few days to plan, at least, so what would the smartest guys he knew do with all this?

Then he thought of a whole new twist. What if, he thought, the touch doesn't really do anything at all? What if it's just the voice? What if you could get a room full of people and C.J. could just shout, or just use a loudspeaker, like at a stadium? Or take it the other way. What if C.J. didn't have to talk? You line all these bodies up on beds or stretchers, dead people and sick people and all, and C.J. just runs between them, touching them. Or better yet, you drive him between them, and he's just touching their toes out the window, thirty miles an hour; wham, wham, wham.

If the kid didn't use the power up or run out of time with it, that is. That was the one thing. Scary.

He turned his thoughts to better things. He thought, I wonder what happens when C.J. touches me right now, if there's energy coming out of him all the time, if maybe something's happening that helps everybody, even if they're still alive. For that matter, he thought, even if I do die, it wouldn't be for long—not as long as C.J. stays healthy.

And the kid could heal himself, too, if he got really sick. Just say, "Be well, C.J." He could go forever that way, Joe thought, grinning. As long as he did not die in his sleep or have somebody shoot him in the head or something. But why would anybody do something like that, shoot a kid who could do what C.J. could do?

He laughed out loud and decided to give News Radio another turn— just to hear the priest and the undertaker's sound bytes, just for fun.

This was so flat-out, spectacular awesome, he felt like he might never go to bed.

If they think they've got a wildfire now, he thought, wait till we bring back a major movie star who's been dead and buried for ten years.

Lynn had asked C.J. if he wanted to sleep in her bed—she and he together. He shook his head no, which surprised her.

She wondered, just for a second, if this was the day she might be losing him as a young boy. She wondered, just for another and more chilling second, if his power could mean that she'd lose him, period.

At 10:30 P.M., C.J. climbed into his own bed, late, and Lynn sat at his side, and they talked for a long time, and in a way, for the first time. He told her again, speaking slowly at first, in the dark, how creepy it had been to hear about Mrs. Klein, and then to be right there and see Mr. Turner moving, even though he knew it was going to happen. He told her how he still didn't feel heat or any special physical thing. And how he didn't talk to God about it, but he figured God must be making it happen. And how his dad had said that they wouldn't really be mad at him or think he should go to jail or anything for doing it. But how, up until then, he was kind of scared.

And, yes, he said, he could do it again. He was sure.

Then he whispered, "Are you scared, Mom? You seem scared."

"No, I'm not scared", she said, trying hard to act the part. "Why do you say that?"

"You look like it."

"No, hon. I'm just thinking, I guess I wish you wouldn't do this again. Okay, honey? I'm not scared, but I think that's really important. Okay?"

He thought about it, uncertain that he wanted the restriction. "Why?"

"Not to dead people, and not to sick people, either," Lynn insisted softly, "even if they're in the hospital, or whatever. Promise me, okay?"

"But why?"

Lynn didn't tell him it was because if he did it again, people might find out it was him, and that if that happened they wouldn't be able to stop the crowds from coming and hammering on their door and coming into their house and making him do it again and again and again and again. She said, "Because it's not something we should just experiment with to see what happens. You know that, too, don't you?"

He thought about it. Nobody had died that he wanted to bring back, anyway, and he didn't even know anybody that was real sick. Finally, he said, "I'll ask you first if I want to do it again. Is that okay?"

"But we won't know. Maybe somebody's supposed to be dead, and just see God and be happy and not come back, you know?"

"I guess."

She nodded and smiled and hoped he accepted what she thought were not very convincing reasons. She stroked his hair in the dark, and they were quiet together for several minutes. Then she asked with a whisper, "If people ever find out what you can do, C.J., what do you think would happen?"

He lay still for a moment, thinking; then he shrugged. "I don't know." He was whispering, too. "They'd want me to bring back important people, I guess."

"What kind of important people? People that are important to you, or just to them?"

"Like, if the president died or something, they'll want to fly me to Washington and bring him back. People like that. I guess."

"And would we still live here, do you think, or would we have to move?"

"I don't want to move. They can just pick me up and then bring me back, can't they? And you'd go along with me, wouldn't you?"

"Sure I would", she said. "Whatever happens. You know that."

In the silence that followed, she thought how radically different the power looked to him from the inside looking out than it did to her from the outside looking in.

"They'll pay us, too, won't they?" C.J. asked. And with that, he nestled toward her.

She could hear the smile in his voice, surprised and delighted and fresh with discovery, as he added, "You won't have to work anymore, Mom."

"That would be nice, hon." She held him close. He was as warm as fresh bread. "But I don't mind working, either."

"But you won't have to", he insisted, whispering again.

Lynn leaned over and kissed him on the forehead and eased him back down on his pillow. "And you know how much I love you, don't you?"

He said, "Okay", not, "I love you, too", Lynn noticed, but just a satisfied "okay", as if to say "So everything's the way it should be."

But everything was not the way it should be.

There was such a thing as too much power. And there would be a terrible price to pay if people found out he had it.

Lynn had never felt more certain of anything in her life.

Nine

It was something like a board game he remembered from when he was a little kid, the one where you take metal tweezers and reach into bloodred holes cut into a cartoon man's body and try to pick up tiny, white, plastic bones. But if your tweezers touch the metal edge of the hole, then the buzzer goes off and the red light in the man's nose lights up and you know you screwed up and you lose. Only Father Mark didn't have tweezers this time. He had thick metal wires. They were gold, like brass. And this time, the man's body with the little white bones in bloodred holes was not just a cartoon painted on a board with a red light for a nose. It was Mr. Turner, his finger still twitching, his eyes still closed, little holes with little bones in them all up and down his body.

He decided to quit playing, though, because every time he reached for a bone with the twisted brass wires the buzzer went off and Turner raised his head and glared at him, wide awake and furious, as though he wanted to shout, "Why didn't you leave me alone?" Only he couldn't say the words because his mouth was wired and glued shut. He had been embalmed.

The real problem, though, was that the buzzer in the game wouldn't stop going off, even after he threw the brass wires into the piles of sheets that lay in mounds along the edges of the room. The buzzer kept sounding, and Turner kept rearing his head up and glaring. Mark was trying to tell him that he wasn't doing it, that he wasn't even playing anymore, when he noticed that the buzzer sounded very far away, and somehow seemed familiar to him. He forced himself to think about that. He even tried to shift his head, although he didn't want to pull it away from its warm place in the pillow.

And then he knew.

The doorbell buzzed again in the hall downstairs. He opened his eyes, hoping he was in a position to see the digital face of his alarm clock. He was. It was 3:50 A.M. He turned on his bedside lamp and got up. He tried to put his pants on in a hurry. His heart was racing. He realized how much he hated to hear a doorbell buzzing in the middle of the night. He hated phones when they rang in the middle of the night, too, although the ringer was turned off on the phone downstairs and they couldn't hear the answering machine from the bedroom, but a doorbell was worse because you knew that somebody was physically there, standing outside in the middle of the night, and they couldn't possibly be happy. Nobody comes for you at 3:50 in the morning unless there's pain.

It buzzed again as he stumbled into the hall. Lord, he hated this.

Father Steve came out of his room in his bathrobe just as Mark started down the stairs. He said, "We still have the 'Do not disturb' sign on the door, don't we?"

"People ringing it for fifteen minutes at four in the morning, something's up." Mark shook his head. "I don't know if I can take much more of this."

His young associate followed him, too curious to stay behind.

Mark turned on the porch light and peered out the thin window next to the door. He saw a man and a woman—the man in his sixties, dressed in a sport shirt and casual slacks, unshaven but looking clean-cut; the woman he recognized as Ruth Cosgrove from Channel 3. "I don't believe this", he said bitterly. "It's reporters."

Worse, there were other people out there who had rushed to stand behind the two reporters now that the porch light had been turned on—the "resurrection groupies", as Father Steve had dubbed them, and other reporters and believers and curiosity seekers who had clearly decided, especially after the Turner resurrection, that Father Mark once again deserved an all-night vigil. It looked like there could be thirty of them already.

He opened the door six inches, just enough to see that the "Do not disturb" sign was, in fact, still in place. The older man crowded into the space offered by the barely opened front door, and Mark snapped, "You can read the sign and you can tell the time. What do you want?" He said it loudly. First, because he wanted them to hear him over the sudden shouting from the crowd, which, encouraged by the opened door, was now moving up to the porch. Secondly, he wanted them to know they were not talking to someone who was glad to see them. The sign said, "Please do not disturb for any reason", and he and Steve had been very much disturbed. The pair had better have a very good reason.

The face in the gap didn't speak. Instead, the man reached his right hand through the six-inch opening, offering the priests a business card. The crowd behind him had pressed onto the porch, most of them talking now, a few calling out, the volume increasing. Ruth Cosgrove jerked heavily into the man's back as someone pushed hard into her. Mark snatched the card and shut the door hard.

The card read "WGRV-TV Channel 3. Kenneth V. Stoddard: News Director". It had an address, phone number, fax number, and e-mail address. He turned it over to read the handwriting on the other side.

"What is it?" Steve asked.

Mark's mouth had opened weakly. His head shook a very slight no. His body visibly sagged. He blinked. He read the card a second time, then a third. He drifted an absentminded step backward and stopped, still staring at the card.

"What the heck is it, Mark?"

He read the card one more time, silently. Then, without looking up and without speaking, he handed it to Father Steve.

The penciled handwriting said: "*Turner Resurrection was videoed. Have ID of boy and parents. Will air video at 5:00 A.M. Do you wish chance to see it and comment first?*"

They settled into the small study that housed the rectory TV and DVD—Mark and Father Steve with Ken Stoddard and Ruth Cosgrove.

Ruth told the two priests that Giles MacInnes had showed up at their station with a two-hour video at 11:45 P.M. Giles told the 11:00 news producer, who was still there, that he had kept the original. The producer called her in, since she'd been mother-henning the story since the Marion Klein incident. They carefully reviewed the entire video, judged it to be a "possible authentic", and called Stoddard at home at 2:15.

There was no more introduction than that. The video was inserted and they waited. There was black. Then fuzz. Then there was Giles MacInnes. And what followed was worse than anything the priests could have imagined.

Giles wasn't in the visitation chapel of the funeral home. He was in his embalming room. He was wearing a protective slip-on gray nylon top covered by a full-length, yellow rubber apron. He had thick, yellow rubber gloves. His expression was defiant, his eyes wide with secrets he was about to reveal. The camera view began as a close-up, covering him from his head to his waist as he gave his name and told where he was. He said, "It is my belief that anything as remarkable as what I have faith is going to happen here at the MacInnes Funeral Home tomorrow, on Friday, May 9, demands to be made public in its most unquestionable form."

Mark slid to the edge of his chair, horrified. He whispered, "Oh Giles, don't do this!"

The lens widened to reveal an old man's body lying on a white porcelain table that tilted slightly toward the man's feet.

"It's Mr. Turner!" Father Steve gasped. "Oh God."

The old man's head was lodged over a red rubber block placed behind his neck. His elbows and knees and ankles were also lodged over red rubber blocks. He was naked. A small, white towel covered his groin, pretending to protect both him and his family from exposure that would be indecent.

Giles was picking up a spray bottle of antiseptic from a table covered with surgical tools and strings and wires and cotton swabs and white linen packing, and he was talking louder than he had to, saying, "I respect the right of the Turner family to privacy, but I am convinced that the gift of their husband and father's new life in resurrection will give them cause to celebrate, with all of us and all the heavenly choirs …"

Young Steve was breathing, "Oh God", again and again in a stunned stream of whispers from the chair against the south wall.

The screen went momentarily black in the middle of MacInnes' sentence, and then he was back, pressing cotton swabs into Turner's nose, still talking. Both priests wanted him to stop, but he wouldn't do it.

"The two-hour version is complete", Stoddard muttered. "This is just an edit to show you basic content."

The thirty-second scenes played out like a theater of the macabre. They were riveting and awful.

The embalming procedure content, to Mark's mind, reflected a breathtaking betrayal. Beyond a clinical procedure, it represented something intrusive and violent—a shameful exposing of final secrets, a parading of ancient rituals never intended for public view, a crime against Turner and his family and against C.J. and his family and even against God.

Turner's mouth was being sprayed and wiped.

Mark was sweating.

Turner's eyes were capped with half circles of plastic.

Father Steve, in the background, kept saying it: "Oh God …"

It was voyeurism. It was numbing.

"He said he had to make sure people believed him this time", Ruth commented in a low voice. "He said he felt bad about it, but nobody would believe it, he said, if it was just you and him saying it was so. Some people might believe you, he said, but not the medical examiner or prosecutor."

Stoddard added, "I'd have to say, that's probably a fair guess."

Mark's criticisms stumbled. It probably was true. He could admit that. And not even "probably"; of course, it was true. So the video was a desperate grab for self-preservation—no more, no less. He turned the criticism toward himself. Why hadn't he seen something like this coming?

Incisions followed in their own series of thirty-second clips. The final invasions. "This will be mostly edited out for TV", Stoddard said. "Some of it will be there, but visually distorted. Over an actual incision, for example. You know how that works."

They knew.

The probing. The metal rod. The trocar button.

"His daughter shot it", Rush said solemnly. "Said his wife wouldn't watch an embalming."

"So he shows the whole country", Father Steve whispered. His mouth was dry. His voice raspy.

"He dresses him and all that", Ruth continued. "But it's getting to the section you're in now, Father."

The priest sank back into his chair.

Turner's body was suddenly on a medical table with wheels, already dressed in his blue suit. Giles was combing his hair. The screen went to black again. Mark held his breath. He realized that he felt sick.

And then he was there—Father Mark Cleary, pastor of Royal Oak St. Veronica parish, standing right next to Galvin Turner's body, now pressing his fingers against the dead man's hand in the visitation chapel.

"Oh God."

Stoddard said, "She was apparently up behind a curtain to your left, Father; up high, you can tell. On a chair or something. Curtain around her. Except for the camera."

Ruth added, "You'll see the camera start to shake when it happens. She breathes real loud, like she's almost started to shout something."

When *it* happens. Mark's heart was pounding as they all watched him press his fingers against Turner's cheek. They watched him press the flesh between the old man's chin and lower lip. They watched him probing and staring, thinking. They watched him pause, finally convinced. Then they watched him back out of the camera's view.

Another moment of black.

The casket again. Motion off to the right side. Hands brushing in and out of view on the right edge of the monitor, and sounds—a shuffling movement.

"The boy and his mom", Ruth said. "She never quite got on camera. The dad does, though, later."

Mark drew a deep and sudden breath. C.J. was stepping forward. He was easily identifiable. There wouldn't be any mistake.

"Who is he?" Steve whispered.

It was C.J. Walker, fourth grader, St. Veronica's, but Mark didn't answer—neither did Stoddard, who had hunched forward and was manually pressing the volume, turning it all the way up.

"Voice is very faint", he said quietly. "Funeral home guy gave us his name."

They saw C.J. move his lips. They heard the outlines of words softly spoken but difficult to make out.

"Be well, Mr. Turner", Ruth said.

"Be well, Mr. Turner", Mark repeated in numbed agreement. He looked around at Steve. There were tears in his eyes. He said, "Mr. Turner just came back to life, Steve. That was it."

Stoddard nodded and drew the volume down to normal again. The screen had gone to black. Then they could see the old man's fingers, up close, and the index finger, twitching.

"I saw that", Mark whispered.

The camera jiggled sharply. MacInnes' daughter had seen it, too. They heard her gasp next to the camera and even begin to utter an abrupt syllable of alarm, but she muffled it in time. The camera jerked again and then settled down. Father Mark, Giles, and Joe came into view together, all of them hovering over the body, all of them wide-eyed, waiting, not really sure ...

Then Turner's hand moved again and the camera jiggled again and the three men were saying things and the hand slid slowly to one side and Giles was making a sharp sound, like an "Aw", and Joe was saying, "Jesus", and in a moment, Mark was exclaiming, like a mantra, "This is really happening. This is really happening. This is really happening."

Father Steve felt tears rushing into his own eyes. Even seeing it on the screen was overwhelming.

"His name is C.J. Walker", Mark offered softly. "He's nine years old."

Driving twenty over the speed limit, Father Mark would be at Lynn's house in less than five minutes, if he didn't get stopped. That should give him just fifteen minutes before airtime to tell her what had happened and try to offer some kind of help, maybe even get her and C.J. out of there.

It was nearly 4:45.

He had no illusions about it. All the attention focused on Fremont Hospital and on MacInnes Funeral Home was an energy desperately looking for outlet, especially with Turner's story breaking that afternoon. When Giles' video hit the air at 5:00 A.M., all of that focus and all of that energy was going to rise up like a flesh eater. It would find this fresh, young focus and thunder down on C.J. Walker like nothing the boy or Lynn or any of them had ever experienced. It would bring a life of its own, and it would be in a feeding frenzy. It would not be calm. It would not be ordered. It would not be stopped.

He sped east across an empty Ten Mile Road, past Main and Rochester, and tried to think of the best help that the Church system could offer. Security from the crowds? A monastery hideaway or a convent somewhere? But he felt like he was trying to think in the middle of a free fall. It was hard enough trying to be brilliant on just a couple hours of disturbed sleep, but to think about uncharted territories in a speeding car and on a five-minute deadline, with no time to review and no room to make a mistake and with someone else's life up for grabs, this wasn't good.

Stoddard and his news anchor had given him first review. They were holding back on showing the video to Lynn Walker and Joe, they said, although they already had news teams in front of Lynn's house and Joe's apartment, because Stoddard was hoping that the priests would agree to "full and open cooperation both ways". He not only wanted to maintain first access to the priest during whatever else developed; he asked if the station could count on airing the priest's first news interview as a Channel 3 exclusive, even if it was just five minutes or so. Maybe, it could even be the first interview with C.J. and his mom, since the boy's pastor, would be an important part of this mix, and a person that Mrs. Walker would certainly turn to for advice.

For the station's part, both Stoddard and Ruth Cosgrove assured Father Mark that they would continue to try to cooperate with him and the Church as the story developed. They would keep him abreast of any and all significant developments, and they would guarantee a disposition of "positive emphasis" for the boy and his family in any resurrection-related stories that they developed over the foreseeable future.

Mark agreed to cooperate within reason; then he told them that he'd appreciate the chance to talk with Lynn Walker first himself, even to the point of giving her the video himself. He wanted to do it, he explained, because he felt largely responsible for whatever was about to happen. He should have seen Giles' video coming. At least he wanted to try to soften the blow. Beyond that, he wanted to be able to offer them some kind of help through diocesan channels. They'd have to go into hiding somewhere, for sure.

Before he left, he also asked Ruth Cosgrove to get a copy of the cut-down version of the video to Monsignor John Tennett at St. Mark

Seminary, a personal delivery, hand to hand, to be delivered immediately. In the meantime, Father Steve was to call the Monsignor, waking up whomever he had to in the process, to let him know what was coming, and why.

He wondered now how many other thousands of deals and arrangements would soon be in the works between people interested in gaining control of the boy who had broken through the ultimate stronghold.

And he wondered who else's life would be resurrected. And who else's life would be destroyed.

Westlane Avenue was dark. A street light glowed at each corner, but nearly every porch light was off. Father Mark slowed, then noticed the camera van parked in the darkness on the right side of the street, nearly at the end of the first block. That would be Lynn's house.

He eased in behind the van. Two men got out and walked back to meet him. They identified themselves in low voices and said that Stoddard had called them and filled them in. Then they gave Father Mark a copy of the edited video for Lynn and asked him for a three-minute interview at 5:10, "before the street gets crowded".

"I won't talk to anybody before you", he said. It was all that he could promise.

The house was an old, five-bedroom house, white, with a long wooden porch. Its sides had long ago been masked with now-aged aluminum siding. It had been one of the area's original farm houses left standing in the forties, after the Second World War, only to have a suburb spring up around it. Now it was no doubt too large and in need of too many repairs for a young mother and her son to find ideal, but, being squeezed into what was now the city's oldest and most industrialized section, it was probably too affordable and too settled to let go of easily.

A white garage stood next to the house on the right side, set into the backyard, which was completely enclosed by a high wooden fence. A dark Volvo was parked in the driveway, four or five years old, at least.

He wondered if Lynn was asleep or if she was still tossing in the night, like he had been and like Joe probably was. He felt his nerves pulling tight.

Once on the porch, he realized that there was a glow from the living room, a TV monitor flickering like a candle. It meant Lynn was up. Or maybe asleep on a couch. He decided she hadn't noticed the news van or she'd be at the door already, or at least at a window, and she'd have seen him and turned on the porch light.

He inhaled a deep breath and tried to settle himself. A knock on the door in the dark in the middle of the night, he thought, worse than a phone call. Somebody there, waiting. Then he knocked three times, but not too loudly. If she was in the living room, she would hear the knock. The doorbell might wake C.J.

Mark waited. No answer. He listened. No footsteps. He watched the window. No light going on. No sound of anyone moving.

The brake lights of the news van flashed on behind him, their red glow momentarily lighting the face of the house; the driver was resting his foot. Then the lights went off, and the house, like the street, was dark again.

He knocked a second time, louder. He hoped she'd hurry and wished he knew exactly what time it was, to the minute, but he couldn't see his watch in the dark. He also wished he'd worn his collar so he'd be easier to recognize, but he just had a dark-blue sport shirt under his beige, spring Windbreaker, and jeans. Too late to think about wardrobe.

The porch light went on, startling him and partially blinding his view. He stepped back and waited, facing the door, trying to look calm, aware that she was peering out from somewhere, looking to see who he was, wondering why he was there.

He tried to relax. He took another breath, and then he saw a light glow brighter in the living room and the front door opening slowly and she was there, the light from the living room glowing behind her. She was looking at Mark through the still-closed screen door. She looked afraid.

"What happened?"

From the glare of the porch light he could see that she'd been sleeping. She had a pillow crease in her cheek, and her short brown hair had been pulled back with her fingers and pressed down. She was wearing green summer shorts and a gray T-shirt with a denim shirt over that, buttoned at the waist with one button—slipped on quickly, it looked like, just before she answered the door.

She noticed the news van on the street behind him and said it again, her eyes insisting on a quick, clear answer. "What happened?"

"It's not what we wanted", he said. One more time that he wished he'd figured out what he wanted to say before he started talking. "It is important, though. Can I come in?"

She didn't answer. Her eyes had dropped. She was looking at the video in his hand, her expression heavy with fresh worry, her shoulders suddenly looking as tired as her eyes. She said it in a low whisper: "What is it?"

He wanted to explain the whole thing, but all that came out was, "It's a video."

Her expression took on the look of a new and desperate fear, but her eyes never left the video. She whispered, "C. J. is on there!"

Mark nodded, feeling hopelessly inadequate. "I'm sorry."

She just stood there, staring at him through the screen. He didn't know what to expect, but she just stared at him, then looked past him at the news van in the street, then back at him. She stared for a long time without saying anything. And then, very slowly, she took a deep breath and pushed the screen door open.

He followed her into the living room. One lamp was glowing in the large, but simply furnished room—nothing flashy, nothing new. It had wall-to-wall tan carpeting that looked worn; a brown couch opposite a TV; a few easy chairs, one light brown and one dark brown, both thickly stuffed; few end tables with modest lamps; a glass-topped coffee table in front of the couch; half a dozen plants in the corners of the room and between the chairs and the couch; a few framed prints on the walls, one of the Alps, two ocean scenes, all places beyond the world of Lynn and C. J. Walker. On the north wall, to the right of the TV, a dozen black-and-white photos mounted on foamcore were arranged in a neat, but irregular vertical pattern. C. J. was in every one of them.

Lynn sat on the far end of the couch, near the phone and the only lamp that was lit, her knees curled in front of her. The video was in her hands. She stared at Mark, looking a lot more weary than when she had first opened the door.

"MacInnes?" she whispered.

He nodded. "I'm so sorry, Lynn."

"When are they going put it on TV? They're here to interview us, I suppose."

He nodded again and sat at the other end of the couch. He said, "In just a couple of minutes. Five o'clock it'll be on the air."

"God Almighty!" Tears filled her eyes. "The first of how many ... ?" She was speaking slowly, as if in a daze. "God!" she said again, "I can't even imagine ..."

Her glance flitted past him to the front door, then to the two front windows, the rug, the video in her lap, the rug again; quick, darting glances, as if they were trying to keep up with her thoughts, as if they were trying hard to find a place to settle, as if they weren't succeeding. "I can't believe this is happening", she whispered. "He won't be able to leave the house. Neither will I."

"It shouldn't have happened", he said. "I feel sick about it."

"This will be so insane."

"I'm sorry."

"He's just a kid, for Pete's sake! Why him, of all the people in the world?" Her eyes were fixed on Mark's. They were brimmed with tears. "He plays soccer. He doesn't get visions. He's not a little monk. He just horses around, goes to school. He gets in trouble. He makes jokes with Burr about girl's boobs. He's nine years old!" She paused, alarmed by a new realization. "He's not even going to be able to go to school again! Ever."

She got up and walked quickly to the front window. The night sky was dissolving; the glow of a new morning was already seeping in like watercolor over the trees. Her arms were squeezed tight across her waist. Suddenly, she looked back toward the dark TV. "I'm not going to watch it", she announced. She was trying to fight off her tears.

"I'm going to see the Cardinal tomorrow," he said, "in the afternoon. Would you go with me?" He rose from the couch and moved toward her. "He'd want to see you, too, for sure, if you'd want to go. He may be able to help."

"What can he do?"

"Maybe help explain things. I don't know. It's a good place to start."

She turned to him, anger flashing. "You think it might have happened before, so they'll have a file with answers for me?" She turned back toward the window. "It could be, though, couldn't it? They just might put the people who can do this in a cell somewhere. Study them. Keep them out of sight." Alarmed by her own speculation, she turned again quickly to face Mark. "What will he want me to do with C.J., seriously?"

"What do you mean, 'do'?"

"Those kids in the past who had visions," Lynn said, "the ones the Vatican decided were real visions, like at Fatima and Lourdes—those kids ended up shut away in monasteries or convents for the rest of their lives, didn't they? I've seen pictures of them. Always in religious habits. Always hidden away from everybody. Don't talk to the world. Don't see or be seen. Did you ever see pictures of the Fatima girl or the kids at Lourdes being let out to run around a beach or play soccer with their friends at school; that kind of thing?"

"That was so different." Mark was shaking his head. "You're not going to Rome. I just mean, let's talk with the Cardinal."

Lynn was adamant, and now, animated. Her hands rose and fell. "But C.J. being able to do something like this, the Cardinal will be just like everybody else. Worse, maybe, because he's the Church, and this is, like, biblical powers. He'll want to have his say over it, won't he? Everybody will want their fingers around him, but my gosh, the Church … when the kid's doing something like raising the dead?" She bit her lip and studied him and asked with audible pain, "That's my question: what's the Cardinal going to want to do with him?"

He took a deep breath. He held up his hand and whispered, "Lynn. Honest. Please don't run away with it in your own mind. I'm just talking about a visit with somebody that might help. That's all, honest. I just don't know what else to suggest right off the bat."

Lynn shook her head. She glanced again at the black face of the TV monitor. "What time is it now?"

He checked his watch. "A couple of minutes to go. Till five."

Lynn said very softly, "I'm sorry. I feel my head's going to spin off."

"Tell me what I can do that would be a help."

"It might not even be from God, you know? It's not like it has to be all thought out, like God's great plan for the world." Her tears were back, even stronger now, rimming her eyes and spilling over. "Why couldn't it just be some freak of nature or something, with no plan to it at all?"

"I don't know yet what can I do to help you," he said, "other than deal with the reporters. They'll be at the door in just a minute. I'll keep them away, but we'll have to come up with a plan of some kind."

"I don't want them on my property."

"I'll tell them."

"What time is it?"

"It's five. It's going on the air now."

"He'll never be able to go out and play with anybody, Mark! Never ride his bike again!"

"I'll do anything I can, I promise."

"Everybody will say it's such a great gift …" She paused for a moment, then rose and walked quickly to the window. No movement yet in the satellite van outside. She turned back to him, her eyes wide and afraid, and she said in a low and urgent voice, as though it was a matter of life and death and it was critical that she not be overheard: "Will you be on our side?"

He looked puzzled. He didn't speak.

She said, "If it comes down to everyone else on one side and me and C.J. on the other, even if it's the Church on one side and us on the other, will you still be on our side?"

Mark barely breathed. Then he nodded. No words, just a single nod.

"That's a promise?" she said, whispering.

Another nod, this time more firmly. "I promise", he said. "You let me know how I can help you, and I'll do everything I can. I promise."

A van door slammed loudly outside, and then another. Lynn turned her head to the door, then looked back at him, her lips pressed tight.

She looked like a little girl to him, like someone soft and wide-eyed and frightened, but she said it with tears in her eyes and her raised voice as sharp as a spike. "You can start by telling God we don't want this thing."

There was shuffling on the porch. Three knocks sounded on the door.

Lynn added, speaking quickly and firmly, "And you can remind God that C.J.'s just a normal kid. He's not to be made into some kind of freak. He's not Jesus, and I'm sure no Blessed Mother Mary!"

Ten

Joe didn't look into the Channel 3 video camera that met him in the apartment entrance when he rushed downstairs to the parking lot. He didn't acknowledge the reporter. He walked with his eyes glazed, straight toward his car. The reporter asked him for an interview. He didn't answer. The reporter jogged along beside him asking, "Please." He didn't answer.

He had gotten the call at 4:50 A.M. They were outside his apartment; they had a video and were wondering if he wanted to see it.

He saw the video and he saw the news, too, saw the whole thing blowing up in his face—all the time he had for planning, all the time for getting ready and doing things right with the biggest thing he'd ever have in his whole life—the whole thing blowing up, as usual, right at the last minute. The embalming on video: holy hell! Right on television, fuzzing out the gross parts, but C.J. right on screen as plain as day, and then Turner moving and Joe and the others gaping like apes and looking stupid, making stupid sounds.

Every time, he thought, right at the last minute; everything I try to do, blowing up one foot from the end zone, and it's never my fault!

He'd tried calling Lynn nearly fifteen times while the news was on. Busy each time. Phone off the hook, for sure. So he had to get there.

The Channel 3 reporter that gave him the video wanted to know, was what he saw accurate? Joe didn't answer. Was that really his son, Christopher? Joe didn't answer. But the guy was waiting for him in the parking lot. Same questions, same response from Joe: no answer.

He was at his car. Was he on his way to see his son now, they wanted to know. Joe slammed the door and roared out of his parking space and peeled away into a darkness that was already glowing in the east with the first light of morning.

The driver of the news van had it running and ready. He picked up the reporter, and they followed Joe, staying with him even when he hit seventy in just the four short blocks from his apartment to Farnum Boulevard, where he squealed around the corner and headed north.

Joe wasn't thinking about C.J.; he was thinking about Giles Mac-Innes. He was hating the skinny weasel's guts. Hating him for lying to them, and having Joe fall for it. Hating him for stealing Joe's time to think and plan and get a handle on this thing. Hating him for being alive. He was thinking he'd like to pound him, hammer his face and leave him bleeding in the street for a while, hoping somebody would come along and run over him; Joe would say to C.J., "Hey, C.J., bring the liar back to life." Then Joe could pound his face all over again.

If it isn't a three-hundred-pound nurse, it's a hundred-twenty-pound undertaker. Always somebody, though. Always at the last minute.

He was less than a mile from Lynn's, still doing seventy, shooting past the early-morning workers easing north toward Eleven Mile with plastic spill-proof coffee mugs in their built-in cup holders. But no cops. He saw the camera van behind him in the early-morning dark-ness, now just a block back. They were clipping along, too, he realized. And they were on the phone, he knew that, telling the others he was coming. They'd be all over C.J. and all over Lynn, and they'd be wait-ing to land on him as soon as he got there, all because of the chicken undertaker who lied and couldn't leave well enough alone.

He swung hard through the red light at Eleven Mile, taking his anger out on his steering wheel. He watched in the rearview mirror as the reporters slowed to wheel around the corner after him. They don't even have to rush, he thought. They had people out in front of him, watching for him at Lynn's house.

Everybody had help but him.

He took in a slow breath, trying to settle down, forcing himself to think, well, it's done. No more secret. Time to deal with it. Fig-ure out how to make the most of it. Figure out how to turn it to his advantage.

He'd like to get C.J. and Lynn away, he thought, but once the media is all over you, how do you physically pull that off? He couldn't just outrun them. Couldn't do that, just get in the car and speed away. Couldn't disguise himself as a delivery man and sneak the kid out in a box or anything.

Four more blocks to Westlane, and then around the corner. Time to slow down. Think. What was Plan B?

There wasn't any Plan B, but there would be. He'd have to make one up. Another deep breath. God, he didn't want to lose his hold of this thing!

He was approaching Westlane. The car immediately in front of him signaled a turn. He wondered if the driver in that car was heading to

Lynn's, too. Then he noticed another TV camera van approaching from the other direction, coming fast, left-turn signal snapping on. Somebody from one of the other stations, rushing to Lynn's, for sure.

As he turned the corner, he saw that there was already the beginnings of a crowd in front of her house—already too many cars plus a couple of pickups and TV camera vans; fifty or sixty people milling around already, and it was only pushing 5:20. People pacing up and down the front walk to the house and pointing, even standing around on her lawn, all of them staying close, everybody talking like they were at a picnic.

No sign of the police, though. Only more cars coming in behind him, and now up ahead of him, too.

He thought about driving past the house and parking in the next block to keep the car away from the crowds, but no way. How'd he ever get out later? He decided, instead, to head right up the driveway and park close behind Lynn's blue Volvo, next to the side door.

When he turned in without tapping his horn, the half-dozen women standing behind Lynn's car scattered and began pointing and fluttering their hands in Joe's direction and talking, all excited. They recognized him because they'd seen him on TV standing by the casket before the boy came on. Now they shouted out who he was and rushed to circle his car. Others were quickly on their way, including reporters who were already loping across the lawn with wires and lights and microphones and cameras.

He jumped out of his car shouting, "No!" He swung the side screen door open and rapped three times, fast and hard. He tried the knob without waiting, then knocked a second time, the same way. She'd know who it was. He'd used that knock since way back, only not quite as hard.

The crowd pressed in. "Is it true what was on TV?" "Is your son inside?" "Will he be out so we can see him soon?" "Is the video a fake?" "Did he heal the other ladies, too?"

Joe kept answering no, rapid-fire, regardless of the question. He hated the crowding, but he did realize, just in those few seconds, even as he heard Lynn's footsteps finally thumping down from the kitchen as she came to let him in, that this wasn't all bad—the crowds and all the raising the dead fever. These people knew what he had, is all. They knew that Joe had the most powerful person in the world inside that house. They wanted to see his son, Christopher Joseph Walker, the boy named after him. Everyone in the country would be like this, wanting to see his son. The whole world would be like this. And some of them, he thought, will give us every dollar they have.

Lynn yelled, "Please get off our lawn!" to the gawkers who had recognized C.J. and surged closer when Joe entered the house, acting as if they expected to be invited in, too.

Joe was flushed. "Didn't you call the police?"

Lynn hesitated. She had a hunted look in her eyes.

"God, Lynn! Call them now!" Joe demanded. He stepped quickly up the two stairs into the kitchen. "Or I will for you, that's fine."

He turned and for some reason noticed that they both had on jeans and a blue oxford button-down shirt, like "the suburban twins do on Saturdays". It meant nothing, really, but he noticed it, and it made him feel good for some reason, like they were in this thing together.

"We'll sit down and figure out what to do next", he said, speaking more softly, sounding confident, which came naturally to him. "Don't worry. We're gonna handle this."

He wasn't just C.J.'s divorced dad anymore, not just soiled goods living somewhere else. He was Joe Walker, back managing his family. They were even in uniform.

Then he looked up and saw Mark.

Caught by surprise, his eyes flashed disappointment and then anger, but only for a split second. It wasn't just that the priest was in Lynn's house but that he'd gotten there first, before Joe, and was already standing there with a coffee in his hand, not even in his Roman collar, but a sport shirt, like just one of the guys, looking right at home—that's what got to Joe.

Mark said, "Hello, Joe." He looked apologetic. He sounded apologetic.

Joe nodded and said, "Yeah. You saw that video?"

Lynn said, "He did. I'm not going to."

Joe was already thinking that the priest would want C.J. for himself now. Like wanting to talk to him before was nothing, but now he'd be after the kid big-time. And the worst part was, Joe had put him in the middle of things himself, back when he was trying to get him to the funeral home, the way he was so careful to make the Church's being involved seem like such a big deal.

So now it wasn't just the priest from St. Veronica's standing there and making himself at home; it was a thousand priests, and a hundred bishops, and even the Pope. The Church brass would come expecting to get C.J. now, along with government brass and every other kind of brass going, and Joe would have to deal with it.

"C.J.'s still sleeping", Lynn said. "Father Mark's here to help. He asked if we'll go see the Cardinal with him tomorrow. You want coffee?"

Joe stopped. There it was already: the Cardinal. But people were shouting outside, and he couldn't stop to work on Lynn just yet. "I want to keep two hundred people from rushing your front door, Lynn", he said. He was glaring at her. He said, "You didn't call the police, but you decided to call the Cardinal?" His voice was sharp and sarcastic.

Lynn started to shake her head no, but stopped abruptly as she noticed movement behind Joe, in the hall.

C.J. was standing in the archway watching them, looking small and vulnerable and still groggy with sleep. He didn't seem surprised that Father Mark was there, or his dad. He was staring at Lynn, the left corner of his lower lip tucked between his teeth, his eyes filled with fresh worry. When he spoke, it was barely above a whisper, just a boy thinking out loud. He breathed, "When are all those people going to go away?"

In the three years that David Cardinal Schaenner had been hierarchical shepherd to the Catholic church of Detroit, he had been awakened before his usual rising time of 5:45 A.M. with a personal visit from his director of the Curia, Monsignor John Tennett, on just one other occasion. That was when one of his diocese's most successful pastors was found robbed and murdered seven months ago, his body clumped in a pile on a side street in southwest Detroit with two .22 caliber holes behind his left ear.

This would be the second time.

At 5:30 A.M., just five hours after the Cardinal had arrived home from his wearying visit to Rome, his housekeeper found Monsignor Tennett on the doorstep with an urgent request that he be summoned immediately.

It was just four minutes before the unshaven sixty-six-year-old clergy-man came down to join him. He was a tall man, and clearly overweight. Soft-spoken and round-shouldered, dressed in his light-brown pullover and black trousers, he looked to Monsignor Tennett like he might be a retired school teacher, an aging Mr. Rogers with more rounded edges. But despite his rounded appearance and a smile that could look as warm as a night light, he was also, Monsignor Tennett knew, a man quick to assess situations, set goals, make decisions and act, an executive who was outspokenly impatient with slow-moving organizational wheels, especially those within his own church.

"What's happened, John?" he asked as he reached the bottom of the stairs. "I take it it's very serious." Without waiting for an answer, he moved into his office and sat in his dark-scarlet chair, gesturing the Monsignor toward the chair facing him.

Monsignor Tennett held up the video disc. "A video", he said. "The original takes a couple of hours. This is just nine minutes' worth. I've watched it, and felt sure you'd want to see it right away, because they're putting parts of it on TV even now. The city's waking up to it."

The Cardinal responded with a simple, "Let's see it", then inhaled, and waited as the video went into the player and the TV went on.

The Monsignor pushed Play. A man in a bright yellow rubber apron and bright yellow rubber gloves came on-screen to say to the Cardinal, "My name is Giles MacInnes."

"It's about the Mrs. Klein thing?" the Cardinal asked. He leaned forward toward the TV.

"Someone else", the Monsignor said. "His name is Turner."

"A second one? Mother of God!"

"With the same undertaker, and that's Father Mark Cleary again. The others are his parishioners. And that's their son, C.J., that all the commotion's about."

"The Lazarus boy ...", the Cardinal said. Then he was silent as they watched the whole nine minutes, silent with the exception of two more "Mother of God!" whispers.

When it ended, he stared at the screen for nearly ten seconds without speaking, then turned to the Monsignor without expression to say, "The statement we put out about the Klein woman still stands. 'There will be no response from the diocese until all investigations into what is now both of these claims have been fully concluded.' You'll take care of that. Nothing more. And make sure Father Mark knows it. Also, get Bishop Ryan to fold this into the diocesan investigations into the Klein woman."

He slid back into thought, his eyes narrowed.

"Fremont Hospital staff and Father Mark", Monsignor Tennett said. "Not people easily made fools of. The hospital has no answers, and Father Mark seems convinced it really happened."

"Even the possibility that it might be authentic stops your heart", the Cardinal said slowly. His eyes were locked on the blank TV screen. He added, "God knows what they can do now with computer-generated videos. But this one ... I don't know. In just a number of hours? I don't know. The Turner fellow would have to be in on it. His family, too. And the doctors."

He was silent again for several minutes.

The Monsignor let him think with no interruptions.

He finally straightened up, looked at the Monsignor, and said, "Just get them here as planned. Father Mark, the boy, and his parents. I'll add a few people when I have more time to think. I'll let you know."

"I'm sure they'll all come", Monsignor Tennett said.

"We can see if we have a stage mother here, pushing the boy and what have you. It'll help to see the boy up close, too." The Cardinal rubbed his chin lightly with his fingertips and expressed once more, "Mother of God!" this time adding, "On my watch!" He thought for another moment, then stood and said, softly now, "I want this controlled, John, however we can. I want this kept firmly in the hands of the Church. I want you to tell Father Mark that. Make him our eyes and ears. Keep him close to the family and close to us."

"We've already talked. He'll stay close."

"Just tell him that's what I said. Stay close to the boy and his family. That's imperative."

The Cardinal of the archdiocese of Detroit found himself wondering, as Monsignor Tennett left, which would be the bigger disaster: to wake up with the news of a half-dozen unexpected deaths among his dwindling diocesan priesthood, or to have authentic resurrections taking place in his diocese only to have the source of the miraculous power slip away to a place beyond his pastoral orbit.

A. W. Cross sat on the edge of his bed watching cable news, a small pad of paper at his side, a pen in his hand. He had seen the video of the boy who supposedly raised the dead at 6:15, and had already called Torrie Kruger, who was watching the replays and follow-up reports in his own room in Detroit, both of them taking notes.

He did not feel like an old man weighed down by his grieving any longer—not now. He knew that there were four people now. He knew that the video was being touted as incredibly strong evidence of an actual resurrection, if not final proof. He knew that the doctors interviewed live at the hospital were as blank-faced as children—without bearing, without argument, with nothing left in their own medical repertoire to put on the table. And he knew now that it wasn't the priest, after all, or magnetic fields in the hospital room, or luck, or magic, or chance. It was supposed to be a boy. It was supposed to be a nine-year-old boy named C. J. Walker.

He had reminded himself, certainly, when he had first seen the video and he was calling Torrie on the phone, that video can be phony; they can be made to show anything, literally. But on the other hand, there was a priest there this time, right on the video itself, and the look on the priest's face when he was close to the body and the dead guy's fingers were moving, the way the priest looked like he was going to die himself of a stroke or a heart attack, and the sound of his voice, the way he was saying, "This is really happening", again and again, all of that, Cross felt certain, could not have been faked.

And so, when the next CNN segment covering the "Lazarus video" came on, Mr. A. W. Cross pushed Record on his DVD and double-checked his handwritten notes: "Giles MacInnes, Funeral H. Galvin Turner. Fremont hosp. Priest—Cleary. St. Veronica's, Royal Oak. C. J. Walker. Christopher. 9 yrs. Joe Walker—dad. Lynn—mother. Divorced."

On the thirty-six-inch TV monitor ten feet in front of him, a young video engineer from CNN headquarters in Atlanta was commenting on the video capabilities of the latest digital technologies, but the elderly man had closed his eyes. He was thinking about Torrie Kruger, who was already on the outskirts of Royal Oak, no more than fifteen minutes from the boy's house and his father's Royal Oak apartment.

Five minutes later, when he opened his eyes again, he carefully drew a dark circle around one of the names on his notepad: Joe Walker—dad.

Eleven

With C.J. awake, the day became an exercise in disaster control. Security, communications, supplies, travel—everything had to be reconsidered while new plans would be made, and all in the face of a crowd that was growing larger by the minute.

Mark put a sign on the doors, front and side. The bold, black letters read "We're sure you understand. Privacy is critical to us. Please do not disturb us for any reason. There are no exceptions."

Lynn had scrawled a handwritten "Thank you" on each one, and signed them, "The Walker family".

Things like that drove Joe crazy.

In the first minutes of daylight, they saw just two police officers, a man and a woman, easing past in one of Royal Oak's gun-metal gray cruisers. Joe called the police station to ask why there weren't more, trying to explain to the officer at the desk why they needed extra attention. The officer told him they'd already received two dozen calls from upset neighbors and had already responded. "Probably down at the corner doing traffic," Joe muttered to Lynn, "or eating McBreakfast. Who knows?"

By 7:30, two police cruisers were parked in front of the house and four officers were on foot, trying to keep traffic moving. The crowd continued to grow and continued to press closer, about 150, all buzzing and spreading like a blanket, folding over the lawn and moving out into the street to press against the police and to slow traffic to a crawl.

Every few minutes, a small cluster would come walking up to the porch to lean forward and read the "Please, Thank you" sign. They'd read the sign; then they'd shrug or nod or read it out loud one or two times to their friends or show no reaction at all before they eased their way back into the crowd that was quivering with questions and would start pretty soon, Joe was certain, to get more aggressive.

He watched them and wondered which one it would be: that first one to come pounding on the door demanding that C.J. come out and be a personal savior for him, right now.

Lynn tried to call Marion Klein. Her room at the hospital wasn't taking calls. Lynn left a message of encouragement with the information operator, explaining that she wasn't taking calls at her own home, either, and that she'd try to call back; then she tried Marion's house. There was no answer, and Marion's answering machine was full. Next, she called her friend Nancy Gould. She asked if Nancy and her son, Burr, would come and spend the day with them, since it was Saturday, anyway. No work, no school. Nancy jumped at the chance. And she'd bring some groceries, she said—lots of them. Who knew how long they'd be stuck in the house?

Joe told Lynn he thought they should move the old TV and VCR, with the video games and some movies, upstairs for the kids and get a new TV right away for downstairs. "We'll need C.J. and Burr entertained and out of the way," he said, "so we can make our plans downstairs, and we might be watching stuff on the new TV that we wouldn't want the kids to see. And I'll pay for the new stuff, so don't worry about that."

Joe was thinking he'd never be short of money again.

When she agreed, he called a friend who worked at Discount City and told him to come over with a new forty-inch TV and DVD player as soon as he could. The man had heard the news. He asked if C.J. was with Joe. He asked if C.J. would still be there when he got there. Then he said not to let the kid go away; he'd be over as soon as he could. Joe told him C.J. had no plans to travel.

"You should go to an unlisted number on the house phone," Joe told Lynn. Lynn said she'd think about it. "Hardly anybody has your call number, I know," he said. "So that's good. But the mail will still get through. Neither snow nor rain nor the rising of the dead ..."

In fact, Joe realized that the mail would start coming in by the ton, and soon. It would come in a morning delivery if they still had their old schedule, about ten o'clock. And in the mail, he was convinced, would be offers. The mailman, he decided, would probably make four or five hundred bucks on the side just from delivering sealed offers handed to him on the street. Why not? Joe would if he had access to Lynn's front door.

Sorting through those written offers would have to be part of Joe's personal Plan A. Bring Lynn on after the deals were on the table, he decided. Find the highest bidder and get some cash to hire the necessary bodyguards, move Lynn and C.J. to the safest place, then make longer-range plans when they had the money to make big things happen. But make something happen quickly, before Father Mark and the Church or the cops or somebody even worse moved in and got Joe squeezed right out of the picture, because that's what they'd try to do. Whoever came after C.J. with smiles and offers would try to cut Joe off at the knees. Never see his own kid again; never make a dime on the whole thing—how could he tell?

In the meantime, they had all forgotten how much Nancy Gould resembled Lynn, and how, even though his hair was a lot longer, Burr looked like C.J., especially to people who had just seen photos of the mother and her son on TV. As a result, when Nancy and Burr arrived at Lynn's house just before noon, their car was mobbed; people were mistaking them for the miracle kid and his mom. The police had to surround their car three blocks away and escort them all the way into the driveway.

Joe's friend from Discount City finally made it with the new TV and DVD player. It had taken him two hours to get there, he said, more than thirty minutes just to work his way through traffic and the police and the crowd between the house and Eleven Mile Road. And the police had been alerted that he was coming.

"At least you didn't have a kid with you that looks like C.J.", Nancy told him. "You'd still be in mob heaven out there, beating them off with a stick."

While the adults settled down after an early soup and sandwich lunch to talk about the crowds and police and Marion and Turner and the TV news and about things to do and not to do next, C.J. led Burr back upstairs to peer out C.J.'s bedroom window and pick out weirdos in the crowd, and even to wave from Lynn's front-bedroom window while people in the crowd waved back and hollered for C.J. to come out.

Lynn heard the shouting and issued the order: all the shades had to be drawn, and no standing at open windows!

As the boys settled down, their careful peeks at the crowd outside diminished to a few intermittent glances spaced long minutes apart and stolen from the corners of the now-shaded windows. When they tired of that, they slid to the floor on either side of the window, their backs against the wall, and eyed each other, grinning.

A moment of silence passed—two young boys getting their bearings on new and exciting ground, two best friends, not quite sure what to do next.

Burr whispered, finally. "God, Ceej. This is so cool." Like C.J.'s dad, he often called his best friend "Ceej", squeezing his two initials together the way C.J. and everyone else squeezed "Brendan" down to "Burr".

C.J. nodded without grinning. "Yeah", he said. Yeah, it did feel cool, and yeah, he was cool because he could do it. He felt that now, with Burr at his side.

Burr giggled. "They'll probably name a church after you."

C.J. giggled back. "Saint C.J.'s."

They both laughed out loud.

Burr said, "You've got police all over the place."

C.J. said quietly, "There'd be people all over the lawn if the cops weren't here." He pulled his knees up to his chest and wrapped his hands around his legs. He bit his lip, thinking.

"They'd be pounding on your door, man."

"Yeah."

Burr pulled his knees up, too. He was staring at C.J. the way he might stare if a rock star had suddenly shown up. He said it again. "This is so cool."

Another nod from C.J. "Yeah."

Burr grew more serious. He asked quietly, already keeping secrets, "But do you know what happened to you? To make it happen? Like what you felt like when it happened, and you could do that, or when it came into you or whatever."

C.J. turned. He pursed his lips. His eyes narrowed. "I guess God did it", he said solemnly.

"But how? Did you hear voices or stuff, or what happened?"

C.J. considered the question for a moment, then whispered, "I think maybe it's something in my blood. I didn't feel anything, but I think it might be that."

Burr leaned forward, getting the picture: something in C.J.'s blood.

C.J. nodded at his own insight and restated the idea, this time louder, and with his finger tracing slowly down his arm from inside his elbow to his wrist. "I think maybe it's something in there, so it's going through my veins." His finger stopped at his wrist. He looked at Burr. "I don't know, but it might be that."

Burr nodded again, his eyes wide. "Yeah!" he said.

They both thought about it.

"God, Ceej", Burr whispered again.

C.J. had been thinking it out even further, the blood and all. He said, "If I cut myself, it might run out."

Burr leaned forward, letting himself be drawn deeper into this vivid, new possibility. "Or if somebody else cuts you. Somebody could stab you."

"Yeah." C.J. nibbled on his bottom lip. He'd thought about that possibility, too. But he'd come up with an answer. "If I said the words to myself, if I was stabbed, I could make myself better, couldn't I? 'Cause if I said it to myself, then I wouldn't be cut."

He wasn't certain, but it seemed that way.

"I guess so", Burr said. A pause for reflection, then another smile.

C.J. smiled again, too. Yeah, it was cool. Still scary, but cool.

They thought about cuts and blood and power for several seconds before Burr giggled again, loudly and suddenly, his eyes wider than before, now touched with nervousness as well as excitement. "Do you think your blood would glow, if you could see it?"

C.J. started to laugh, but the humor in the idea quickly drained away. His eyes widened slightly. "I don't know", he admitted. And then, "No, dumb ass, it doesn't glow."

"Well?" Burr laughed defensively. He paused again, waiting, not sure how to ask it but wondering if they could find out.

They were silent for more than a minute, their imaginations going places only nine-year-old imaginations easily went. Then Burr said, "Ceej? Show me how it works."

He turned to C.J., grinning, the look of wild adventure in his eyes.

C.J. tilted his head. "What do you mean?"

"Show me."

"On who? Who's dead?"

"We can get something."

"No. I'm not gonna get something!"

"Why not?"

"I don't know. You don't have to see it."

"We can go out in back. It's raining all the time. You'll have those worms up on the concrete walk along the side of the garage, going up to the garage door."

"You want me to try it on a worm?"

"Why not?"

"I'm not gonna do it for a worm, is why not." He laughed.

"Are you afraid? What can happen?"

C.J. thought about it. He shrugged and said, now more thoughtfully, "I don't know."

Burr was on his feet. "C'mon! Let's go!"

C.J. shook his head. "We can't. Not now, anyway. I don't know. Maybe when they're not all watching us, but I know we can't try it now."

Burr considered the risks. He was still grinning wildly, but he finally sat down hard. "Okay, man. But later today."

"Maybe tomorrow", C.J. said.

"Later today or tomorrow, for sure. Oh man, I can't wait."

C.J. shrugged and fell silent. His lower lip eased between his teeth. He held it there, thinking. Then he said, looking worried. "I just thought ... do you think somebody could try to kidnap me?"

Burr had not thought about that one. He said, "Well cripe, Ceej." He kneeled and peered out of the window again, starting to look for bad guys. "Do you think so? With all these people here?"

"I don't mean right now", C.J. said. "I mean later. 'Cause if they kidnapped me, they'd do a transfusion. Then they'd have my blood in them. Then they'd have the power themselves."

Burr stared at the floor for ten seconds, thinking hard. When he raised his eyes they were smiling again. "Hey, Ceej. This is so awesome!"

C.J. and Burr laughed once so loudly in the upstairs front bedroom that Joe, standing at the white-draped living room window to study the crowd, turned his eyes to the stairs. He couldn't help smiling. He really loved that sound. C.J. had that weird little kick to his laugh that made it jiggle on the way out, really fun to listen to, and for a second there it was sharp with all the energy of a nine-year-old operating on too little sleep, and forcing it, so it kicked even higher and hung there, and it was so great to hear—Joe's own son and his sharp, little, goofy laugh.

He grinned and turned to study the crowd one more time.

Lynn and Nancy were upstairs with the kids, and the priest, too, all of them watching a movie now, he thought. Lynn had said she didn't want C.J. to get lost inside his own house. Joe had said, "No. I guess not." But he'd rather be alone.

The sound on the new TV was down low. No coverage at the moment. Local shows paying the station's bills.

He watched for the mail. He watched the crowds. He watched the police. He watched the TV for more than fifteen minutes, switching channels, stopping to hear anything that related to the siege at the house or to C.J. or to Marion or the Turner guy.

And then, something new. Something breaking with new visuals and a trailing "News 8 Alert" running across the bottom of the screen. New supers, all of a sudden, with a news anchor back again and computer graphics popping on that he hadn't seen before—pictures of lungs and the heart and the stomach, like a cutaway body, but with a lot of moving arrows and circles popping on and off here and there, all over the place, and the words across the top now reading "Metallic tracings".

He grabbed the remote and turned the sound up louder.

Metal in Marion Klein, they were saying—microscopic tracings found all over the place, in her and in the other guy, too. The reporters were saying that when the surgeons go in and get it they'd be able to analyze it and know if it was from the undertaker's metal tools. They didn't do it yet, they said, but they'd be doing it for sure as soon as they got the okay from Marion or Turner, either one, whoever nodded yes first, and then they'd know, they said. Or at least have the first hard evidence that an embalming might have actually been done, which would blow the roof off things any way you looked at it.

Joe bit his lip and slumped on the couch. Everything was happening too fast. He watched the whole report, seeing how it would all be done in the computer graphics, listening to the whole thing right up until they promised to stay on top of it and cut away to catch up on the weather.

He felt trapped. Everything was closing in, things were going to break totally loose at any minute, and three hundred people were already outside keeping them pinned in the house. The first day, he thought, and most people still wondering if anything real happened at all, but still, there had to be four, five hundred people out there, and more still coming, pressing in all the time, stretching now way down the street on both sides.

He was back at the window, his mind churning, thinking, Saturday. Everybody off work, comin' here instead of going to the mall or a show or watching a game on TV. A lot of them setting up folding chairs on the lawn between the sidewalk and the street like C.J. was gonna come out and put on a show. Folding chairs, for God's sake.

He muttered, "This is going nowhere but bad."

From across the room, the TV weatherman told him that showers were moving in, with thunderstorms possible over the next two days. "A threatening pattern", the man called it.

Sounded about right to him: a threatening pattern, going nowhere but bad.

Then, looking back over the crowd, he noticed a new banner going up on the face of the porch across the street. One with sloppy, foot-high letters painted on a white sheet, hanging down, over the side of the low porch wall, directly in front of a frizzy-haired lady sitting with about fifteen people crammed in around her. She was watching Joe through binoculars, and now pointing at him, with all of them now laughing and pumping their fists straight up.

The sign read, "Christ Jesus: The Second Coming!"

All the letters were black except two. The "C" and the "J" were flame red.

It hit him like a fist. It hit him so clearly and powerfully that it stunned him. He had the grand plan. Right. He always had a grand plan. This time, do a few risings with the relatives of the superrich, presidents, dictators, financial kingpins, whatever. Live in a safe place, totally guarded. Take in enough with just half a dozen risings of their dead to live ridiculously rich ever after.

He saw the grand plan, but all he had right now, as the zealots watched him with binoculars, for God's sake, were two hundred dollars in his pocket, and no real friends, and no real connections, and no real place locked in place to get the three of them safely from "here" to "there".

And surrounded now by the kind of people who'd raise a "Christ Jesus Walker" sign, for God's sake, with all of them pointing and ogling and hell-bent on getting a touch of C.J., and with a hundred million people already knowing the kid's face from television or the Internet, all around the world, which meant it would be billions of them before the story plays all the way out, and most of them determined to get their own dead person back, or maybe tear off a piece of C.J.'s shirt, or rip out a tuft of his hair, or scratch off a patch of his skin, like a relic. "Christ Jesus Walker: the Second Coming". He imagined little plastic boxes with "Actual Fingernail Clippings of C.J. Walker" being sold from a card table at their corner and mobs blocking the roads so bad that even the police couldn't get them out.

And there were other kinds of binocular people, he suddenly realized. All the fanatics who were probably seeing C.J. as being in direct competition with Jesus himself. Seeing him as the biggest competition to Jesus in history, a devil kid or something. That'll happen, too, he thought, for sure. Probably already was. Thinking he's a demon kid being used by the devil to tear down Christianity. With maybe no bonfires to end the blasphemy this time, but with long-range rifles and scopes probably selling fast.

So how can he possibly keep C.J. safe for even a day and a half, let alone until they start to get to him? How can he possibly do that?

He sucked in a deep breath, closed his eyes, let the breath out with a soft whoosh, gathered his thoughts, and, for the first time since grade school, he prayed. He said a real prayer—Joe Walker, needing help and praying to God.

He thought, speaking as honestly as he could to God, who knew it all anyway, "I didn't do this right so far, did I?" Another deep breath and exhale. A moment to focus again. "Not smart. I know that. I'm not taking care of what you have going on here, am I? But I'm asking you right now, show me what to do. Open a door. Give me the answer, please. There's gotta be a way to play this out smarter."

With his eyes still closed, he bit his lower lip and lowered his chin, thinking hard for nearly two minutes. Then, resigned, he said out loud, in a very soft whisper as he raised his head and looked out of the window again, "Or, if you won't do that . . . at least show me how I can keep him safe. From all of them. At least that much . . ."

C.J.'s laugh suddenly sounded again from the bedroom upstairs. Joe opened his eyes, listened for a second, and smiled an easy smile again, just like he'd smiled so many times at that hopping thing that happened in the kid's laugh. He couldn't help smiling. In the middle of all this, with his grand plan ready to maybe tumble totally out of his control, C.J.'s laugh was still his favorite sound ever.

He instinctively looked across the street again, and at the sign again, and at the waiting people crowded on the porch again, and he lost his smile.

He was watching the binoculars.

The binoculars were still watching him.

Lynn and Nancy were seated at the kitchen table, their coffees getting cold. They had made lunch, visited with the boys, watched a movie with them, in fact, or at least the last half of one, come back down to watch the crowds and worry and wonder. They tried again without success to contact Marion Klein or one of her family, and made a fresh pot of coffee, yet in all that time had managed to avoid being alone and looking in each other's eyes and actually talking in serious, best-friend's terms about "it".

Lynn sipped her cooling coffee, cradling the cup in both hands, keeping it close to her lips. "Nance?" she asked softly.

"Yeah, hon?"

"What would you do?" A long pause. "If it was Burr?"

Nancy drew a breath slowly and tried to think, buying time with an encouraging response, if not a real answer. "Oh gosh, Lynn", she said. "You'll know what to do. You will."

Her hand reached and touched Lynn's hand, and Lynn took hold, very lightly.

Nancy, still speaking tentatively, said, "I'm sure I'd try to keep him from getting hurt more than anything. But I'm not really sure how, you know?"

Lynn nodded, then nodded again. "I know."

"I'd pray like crazy. It's such a miracle, you know. There must be a plan."

"You think so?"

"Of course. What do you think?"

Lynn said, "I feel like the plan must have broken down. Like God got the wrong person. If it is a plan. I don't know."

Nancy pressed her lips together and nodded. "Sure it's a plan", she said. "You'll be more than okay, Lynn. So will C.J. You'll see."

"I'm down to one-word prayers", Lynn said. "First it was 'Help'. Now it's 'Why?'"

"I'm sorry. I think I understand what you're feeling. I really do."

"I don't want it", Lynn said, staring at her coffee. "Is that something you can understand? I really, honest to God, want it gone, Nance."

Tears rimmed Nancy's eyes. She waited nearly half a minute before she whispered, "Yeah, hon. I know. I understand. And I'll do anything to help you. You know that."

Very softly, Lynn said, "I just don't want anybody taking C.J. and using him—taking him physically, taking control of him, taking him any way at all."

"Then we won't let them."

"That's what's coming, though. I feel it so strong, sometimes I can hardly breathe."

"We don't have to let them, Lynn."

A police siren sounded a single, cascading whoop in front of the house and then, from the distance, sounding like a soft pulse at first but growing nearer and harder, quickly, a brand-new entry: a helicopter thumping toward them. In just a matter of seconds, it seemed to be circling overhead.

Lynn raised her eyes to the ceiling briefly, then lowered them again. She whispered flatly, without changing expression, "Oh, that's great. Something new to resent. Thump, thump, thump, right over our heads."

She released Nancy's hand and took another sip of coffee. "You'll stay, won't you? I've been assuming you would but haven't asked."

"You mean overnight?"

"Whatever you can manage."

"We're not going anywhere, Lynn."

Their eyes met, and both of them smiled lightly, like a contract being signed.

"I told Father I'd take C.J. to see the Cardinal with him tomorrow", Lynn said, looking down at her cup again. "See what he has to say."

Nancy studied her silently for a moment, then asked, "What'll he want to do, do you think?"

There were footsteps approaching the kitchen, and then passing by the closed door. Joe or Father Mark, one or the other.

Lynn stared at Nancy. She shrugged. Then she put her coffee down and nestled her face in her opened palms.

While tens of millions of people around the world were asking whether a boy named C.J. Walker could really raise the dead, Father Mark felt pinned to a different question. He, too, wanted to know why. Not why would it be happening, but why C.J. Walker, of all the people in the world? Why not some holy person that had worked with the homeless round-the-clock for about twenty years? Or somebody who gave up some significant piece of his life every day to help people in some godforsaken slum or desert or jungle mission? Or some sweet old lady who fell on her knees and prayed every day of her life for all of her ninety years on earth?

And so, as their first day together snuck toward evening, he found himself alone for the first time with this most extraordinary human being: the nine-year-old wonder child whom he had baptized and seen on the playground and talked with at church and who, alone among all the people on earth, could now raise dead people to life again.

They were in C.J.'s bedroom, sitting together on the boy's bed, Father Mark near the foot on an orange-and-blue bedspread splashed with soccer players scoring goals. C.J. was resting against his headboard, his knees spread wide and pulled up toward his shoulders, his hands between his legs, his expression saying very clearly that he would rather be somewhere else.

"We haven't really had a chance to talk together about what's happened, have we, C.J.?" he began. He was glad he was in a regular shirt and not a Roman collar. He knew that young kids from Catholic schools can easily freeze in front of a Roman collar.

C.J. shook his head and said, "Uh-uh."

"I'm glad we can talk now."

C.J. answered with a soft, "Okay", and started, very gently and very slightly, to rock.

"But I've gotta tell you, C.J., I'm not sure what to say; what happened was so incredible."

C.J. stopped rocking. "Yeah", he said quietly.

Mark looked around the room. There were four posters, two of them photos of the Detroit Red Wings, both showing hard collisions, and two illustrated soccer posters—one showing someone on the U.S. World Cup team jumping with a player in green to contend for a ball in midair, the other a player in a blue-and-yellow uniform running over a sliding player in a red-and-white uniform. High action, hard collisions. No angels. No saints. No crucifix. No Bible pictures.

"What do you like to do most, C.J. Just for fun?"

C.J. pursed his lip, thinking. "Nothing", he said. "I don't know. Play soccer."

In a red-and-blue apple crate in the corner of the room, action figures were piled along with metal model cars, various balls, and an old baseball cap.

Mark wondered if C.J. knew who Saint Christopher was, his own namesake. "I notice you have action figures in the box there. Do you like superheroes?"

C.J. gave a hesitant smile and a short nod. Cool memories hidden behind young eyes. "They have video games with them", C.J. said.

"Most kids like those best, don't they; the video games?"

C.J. nodded. "I guess." The rocking stopped, but his fingers didn't. He picked absentmindedly at the tops of his fingernails. His head was lowered.

"Did you ever pretend you were a superhero that did things nobody else could do?"

C.J. thought, sniffed, and nodded. He raised his eyes but not his chin. "When I was little I liked to be one that's invisible", he said cautiously. "Matt Bunger."

"Matt Bunger?"

"He's one I made up when I was little", C.J. said. "He's a person, like a detective. And he's strong. But the main thing is, he can make himself invisible."

"That's so great". The priest's smile was genuine. "Matt Bunger."

C.J. nodded.

"I made up some when I was little, too."

"Superheroes?"

"Fire Hand made a fist and shot fire."

"You called him Fire Hand?"

The priest nodded, remembering games he'd played in the railroad yard by the river in Monroe, so many years ago. "He'd hold out his fist, like this, but when he made his fingers straight . . ." He did it. "Shhhiew! Fire shot out."

C.J. grinned. His hand formed a fist slowly, then opened with a snap. A nod of approval. "Fire Hand."

The priest's smile lingered. C.J. made him feel that way, like smiling. He wondered how much of himself he was seeing in C.J. Walker. It was like a replay of his nine-year-old self in a lot of ways. He was not outwardly spiritual in the usual sense of the word, not as far as he could see. And lonely somehow, with some anger, as C.J.'s fighting in school showed.

Probably from missing his dad in the house, the way Mark had missed his own dad, who was killed in a car accident when Mark was twelve.

He also guessed that C.J. was one of those kids who thought things that adults didn't guess he was capable of thinking.

"Do any of the heroes you made up have the power to bring back dead people?" he asked.

He tried to smile with that one, but fell short. He wasn't good at faking it.

C.J. squirmed and slid sideways on the bed, his legs moving around slowly to hang off the side. He shook his head casually from side to side and said, "Nobody does that."

"Not even Matt Bunger?"

"Nobody does that."

That was clear. Nobody does that. Not even in C.J.'s imagination.

"If they came back from the dead," C.J. said, "then they wouldn't try not to get killed because they'd never stay dead, and you would know that."

"Yeah, I guess you would."

"So they could just let the bad guys kill them because they wouldn't care if they got killed or what. Except it might hurt. But you'd know they'd always come back."

"So that wouldn't be as much fun."

"All of them can die", C.J. said, sliding off the bed and then hopping back on again to sit sideways. "Even aliens can die", he added.

"If there was a character like that, C.J., maybe one that could die himself, so the story would still be good, but he still had this power to bring back the dead, what would he be called, do you think?"

C.J.'s brow furrowed. "His name?"

"Yeah."

C.J. gazed past the priest to an imagined place where superheroes might get their names. Ten seconds passed. Finally his smile widened and his eyes lit up, and he said with a touch of hissing and more than a touch of dramatic satisfaction, "Deathbreaker."

"Deathbreaker?"

C.J. nodded with a wide smile.

"Deathbreaker and Fire Hand. And Matt Bunger."

"And Matt Bunger."

They looked at each other for a long, sweet moment. Sweet for both of them. Both of them approving.

"C.J? Why do you think you're a Deathbreaker? Because that's what you actually are, isn't it?"

C.J. furrowed his brow and looked away. Then he shrugged and lowered his head to stare at the bed and at his fingers.

"Did you ever say that before to anything?" He asked it softly, moving to something the boy could answer easily. "To a dead bug or anything?"

"Before Mrs. Klein, you mean?"

"Before Mrs. Klein, yes."

C.J. shook his head. He was still staring at his fingers, looking solemn, looking accused. He said, "Uh-uh."

"Then why did you say it to her, C.J.?" he asked. His voice had taken on a pleading tone. "What happened to make you say it to her?"

C.J. shrugged. The lip-biting again. But this time, he looked up, meeting the priest's gaze. "You said we should pray for her to be well again," he whispered, "so I did. I just did it because you said so."

Mark struggled to remember clearly. He'd said the same prayer he usually said at wakes, he was sure. The same thing, in one form or another, nearly every time: praying that the person would now be completely healed in God. But that meant in heaven. He meant in heaven, not that they'd be alive and well again here and now. He'd never pray about it happening in the here and now, not with a person who had already died and been embalmed.

The absurdity of it took his breath away. He smiled weakly at C.J., not knowing what to say. He wanted to laugh and cry at the same time. He wondered if God was sitting around with his friends, laughing— God with a sense of humor, after all, dropping this unspeakable power into the great, cosmic plan like a pinball, knowing for eons that it was coming, dropping it with a wink of his eye into little C.J. Walker, who would rather be outside playing a hundred different games in a hundred different places than be here with his parish priest right now, or even be in church. Maybe least of all, be in church.

He felt like he was standing on a railroad track watching some eternal galactic plan bear down on them all with unthinkable wisdom and depth and complexity while he suddenly wanted to raise his arms and shout, "Excuse me, but C.J. misunderstood me! There's been a mistake!"

The last of the day's sunlight was nearly gone. The sun had slipped into the treetops of western Royal Oak—the bottom ridge of clouds above it already edged in pink, the rising upper folds changing quickly to oranges and violets and bright reds. There was just enough evening glow to let Lynn, standing at the dining room window, see the expressions of the people milling at the end of the driveway and in front of the neighbors and across the street. So many of them now, a lot more than before, it seemed to her, with a lot more signs. But now even the signs had changed; she could see that, too. Now, in addition to words like "End Times" and "Lazarus Boy", she saw words that seemed to fairly tremble with pain, circling over the heads of the crowd like slow-moving birds, words like "Leukemia" and "Lung Cancer" and "Cancer of the Throat" and "For God's sake, do something!"

She found herself staring at a single, large sign held up near the end of the driveway—black letters on a yellow poster board being held up stoically by what looked like a teenaged girl in a light-red sweater who seemed to be staring directly back at her, looking so sad that she looked nearly wild.

The sign read: "2 yr. old daughter. 2 months to live. PLEASE!" Lynn's heart ached for her. She bit her lip, but she didn't turn away.

Joe came up quietly behind her, standing over her right shoulder, watching the crowd with her. Then she heard him murmur, almost as if he was speaking to himself, "Have they found anybody looking for real trouble yet, I wonder. Coming with guns or anything like that?"

"Don't say it, Joe." She was still staring at the sign and at the girl who held it. She was watching the girl's eyes darken and fade with the setting of the sun. She said softly and firmly, without turning around, "I don't want to hear any of that."

Twelve

The police escorted Joe as far as Hilton Avenue; then he was on his own. He'd seen them do the same for Father Mark, who had parked in the street in front of the house next door and got away before him. No incidents from the crowd with either of them, as far as he could see—just a lot of pointing and calling out and a lot of shoving along the edges of the street, people trying to get a look.

They just want to make sure I'm not smuggling C.J. out, he thought. They'll save their serious moves for him.

There were vehicles following him, and he knew that reporters would be waiting when he got there. For a minute he considered not even going home—just driving around for a while, maybe even lose the cars tailing him and check into a motel, avoiding all the hassle. But he had to be at his apartment in case Lynn called. Things could get crazy real quick at her place, and he realized that he couldn't get through to tell her if he was at a motel, not with her phone off the hook.

He should have figured that out sooner, he thought. Should have had his buddy bring a cell phone with the TV; set something up like that.

He clicked on the radio to see what else the talk-radio shows were coming up with. WXYZ. Wixie Night Talk, they called it. Two cohosts, Bri and Di, filling Detroit's night with gossipy chatter. "How many people do you think have been saying it to whoever's passed away, though?" Brian whatever-his-name-was saying. "Don't you think other people are trying it?"

Di, the woman, said, "Oh, do we want to get into this?" Laughing.

The brains of a hen, Joe thought. Both of them. For this they get paid.

He snapped off the radio and pressed harder on the accelerator. Everything was moving faster now, including him.

At his apartment, he pulled into handicapped parking. So give me a ticket, he thought. He jumped out and jogged to the door without looking at the reporters and without answering their questions or acknowledging their appeals for "Just a few words, please." With just a little pushing he was safe inside.

The building was quiet. Nobody was hanging out of doorways to nail him on the way up to his room. He realized, climbing the stairs toward 215, that he was incredibly tired. He hadn't felt it that much before. Maybe his body sensed his bed closing in.

As he stepped through the stairway door on the second floor, he stopped abruptly. A man was standing there, arms crossed, leaning against the wall, coming straight up as Joe came through the door, his arms dropping slowly to his sides. Tall, muscular, dark suit, dark hair, thirty-something, a bland expression, and a low voice as bland as his expression, now saying flatly, "Mr. Walker."

"Who are you?" Joe asked. He moved past him without waiting for an answer, and noticed another guy at the other end of the hall, looking like he could have been the first guy's twin. He was not moving toward them, just watching from outside the far-end staircase.

"Security", the man said. "Everything's fine."

Joe didn't bother answering. Just so they left him alone.

He slipped his key into his door, glanced again to make sure the two men were not moving, started to push his door open, and froze.

He hadn't even noticed it: his lights were on.

He glanced uneasily at the man at the stairway, the man still not moving, just watching; then he eased the door open and stepped inside.

The first thing he could see as he came into the apartment was the table in the dining "L". It had money spread out on it. A lot of money. Big bills, it looked like; fifties, all fanned out left to right in a half circle, like a deck of cards.

Then, motion.

Joe spun to his left. A man was in the living room, getting up from the couch—a thin guy in a black suit, looking right at home, looking right at Joe, not looking like he was there for any kind of breaking and entering but not looking like a reporter, either. Guy looked more like a lawyer, Joe thought, one with his hair all slicked down and run straight back. Sharp nose, sharp chin. Eyes sharp, too, and not real happy. A man with money, though, he could tell, with some of it spread out already, nice and neat, right on the table. A man with two friends in the hall, too. Or maybe not friends. Maybe just weapons.

He couldn't help it. He wanted to look tough, but he grinned, instead. This was a guy who didn't have to sneak an offer in with a mailman, and Joe was ready to listen.

Torrie Kruger said, "It's one thousand dollars, Mr. Walker, for three minutes of your time." He stood in front of the couch like it was his own apartment and Joe was the visitor. His voice was as sharp as the edges of his face, and it came out quietly. "Twenty fifty-dollar bills. You keep it if you give me three minutes of your time, starting now."

So far, so good. Joe slid the door closed behind him.

"Who are you?" he asked, trying to sound casual.

"That works out to twenty thousand dollars an hour, just for listening to me talk. My name is Torrie Kruger."

Joe nodded toward the money. "That's real nice. How'd you get in?"

"Since I only have a little over two and a half minutes left, let me tell you that I represent a man whose son is dying. May be dead right now. The boy is very sick."

"Hearing from a lot of people with sick kids these days", Joe said. He had all the cards and he knew it. So did Mr. Slick.

"The boy is fifteen years old. My employer is offering to give you one hundred thousand dollars cash to have your son pray for the boy, however he does that. In person, of course. And that hundred thousand is yours, or your son's, just for the prayer, regardless of results. Then it gets even better."

Joe sat down. He almost grinned again but held it back this time.

"If my client's son does return to full health, no more signs of leukemia, which is what he's dying from, and if his recovery is verified by his doctors within seventy-two hours of your visit, my client will deposit five million dollars—over and above the initial one hundred thousand dollars, and over and above this one thousand dollars that you've already earned just for listening—five million U.S. dollars in any account you or Mrs. Walker choose, either jointly or separately, anywhere in the world. That day. No waiting."

Joe felt numb; it was so good.

"That's a total of five million, one hundred and one thousand dollars, coin of the realm", his visitor said. "For a five-minute visit to the man's home."

Joe still didn't move, but he did inhale slowly and deeply, and, with an effort, he kept himself from jumping up and shaking on it. He thought how his ticket wasn't in sight all day, with him wondering how he was going to find it in all that crowd and with the phone off the hook at Lynn's and not a lot of time to wait for mail deliveries, and then, all of a sudden, when he was getting scared it might not happen at all before the priest and the Cardinal or whoever else tried to hide C.J. in the Vatican or something, and bang: the ticket drops into his lap. Five million dollars and way more. "Coin of the realm", the man said. He liked that. Two and a half million for him and two and a half for Lynn. A five and six zeroes, all told. And he keeps the hundred and one thousand, like a finder's fee.

And after that, there would be so much more!

Torrie moved across the living room with two envelopes in his hand, long ones. "This", he said, offering Joe the first of the two envelopes, "is a sealed letter from Mr. Cross to you and your wife—and your son, too."

"Cross, huh?" Joe murmured. Was it too good to be true? He'd have to look for the catch.

"He's asking your son to try and save his son, simple as that. He's not even demanding that it happens. Just asking that you try. He's a nice man."

Joe took the envelope addressed to "the Walker family" and stared at it without opening it. He said, "You want a beer?"

Torrie shook his head no. "You go ahead, though", he said. "You've had a rough day, I hear. Mr. Cross can fix it so you don't have any more of them. You or your wife. Or your son."

Joe said, "Is that right?"

Now Torrie smiled. Not even an answer, just a satisfied smile. And, with that, he held up a second envelope. "This one is the contract. Drawn up in the terms I've just outlined. Two copies, already signed by Mr. Cross. You sign them, the boy's mother signs them, you get one back to us, and the deal's binding."

"Then we should get the hundred thousand up front", Joe said, trying to stay poker-faced. "Since we get it even if nothing happens, we should get it up front, as soon as we sign the contract."

Torrie smiled again, just with his lips. "I've gone over three minutes, haven't I?"

"Don't worry about it. Do we get it up front?"

"You get one hundred thousand in cash, on the spot, as soon as it's signed by both you and your wife and we have our copy in hand. After that, you bring your son with me to New York in our private jet. Takes just a couple of hours to fly, another thirty minutes to drive to the house. You have your son try and help Tony; the boy's name: Anthony Junior. If he recovers, you have another five million dollars. Unreported, at least by us. Less than nine hours of your time, total."

Joe breathed in as deeply as he could without being obvious. He took the envelope in his left hand and reached out his right to grab Torrie's hand and shake it quickly. "Done deal", he said.

"You'll get Mrs. Walker's signature?"

"Done deal. First thing tomorrow."

Torrie walked to the side of the couch and picked up his attaché case. He carried it to the dining table, dialed a four-number combination, and opened it. What Joe saw was six stacks of fifty-dollar bills, each several inches deep. He also saw a cell phone.

"Two thousand fifties", Torrie said. "As soon as we receive the contract, it's yours. We arrange getting you to the flight immediately afterwards."

Joe said, "Done deal, absolutely", then added, "Is that cell for me?"

"It's probably more secure than yours. It's for you. Call us on this one, nothing else."

Joe nodded and took the phone, flipping it open to look it over.

"It's programmed with my number", Kruger said. "Number one. If you see this light blinking, it means I've tried to call you. Get back to me right away."

"Why don't you just come with me to the house tomorrow? See Lynn yourself? That'd be the best way."

"I understand there's a small crowd there", Torrie said, locking his case again. "Anyone that comes to your wife's house gets on TV."

"Oh", Joe said. "I guess so." He smiled again. "How'd you get in here, anyway? You pay off the building manager? Abe let you in, right?"

Torrie turned and went to the door. "I'll expect to hear from you tonight or tomorrow. Tomorrow morning at the latest."

"You didn't tell me what this Mr. Cross does", Joe said. "I'd like to know who I'm doing business with."

"What he does is," Torrie said slowly, "he loves his son. He misses his dead wife. He manages a lot of money. And he keeps his word. Like a blood oath. He's from the old country, you have to understand, where a man's word is his blood oath."

"What country?"

"Have a good day. You're now a rich man."

Lynn was asleep ten minutes after lying down, but she didn't sleep well. She heard a knock on the door, more like a pounding, and she was the only one in the living room, so she opened it, and the Pope was there. He'd come all the way from Rome because he heard about C.J. Only it wasn't just him. He was holding a body in his arms, all bones, and dead, the face already a skull. It reminded Lynn of one of the bodies from those old pictures of the German death camps in World War II, just bones and stretched skin and big eyes, no clothes left, just bones. And the Pope kept asking her to please bring C.J. downstairs, but she didn't want C.J. pulled into this, not with the bones and the eyes, and especially not with the people behind the Pope, because she saw the crowds were pressing forward again, and they were just waiting, all grinning and watching and hunched over. She knew they'd rush C.J. if he came out. But this was the Pope.

Then Joe was there, standing behind her and shouting at them to all go away, but then she saw that the Pope was dying, too. He just sank down on his knees with the body in his arms; he was dying, too, and he kept asking her to, please, go and get C.J.

There was a lot of shuffling on the lawn, and she saw that what must have been two or three hundred more of those same death-camp people had come up around the porch, or the whole crowd had been these same people all along, she didn't know; but they were all bones and big eyes, and now there were hundreds and hundreds of them, like the march of the living dead, just shuffling toward her, begging her, please, to bring C.J. down.

She turned and ran, hardly able to breathe. She ran through the house, trying to find C.J. because she didn't know where he was and she wanted to get him out the back way, but none of the lights would go on, and they followed her, and in the dark she could hear them shuffling through the hall right behind her and getting closer, but she still couldn't find C.J.

When she woke up she was sweating in the dark and trembling. The house was quiet. It was 2:15 A.M.

She lay very still. She wished she wasn't alone with all of this—trying to figure it out, trying to make the right choices, trying to be both parents for C.J. She wished it so much, she hurt.

She shifted her weight and slowly kicked her sheet off, then slid her legs over the side of the bed and sat up.

She remembered the day her mom died. She had had cancer, too, starting in her breast. C.J. could have saved her, but that was before he was born. And her dad's death, the day she was nobody's little girl anymore. That was the first time she ever felt really alone. There had been other days since.

She rose, still shaky, and moved toward her window, wondering with a new surge of heartache if C.J. might call her mom and dad back to life even now, and she briefly pictured them climbing out of their coffins after all these years. But she felt sickened by it and shook the thought from her mind.

She realized, as she got to the window, that she was cool with perspiration.

A large group of the watchers and the waiters, she noticed, were still out there. People were in the street and pressing up her driveway and along the sidewalk as though they were waiting for a ticket to a concert, only there were more than she had expected, maybe two hundred of them even in the middle of the night, some with candles, holding a vigil. And every one of them wanted the power.

Everyone in the world wanted it, or would when they all realized that it was real. Everybody wanted it but her. And she was the one responsible for taking care of C.J.

She began to pick out individuals in the thin light of the street below—the man bent over in his lawn chair, head down, next to the neighbors' driveway; the woman with the book, possibly a Bible, standing by the Channel 62 camera truck, staring at the house, standing and waiting at two o'clock in the morning; the man on the other side of the same truck, just staring.

Someone out there, she felt certain, was thinking that if the person they loved died, they'd bring the body here to the house to find C.J. Walker. Of course they'd be thinking that, she thought; who wouldn't? Right now, she thought, somebody had that plan in mind, to bring a dead body here to C.J.

Then the questions were there again, questions without answers. Impossible questions, like, once the healing line to the house began, how could it ever be stopped? And, if C.J. brought back a hundred of them, what would he do with number 101? And, if you do cut if off at some point, don't you have to end up selecting who lives and who dies? And if so, who would possibly do that? And based on what criteria? Or was no one ever supposed to be dead again? Could that be it? she wondered.

Her mind was racing faster, the questions tumbling one on top of the other. Was C.J. supposed to sit there and let armies carry the dead past him all day long? Would they assign him hours? Would rich people get first-in-line preferences, or Americans, or scientists, or Catholics, or people who win some kind of lottery? Or would it just turn into one huge rotation, with C.J. keeping himself alive until he's hundreds of years old and with millions and even billions of other people being four hundred and five hundred years old, and each coming around to be touched by him again and again—little, shriveled remnants by the tens of millions being carried again and again to C.J.'s door, and she, of all people, being kept breathing by her son for six hundred, seven hundred, eight hundred years . . .

She felt suddenly nauseated, and, for a brief moment, weak enough to faint. She stepped back from the window and from all the people and all of their pain.

Why didn't Mark or Joe or any of these other people realize what she realized, about the power and about where it was leading?

She clutched the curtain and whispered, "Why are you doing this?" but she wasn't even sure who she was talking to. She might have been talking to that person she knew had to be out there already and making dark plans. Or maybe to the whole crowd. Or maybe she was talking to God. Or maybe, to herself.

Whatever the case, she was not getting an answer.

Joe didn't even try to sleep. He kept working out the totals. First, just in his mind, then, when the numbers got too tough to keep track of, he turned on the light and settled into his pillow with his calculator. He was hyped. The way he saw it, it wouldn't take C.J. even ten seconds to say what he says and to touch the kid. Tony, it was. Five seconds seemed more like it. He timed it. "Be well, Tony." Touch. No, touch at the same time. So not even five seconds. But let's say five, just for figuring. C.J. might say it slow or something. So. He keeps the thousand he already has. He keeps the hundred grand he gets for showing up. All cash. And he gets five million on top of that. That's $5,101,000 for five seconds' work.

Then you figure that out on an hourly basis. How many five seconds in a whole hour? Okay, there's 720. So that's 720 times the $5,101,000, just to figure out the hourly rate, and it comes out to, what is that? It comes to $3,672,720,000 an hour! Over three and a half billion dollars an hour!

He laughed and rolled over into his pillow and laughed again, out loud, this time pounding the back of his fist into his mattress. Three billion six an hour. And he started working when he was thirteen at Food Fair, stocking juice shelves for $2.10 an hour.

So how much did that mean that C.J. was making an hour more than Joe did when he was thirteen, with C.J. being just nine years old, four years younger than Joe was?

Back to the calculator . . .

He fell asleep smiling.

Thirteen

Lynn was just beginning to fix bacon and eggs and toast, a real breakfast for a change, when Joe pounded at the side door and rushed in grinning. He had called the police a half hour before, he said, from his apartment. He told them he'd be showing up at about 7:15, in a black Monte Carlo, license plate 474 YVJ. "They watched for me and cruised me in, crowd parting like the Red Sea."

She could picture it. She said, "Yeah", but didn't smile.

"But I've got to talk with you, Lynn", he said, dropping his voice. "Now, if we can, okay? Get Nancy to finish up the eggs and all, or let it wait ten minutes, okay? This is really important. Please. Maybe even upstairs, in your room, if that's okay."

In the past, that wild, bright look in Joe's eyes had too often meant Joe had found another easy way to get rich, one that had shady edges and always fell through. Always. So Lynn had not only grown to distrust it; she'd learned to resent it. She had always wished he'd gotten that excited about other, more important things.

"The back porch will be better", she said, putting the carton of eggs down on the counter by the sink. "The kids are upstairs with Nancy. No one else is here."

"No priests of the holy order?"

"It's Sunday." She moved toward the back door. "He'll be here later", she said.

On the porch, which was fully screened, a favorite place for them in better times, Lynn sat down on the old church bench that she and Joe had bought just after they were married. Nothing religious about it; it just seemed arty to them at the time: wrought-iron vines and grapes in rust-colored paint at both ends of a six-foot-long oak pew.

Joe sat next to her and leaned close. "I want to show you this", he whispered. "It's fantastic!" He reached into his back pocket and pulled out the folded letter from Cross.

"What's this?"

"Before we read it, let me tell you, Lynn, God has really come through for you and C.J."

"We got a letter from God?" she asked coolly. She knew that when Joe talked about God it really meant he was working on her, saying, it's not me that's about to ask you to do something; it's really God, so you'd better go along.

Joe grinned wide, like a kid. "We got a ticket from God, that's right." He was holding the envelope up in front of her, waving it in quick, intermittent bursts. His smile widened, his whisper strained with fresh conviction. "As of right now, you got all the money you'll ever need to move C.J. anywhere you want."

Lynn guessed that the "you" really meant "me, too". Joe was working on her, all right, but obviously proud of something he'd done.

She'd seen that before, too.

"Just like the cop said last night: you have to move, right? Well, now you can; be safe and alone and comfortable. Move wherever you want, then take whatever time you need to think this out, have people come in and give you advice, whatever. And you can have it all without having people who don't really care about C.J. swooping down and hiding him away and using you like the Cardinal's going to want to do. Make life miserable for both of you, honest to God."

She reached for the envelope. It was addressed to "the Walker family" and was still sealed. Lynn saw the name "A.W. Cross" in the upper left corner.

"You haven't read it?" she asked.

"Not a word", Joe said, looking surprised. "It's to the family. I didn't want to open it without you."

Her antennas were up, the instincts Joe once called her crap detectors. Part of the damage of their marriage was she never really listened to him anymore without suspecting an angle.

She pulled out the letter and began to read out loud, speaking quietly.

" 'Dear Mr. and Mrs. Walker. I write this from a place of anguish. Like you, I have only one child, my son, Anthony.' "

She sighed, seeing her nightmare again, flesh and bones and pain and deep-set eyes filled with panic. The carrying of the dead.

"What's the matter?" Joe asked.

"Nothing."

" 'Tony's mother died a number of years ago. He is now fifteen, but doctors tell me that he will not live to be sixteen.' "

She squirmed. It wasn't the Pope bringing them across the lawn. It was Joe.

"He's got leukemia", he said.

She paused again, wondering how he knew that, but she didn't ask.

"'*Tony is dying of leukemia. He may be dead by the time you read this letter. Mr. and Mrs. Walker, I have only two things in this world, my wealth and my son. And only one of them that I care about. I am begging you as parents of a son of your own to take pity on me and my son. Please let Christopher come to us and pray for him. Should God give Tony this miracle, I will consider it my sworn oath to make you financially secure for the rest of your lives. Mr. Kruger has details of my guarantee in the contract that accompanies this letter.*'"

"Who's Kruger?" Lynn asked quietly.

"He's the guy's lawyer. Torrie's his first name. I saw him last night."

"Last night?"

"They came to see me at my apartment, this lawyer and two other guys. Finish the letter, I'll tell you the rest."

She glanced down again. "'*I pray for your generosity. I am sorry that I do not have enough words to describe our thanks. God bless you. Anthony W. Cross.*'"

She put the letter back into its envelope and handed it to Joe. "He made out a contract?"

"It's amazing grace, I'll tell you." Out came the contract from his other back pocket. He was beaming. "Want to know what 'financially secure' means? It means five million dollars, honest to God!" He held the contract up for Lynn to take, but she didn't reach for it right away, so he kept talking, now faster than before, still holding it in front of her. "We go there with C.J. He lives in New York, but he has his own jet. Zoom! Right to the house, total comfort. Five seconds we'll be in there and out. That's all there is to it. Then, if the kid recovers, and he will, we get five million dollars! Five and six zeroes, Lynn, cash!"

He paused.

No reaction from Lynn.

Joe cocked his head. "It's what we were praying for, Lynn; you see that, right? This isn't a TV gimmick or something. Nobody else even knows about it. And then, five million dollars, and you can go anywhere. You're in total control of your own future. *You* are, not these other clowns. You can keep C.J. out of everybody else's hands, keep people away, figure out what's best for him yourself, live the way you want to and not have to stay holed up like a hostage."

Lynn was staring at him.

"Listen", he said. He was starting to talk louder now, starting to plead with her not to think whatever it was that was making her hesitate, looking confused and a little desperate. "I figured it out on an hourly basis, like an hourly wage. We're talking more than three and a half billion dollars an hour! I mean ... good God, Lynn! What the hell's the matter?"

She looked at him, startled by the outburst and suddenly feeling sorry for him. She said, "Joe. I know it looks good, the way it seems to you. But I really don't want to do this kind of thing."

"Lynn!" he said. He looked like he'd been kicked. He dropped the contract in her lap and took her hand, squeezing it tight. "This Cross boy's got leukemia", he said. "For God's sake, honey. I see what you're saying, like if we made C.J. into a carnival act or something, but please! God, Lynn! This isn't like that at all. This is a man who gets his son back, and a boy who doesn't deserve to die gets his life back, and we happen to get our life straightened out for doing that good, good thing!" He shook his head; his mouth opened. "And that's not something you want to do? You'd rather trot him down to the Cardinal this afternoon and have him sent to Rome so a bunch of old men can put him away and study him forever, or lock him up because he's in competition with Jesus Christ, which is the way they'll see it."

He let go of her hand and rose to his feet, too agitated to stay seated. "You think they want somebody going around raising the dead, people following C.J. like he was Jesus' Second Coming? You think they won't bet it's the devil doing this; put the kid through fifty exorcisms, hide him away and shut him down if they can't scare the power out of him, keep him shut up for fifty years while they get twenty commissions to study him like ... forever? Grow up, Lynn! I can't believe what I'm hearing!"

"Joe", she said, really wanting him to understand, wanting, most of all, to sense some kind of ally in him, some signal that Joe might understand with her that once they started down that road, they would never be able to stop. "Give me some credit here, okay? I see what you're saying. I do. But if you go this route ... Joe, don't you see what you'd be doing to him? I've been thinking hard about it, about everybody trying to live forever, and about C.J., and you have to look where that leads. Think about every person in the world grabbing for your son, everybody screaming for him, all lining up with their dead. Think what that would do to him, Joe, my God!"

"But this is private! This isn't on some second-rate TV special!"

"Joe!" she snapped, angry now, because he still didn't get it at all. Even more than that, because he didn't seem capable of thinking about C.J. first, and just like he had never been able to put her first, or their marriage first. Old issues roaring back in her, old arguments and old hurts coming alive again as certainly as Marion Klein and Galvin Turner came alive again. "You really think doing this deal with whoever this Cross guy is would be private?" she stormed, letting out all the tensions of the last few days. "What's the matter with you? You're going to, what? ... sneak him out to an airport for a flight to New York, and you're going to do that in private, for God's sake? Are you insane? And what happens when he gets on the plane? Do you know where it's flying to, really? Are you 'Pilot Joe' now, going to fly the plane yourself?"

She jumped to her feet to face him, dropping the contract to the floor at her feet, not caring about it, not caring about Joe or the Cross kid, if he really existed, or anyone else now—just C.J., caring about him totally, because she knew that no one else did. "How do you know where it's really going to land? How do you know the man's good for his word?"

Joe was talking fast, trying to make up in speed what he felt he was losing in ground. "He's old country. Italian. Keeping his word is like a blood oath to those guys. You'd be saving his son, for God's sake. He'd give you his legs if that's what you wanted, a guy like that."

"Oh great! And he sends a German so-called lawyer, and who else, to get you to sign a contract? You said 'they' came. How many were 'they'?"

"I can't believe this", Joe protested. "Three of them. So what? You're screwed into the ceiling just because the guy's from Italy or what?"

"Who were the other two? Did they sit down and smile and show you pictures of their kids, Joe, or did they stand by the door in dark suits and sunglasses with their arms crossed? Which is closer?"

"They were guys!" His face was flushed, he getting as mad as she.

She could sense it, though: Joe in his defensive stance. And sensing it, she was even angrier because she realized he was gambling C.J.'s life on some story with nothing more to it than five million dollars in the last sentence. That was all he knew. He knew nothing!

Her head shook from side to side, hard. She said, "They were body-guards, weren't they? This guy and two goons come and want to take C.J. on a private plane, for God's sake, and you're so incredibly con-sumed with easy money that you believe them. The superbrain Joe Walker."

"He's not with the mob or something, if that's where you're going", Joe said loudly.

"How do you know? Did you call the FBI in New York? Did you even find out what city he's supposed to live in so you could call the cops there? Has it even once occurred to your galactically superior intel-lect that this may just be a con, that it may be—as incredible as this may sound, Joe—that it may actually be a way for somebody who is smarter than you are to get your son on a plane and kidnap him? At which point, if they can duck under the radar or whatever, they may just decide to drop you into Lake St. Clair, and me with you? You get greedy, Joe, and that's what happens; you get mindless!"

She took a deep breath and tried to calm down as she saw his nostrils flare and his eyes blaze, and she thought, he'd fight me physically right now if he thought it would do any good. But she didn't care about that. It was all too much—too many people outside, too much to be afraid of, too much she didn't know about, too much being alone, just too much. And Joe would never put anyone else's interest before his own, she thought again. Not even C.J.'s. It just was not in him.

"I won't sell him, Joe", she said in a stony voice after a long and silent moment. "I'll do whatever it takes to protect him, and putting him on the block for the highest bidder won't do that. I'm going to protect him. I'm his mother. That's my job."

Joe dragged his palms down his face. His eyes were dark with frustration, his lips drawn tight. He looked angrily to the floor for just a second, then raised his eyes to confront her. "Did you hear about the metal traces yet?" Joe asked. He shot it out like a threat.

The surprise in her eyes and the way she tilted her head told him no.

"You should go back to watching the news." He spit the words out like they'd been something caught in his teeth. "The tool MacInnes used to do all that embalming stuff left metallic traces inside Marion and Turner both. It's in a hundred different places, all from when they were embalmed. The doctors are just waiting now for one of them to give his okay; then they're going to stick a probe or something in there and scrape enough metal to analyze it. And that'll be it, Lynn. Listen to what I'm saying, now." He eased even closer. "What it means is, any minute now they'll have their proof that the metal's from the thing that MacInnes used. They compare the two, the metal and the tool. They nail it down. End of story. End of time to think. End of you keeping C.J. safely in his little bedroom. End of any chance to get away. Because at that point, babe, somebody'll come and take C.J. outta here. It could happen today. It could happen tomorrow. But it's sure as hell is going to happen!"

She stared, her mouth slightly open, her eyes wide and dark and startled—a hunted look.

Joe shook his head. "So you haven't got time to be noble, babe, or whatever it is you think you're being. You haven't got time to wish this away like a twelve-year-old, and say, 'Oh, let's not do anything and maybe the hard part will all go away.' You'll give him to a church that's had two thousand years' practice at hiding people, where he'll be seen as a kid who's in flat-out competition with Jesus Christ, and which is a government, Lynn. Don't forget that. It's a country, the Vatican, all its own. So you'll do that, or you'll take Cross' money right now, before they know for sure about that metal, and you'll run. Take your chances. 'Cause there's one other real good possibility, and you know what that is?"

She waited.

"When they get their proof, the next country to step in will be the good ol' U. S. of A. The government will take him, and they'll do it in a heartbeat. A kid that raises the dead? Oh yeah. The same good citizens who gave us Waco and Ruby Ridge and Little Havana and the IRS and the ATF and just a whole list of big-time hits." He raised his index finger like a flag. "They come in? End of story. So make up your mind what you want. Right now. What do you want?"

She stared at him, then turned her head to stare silently at the back-yard. She looked at the garage for a long time, and at the picnic table and the elm by the back fence with a swinging rope tied to it, and at the neighbor's house in back where the only things they had to decide were what to cook for dinner or what color the bedroom should be.

When she turned to look at him again, the anger had left her eyes. The sadness had returned. Her arms were limp at her sides.

"If you want to help us, Joe, help me figure out how to get him a normal life again. That's all he really wants, you know that. And that's all I want, too." She pressed her lips together tightly; then she said, "I want to see him graduate from grade school. I want to see him grin when he gets his driver's license, and worry about him when he takes the car out on dates. I want to see him go to college, Joe. And I want him to be safe. I want him to not be hunted, and not be kept, and not be owned, and not be used or poked at or analyzed or experimented with."

She stared at him, still hoping that he'd understand and somehow move to join her.

Joe shook his head and sat down. He lowered his head toward his knees. His shoulders slumped.

She said, "I want you to tell me what you think. Is it the person with absolute power who gets corrupted absolutely, like the saying goes? Or is it more the people who come running after that person because they want that power for themselves?"

When he raised his head to look at her again, all he said was, "Maybe you better get C.J. to say those words over you, Lynn. 'Cause you've gone brain-dead, honest to God."

It was a long morning for Joe. He overcompensated for his anger at Lynn, smiling too much and talking too loudly, not only to Lynn but to C.J., and even to Nancy and Burr Gould.

Then he noticed, when Father Mark showed up just after ten, that Lynn took her priest-buddy by both hands and thanked him for coming.

Nice little hand dance, he thought. Just what they all needed. No good plans on the table, just a little hand dance after having thrown five million U.S. dollars right down the toilet because she was afraid to get off the dime. No other reason.

He quit smiling. Hold the priest's hand and kiss the Cardinal's ring, he thought, all in the same day. Wonderful.

Father Mark was explaining to Lynn and Nancy that his Sunday Masses were overflowing, but with a quieter crowd. Everyone pretty "reverential", was the word he used. He was also saying that he could say Mass for them right there in the house, if they'd like, since he knew they couldn't get out.

Joe excused himself. One reason he wasn't a perfect salesman: he couldn't really pretend he was happy when he wanted to smash things, and maybe smash some people, too. "I'll go upstairs and check the kids", he said.

Lynn didn't even turn to acknowledge him. He noticed that, too.

Upstairs, he stuck his head into C.J.'s room; saw they were fine with the DVD, playing something with lots of explosions for about the fifteenth time; and slipped over to enter the next room, which was Lynn's bedroom.

Her purse was where she always used to leave it, hanging on the closet door. He opened it, took her driver's license out of her wallet as well as one of the pens she always carried around. He crossed to her dressing table, where he sat down and pulled out the contract.

He knew he had time. He could hear C.J. and Burr and the roar of the TV game's desert tanks through the wall, and the priest was still keeping the girls busy downstairs. Probably holding Nancy's hands by this time, he thought.

He heard the doorbell ring, faintly but sounding insistent, one ring after the other. It startled him. Probably the police or somebody else he didn't want to see. But that would be okay, at least for a minute or two, which was all he needed. Keep Lynn extra busy.

Lynn could hold hands with some cops, now, too.

He realized his heart was racing. With five million dollars at stake, you get nervous.

He had read through the contract already and knew it wasn't so much "legal" as "binding", one person to another. What it said was that if he and Lynn take the hundred thousand dollars, they guaranteed that C.J. would be on the plane to Cross' house within seventy-two hours from the date and time of signature. It would be their blood oath, but not in those words, to A. W. Cross. "A" for Anthony, Joe thought; Anthony Sr. because it was Anthony Jr. dying of leukemia. He wondered what the "W" was for.

No one coming upstairs yet.

Studying the signature on Lynn's driver's license, he signed her name to both copies of the contract, trying to be careful. He doubted Cross would have anything to compare them to, but you never could tell; sharp guy, and five million dollars at stake. Then he signed his own name and stuck the driver's license and the pen back into Lynn's purse.

"You can have the Cardinal and his buddies study C.J. for ten years", he whispered, snapping the purse shut. "I just need him for eight hours."

Putting the purse back on the doorknob and the contract into his pocket, he stepped into the hall. No one had noticed. All of them were busy downstairs with whoever had come ringing the bell. Something finally going right.

He wondered as he closed the door behind him how he'd do it. He thought of going out in the middle of the night with C.J., over the back fence, or even right into the car; how would anyone know right away that Lynn had not okayed his taking the kid out? He thought of giving her another day or two to come around, too, which she might; things get tougher at the house with the crowds and all.

But it'd happen. He'd make it happen one way or another, he was sure of that. He wondered, too, going down the stairs, about blood contracts with A. W. Cross, who had five million dollars to give away and private jets and German lawyers with—Lynn was right—a pair of hard-nosed bodyguards, was what they were. He wondered if the guy's name was originally Crossetti or Crossano, something he or his dad or grandfather changed when they got over from the old country. Probably had a nickname, too, he thought. Probably the name of a city. "Tony Chicago" or "Cincinnati Tony". Or maybe the name of a weapon. Or maybe a tool. Tony "the screwdriver" Crossetti. Or, even better, "Tony the hammer".

He could hear it now. "Hey, any you guys ever heard of A. W. Cross?"

"Oh yeah, you mean, 'Tony the hammer'. Big in concrete. Place in the Catskills."

He smiled as he reached the bottom of the stairs.

For three and a half billion dollars an hour, he could afford to take a few risks.

Fourteen

Two men got up from the kitchen table and moved to shake Joe's hand as he entered the room. Lynn said as it happened, "Joe, these men are from the government." She looked quietly desperate.

Joe nearly reeled backward. Had they pulled off the surgery on Turner already?

The taller of the two, in his dark-blue suit and dark-red tie, stretched out his hand to Joe and smiled. He was a tall, fortyish man with sharp Italian features and perfect teeth and close-cropped dark hair and hard-looking eyes that flashed over a thin and practiced smile.

Joe pushed a few words out, saying, "Which government?" Trying to act cool. Trying not to look rattled. Feeling shaken.

"I'm Paul Curry", the man said, taking Joe's hand. An ID came up in his left hand. It read "Deputy United States Marshal".

Joe shot another glance at Lynn, who was getting ready to fight, he could tell.

The marshal nodded toward the square-shouldered, middle-aged man with gray hair cut short and lazy eyes who stood beside him and said, "This is Captain Michael Shuler, United States Air Force."

At that, Joe managed the beginnings of a forced smile. Working his way back into control. "You kidding?" he asked. "The Air Force?"

Their expressions said, No, Joe, we're not kidding at all.

"I'm assigned to the Department of Defense", the captain told him. He took his seat again. Then he smiled, too. For the moment, lots of smiles. "We were just talking about your son."

"How did I know that?" Joe said, trying to sound carefree, even entertaining, but thinking as he said it, all the power in the world, from the Vatican to the White House, looking down the barrel at C.J. right now, and me with a ticket for five million dollars parked right in my back pocket.

He pulled up the sixth chair. "You want C.J. to be a pilot, or what?"

The captain stopped smiling. "We were telling the others that we've set up a process to establish the authenticity of your video", Deputy Curry continued.

"It's not our video", Joe said, relaxing for the first time.

They didn't know yet, he thought. Not for sure. Thinking about it, and snooping around, but no operation yet.

"We've also been spending some time at the hospital", the captain added. "Reviewing the medical reports for both people with death certificates and both women in remission. And spending several hours with attending physicians."

"And with Mrs. Klein and Mr. Turner", Curry said. "And their families."

"You talked to the Kleins?" Father Mark asked, sounding protective.

"The Kleins. Turners. Mrs. Welz. Mrs. Koyievski. Their families."

"You must be tired fellas", Joe said, smiling now and meaning it for the first time. They were close, but still fishing.

"We enjoy our work", Curry said, smiling back at him.

"The video", Joe said. "You'd need the original. You took the original from MacInnes?"

"We have the original, yes, sir."

"You confiscated it", Joe said. No more pretense about cordiality. What did he care? "He didn't offer it to you to be a good citizen, did he?"

Lynn shifted in her chair, eyeing Joe.

"The state police requested it", Captain Shuler answered. "There's a criminal investigation underway, as you know."

"I said, 'We have it'," Curry added, "but we're working with the local authorities."

"And what's your take on it so far?" Joe asked.

Curry answered after a slight pause. "Well, we're impressed or we wouldn't be here."

"What do your bosses say?" Joe leaned forward. This one meant a lot.

"They know we're here", Curry said. Nothing more.

More relief. The guys were definitely just circling. Trying to get enough to convince their bosses, who probably thought exactly what the doctors were saying to the cameras: no way this resurrection stuff could really be true. Which meant Joe still had time. Maybe not much, but he still had time.

The largest worm drowned by the rain was on the concrete just outside the garage door. Burr found it and motioned C.J. over with a wave of his hand and a whispered, "Here!"

Burr and C.J.'s parents were in the kitchen with two guys who came to the house. The boys had seen C.J.'s dad going downstairs and heard him join the others; then they sneaked into the backyard to hunt for dead worms and a resurrection of a whole new kind.

"It's perfect!" Burr announced, being careful not to speak too loudly. He waved the worm like a short strand of spaghetti and giggled. He rushed over to place the worm on the picnic table and spoke in a high, whinny, grinning voice. "He's got a little worm family and everything. He's got little wormy kids crying right now, 'Oh Daddy, Daddy, will the boy bring you back to us, please?'"

C.J. giggled and shot a quick glance to the house. Then he looked back at the worm and his smile faded. So did Burr's.

It was dead. And it was waiting.

C.J. pressed it to make sure. Now he looked very serious. He licked his lip and stared for several more seconds.

"Do you want me to squash it?" Burr asked. "It's dead, man."

C.J. did not take his eyes off the worm. He shook his head. "No", he whispered. "Shut up."

"Well do it, C.J.! Is staring at it part of it, or how do you do it?"

C.J. waited another few seconds. Then he reached to touch the worm with his index finger. "You say, 'Be well, worm'", he whispered.

Burr laughed. "Is that all? Man, I could do that."

C.J. was standing still, his hands at his side again, his expression flat and dark.

"Well, do it!" Burr pleaded.

"I just did", C.J. whispered.

Burr stared at the worm. He breathed, "Oh man", and his voice trailed off. They watched like statues. One minute. Two minutes.

The worm was motionless. But not entirely. Suddenly its tail seemed to quiver, just slightly, with the will to live.

The boys strained closer, their faces no more than a foot from the table. They held their breath.

The tail twitched, definitely.

A gasp from Burr. A quick, "Oh crap!"

C.J. stood with his mouth open, not breathing.

The worm moved slowly at first, as though it might be afraid to break. Its tail scraped ever so carefully from side to side, drawing streaks with dreadful patience on the table, in the moisture from the rain. Then the whole, long body twitched sharply and moved to take hold and drag itself back to life while its head raised from the table and curved in an arc that swept slowly from the right to the left and back again.

Burr watched the worm raise its head and start to slide across the table, and he whispered, "Oh, wow, C.J.!", very lightly. Then he suddenly started to laugh out loud. He sounded as scared as he was impressed.

He turned, inviting C.J. to join in his delight. But C.J. wasn't laughing.

C.J. had tears in his eyes.

"If the video is actually a computer generation," Captain Shuler said, "we'll know it. Right now, it's the medical histories that are most impressive, because they're documented over a long period of time."

"An important part of the mix", Curry agreed. "We'll see."

"I guess", Joe said quietly.

He wondered why Lynn and Father Mark and Nancy weren't saying anything. Intimidated, he decided. Nine-tenths of the country were afraid of guys like this, and, he thought, for good reason.

"You must be wondering how you can learn more about what's going on with your son", Curry said to Lynn, sounding especially concerned.

Father Mark interrupted. "But why your involvement, deputy?" he asked. "Why a federal interest?"

Joe wanted to grab the priest by the neck and shout, do you even begin to understand that C.J. actually takes real dead people and brings them back to life again, and that whoever controls him controls who lives forever, for God's sake!?

The captain leaned forward. "The government is very interested in the potentials of what you might call 'paranormal experiences'. Clairvoyance. Astral projection. Levitation. That kind of thing."

"Flying saucers?" Joe asked.

"Intelligent extraterrestrial life, yes, sir."

"Miracles?" Father Mark asked.

The captain hesitated. "That word begs definition in our circles, Father. We're especially interested in paranormal activities that might be brought somehow under control. The word 'miracle', as we assume it's used, doesn't fit that definition. But if this young man is undergoing authentic experiences, it's clearly in his best interest that you find out everything you can about it. And the fact is, no one will be able to help you do that better than us, with facilities we've already developed."

Lynn said, "At the Department of Defense?"

It was Curry's turn. He laid his hands flat on the table. "Mrs. Walker, do you think you really understand everything that boy of yours may be capable of doing?"

"I saw it", Father Mark said.

Joe glared at him. "We saw it", he said.

"Then let me ask you", Curry said, now looking at the priest as if he was daring him to follow where he'd lead. "Can the boy say whatever words he wants, or are the words he used the only words that give him this power? Does he even need words? Or does he really need to touch people? And can he bring back more than one person at a time?"

Joe was smiling again but not talking, thinking, or can he bring them back from the long dead, back from a year or ten years or whatever? He wondered if they'd thought of that one yet.

"You might call it a miracle, Father, but we might be able to help you find out what form that miracle might take. Is it an energy field? Is it psychic? Is it magnetic? Is it electrical? What levels of consciousness are involved? What's happening physically to the boy when he exercises this power?"

Lynn raised her eyebrows. What did that mean: what's happening to him physically?

"We don't have all the questions yet," Curry said, "let alone all the answers. But what if it does turn out that this power involves some kind of energy that's subject to analysis, and even duplication?"

They stared, confronting whole new scenarios.

"You're saying you might be able to clone it?" Lynn asked.

Nancy Gould thought, and almost said, that's why you're from the Department of Defense. But she just fidgeted silently in her chair.

Shuler said, "If an experience is measurable, yes, it may be subject to duplication. It's at least possible."

"So you want the government to take him and find out if the power can be cloned", Lynn said. She got up and started to pace, her face flushed, her jaw set.

"Everybody being raised all over the place?" Nancy whispered to no one in particular.

"That's not the point." Curry put his hands flat on the table again. "The point is, no one in the world can help you find out what's going on as well as we can. There's that to consider on the positive side. But you have to know, there's a negative side, too, if you don't let us help."

Lynn stopped and waited, holding her breath.

Joe pulled back in his chair and crossed his arms.

"In our opinion, ma'am, if the medical community establishes that the metal tracings in Mrs. Klein and Mr. Turner is identical to the trocar rod at the undertaker's, and not consistent with anything else they can identify ..."

Nancy's eyes bulged. Like Lynn, she had made it a point to avoid the TV news.

"... at that time your son could be in serious danger. Because someone may well try to take him from you. And I mean take him physically."

"You mean kidnap him", Joe said. He was wondering how many people the government had kidnapped over the years.

"Picture anyone of great power", Curry said, ignoring Joe. "Take a dictator. Middle East, maybe, but could be anywhere. He is dying, or they have someone else dying that's really important to them. Then ask yourself, what would this person be willing to risk in order to have that boy of yours sequestered away in their own grounds? How many agents would that person, or that government, put on the firing line for that kind of prize?" He leaned across the table toward Lynn. His voice slowed. "Let me say this clearly. If your son can do what you claim he did, then, yes, the bad guys from *somewhere* will want to take him."

Lynn began pacing again, moving slowly. No one spoke. She walked to the sink. She drank a half glass of water. A siren sounded outside. She turned slowly, crossed her arms again, leaned back against the sink, and stared at the deputy with dead eyes.

When she didn't speak, Curry did. "It doesn't have to be a foreign government threat, Mrs. Walker. Be concerned about whoever's watching this on TV right now, here in this country. Right here in Detroit. Wondering, as we're talking right now, what it will cost to pull it off? Already figuring how they'll go about it, for all we know."

When Joe looked up, Lynn was staring at him, and he knew exactly who she was thinking about. He looked away.

"So what are you suggesting?" Lynn asked the U.S. marshal.

"We'd like to arrange transport for you before anything happens. Get you and your son, and the boy's father here, if you'd like, to a safe facility. Do it tonight. Make you comfortable and safe, both. We don't want any unnecessary risks to your son's welfare. We know you don't, either."

Lynn took another deep breath and started for the hallway, her arms still pressed around her waist. "I'm going upstairs with C.J.", she said.

The captain and deputy marshal rose, not happy, but not saying anything.

Lynn turned to face them. "You'll leave some way to get in touch with you, okay? We're going to see the Cardinal this afternoon. I'm not sure we can decide anything before that."

Curry nodded. He had business cards out. He handed one to each of them. "Call us at any time", he said. "We'll be right outside, too, and close by all the way to the Cardinal's and back."

Lynn said a soft, "Thank you", glanced at the card she'd been given, placed it in the drawer in front of the coffeemaker, and left the room.

She didn't say good-bye.

"I need you to talk to me again about meeting with the Cardinal", Lynn said. It was nearly one in the afternoon. She was sitting across from Father Mark at the kitchen table, speaking over a coffee held in both hands. Her voice was hushed like everything else about her. Plain, gray T-shirt; faded jeans; old deck shoes—she was a woman not wanting to be noticed.

Mark had a coffee, too, but wasn't drinking it. His chair creaked when he shifted his weight.

"Joe says the government will take C.J. by force as soon as the metallic stuff is analyzed", Lynn said. "Which means as soon as they get surgery on either Marion or Turner." She leaned forward slightly. "Did you know about the metal tracings before the federal guys brought it up?"

"Yeah. I heard it on TV."

Lynn said, "Joe told me about it. I should watch more television."

"No, you shouldn't."

"It could be happening now."

He nodded, waiting for more.

She said, "The thing is, Joe can be cynical and still be smart at the same time, can't he? Like the joke, just because you're paranoid doesn't mean they aren't really out to get you."

"I think that on this one, Joe's right. I think this time there's a lot to be concerned about. It's hard to see the government rolling over and just watching him from a distance once they know for sure."

"You don't have to be paranoid to figure that out."

"Even more reason to get with the Cardinal, Lynn. I still believe he may be your best possible connection. Let him move you where you'll be safe."

"It isn't the Cardinal I'm worried about. It's who gets C.J. once the Cardinal's out of the picture. And how they're going to feel about him and treat him."

Mark's smile looked forced. "I don't think I'm being naïve, Lynn, but I'm telling you, as far as Rome goes, they'll treat C.J. as someone very special. He won't be a prisoner."

"Joe isn't much kinder about the Vatican than he is about the government. If he's right about this one, maybe he's right about the other. He says they'll really welcome C.J. in Rome, but the whole reason they'll welcome him is to shut him away in a monastery, so no one can ever talk to him again, because they'll see what he can do, and they'll realize he's in competition with Jesus ..."

"In *competition* with Jesus?"

"Whatever. They'll see him doing what Jesus did and that will bring up whole bags of worms for them about what Jesus did, and about the Bible and all that. He says they won't let him loose to be running around with this kind of power. At least when he's not a saint or something. He never even said God did this through him, is Joe's point. And they'll know that, and land on him for it."

The creaking chair. Mark was leaning back, shaking his head. "He won't be in competition with Christ until he brings himself back from the dead", he said. "And that's not going to happen."

Her eyes focused on the edge of her cup. "I never thought of that one: somebody getting the idea to kill him because they'll want to see if he can raise himself from the dead." She thought about it another few seconds, then breathed, "The hits keep on a'coming."

Mark studied her. "I'm not sure where you're going with this, Lynn. I'm sorry."

She sighed and met his eyes. "I guess I just need to talk." She shrugged. "The problem is, where I want to go is about five days backwards into the beginning of last week, but I can't get there from here."

He reached for her hand. She let him hold it. She was staring at the table. She said quietly, "Everybody will want to take him, Mark." Tears formed in her eyes. She wiped them as they started down her cheeks. He held her hand tighter.

She said, "People with money. Anybody with enough money. Anyone with enough power. The government. Other governments, for Pete's sake. Nutcases invited. Crummy potentates from God knows where, got a billion dollars and a private army: 'Get that kid that can raise my kid from the dead', you know? 'Twenty million dollars to whoever delivers him!' Do you think there's any chance in the world that's not going to get in somebody's head? It's a nightmare."

"Can Joe help?" Mark asked—then felt stupid for asking it.

And Lynn jumped on it. "Joe will want to take him himself."

"I'm sorry."

"Joe wants to take him and auction him off, I guarantee you. Go to the highest bidder. Get a billion dollars himself. Get his own army. Protect his property." She stopped, shaking her head, staring at the table, tears in her eyes.

"There ... is ... no ... way ...", she said, "that I can protect him from everybody that will want him at all costs. Except maybe to run and hide with him, and never stop running, and never get caught."

Mark strained to think of something supportive and realistic, something that would let him say, "Oh my gosh! Here's a perfect solution!" But there was nothing. He could just listen, and as much as he hurt for her and C.J., he knew that what Lynn was saying had much more truth to it than fantasy.

"So tell me, Pastor Mark", she said in a whisper. "What kind of gift is it if we can't give it back?"

They sat in silence for a long several minutes. Then Mark did his best.

"Maybe that just says how important it is", he said. "Most people would kill to have it, you know? Maybe C.J. has it because he wouldn't. And because you wouldn't, either. Maybe if you wanted it, you'd never find out what good it could do. I don't know." He sighed. When she didn't respond, he said, "I don't know anything, and I'm sorry. I don't know how animals talk to each other, or bees find their way home, or even how to operate all the stuff on my TV remote, for Pete's sake. I don't know how life began the first time around, Lynn, let alone how it begins a second time, other than to just say, 'Well, God did it.'"

Another pause. Still no response from Lynn, aside from wiping away more tears.

He continued, "I know I believe in God, and I believe God's good, and I believe that this isn't a mistake; that's all. But that much, I believe. And I believe that the Cardinal is a good man. And I believe you'd be smart to talk with him."

A car horn sounded from the street. Lynn realized she couldn't hear C.J. anymore. Or Joe. Or Nancy. Or anything much at all.

She looked at the edge of her cup again, holding it motionless. Finally she said, "I've been thinking about C.J., and about my own dad. How he wasn't ever comfortable being at home, either. With either me or Mom. Just never comfortable. Like living up in the air. And I didn't figure out for such a long time that it wasn't like he was mad at me or Mom for something we did wrong. I always thought that, for a long time. What are we doing wrong? Because he was gone a lot. But no fights. Never a divorce. Just ... not that interested in us. One of those guys that were off somewhere else, other plans, other gimmicks, other people, whatever ... Just kind of gone even when he was home."

She held her sad vision for a brief while, then pulled her hand away from his and stood up slowly. She smiled a weak smile at him and said,

"Thanks for listening. And thanks for being here and on our side. It helps, really. And I appreciate it."

Mark said, "I'm sorry I'm shooting blanks as far as, 'Here's what you should do,' though."

"No. You're not", she said. "I'll talk with the Cardinal. Me and C.J., too, if you think that'd help. And Joe, I'm sure. And I'll consider anything he can offer. But I want you to know this going in, okay? You and him. I want you to know that C.J. is not going through one day of his life without knowing that he's worth my doing everything I have to do to be there with him if he needs me. If he needs me, how he needs me, when he needs me. Because he's worth that to me."

It was strange, but it seemed to Joe like he could actually feel the air pressure in the house squeezing harder against his skin, like it had oozed through the wall from outside and filled the house like water, pressing against him. The feds wanted C.J., no two ways about it, just waiting for their bosses to give them the nod. And now waiting for the results from the surgery on Marion and Turner. It was driving him crazy. That's what they were all waiting for, but the TV people were just going in circles repeating all the side stuff. Asking tacky gossip questions, like, why didn't Marion and Turner experience the same thing in their "nether state", or whatever the hell the Adonis wannabe on 62 was calling it, with Marion not talking and Turner talking about tunnels of light. Who gave a care? Was one of them going to pop for the surgery today or not, was what they should be telling people.

With all of that pressing in and with no real plans locked in, with Lynn still driving Joe crazy by not seeming able to get hold of what she wanted to do about C.J., with her still asking questions about what other people would do and still talking about seeing the Cardinal, with Kruger and his wise guys out there wondering what was going on the same way Joe was wondering, and with him still bouncing around from Plan J to Plan K or whatever he was up to, and still not having a clue how to get C.J. out of there, even without Lynn's okay if he had to, he felt like he was going nuts.

He breathed in as deeply as he could and took another look outside. A mob now. Too much TV coverage, so much of it hype.

His tongue raced back and forth over his lip in quick, nervous stabs. Faces and cameras and signs and yellow tape and more faces, all the way down the street, all waiting for the "Lazarus Boy", which is what they were all calling him now. The Lazarus Boy. And C.J. not even being one of the people that was dead.

But the crowd was definitely bigger now, and still growing, with some of them getting mad; Joe could tell from the signs and the looks in their eyes, the ones who had been waiting longest getting sick of waiting. Maybe all the dying ones were the ones pressed closest to the police tape and the house. Or maybe the whole mob was getting madder now because they heard that it was gonna rain and saw the dark clouds already moving overhead. Everything turning cooler, with the wind starting to blow harder to remind them that nobody inside the house was paying any attention to them at all. The mood all screwed up because ... what were they all supposed to do now?

He even wondered for a second what they'd do if they were waiting in a thunderstorm when C.J. and the rest of them came bouncing out of the house in an hour or so now, and hopped into the church Chrysler and drove right past them, maybe blowing the horn at them to clear them out of the way, but went by without stopping on their way to see the church brass. How will those people feel then?

Nothing but tension now.

And it was then, while the afternoon pulled him toward the meeting with the Cardinal and the crowd started twitching under the first drops of rain and a police bullhorn barked words that he couldn't understand, that it hit him with more force than it had hit him at any other time.

He thought, *my son raises the dead.*

He was stunned by it, like he'd never thought it before. He found himself repeating it in his own mind, but doing it very cautiously, like a man might tiptoe along the edge of a cliff: *My son raises the dead!*

His heart was racing. He wanted to speak the unspeakable words out loud, and so he did, but just in the faintest whisper, like he was whispering a secret behind the back of God. He framed the words ever so carefully and spoke just loudly enough to hear the terrible words with his own ears as he stared out the window at the crowd now being pulled apart by a dark and building rain.

"*My son raises the dead!*"

Lynn stood behind C.J. at her bedroom window. The storm had turned the afternoon ugly a half hour ago, at nearly two o'clock. Its thunder and lightning had scattered much of the crowd. Only 150 or more remained, a remnant pressed together and standing straight and stock-still, like survivors in a minefield. They stood under umbrellas and in rain gear and in no gear at all, demonstrating their need. They had earned their places against the police tape and they knew it. They had earned their right to a miracle, and they wanted C.J. Walker to know it.

Lynn noticed that the young girl with the yellow-and-black sign that read, "2 yr. old daughter. 2 months to live. PLEASE!" was right in front of the house now. She was wearing a black garbage bag as a raincoat. Lynn wondered if that's what waiting in the rain and getting no response made the girl feel like: a kind of garbage. Then she wondered about herself, about what kind of person made a girl with a dying two-year-old wait in the rain with a yellow-and-black sign begging for help and still did nothing to help her?

She felt herself shudder. Her hands were over C.J.'s shoulders, against his chest. She pressed him tightly against her stomach and wondered what he was thinking, staring at the crowd so quietly, not moving, not saying anything.

A siren sounded in the distance, and C.J. stiffened. "Is that them?" He twisted to look up at his mom.

Lynn leaned closer to the window and looked down the street. She could see the reds and blues lighting up the trees and street and houses to the south, getting closer. She knew that the Cardinal's black Chrysler would be right behind the police escort vehicles with a seminarian at the wheel and Father Mark's friend Monsignor Tennett in the passenger seat. She bent down and whispered, "You'll do fine, C.J. We're all together in this, okay?"

C.J. stared ahead without answering.

Lynn pressed her lips into his hair. She knew him well enough to know when he was really scared. "Let's get a jacket on, for the rain", she whispered.

But C.J. still didn't move. Instead, he asked softly, "What if I could do it, not for people, but for other things, Mom?"

She moved to his side and went down slowly on one knee, looking up now, into his eyes, saying nothing.

C.J. said, still very softly, "I promised I wouldn't do it to any more people, but what if . . . ?"

"What other things?" Lynn asked, interrupting him.

C.J. bit his lip. He shrugged and looked away. He released his lip, and Lynn saw it quiver. "I mean, if there were . . . like, if it worked with dogs or cats. Or worms and stuff", he shrugged again, limply, as the tears formed in his eyes. "I don't know."

Lynn's heart broke. She put her arms around him and eased him near.

C.J. looked in her eyes, hurting too badly to hide his feelings but feeling so ashamed that she could see him cry. He choked back his tears and said, as if he was suddenly pleading with her, "What if it worked with trees and stuff? Grass and trees?"

Lynn felt overwhelmed, and she felt tears forming, too. She groped for something to say, something wise and wonderful, but all that came out was, "Oh honey ..."

"What's happening to me, Mom?" C.J. pleaded. Then he put his arms around her neck and pressed hard into her shoulder.

Fifteen

The Cardinal's residence was a classic English Tudor, a chief executive's mansion positioned on one of Madeline Boulevard's perfectly manicured lawns in the middle of Palmer Park, the northern Detroit border's plush residential district.

C.J. "wowed" softly at the house, then, as they drove up the driveway, "wowed" again at the inground pool that could be seen bubbling in the rain through the wrought-iron fence that guarded the backyard.

Joe looked at the house and the grounds and figured six hundred thousand as is, but set it all down in Bloomfield Hills, and you'd be getting a million-five, easy.

"He's not alone, is he?" Lynn asked, studying the four empty cars in front of the house.

"He's not often alone", Monsignor Tennett said. "He's invited four other people today. But you'll like them. A nun, two priests, and a layman."

Lightning lit up the western clouds and thunder rumbled.

Monsignor Tennett swung his door into the still-driving rain and said it again, this time a little louder, "You'll like them!"

The front door was held open for them by a very young seminarian who, in his Roman collar and black clerical suit, might have easily passed for a tenth grader forced to play a priest in his first high school play. He grinned and welcomed them, pointing down the hall and whispering to the Monsignor.

As Joe stepped across the maroon-tiled foyer, he reviewed the rich interior of the house, and he revised his estimate: nine hundred thousand here, two million and change if you dropped the house on a good-sized lot in Bloomfield Hills.

A mahogany table thick with wood and polish and history dominated the conference room where Cardinal Schaenner and his friends waited in an anxious cluster for C.J. Walker and his parents. The table's two longer sides were lined with high-backed red leather chairs, ten in all. Six leaded glass windows rattled under the relentless rain on the west side of the room. The overhead lights were on. Three Church Fathers stared down from gold-leafed frames on the north wall: Saint Thomas à Becket, Saint Augustine, and a monk identified by nameplate as Saint Columban.

All three were dead but all three were watching, C.J. noticed. It was as though they were waiting to be called back themselves.

The Cardinal wore a standard black clerical suit with a regular Roman collar—no scarlet trim, no bright reds of high position. Only his ring stood out: the raised cross and clusters of grapes as a single, gnarled sign of an authority beyond his own.

Tall and heavyset and slightly round-shouldered, with his thinning black hair combed flat and straight back, he smiled at C.J. with his own touch of pleasant surprise and hurried to grasp the small hand that so many people insisted was strong enough to pull the dead back to life.

Sister Melonie, dressed in a plain, gray suit and white blouse buttoned to the collar, was a smiling woman in her early sixties who carried her plump self like a kindly caricature: Sister Nice Heart, growing gracefully old.

Monsignor Nesbitt was rector of St. Mark Seminary. He was also caricature-like: an academically prim and uncomfortably proper man, with short, graying hair pressed flat over a high brow, deep-set eyes, and neatly placed wire-framed glasses. He had the kind of darting smile that looked like it was either too brittle to have enjoyed much use or too nervous to be shown comfortably in present company.

A second priest, Father Killian, was tall and young and friendly, with light-brown hair cut short and brushed back without a part. He was, they learned, the Cardinal's secretary—a young man on his way up.

The layman, whom Father Mark had met before but greeted coolly, was Bennington Reed. At six feet, six inches, he was as tall as his close friend, the Cardinal, but, unlike the Cardinal, Reed was a loaf of a man, thick and round at every point and imposing in every way. He appeared to be in his early forties. He was expensively dressed in a deep-brown double-breasted suit that looked like it had never known a wrinkle and never would. His light-brown hair, glimmering with hair treatment, was close-cropped and thinning high into his temples. His shining, wide-open smile and rounded, pink cheeks reminded Lynn of a child's bedside clock. Only the intensity of his eyes broke the spell.

He was introduced as a close friend of the Cardinal and of the Church in the archdiocese, which, Joe and Lynn both realized, had something to do with financial contributions as well as personal camaraderie. The president and CEO of Bruce Exporting Company and owner of one of the local hierarchy's preferred retreat centers, located on Bruce Lake in northern Michigan, Reed was, according to the Cardinal, an "enormously knowledgeable, resourceful and energetic friend" who had successfully come to the Church's assistance in a number of special circumstances, most notably as coordinator of sensitive transportation and security issues relative to the Pope's last visit to Detroit. He also possessed, the Cardinal noted, "an inquiring, metaphysical mind in his own right".

The huge man greeted Joe and Lynn with a strong right hand that shook their bodies with welcome, but when he got to C.J. he was as gentle and reverential as a child.

As they prepared to seat themselves the storm closed over the house with such dark insistence that Cardinal Schaenner asked Monsignor Tennett to dial up the overhead lights. Then the Cardinal took his place in the middle of the table with his back to the windows. Sister Melonie and Mr. Reed sat to his left; the rector of the seminary and the Cardinal's young secretary sat to his right.

Location being everything, Joe grabbed the middle chair directly opposite the Cardinal, facing him, and letting Lynn and C.J. sit on his left and Father Mark and Monsignor Tennett on his right.

The Cardinal began with a short, soft-spoken prayer. Then, with his fingertips forming a tent under his chin, he smiled at Joe, Lynn, and C.J. in that order and acknowledged that he was now prepared to give the news stories, the video, the hospital records, the doctors that he knew, personally, Joe and Lynn, and Father Mark Cleary the benefit of every doubt regarding the authenticity of C.J.'s astonishing powers. "That being the case," he assured them, "the purpose of this meeting, today, is simply to explore God's will with you, and to offer my help to you in this most extraordinary time."

With that, he asked C.J. and the others if they would begin by sharing their own accounts of the events of the past several days, which they did, each telling what they had done and seen and heard without theatrics or any great amount of detail.

When they finished, the Cardinal's eyes smiled again, his fingertips formed another tent against his chin, and he thanked them and added quietly, after a long moment's thought, "May we put a few questions to you now? Starting, I'd suggest, with Sister Melonie?"

Over the next few minutes, Joe evaluated his son's inquisitors, and their questioning, this way: Sister Melonie wanted to talk with C.J. about feelings. Probably a child psychologist, Joe thought, but for sure, a child of the sixties. All buttoned-up tight in her little black habit back then, and one day, all of a sudden—Bam!—the Church shuffled its deck and she was suddenly into pinstripes and *feelings*, stuck there ever since. She walked C.J. all the way through his description of the resurrections again, asking things like, "And what did you feel then, C.J.?" "What do you think Jesus is feeling about all this; do you think you might be able to guess for us?" C.J. was nibbling on his lip the whole time. Joe could picture the nun breaking into "Michael Row the Boat Ashore" at any second.

One down. No problem.

Thunder rumbled again, but this time without lightning that any of them could see, and now more distant than before.

The rector of the seminary was all church. Locked in his church books, Joe decided. No vision past the two covers. Had the wonder kid of all time sitting in front of him, but still asked Father Mark all the questions, not Joe or C.J., just one priest to another. Kept wondering out loud what Father Mark's theology of healing was, and his theology of life after death; things like that. Lost C.J. completely. The kid hadn't clue number one what the guy was talking about.

But then, Joe wondered, who did? Two down.

Surprisingly to Joe, the youngest member of the group, the Cardinal's priest-secretary, went the darkest route, and he talked to C.J. exclusively. He began with harmless stuff; he wanted to know how much he prayed and went to church. But then he moved into things like whether or not C.J. believed in the devil, or was afraid of him, and even whether he knew any kids who ever talked with Satan, that kind of thing. Not fun stuff to listen to, and, Joe could tell, turning C.J. off big-time, and Lynn, too.

C.J. was answering the priest with, "Uh-huh", and, "Hmnh-mnh", the way he did when he wanted to get away from someone, badly.

Then the young priest turned to question Lynn and Joe, looking friendly but asking them point-blank about any instances of occult activity in their family backgrounds—séances, unusual spiritual powers, visions, spells, any of that stuff. Lynn didn't even bother answering with sounds, let alone words. She handled her negative responses with expressionless shakes of her head, quickly delivered. Her jaw was tight, and her eyes looked hard and dark.

The whole line of questioning alerted Joe to something he'd have to talk with Lynn about when they got out of there. If the Church higher-ups decided that the devil made C.J. do it, they might say he had to go through an exorcism. Joe didn't know how that worked, but it would freak Lynn totally out, and Joe knew it. He'd have to remind her about that, making sure she thought about it before she got too much into the Church's pocket.

With that, the Cardinal thanked them and suggested a minute or two break, which they took, but just to stretch and get C.J. another glass of Pepsi.

One other thing Joe realized, and it seemed important, was that Bennington Reed was conspicuous in his silence. The man-mountain had just sat there staring at C.J., his eyes burning one minute and dancing the next, the beginnings of a smile edging his lips with no apparent reason, then fading, then easing back again, all of it making Joe wonder what he was thinking, his thoughts coming and going like that, and his smiling and then not smiling, but always staring at C.J.

And if he wasn't there to ask questions, what was he there for?

The Cardinal turned to check on the rain as they sat down again, saw that it was finally letting up, nodded his approval, and invited immediate feedback from anyone in the group.

"I think you should know, the government was at their house today", Father Mark said abruptly.

The Cardinal's eyes glistened suddenly, and narrowed. His fingertips joined under his chin. He waited several seconds before asking, "The federal government?"

"The Defense Department", Lynn answered, nodding.

C.J. sat up straighter.

Reed's eyes flashed and darted to the Cardinal.

Father Mark said, "A U.S. marshal, and somebody from the Air Force."

C.J. nudged his mom's arm hard. "The Air Force?" he whispered. "At our house?"

Lynn nodded, but raised her hand to signal no more questions, not right now.

"They say there are national security issues involved", Joe said.

C.J. nudged Lynn again; his lower lip stuck out to protest her secrecy, but he didn't say anything.

"Those people say anything they want, and they do anything they want." It was Joe again, speaking to no one in particular, sounding bitter.

Lynn said it apologetically, as though she'd said it a hundred times to a hundred different people: "Joe's not a big fan of the government."

The Cardinal turned to Reed without speaking, his eyebrows raised, inviting comment.

And so, for the first time, Bennington Reed spoke. He leaned forward, his large fists closed on the table, close to his chest. His eyes were narrowed and his head was nodding very slightly, as though he was, with every passing moment, realizing something new and important that could change their situation dramatically. "They'd be from a paranormal activities unit of some kind", he said. Another nod. "The government investigates the whole universe of paranormal experiences. The black budget; other special, hidden budgets; secret facilities; everything they need. Looking at UFOs. Psychic powers. Anything involving the paranormal that could affect the body politic."

"And the power to raise the dead could affect the body politic", Cardinal Schaenner whispered.

"Oh yes indeed. For example, the first and most obvious thought: what if they could identify a genetic aberration behind the power? Learn how it works? Oh for heaven's sake, yes."

As the group wondered where Reed's vision was leading them, with his "oh for heaven's sake", there was a soft knocking at the conference room door. It was an apologetic sound: three soft raps.

Monsignor Tennett opened the door to the seminarian, who looked as hesitant as his knock sounded. He held out a single sheet of paper and said, as though asking a question, "They said to bring this in right away?"

The Monsignor took the note with a quiet "Thank you" and passed it across the table to the Cardinal without reading it. With a second, "Thanks", quietly spoken, Monsignor Tennett closed the door.

As the Cardinal read the message in silence, his eyes lost their natural edge of pleasant surprise and narrowed. He looked as though the paper was too bright for the naked eye. He read it a second time, nodded slightly, then raised his eyes briefly to look with quiet concern at C.J. Then, looking at Lynn, he said quietly, "Things are changing quickly."

Lynn started to stand up. "What happened?"

But the Cardinal was smiling again, this time speaking to C.J., and speaking in a normal, even cheerful, voice. "What would you say to this, C.J.?" he said. "We could ask our seminarian to get you some ice cream and show you the video games we brought in for you. Mr. Reed thought of that. They're in the den, right down the hall." His smile widened. "I'll bet you did not expect to find video games at the Cardinal's house, did you?"

There was only Cardinal Schaenner and Mr. Reed on the window side of the table when they gathered again, without C.J., ten minutes later. The nun and the other two priests had to leave, the Cardinal explained, because of pressing business elsewhere. He said they had asked him to convey their thanks, prayers, and best wishes. Mr. Reed, he assured them, was still available, and, as they would see, was uniquely well qualified to contribute to whatever discussions and decisions might ensue.

Lynn interpreted the exit of the two priests and the nun differently. She thought that they'd been there to ask the Cardinal's tough questions, to find out if C.J. was hallucinating or crazy or what, and to ask things like, does C.J. talk to the devil? That's why the younger priest took off on the dark side, she thought. He was told to. It left the Cardinal as the good cop.

But now the real business was about to begin. And it would begin with the note the Cardinal had read and not yet shared.

He got to it quickly. "I'm afraid", he said, sliding the paper across the table to Lynn, "that we may have a much-narrowed window of opportunity, at least as far as offering help without government involvement. Or interference, I think we could say, in whatever form that might be developing."

Lynn was reading the note. Her eyebrows were furrowed.

Joe leaned to get a look.

The Cardinal said, meeting the stare of the others, starting with his friend Mr. Reed, "The note is from our Communications Office at the Chancery. Mr. Galvin Turner, the subject of the video we've all seen, has just accepted seven and a half million dollars to undergo exploratory surgery in Philadelphia on Friday. Ten in the morning. The object of the surgery will be to scrape his internal wounds for metal traces and determine once and for all if the metal found is identical to that of the undertaker's tools, which won't take more than an hour from the start of the surgery."

The announcement hung in the air for nearly ten seconds.

The Cardinal said, "You all see what that means. If the surgery confirms what we all believe it will confirm, the scientific community will have hard evidence of a genuine embalming. Which in turn points to a genuine death, of course, and a genuine resurrection. In and of itself, the video is compelling, but digital videos leave room for too much mischief. This time the evidence will be hard to ignore, and its implications hard to deny, for anyone." He was staring again at Lynn, looking sad. "Which means, Mrs. Walker, that you'll have to decide very soon exactly who, if anyone, you're going to turn to for help. It's my absolute conviction, for whatever that may be worth, that the government will be ready to issue directives to take C.J. into federal protective custody by noon on Friday. And God knows who else will be ready to close in on you and the boy at the same time."

"They can't do that", Lynn protested. "We won't go with them." But the tentative tone of her voice and the deep fear in her eyes told them all that she knew it as certainly as any of them: of course they could take C.J. against her will. A boy that could give them the secret to the power of life over death? Of course they could, and of course they would.

"The Cardinal's right", Bennington Reed said, diving in again. His voice was louder now, and his expression was a far cry from the smile on a child's bedside clock. "A metallic match from surgery will be their kind of evidence. Solid. Demonstrable."

Lynn protested again, but with an air of quiet desperation in her voice. "You're talking about kidnapping, though. I mean, if I say publicly we don't want to go ..."

Reed began to answer, but Cardinal Schaenner had leaned forward, his hand raised to silence Reed abruptly.

He was staring at Lynn again, and leaning forward. No smile now. He spoke slowly but firmly. He said, "There's something I'm begging you to come to terms with, Mrs. Walker. I honestly don't know that you've been able to do it yet." His hands spread slowly on the table, palms down, his fingers moving like spreading water. He said, "If your son really has the power to raise the dead at will, just at the sound of his voice ...!" He straightened slowly in his chair. "Well! This will make people do extraordinary things. Possibly dreadful things. Stopping at nothing. You have to come to terms with that. Stopping at nothing. Not kidnapping. Not murder. Not treason. Not anything." He shook his head, staring at her sternly, still speaking very slowly. "How could you think for a minute that there will be any boundaries to what a government, ours or any other, will do in order to hold and control your son? If, in fact, they become convinced that he can do these things? No, ma'am. For good or ill, this is about to bring about reactions that have no limits. Do not doubt it."

He withdrew his hands from the table. He looked at Joe, then at Father Mark, then once more at Lynn. He said, "You have desperately little time to find your safe haven, Mrs. Walker. Do not doubt it."

Lynn had stared silently at the Cardinal for nearly two minutes. She was immobile. Her dark eyes were narrowed. Her lips were dry cords, stretched tight.

Joe squirmed in his seat, watching her.

She could feel the Cardinal, and Reed and Monsignor Tennett, all staring, waiting for her response.

She wanted to bolt. Tears crept into her eyes. She said, in words nearly whispered, "Why is this happening?"

The Cardinal's expression softened. He nodded and slowly repeated her question. "Why is this thing happening?" Another nod. Time to think. Then he said, "I was in the woods once, as a boy, with my father. I was only about C.J.'s age. My father was a hunter. It was autumn, and cold, and we had set up a kind of lean-to by a pair of trees, up by William's Bay in Wisconsin, while we waited for deer. And I didn't know until the water leaked in the top laces of my boots that a stream had broken off from the river, and Dad and I were standing in four inches of water, running down from that stream.

"There are streams that overtake us, coming from God knows where. They're just there. Like this thing. All of a sudden, and we don't know why. And we don't know how big they'll grow. And we don't know when they'll just dry up, or if they'll dry up. There are just things we don't know.

"I heard about a drug dealer, true story, his mother dying of throat cancer, and sick himself, too, with emphysema. He took her to a healing service. Not for himself. He said after, he didn't believe a thing. They were at this service, though, everybody praying for healing, and his mom went home still sick, but he was healed of his emphysema. Totally healed.

"I say, well, was he a secret saint? Was God paying him off for being so holy? It couldn't have been that. But somehow, that stream crept up on him where God heals, like a River Jordan. It happened when he didn't even believe it was possible. And it happens so often that way. Ordinary people, caught by the extraordinary, the unexplainable stream. The Spirit blowing like the wind. We don't know where. We don't know why. Probably so we won't be able to control things, which is what we want to do with everything. But not this. Not something like this. This Lazarus Stream, this is God's secret."

He was shaking his head slowly, persistently. He whispered, "I wish I could be a wiser man for you. I really do."

Lynn sighed. She drew in her lower lip and held it there, between her teeth, her tongue moving over it, back and forth. Then she sighed again, glanced at Joe, looked again at the Cardinal, and said, "Then tell me what you can, okay? Tell me what happens if we go to Rome. Or to wherever you think would be some kind of safe haven. If there is such a thing."

The Cardinal's smile eased back into his eyes. "I truly believe that Rome would be the best possible place for you. Certainly you have to get out of the country, in my opinion. And Vatican City would be perfect. The only place, I think, that would be."

Joe said, "Think that one over real careful, Lynn." His voice was low, with an edge of tension.

Lynn set her jaw. Her eyes were on the Cardinal, but her mind was moving like a scanner radio, already racing in search of other, last-second alternatives. She had four days until Turner's operation. She knew that the door would close on her then because she knew what they would find. Four days, with everybody in the world watching her and with no one she could turn to for help, no one that really cared about her and C.J., personally. Her parents dead. No relatives that she'd kept in touch with. Even her friends were limited. Nancy Gould was close. And there were six or eight second-tier friends scattered around work and church and the neighborhood. But they were more like acquaintances, not real friends. Even the last few guys she'd dated were just casual dinners, going nowhere.

Like a lot of single mothers, she was more alone than she wanted to realize.

Bennington Reed sniffed lightly, watching Lynn.

Monsignor Tennett slowly moved his coffee cup from one spot on the table to another, watching Lynn.

Joe drummed his fingers, watching Lynn.

Father Mark and the Cardinal sat in silence, watching Lynn.

Four days. With no more time to plan. Knowing that her boy would never be safe if she just hired private guards to be his protectors. What bodyguard could she trust not to turn on him and take him for themselves if they were just there as hired guns? No matter how much she paid, how could she ever protect him from his own, hired protectors, and from people who could and would be willing to pay more?

Random ideas were suddenly shooting through her mind. Impossible ideas, like sneaking C.J. away from her house in the dark, in the middle of the night. Absurd ideas, like smuggling him out of the Cardinal's house dressed as another young seminarian. Hopeless ideas, like getting him out right away, on the spur of the moment, without planning, just grabbing him from in front of his video games in the other room and hopping over the Cardinal's back fence and pounding on the nearest door to beg for a miracle and a hiding place.

"Could I ask you to consider one plan that seems to make sense?" the Cardinal asked, breaking the spell.

Joe whispered her name like a sharp question and shifted in his chair. More silence.

"If you need time to think it over, or if you feel like you have to get C.J. used to the idea before you suddenly get up and move to Italy, I understand. I wish it was different, but I understand. But we could still get you and C.J. away from the chaos of your own house for the next two days. And from the clear insecurity of it. We can house you in St. Mark Seminary. Or St. Matthew's in Plymouth. It's new and would be entirely secure. Or, Ben here; go to his family's estate on Bruce Lake, a retreat house, way back in private property. It would be more like a vacation."

Reed was beaming.

"Then, come Friday, before the Turner surgery, we all take a flight to Rome. Simple as that. We're at your side the whole time. You get to rest and get adjusted; I get a few days to make full arrangements; it's a godsend. What do you think?"

Reed rose to his feet like a wall. His eyes were dancing. "My place is perfect", he said. He pulled half a dozen photographs from his suit's coat pocket and began to display them in the middle of the table with fumbling fingers.

Joe, whispering again: "Lynn?"

Lynn turned and snapped at him. "I know, Joe!" Then she breathed deeply, held up her palm to slow Reed down, and said to the Cardinal, "Please. I appreciate it, but moving out for three days would just be even more confusion for C.J. He's in his own home; he's safe in his own bed; the police are all over the place, like flies; it's okay there. It's noisy, but I'm not afraid. So ... if we go to Rome with you, we'll leave from there."

Reed looked embarrassed. Like a child. He looked at the Cardinal for directions.

"It's okay, Ben", the Cardinal said quietly. "Thank you."

Joe was smiling.

"I'm sorry", Lynn said. "But that's best for us. I'm sure of it."

Reed gathered up his photos. "Well," he said, forcing a smile, "maybe there'll be a day ..." His voice trailed off as he lowered his wide frame back into his chair.

"Those were just suggestions", the Cardinal said to Lynn. "But this is a request. This comes with thought and with a very large 'Please' in front of it."

Lynn crossed her arms.

"Since we have three days, and while I go ahead, with your permission, and make arrangements for travel to Rome, pending your final decision, of course, please Mrs. Walker, let us have the best doctors in the city give C.J. a physical. With all the best technologies and processes. Let us arrange a physical for him tomorrow, here in the city, in our own St. Paul's hospital."

Lynn stared, momentarily stunned.

Joe asked loudly, "Why? There's nothing wrong with him."

Father Mark and Monsignor Tennett raised their eyebrows and waited.

Only Reed smiled. He even nodded approval.

"Why do you think he needs a physical?" Lynn asked the Cardinal.

"I'm just thinking, you'll certainly want to have him get a thorough physical anyway, either here or abroad. And with all due respect to Roman medicine, you'd rather have it done here, believe me."

"Why, though? Why a physical?"

"Because any time there are extraordinary physical experiences, Mrs. Walker, it's very wise to check for physical and physiological influences first. I'm sure you haven't thought about it yet, but I'm asking you, please, to think about it now."

"You really think your 'Lazarus Stream' might be some physical quirk?" Lynn's voice was shaky. "You mean, something growing in his brain? One of those deals?"

The Cardinal thought for a moment, then said, "What if there's something else to rule out? What if exercising this kind of unthinkable power ... is altering C.J. in some way?"

Lynn's lips parted. She stared without moving.

"What do you mean, 'altering him'?" Joe snapped.

"I'm simply saying that a physical is the first, and safest, and most responsible action you can take while you wait for the Turner operation. What else will you do, Mr. Walker, over those three days?"

Joe narrowed his eyes. He didn't bother hiding his anger.

The Cardinal pressed in. "Do you realize the risk in not having a physical? Do you think a doctor coming in with a fever thermometer is going to be able to read the physiological signs in a case like this? Do you have any idea of what taking the boy to a hospital in Italy, for heaven's sake, after the Turner operation proves that the metal in the man's body is from an embalming rod, is going to be like for the boy? In an Italian hospital? After a thing like that goes public?"

Reed rose abruptly to his feet, looking dissatisfied and impatient. He jutted his round chin forward and muttered, "Excuse me. For just a few minutes. Please." He began to work his way awkwardly around the table. "I have to make some phone calls." His face was flushed. "I'll be back soon", he said.

The Cardinal's startled expression told him, no permission needed.

It also said, but why in the world would you want to make phone calls at a time like this?

Sixteen

Reed moved down the hall like a hunter. Listening. Knowing where C.J. was playing the digital pinball the boys now called video games. Walking past the stairway. Entering the den so silently that neither C.J. nor the seminarian noticed him.

He stood behind them for nearly two minutes, not only watching their game but rehearsing his plan. Then he startled them by saying, in his most soothing voice, "C.J.? Would you come with me for just a minute, please?" He smiled at the young seminarian and added, "You wait here for us, okay, Brian? We'll be right back. Just a couple of minutes."

His face was flushed.

The seminarian said, "Sure", and fell silent.

C.J. shrugged and got to his feet. Then, walking slowly, he followed the Cardinal's friend with the big body and the big hands out of the den and down the long, tiled hall to the kitchen in the far back corner of the house.

In the meeting room, Joe cracked open a 7 Up and stared at the little plastic glass. Not even good glasses, just little plastic crap.

He couldn't believe how quickly it was all slipping away from him. He felt like saying to them, "You wouldn't even know about C.J. if it wasn't for me!" He felt like saying to the Cardinal, "What do you give us half-cup plastic glasses for?" He felt awful.

And then, he didn't feel so bad after all. Then he thought, all this new pressure, and the Cardinal and everybody saying just what Joe had been saying to Lynn about the government—maybe this was just what he needed to change Lynn's mind about things. Get her to reconsider going with Cross. Her not only starting to feel the heat of a Friday deadline, but now the full court press coming at her about the hospital. All of that pressure in her guts now, not just in her head, about how everybody around her was dead serious about this, and now really closing in on her. People actually wanting to do things to C.J. physically, right now.

And so he decided, standing there with a 7 Up in his hand and the Cardinal's voice droning on behind him, that, yeah, this could work for him. He'd go ahead and do the deal with Kruger. And then he'd make it work with Lynn—get her on board about how the Cross kid was really her best way out later. Talk to her about it tonight or early the next morning, before the hospital trip, which it looked like she just might be worried enough about to go along with right now. He could tell, after the Cardinal tried to plant that stuff in her head, like a bad seed, about some terrible things the power might be doing to C.J.

He had just poured his soda and picked it up in its cheap plastic glass, thinking about the timing of when he'd talk with her, and about the hospital and all, when an entirely new idea hit him: a whole new world of possibilities heard from. He thought, what if C.J. could do this because of something in him, something that came from Joe? What if it was genetic, something in Joe's family, back ten generations maybe? Which meant, what if Joe could do it, too, but never did it only because he never thought to try it? Holy hell!

He drank the glass of soda without taking a breath and poured another.

Maybe C.J. could have done it any time in his whole life if he'd tried it. But he never did. Of course, he didn't. Why would he? So why not the same thing, maybe, for Joe? A chance in ten billion, but a chance.

It was as he was walking back to his chair, just passing by the two priests that he decided to find out for sure. He would get on board the hospital idea. Tell Lynn, why not? Let 'em check C.J. out, he'd say. Let's go to the hospital together, get the police to escort them over there, tomorrow, first thing, like the good Cardinal was saying. Get over there where all the sick people were. All of the waiting to see if anybody could heal them.

Not really a chance in ten billion. A million times better than that, probably. He was C.J. Walker's biological father!

Bennington Reed shut the kitchen door behind C.J. and clicked on the light. "The Cardinal has a cook that comes in to fix his meals", he said to C.J. He had moved as softly as he was speaking. He was very close to the boy now, dwarfing him, both of them easing into the empty room. "She should be getting here in about fifteen minutes, fixing things for sandwiches when the Kleins come, so I thought if we came in right now, we'd still have a few minutes to be alone."

C.J. shifted his weight and slipped away, toward the counter by the refrigerator, his hands deep in the side pockets of his tan slacks, the ironed ones, put on especially for his visit to the Cardinal.

"C.J.?" Reed asked, moving again, this time toward the refrigerator. "I brought the video games for you today, when I heard you were coming", he said, smiling again. "The Cardinal told you that, huh?"

C.J. nodded and reached with his right hand to scratch his left arm, just below the shoulder. He waited for more.

Reed opened the refrigerator door. "Well, I brought the Cardinal something he likes, too. I brought him some wine, because he likes wine."

As he spoke, he withdrew a long package of something wrapped in slick, white paper. His voice dropped to a whisper. "And I brought him this."

C.J. drew closer, his eyes on the package.

Reed turned to place it on the counter between the refrigerator and the sink; then he began to unroll it. His smile wouldn't go away. "I was so thrilled when I heard on television what you did for those ladies," he said, talking faster, "and for Mr. Turner, you know? Everyone was thrilled, weren't they?" He sounded like he had been climbing stairs. He looked like it, too, all of a sudden, his face flushing again as his smile finally faded. "I have friends who were even more excited than the Cardinal," he said, "because some of us know something about this that even the Cardinal doesn't know yet. About you, and about evolution, C.J."

He stopped abruptly, staring at the boy, his eyes wide and dark and reverent.

C.J. looked away from Reed, back to the package. "What is it?" he asked softly.

"I was just wondering, C.J. . . ." He held the last sheet of paper. One more fold.

"Would you do me a great favor, son?"

With that, the last corner was folded back.

C.J. could see the trout.

It was a big one, and he was fascinated. He had never seen a whole fish up close. His mom never bought one, and no one took him fishing.

"Would you show me how the power works, please?" Reed whispered. "Just here, with the two of us?"

The fish smelled; C.J. noticed that. And its eyes were open, even though it was dead.

Reed reached to the cabinet overhead and slowly withdrew a plate. He placed it on the counter and slid the fish onto it. His eyes left C.J. only for quick, darting glances at the plate and the long, shining fish that was dead.

C.J. stared, his eyes narrowed. He nibbled at the corner of his lip, his hands still in his pockets.

Reed edged the plate closer to the boy. His voice was soft and warm, folding over the boy like a blanket. "Just say the words and touch the fish, and you can show me how it works. Please, C.J."

C.J. squirmed, turning a little to his left, away from the fish. "My mom asked me, no more resurrections", he whispered.

"But that was for people, I'm sure, wasn't it? Did she say 'fish'?"

C.J. shook his head slowly. Then he shrugged.

"So it wouldn't hurt anything to do it with a fish, would it? I'm sure it wouldn't."

"I never did it with a fish."

"But it wouldn't hurt to try, would it?"

C.J. stared for another several seconds. Finally, he nodded and whispered a tentative, "I guess not."

Reed drew in a deep breath.

C.J. looked at him, his eyebrows raised, waiting for a final okay. Reed nodded. "Yes. Now."

C.J. smiled and reached out cautiously. He touched the cold scales, laying his fingertips on the fish's side. It felt hard and dry. He waited—four seconds, five seconds, as though he wasn't sure what to say. Then he whispered it the way it seemed right, the only way to say it. He whispered, "Be well, fish."

It didn't take long—a minute and a half, no more. The tail moved first, a twitch in the tail, and then a twitch in the fin.

Reed's eyes filled with tears. His face flushed to crimson. He didn't blink. He barely breathed.

"It's alive", C.J. announced quietly. He sounded as though he was mesmerized, too, but he was smiling.

The creature's tail twisted slowly and then fell flat. As it raised its tail for a second time, its mouth opened slowly, and then its whole body flapped hard, once, all of a sudden, and the fish was bursting with new life, slapping off the plate and onto the countertop, frantic for water.

C.J. jumped backward, and Reed whooped in a whisper and rushed to sweep the fish into the sink and fill the sink with water as C.J. reached out again to feel it. His eyes were wide, and his grin was wide, and Reed laughed hard but quietly, not wanting to be heard by Brian or the others, and in a matter of seconds the fish had enough water to submerge and was flapping fresh water on the huge man and the little boy who looked so very proud of what he'd just done.

"Oh my!" Reed chuckled, holding his hands out to minimize the splashing. Then he held a dish towel over the sink. "Oh my! Oh C.J.! Thank you so much for doing that for me! Oh my!"

He turned a beaming face to the boy and then reached a huge hand around C.J.'s shoulder, letting the towel hang in the water. "Oh my word! Thank you, son!" His other hand dropped the towel beside the sink and pressed against his chest as if it was holding his heart steady, but the fish flapped hard again, and Reed quickly reached to lift the towel over the sink again as a shield.

C.J. giggled at the sight.

Reed let the towel settle onto the water and the living trout, and then he bent down to rest on one knee in front of the boy. His great, round hand reached out and rested on C.J.'s left shoulder. A very light touch for such a big hand.

"C.J.?" he asked, looking into the miracle boy's eyes. Now his words were barely a breath.

C.J. looked at him, still grinning.

"You know some of the questions people are asking on TV, and I know your dad and mom are asking about, too, probably . . . like, could the power work if you just said the words but didn't actually touch the person? Did you ever hear your mom and dad wonder about that? Or did you ever wonder about that yourself? Because, I know the rest of us wonder about it a lot."

C.J. scratched his ear and said, "My dad said stuff about that."

"Oh yes, we're all wondering."

"Or if the touch would work," C.J. said thoughtfully, "but without me saying anything, just thinking it and touching somebody. Or something like that." There was a hint of new interest in his voice.

"Yes", Reed said, stretching the word out slowly, nodding and huddling closer. "That's right, son."

"I don't think that would work, though", C.J. said. "The one without me saying the words at all. But I don't know. Saying the words by themselves might work, without the touch."

"C.J.?" Reed said. It was the same way he said his initials before, when he was about to ask him to bring back the fish. "Let's try it with just the words to the fish, okay? Let's do that so we can tell your mom and dad and the Cardinal, okay?"

C.J. was silent. Thinking again. Then he nodded, a look of new determination on his young face. "All right", he said. Then he added, as if to get the directions straight, "So I'll just say it. But don't do the touch. Okay?"

"Oh!" Reed said quietly, sounding suddenly startled. His eyebrows raised. "Of course, if we do that, the fish will have to be dead again, won't it?" He held his breath and watched C.J. carefully. "Why didn't I think of that before?"

C.J. nodded slowly. It was true: you can't get something back to life again if isn't dead before you do it.

Reed's eyes stayed on the boy.

C.J.'s eyes slid to the towel. It was still swishing over the fish, getting in the fish's way, being pulled down into the water.

Reed rose to his full height, and, with a deep breath, pulled the towel from the sink and closed his huge hands tightly around the trout, lifting it slowly out of the water.

He held it in front of C.J., nearly touching the boy's chest with it. The trout was trying to free itself, but only its tail had room to flap. Drops of water were splashing on C.J.'s shirt again, and on his ironed tan slacks, his good ones, worn to visit the Cardinal, and on the floor.

Reed, bending down with his victim in hand, whispered again, so quietly, "Just say, 'Be dead, fish.' Just like that. Say it, C.J. 'Be dead, fish.'" His face was on fire.

C.J. eased backward. He looked at the fish. He looked at its eyes, still wide open. He looked again at Reed, and his own eyes filled with questions. He stared at the fish again, saying nothing, thinking as hard as he could, not knowing what he should do. "That wasn't what my dad talked about", he said softly.

Reed pressed closer. The fish flapped its tail again, splashing them both lightly. It was hardly a protest worth noticing, but Reed feigned momentary surprise at the fish's little outburst and grinned. "But we're going to kill it anyway, aren't we?" He bent lower, still smiling, his voice thick and gentle. "I mean, somebody has to do it. And better you than the cook with her knife. Besides," he said, "it won't stay dead for more than a minute, will it? So what's the harm, son?"

C.J. bit his lip and twisted to the side, easing backward. "Its eyes are wide open", he said cautiously.

"Even Jesus ate fish", Reed grinned. "He certainly didn't eat it without killing it, did he?"

C.J. stopped moving.

Reed stopped moving.

C.J. watched the fish trying to curl and slap at the air one more time. He was looking at the fish's eyes again, and how they were so wide open and could not shut. He moved backward with excruciating care. Just one step. Then another, now turning slowly toward the door.

Reed said, "C. J.!" sharply, then caught himself and said it again with a soft lilt, as an invitation, a smiling invitation from a friend as he moved to stand with the dying fish between the boy and the door. "C. J.?"

C. J. took another step, this time to the left and this time determined, and then, all of a sudden, two, three, four more steps to the door.

Reed stood to his full height. His smile was gone. He said, "All right, C. J. But this will be our secret, won't it, son; what we just did here?" He took a single step toward the boy and stopped, the fish barely moving in his massive hands. "I'm asking it as a special favor. You go back to the video games I bought for you, just as a present for you, and you can take the games home with you and keep them, if you want, because that's what they are, a present for you. Would you like that? But what we did here will be our own secret, is that right, son?"

C. J. looked at the fish one more time before he opened the door and left. The fish still could not close its eyes.

Seventeen

With everything going his way, the Cardinal was very satisfied, indeed. The physical for C.J. had been approved, if reluctantly on Mrs. Walker's part, for early the next morning. Bennington Reed had already begun putting into play and coordinating the necessary arrangements. C.J.'s transport to Rome seemed secure, if not specifically agreed upon to that point. And now it was time for the "gift" he had been waiting like a child to present to the others, and to Lynn and C.J. especially, all day.

"A surprise I think you'll be very excited about", he announced, rising triumphantly from his seat at the conference table.

He had their attention.

"Mrs. Marion Klein has been released from the hospital. No, she is not going to allow surgery to explore anything more, including metallic tracings. And, yes, she is being escorted by Royal Oak police at this moment to share our dinner with us, here, today. She should be arriving in about fifteen minutes from right now!"

Lynn was on her feet with a gasp of delight.

The Cardinal was grinning like Father Christmas.

The first two things Lynn thought as she watched Marion and Ryan walk slowly behind two policemen from the cruiser in the driveway to the front door were that Marion had lost so much weight, and that she looked radiant—more filled with life than at any time she had ever seen her before. She saw that the rain had stopped, and that a huge crowd was building up now in front of the Cardinal's house, the word having gotten out that not only was C.J. Walker at the house, but that the first woman he raised from the dead was there, too, and that Marion had a wig on, and she saw that she looked wonderful—not at all like the last, terrible time that she had seen her, when her face had been puffed gray and hard under too much makeup and Marion herself, the living person, had been gone.

To see her now, to watch her alive and suddenly closing in on the doorway of the Cardinal's house walking and seeing and laughing and crying and saying Lynn's name with tears in her living eyes, and to watch her reaching out with living arms to embrace Lynn like a sister, struck her so hard that she felt her knees turn to rubber.

Yes, she had believed the news reports, and, yes, she had seen Marion alive again on television. But to see her here actually moving toward her in her plain white blouse and plain gray skirt and black high heels and dark brown wig and to hear her voice again and to know that it actually was Marion Klein . . .

Lynn staggered and began to cry hard as Marion swept close to her with love and a firm embrace and kissed her on the cheek five times, quickly, pressing hard, her laugh ringing like bells.

Marion's husband, Ryan, watched from a few feet behind his wife, laughing and teary-eyed, himself. Father Mark watched, and fought back tears, and was silent. The Cardinal watched smiling and transfixed, as though unable to move. Reed was also transfixed, his arms limp, his eyes open wide, his mouth opened slightly. Monsignor Tennett hovered farther back in the entranceway, his expression locked in a wide, unchanging grin. Joe stood next to Monsignor Tennett with his arm around C.J., his eyes narrowed and laughing, shaking his head, seeing again what he knew before any of them: that it was all real.

C.J. watched and waited. He was not in a hurry. He was the only one among them who looked nervous.

Marion embraced them all in turn, and Ryan did the same right behind her. And when she came to C.J., she took his young face in her hands very lightly and stared into his eyes for a long half minute. Then she whispered a soft, "Thank you, C.J.", through fresh tears, and she kissed him with barely a touch, once, slowly, on the forehead.

He let her kiss him. He did not try to move away. He whispered, "You're welcome."

In the living room they ignored the sandwiches and cold drinks and visited like a family hungry for other things. They sat close and spoke about miracles, Marion's and the others, and others beyond that—about C.J.'s school and about crowds and police and the physical exam C.J. would be taking and about the upcoming surgery for Turner and about the possibilities, maybe now even the probabilities, of Lynn and C.J. and maybe even Joe going to Rome with the Cardinal. Then they talked about Marion's decision to forego surgery on herself so that she and Ryan and the kids could simply disappear into the homes of distant relatives far away in order to, as Marion put it, "find a life that's not only up and running, but peaceful and normal, or at least, as normal as can be".

Lynn knew exactly what she meant.

It was at that point that Marion paused and looked at C.J. and quietly asked, "C.J., would it be okay if we talked? Just you and me?"

"How about Marion's teeth, did you guys think of that?" It was Joe, trying to fill a void in the conversation. "Maybe, before she gets out of here, I'll ask her if she had any fillings going into this thing, and if they're fixed now."

In a different place and a different time, Joe, Father Mark, and Bennington Reed might have been members of a male-only club gathered to sip brandy, smoke cigars, and discuss the day's financial or other news events gravely. Today, they were three men from very different backgrounds and with very different agendas thrust together on an extraordinary Sunday afternoon in a Roman Catholic Cardinal's living room. They were now waiting for C.J. and Marion Klein to finish their private talk and for the Cardinal and Monsignor Tennett to finish whatever business had unexpectedly urged them into the den for a series of conference calls. Lynn had left them, too, choosing to spend a few minutes sitting close to the house in the backyard, lost in thoughts of her own.

"By 'fixed' I mean are Marion's teeth back being real whole teeth, is what I mean", Joe said. He leaned back in his dark leather easy chair and took another swig from his fourth can of 7 Up, which he wished for the tenth time was a cold beer, but he kept his index finger raised to hold his place on the conversational stage. "Little things like that, we should know, too. Along with the main things, for sure, like whether it works on people who have been dead a long time, or if C.J. can just shout it out to a crowd through a loudspeaker, without touch. Or even do it over the phone, which would, seems to me, be Katie bar the door. You think about that."

Father Mark dragged his fingertips across tired eyes.

Reed, sitting on the long, beige, living room couch, leaned forward in a kind of controlled collapse that carried him closer to the other two men by nearly twelve inches. His eyes were dark and bright. "I would like to know, among other things, if it works for plant life as well as animal?" He let the question breathe in the open air for just a few seconds, then added, "But most of all, I would like to know if it is, in fact, a 'gift' in the way most of us have been talking about it, meaning that God has given this gift to this young boy in a very selective way and with a very selective purpose. Or, might it possibly be—an enormous possibility here—might it possibly be an entry into a new stage of human evolution? Not just a gift given to one person, but a process that will involve, in the next three, four generations, for perhaps every person on earth?"

The others raised their eyebrows.

Joe was still focused on more immediate things. "Well, let's go through the ideas one at a time", he said. "What do you think about checking Marion's teeth?"

Reed squirmed. His voice was edged with irritation. He said, "I don't believe that dental health is the highest issue, right now, Mr. Walker."

Joe sensed competition in the air. He sat upright. His eyes flashed. A hard smile pressed his lips tight. "Oh, excuse me for thinking if my kid can heal somebody's teeth as well as their cancer; that might not be a high issue", he said. "In addition to arranging physicals for the Cardinal, this is what else you do, Mr. Reed? You decide what's the issue we should think is high enough to talk about?"

There was a brittle silence.

Father Mark studied Reed. Reed studied Joe, staring back at him hard-eyed. "I don't mean to dismiss other questions," he said in a calm and unapologetic voice, "but in the short time we have alone, please consider with me the possibility that the boy might really be the first of many. You, and Father, here, please think what it would mean if he was a template, rather than a unique individual receiving a selective gift. That's bigger than Mrs. Klein's teeth. Believe me."

Father Mark had lifted his feet from the footrest and sat upright. He was leaning forward.

Joe noticed the priest's interest in Reed's proposal and thought about it himself. "So what's your idea?" he asked. "You're saying C.J. is just one of a whole bunch of people who are going to be running around, now, all of them able to bring back the dead? Like there's, all of a sudden, a resurrection flu going around?"

"I was hoping we could have a serious discussion of the possibility", Reed said flatly. "I was hoping you could see a little further than that." He stared at Joe, trying not to dislike him but not succeeding. The man was a cheap suit, he concluded, a salesman looking for a hustle, be it aluminum siding, used cars, replacement windows, or even his own son. He was a bad father, Reed suspected, the reason his wife left him. And he was vulgar. Modestly clever, one might grant him that, but not intelligent. Not intelligent and not caring and not sensitive to anything deeper than the pocket he carried his fifteen dollars cash in, and certainly not worthy of having someone as unthinkably significant as C.J. as his son. "I happen to suspect that in C.J., Mr. Walker, we may well be seeing the beginning of a whole new human experience. It's a possibility.

It's possible that he's the breakthrough we've been waiting for, and that a whole new humanity may be evolving at this very moment, like a new Lazarus rising, all of us rising to a level more divine than human. Right now, here on earth."

Joe stared, trying to take it in, now silent.

Father Mark said, "It's a theory. I know it's been suggested, this divine evolution idea, but I'm surprised to hear it suggested here, to tell you the truth."

Reed's eyes danced in front of his unorthodox vision. He was smiling a proud smile.

The priest continued, "As far as what we do next, you think we should sit tight and prepare for the other C.J.'s to be discovered? Would that be your advice?"

Reed studied him. His smile faded. He nodded slowly and said, "I would advise you, if you're seriously asking me, Father Cleary, and I hope to advise the Cardinal in this same way, that we not sit tight at all. On the contrary, I would hope that certain elites among us would be invited to be gathered together and form the boy in the selective use of his powers."

Father Mark said, "You've been giving this some thought."

"Oh yes indeed!"

Joe placed his soda on the table next to his chair and said, "And who are these 'elites', my man? You and the Cardinal are probably 'elites', right?"

Reed eyed him. "Maybe not myself at all; that wasn't my point. My point is, we should invite the finest minds and highest spirits that God has provided. Not just Church leaders, although certainly we need spiritual people, too. But we should broaden the boy's input. Set up a model of formation that we can then apply, if and when cases arise, for other people empowered in the same way. Which I expect we will see soon. There should be outstanding scientific minds involved. Teachers and doctors. Artists. Poets. The right people can be identified, I promise you."

"What did that mean: the 'selective use' of C.J.'s powers?" Father Mark asked. "You mean this group of experts would select who gets resurrected and who doesn't?"

Reed raised his chin. "Well, Father, someone will have to decide how the power is used, won't they? Isn't that where this whole process has to lead? It may be you, Father. It may be the boy's mother. Or his father, here. Or it may be, and I believe it should be, a group of very special advisers. But it will have to be someone, won't it?"

"Someone will advise him, yes."

"Well then, all I'm suggesting is that we should identify our very best talents and spirits, if you will, and then let them direct the power. Not leave who does or doesn't get resurrected up to a nine-year-old boy."

"And the criteria they'd use to decide these resurrections would be ...?"

Reed looked incredulous. "We'd select those individuals who would most benefit the human community, of course. Who else would you possibly choose?"

"Oh Lordy", Joe grinned. He wasn't so much shocked as he was amused. He picked up his soda and drained the can, a guy who suddenly realized he was at a prize fight. The atmosphere had been charged. It was palpable. It had happened all of a sudden, and he was not even the one doing it.

Father Mark said, "Have you given the Cardinal this advice yet?"

"Not specifically, no."

"And poor people, or helpless people, the little people back in the shadows, the weakest ones, they'd be left to die off, then; is that right? So the elites end up selecting ... what would you call this new human race? Could we call it a divine race? Maybe a master race?"

Reed tilted his weight forward and rose slowly to his feet. "You choose to put things in very defensive terms, Father, and I'm sorry for that." He paused, as though hoping for a response, perhaps an apology. But the priest just stared back at him, his brow still furrowed, his lips held tight.

Reed continued in a mild voice. "For the record, I believe your choice of words is uninformed and unfair. But the fact is, yes, of course, that is what will happen, given a long-term view. But don't you see, Father? I'm simply talking about God's plan for evolution. It's not my plan. The weak *will* die off, yes. And I'm not evil in acknowledging that. The weak, the destructive, the criminal, the twisted, yes. That's the way evolution is meant to develop. The survival of the fittest, the survival of the elite, it's all the same thing; choose whatever word you want. But recognize, please, Father, that right now, today, beginning through this unspeakably priceless child, we may in fact have the chance to experience not just the *survival* of the fittest but the *elevation* of the fittest, the elevation of the best of our species into true, holistic fitness. Holy fitness. With no more wars. No more slums. No more homeless, wandering shadows. No more diseases. And even, as unthinkable as it may have seemed just one week ago, no more physical death!"

Father Mark stared, motionless.

Joe had lost his smile. His lips were parted, his eyes, wide.

A noise came from the back of the house: Lynn returning, or maybe the Cardinal and the Monsignor.

Reed hurried to add, in a low but fiercely insistent whisper, "What I'm describing has a name, Father. What I'm describing is heaven on earth!"

"What you're describing isn't heaven", Father Mark said. "It's hell."

Marion Klein paused. They were sitting close to one another on the beige couch in what the Cardinal called his den, sitting in front of the fireplace, which had logs in it but no fire, not in the late spring, and they had been talking for a long time.

She had thanked C.J. again for what he had done for her, and asked him how he felt about the attention he was getting, and tried, rather unsuccessfully, she thought, to answer his questions, most importantly, what it was like in the "waiting place", as she called it, the waiting place that wasn't heaven, but something less, like an entry place but not a completion. "If it had been heaven," she told him, smiling, "I don't think I would have come back even if you opened the door. Not if I had really seen the face of God, the way I believe God is."

C.J. thought about that. "Could you really have said no and then just kept going into heaven?"

She smiled again. "I wonder about that, myself, C.J., but we're into things I don't have a clue about", she said. "I'm not really that kind of personality, that I'd argue much with God. You know?" She laughed. "I'm glad I'm back, though. I'm glad I'm here. But someday I think I'll be glad to go back there, too, to someday go all the way back."

C.J. nodded. Mrs. Klein was smiling, but he wasn't. He had wanted her to have seen Jesus and the angels, and to have seen his grandmother, most of all, and so he told her that.

"I'm sure I would have seen her, honey," she told him, "if I had gone farther. Boy, I would have liked to see my grandma, too, and my mom and dad. But like I said, I guess it was probably like where Lazarus had to wait, in the Bible, before he came back, because God wanted him back so all the people could see him. You know who Lazarus is, don't you?"

C.J. nibbled at his lip and nodded his head. He knew who Lazarus was. He even knew, from that first time they talked about Mrs. Klein on TV, that the announcer in the red dress had called her that name: "The Lazarus Lady".

She slipped her arm around him and said, "I know there's a lot we still don't know, C.J. But there is one thing I want you to know, for sure. It's why I wanted, most of all, to come today and visit with you."

He turned to look at her. She looked like his mom, he thought. Not the way her hair was or her face, really, but the way her eyes were looking at him.

"People who get that close to God, C.J., and gosh, people who get to go past where I was and actually see God's face, I want you to know how good that is, okay? And I want you to know most of all—especially with everybody saying how you've got to bring all these people back again, because I see it all over the TV; what they're trying to force you to do—I want you to realize that if you don't bring people back like they all want you to, it's still going to be okay. I want you to know that, honey, because it really is. Those folks are still going to be okay. Because dying really is just the next step into another life. Like being born. You leave your mom's body and go into a whole new place. And it's wonderful being taken back to God, C.J. It really is."

She paused, studying him, hoping to see his eyes light up with some sign of understanding. But what she saw was a nine-year-old nibbling at his lip and not saying anything, as though he might be waiting for more. She said, "Do you know what I'm trying to say, C.J.? I don't know if I'm saying it real well, but do you know what I mean?"

He stared at her. He nodded once. Then he said very tentatively, "Yeah. You mean ... it's okay if we die."

Marion took a deep breath. She didn't answer for several seconds. Then she shook her head very slowly and said in a whisper as light as a sigh, "Not exactly that. Not that. What I'm trying to say is, we *don't* really die. That's what I want you to know. They say we do, but we don't really die. That's the gift."

For the first time, Joe was driven back to his apartment with a police escort. He had to be. Getting back to his car at Lynn's house was nuts enough, but getting away again on his own would have been impossible. The crowds were bigger than ever; news of the Turner operation was hyping things like crazy; and the visit to the Cardinal with Marion Klein was throwing gas on the fire worse than ever before, making it seem certain that the Church took C.J. Walker seriously enough, and Marion Klein's recovery seriously enough, to make the Cardinal want to spend the whole afternoon with the Lazarus Boy.

So the police got him into his car and through the crowd, one cruiser in front and one in back. They told him they'd get him all the way home. They told him they'd get him back the next morning. They told him that he and Mrs. Walker better find another place for C.J. to live real soon. *Real* soon, they said, hitting the "real", saying that with that new surgery coming up with Turner and all the frantic stuff people were capable of with something like this, they didn't think the Royal Oak house would be secure enough, like the family needed.

On the way home, he found himself turning over Reed's ideas again: everybody someday raising the dead just like C.J., resurrections all around, heaven on earth. Nope, he didn't like the guy. Something loose cannon about him. And he knew the guy didn't like him. Fair enough.

He also wondered if the Cardinal would ever get the full story about what his big buddy was thinking, the way he and Father Mark just did. And he wondered if the Cardinal would be as freaked out by it as Father Mark was, the local padre looking like he was going to puke.

He laughed. Maybe cracks in the old church walls, after all, which would be all the better for him.

The fact was, he thought, the day hadn't really gone one hundred percent bad. At least Lynn hadn't signed on the dotted line to let them take C.J. into some stone-block monastery in vino country. Not yet. And at least he wasn't forced out of the picture yet. He'd still be close to C.J., still go to the hospital with him for a physical, and, when he thought about it, it was still only Sunday. Having four days before Turner's operation gave him time to turn Lynn around and get the kid to Cross for the five million bucks, after all.

But he still wondered about the way the physical was being set up, for one thing. He wondered why nut-man Reed was the one to set it up, and why he didn't set it up for the middle of the night, when fewer people would be around. Maybe the big guy's appetite to be at the center of anything and get himself on TV played into it, the guy like a little kid in a way—maybe wanting as big a parade as possible just because it made him feel important. Maybe it was because it made him look all the more indispensable to the church brass; making easier for him to lean on the Cardinal to let him call in some of his "elite" friends.

He wished the physical was going to take place at Fremont, in Royal Oak, too, rather than at St. Paul's Hospital on Detroit's east side, which put it forty minutes away, even with a police escort. But that part, at least, he understood. St. Paul's Hospital was Catholic, their best place in Detroit, and the Church would try to keep everything controlled from here on out, he had no doubt about that. Having the physical on their own turf was only step one.

The Church and the government, too, he thought. Both of them squeezing now. Sitting around making plans even as Joe turned the corner onto his street, his apartment complex down just a quarter mile on the left.

Arriving at his apartment building, he parked in the handicapped area again, even though the police were right behind him. What would they do, ticket him? Then he bolted for the door, pushing himself without comment through the wall of reporters armed with cameras and mikes and loud questions.

No stopping. No talking. No time for reporters. Not tonight.

Safely inside, he mounted the stairs two at a time. The two goons with Kruger weren't in the hall, and he worried that something had gone wrong. Then he noticed that the light in his apartment was on, glowing along the floor at the bottom of his door. Fantastic, he thought. He thought, that'll be my hundred thousand dollars, lighting up the night.

Kruger was in the apartment, as expected. Looking cool, also expected. Only this time the two other guys were in the apartment with him. There to look serious, Joe thought; there to make Joe think twice about jerking Cross around on the hundred thousand dollars.

Joe wondered again about Cross' name being something like Crossetti, and about maybe being called "Tony the hammer".

Kruger didn't bother introducing the other men. He just said, "Hello, Mr. Walker. You have the contract signed and ready?"

Joe grinned and gave him the contract with Lynn's forged signature and told him the news: they'd be having a physical tomorrow, a lot of attention, something they couldn't get out of, but after that, it looked golden. After that, they'd set up the boy's trip to New York.

Kruger stared at the contract. No smile. No look of satisfaction. "Maybe tomorrow night? You and the boy and your wife?"

"Maybe. But we got seventy-two hours, you said, from now until the time we have to be in New York."

Kruger nodded. True enough. With that, he snapped open the leather attaché case, and Joe was staring at $100,000 cash for the taking: two thousand fifty-dollar bills, all in one place.

Joe was feeling his nerves clicking in. Serious money, seriously happening. "Looks good", he said.

"We trust it's money well spent", Kruger said flatly.

The two guys that had come with Kruger stood by the door without expressions, their hands folded in front of themselves like soccer players, guarding their crotch.

Joe thought, these guys don't believe C.J. can do anything at all. They think their boss is being conned.

He didn't say anything more.

"Okay", Kruger said, starting to smile and then not bothering. "We'll see you and your family real soon." He held out his hand and Joe took it.

The other two men didn't offer to shake hands. They just moved to the door.

"One more thing", Kruger said, holding the contract Joe had given him and waving it once, waist high. "This piece of paper isn't meant for a court appearance, you know that. This is much more serious than a court appearance."

Joe waited for more. He got it.

"See, if Mr. Cross' son dies, and your son hasn't shown up, that would be worse than breaking a legal contract, if you understand what I mean."

"If he doesn't show up and at least *try*, that's right. But he'll be there."

"Because that's in the contract, isn't it?"

"I understand", Joe said, sounding irritated. "Blood oath. Good Italian family. I got it, believe me. No problem." He didn't like it, but he could feel himself stiffen. His voice sounded stiff, and his body stiffened; not a lot, but maybe enough to be noticed.

He thought, stay cool.

Kruger nodded, then followed the other two men out the door.

Nothing more was said.

The door clicked shut and Joe stood very still. He stared at the money for a long minute; then he shut the case and snapped the latches tight. "I'm the only one around here who *does* understand, pal", he whispered bitterly.

C.J.'s mom was in the shower across the hall. Burr was with his mom in one of the other bedrooms. C.J. was alone.

He stood with his bedroom light out, looking out his side window, over the garage, over to the Ackerstons' house next door, and all the other houses. The people in the street were only visible from that window when he pressed close to the screen and looked straight right, or when he pulled the screen up and stuck his head out, and he didn't feel like doing that. But he could still hear them. Things being moved. Talking. Calling to each other every now and then. Like his mom said when they got home: more of them now than ever. So he knew they were still there. He knew they wouldn't go away.

He watched the moon hiding its upper half under slow-moving clouds that looked like torn rags. He watched the moon, and then he watched the fly that was buzzing against the corner of the screen in front of him, trying to get out to where there were a few sharp lights in other houses and in the street, and cooler air.

He watched the moon, and then the fly, back and forth. And then, just the fly.

He wondered why everybody kills flies. They carry germs, his mom said. Maybe. They don't bite, though, like mosquitoes, he thought. Still, everybody kills them. They make a little noise and bother you, is all.

He wondered if Jesus killed flies, or the saints he was always hearing about in school from Mrs. Sawyer.

Probably, he thought, because everybody kills flies. And he could, too, he decided, probably with just his words and his touch, and maybe even with just his words, if he wanted to. But he wondered. He thought he could have killed the fish, too, like Mr. Reed wanted him to, only it had eyes and made him feel creepy, so he hadn't done it. But flies would be different, wouldn't they? They had eyes, too, but you couldn't see them staring. And their eyes were different. He saw a picture once, how a flies sees. A million things at once. A fly looks at a pencil; it sees a million pencils all at once. Weird. And everybody killed flies.

The night breeze was cool on his face, a light, clean breeze moving into the house from over the restless neighborhood.

The fly kept trying to get out—buzzing and bouncing off the screen, stopping, circling, buzzing again.

C.J. began whispering absentmindedly in a thin breath, as though several very small thoughts had just escaped accidentally, "Somebody will kill you, anyway. Mom will swat you or something. Or tell me to do it."

He turned slowly to glance out his open bedroom door, into the hall, and listen to the shower water running in the bathroom where his mom must be about finished with her shower; then he turned back to the fly.

It had landed again, up by the corner of the screen. It might be thinking about something. It wasn't moving.

He whispered again, now a murmur. "Even if I let you outside, what are going to do? A bird will catch you or something. Spiders will catch you or something."

The fly moved in a small circle, pacing.

C.J. wondered if it was listening. He wondered if flies' ears made everything sound funny, the way their eyes made everything look funny. He wondered if they heard a million things at once.

He whispered, "I wouldn't want to be a fly."

He heard the water in the bathroom stop running under the squeak of a faucet handle, and he turned again to look at his open door, this time quickly. His heart had sped up. He noticed that, too, like he was scared or something. But, he thought, I don't feel scared.

Then he thought, maybe I do.

He turned back to the fly, still listening for sounds from his mom. Hearing noise from the bathroom. Things clicking, being put away. His mother, getting ready to come out.

His heart was pounding.

She'll do it with a paper or something, anyway, he thought again. What's the difference?

He held his breath.

His index finger was outstretched. He was trying to figure out how he could touch the fly with his hand, so he could touch it and say the words. Trying to figure out if he really wanted to.

Then a sudden click sounded in the hall, and he whirled to see Lynn stepping into his doorway fresh from her shower, dressed in her light-blue bathrobe, still rubbing her hair with a white towel.

"What'cha doing, hon?" she asked.

"Nothin'."

Eighteen

For three years, back when he was at Royal Oak's Kimball High, Joe had worked at the Amoco station at Thirteen Mile and Woodward. He worked with Rich Weinert, whose uncle was night manager of the Sycamore Motel on Southfield Road, and a bookmaker. He also got to know Amy Conklin, the fifty-eight-year-old owner of a mediocre thoroughbred named Ebony Hill, and a racetrack groupie who enjoyed the idea of having teenaged male gofers at her elbow in the denial of her sunset years, and who was a regular Amoco customer.

Before long, Joe and Rich were driving Amy and her tired dreams to the track, placing her window bets, and, best of all, acting cool in her reserved box at the track, where they waited for those adrenaline moments when Amy would whisper what was usually solid information about horses that had been held back and were magically ready for a big payday.

One day in June, Amy told Joe and Rich, "I'm gonna put you boys through college in August", and she was serious. She said, "In the last two weeks in August, we're going to have a horse that's going to win us the limit", which Joe knew meant 32–1 odds through a bookmaker. "And nobody'll know about this one," Amy said, "so the odds will be there, guaranteed."

Joe had $1800 saved from working paper routes and gas stations since he was twelve, and he made up his mind on the spot to put it all down on Amy's tip, which would make him $57,000 plus.

And Joe, barely seventeen years old.

Then, on a steamy Thursday late in August, Amy told them, "Saturday's the day. The horse is Kirk's Kiss. Get something down," she said, "but not till the last couple of hours. And don't tell anybody, you understand?"

The problem was, it started to rain Thursday night, and it kept coming down really hard all Friday and even Friday night, right into Saturday morning, turning the track into a foot of mud. And they said it would keep on, nonstop, all day long. And Joe didn't know if Kirk's Kiss was still going in the mud or not.

The other problem was, he couldn't find Amy to ask her if the horse could still win in a foot of mud. She and her best track pal, Sarah Lee, named like the cakes, were both staying out of sight.

Rich's uncle, the bookmaker, said the boys shouldn't risk it. "There are four other horses in that race that've won in the mud", he told them. "Kirk's Kiss has never even showed, not in heavy slop like this." He said he wasn't risking it himself. He told them, "I'll put down what you boys want, but there are mudders and there are others, and Kiss is not your mudder."

So Joe ended up betting ten dollars at the track, just for fun, and Kirk's Kiss ended up winning by a neck and paying $48.20. Not the limit, but a solid 24–1, which would have meant more than $43,000 if Joe had gone ahead and done what he'd planned right from the start.

What he ended up with, besides the $241 from his ten-dollar ticket, was the hard-and-fast lesson that you don't get many chances in life to cash in a big hand, and some people don't get any. So if he ever got another chance, he told himself even then, he'd never back off, ever.

Joe Walker would never "do a Kirk's Kiss" again.

He was thinking about that, about Amy all painted up and talking loud and wearing perfume like syrup, and the smell of the track, and about Rich and his uncle and Kirk's Kiss charging down the straight with Joe thinking, don't win now! He was thinking about that Saturday in August and about his lost forty thousand dollars, which was still the way he looked at it, the whole time he crawled behind the police through the morning crowd with their signs and their shouts and their frustrations, which he could see so easily now. He thought about it as he approached Lynn and Nancy in the living room at 7:40 A.M. and asked Lynn to follow him, please, out to the back porch for just five minutes— he with his black athletic bag, she with her second early-morning coffee, looking reluctant, eyeing him and the bag suspiciously. He thought, Kirk's Kiss. The money going down, long shot or not. He thought, no use waiting for the track to get dry. The track, he knew now, never got dry enough.

As they moved silently through the den to the back porch door, he assured himself that it was a good time to hit her with the Cross alternative again. She'd be feeling especially protective about C.J., he reasoned—all the mother juices clicking in with the hospital just a couple of hours away.

Hell, he thought, it's the only time I've got.

Lynn's denim shirt was wrinkled, and her eyes were still tired, but she was beautiful to Joe, moving quietly onto the porch, glancing around, pulling her hair back, moving it easily over her left ear. Beautiful. Always had been, always would be. He thought that, too, as he pulled up a white, molded chair so he could face her as she sipped her coffee on the old church bench with the red metal arms at each end.

"Just a few hours to the hospital", he said, putting the bag on the floor between them.

"I know that."

He nodded, then smiled. "They won't find anything."

She shook her head and took another sip of coffee. "Nope. I hope not." Then, looking again at the black bag, she said, "But this is about the bag, Joe. What's in it?"

"Something new that's come up, Lynn." Joe started unzipping the bag, wrapping the zipper around the top. He was still smiling. "I just thought you had a right to see it right away, is all."

She took another sip of coffee, waiting, now shifting in her seat.

Joe reached inside. When his fist came out it was stuffed with fifty-dollar bills.

Lynn blinked as Joe held his hand over the bench seat at her side and opened his fingers. Fifties rained onto the seat, fluttering onto the floor.

Joe was grinning as he reached in and dumped more bills on the seat. Every one a fifty. He reached in a third time and then a fourth; fifties were piling up four inches high as Lynn sat stunned and staring.

She said, "Where did you get that? What is this?"

"It's for you, babe. You and C.J." He tilted the bag toward her, showing her; the bag was still choked with cash. "One hundred thousand dollars in honest-to-God fifties, Lynn. Take it."

Lynn's eyes turned fierce. She glared at him. "Tell me where this came from in three seconds or I'm outta here, Joe, and I mean it."

Joe held up his hand, empty now, trying to freeze the moment, forbidding her to leave. The bag tumbled onto the floor between them. "We already own this. You do. You don't have to do anything for it."

"One!"

She was getting ready to stand up, he could tell. It was time to make it happen. He had to change her mind about Cross right now. His voice was rising. "You think you're the only one that cares about C.J., Lynn, but I care about both of you."

"Two!"

Lynn stood up, moving slowly, holding her coffee steady. Joe stood with her, moving now to the side, easing to the right, ready to cut her off if she bolted for the door, talking even faster, starting to look mad. Or maybe just pretending to be mad; how could anyone really know?

"The Cardinal talks like you only have two choices, like it's Rome or Washington, but that's a crock, Lynn." His index finger was jabbing toward the money. "This is your way out! That's what this is, ... it's your and C.J.'s freedom!"

Lynn shot a furious glance at the money on the bench. A hundred thousand dollars cash.

Joe didn't pause. "You don't have to let the kid get swallowed by anybody, honey. And you don't have to belong to anybody. You can fly, Lynn! You and C.J., and me, too, we can all get up together and we can fly!" He reached down and scooped up another handful of bills. "Touch this! Hold it in your hand! This is just the beginning, what you see here."

She stared back at him, now with a fire of her own. She said bitterly, "I do know where it came from, don't I, Joe?"

That's when Joe felt it all slipping away again, in those few sickening seconds. He felt it all slipping away like the fifties he let fall from his fist, this time right to the ground. He shook his head. He licked his lips. "Lynn, I'm the only one that's offering you a way to keep C.J. from being locked up in somebody else's total private vault for the rest of his life. Why can't you see that?"

"It's from the New York guy", she whispered. "After I told you, never again."

"I'm gonna admit something to you, Lynn, honest to God", Joe lied. "I got this money before you and I even talked about him that very first time. Honest to God."

She cocked her head. Her eyes narrowed. She was still speaking softly, but the heat was in her eyes. "You made a deal with him about C.J.'s life before you even talked with me?"

"Honey", he said, trying to scramble so she couldn't stop to think, talking louder and faster and moving his hands now, jerking them, palms facing her, the sign language of the desperate: "When I talked to these guys, I thought, wow! ... that teenaged son of this guy is dying, you know, just like you and I have an only son, and I thought, hey, C.J. can save this kid's life, and ...."

"You wretch." She said it so softly it startled him.

"And ...", he hesitated, but just barely, "... and at the same time, this guy says, 'Here, you take this to Mrs. Walker.' And Lynn, the guy gives me ..."

Lynn was shaking her head slowly from side to side. A deep sadness was rising inside of her, showing itself now where the fire had been, rising in her eyes like water. "He's not going, Joe", she said.

"Just listen! He gives me a hundred thousand dollars, Lynn, one package, right in my hands, honest to God."

She spoke slowly and evenly. Her voice was colored gray. Her eyes were filled with tears. "I will not sell C.J. to the highest bidder, Joe. I will not put him on the block. I will not drag him to people who send bagfuls of fifties to his father, and I will not let them start parading their dead to my door. I will not buy mercenaries to protect my son. I will not be the one to decide who lives and who dies. I will not decide who else should be given that right. And I certainly will not put C.J. on a private plane with some strangers from New York, men that you don't even know and that I don't know and that maybe nobody knows but the FBI, and who may not even have a dying boy to go to, and who may really be planning on dumping your body and mine into the Great Lakes so they can disappear with our son. And I don't know why you don't get that! For God's sake, Joe!"

Joe reached fast and grabbed her arm, but she twisted hard and pulled away.

Her tears were suddenly on fire. "Stop this!" she snapped. "Think about C.J. for once in your life, and stop thinking about yourself!"

"I am thinking of him. And I'm thinking about you. I'm thinking there's a zillion dollars ready to drop right into your hands, and every penny would be for saving people's lives. Is that a bad thing? Is that what I hear you saying? That's what I don't get: you're throwing those people away, too. And all the safety that money would buy, and you're acting like I'm some animal and you're some kind of ... 'Oh, am I the only brilliant and wonderful parent on this planet, or what?'"

Lynn turned and walked to the door that led back into the den of the house. No expression.

He let her go. He felt like crying, himself.

"We had a deal first, Joe", she said softly, standing in front of the still-closed door. "You and me. Way back. We made a deal always to be there for one another first. That was our deal, yours and mine."

Joe whispered, "Oh God, Lynn."

She said, "Why is it that you always want to break your deal with me instead of the other person, when it was you and me who had the best deal first?"

He closed his eyes. It was so incredible to him, so stupid and impossible. He turned away. Then he began to stuff the fifties back into his bag in slow motion.

Lynn said, "I'm sorry for this other boy, if he's real. And I'm sorry for his dad, if he's really somebody's dad. But when I say nobody will buy or manipulate or control my son, that includes you. Because I think you're incapable of putting C.J. in front of yourself, Joe. I think you've never been able to put anyone in front of yourself, and you never will. I think you're broken that way, and nobody will ever be able to fix you."

She turned the handle of the door.

"You've already given them control of him", Joe said bitterly. He spit it out. He didn't look at her, just at the money he'd have to give back, staring at it dead-eyed and dead-voiced as he shoved it back into his bag. "You're just too stupid to know it." He continued to stuff fifties into the bag like a man in a daze, talking as though Lynn wasn't even on the porch with him. "They haven't decided which owner takes him, is all. But you sure don't own him anymore."

A few bills scattered to the floor. Joe bent to pick them up, noticing as he did that Lynn had stopped. He straightened and turned toward her one more time, ten fifty-dollar bills in his hand. His voice was as flat as a knife. "If you honest to God think those people don't already own him, Lynn, try making a run for it. Try it. Go out the front door and run. Or walk out of the hospital. Just tell them, 'I'm going for a walk with C.J. I want to be left alone now.' That simple. Just you and him. Try walking away from them like nobody owns him but you. See what happens to Momma and her boy then. The moment of reckoning. The moment of reckoning, babe."

He turned away again, shoving the last of the fifties into his bag.

She heard him mutter, "They wouldn't let you get ten feet. You try that, they'll eat you for lunch!"

Joe gave it some time. He had some toast; stayed quiet, letting Lynn calm down. He kept the TV off too. Kept it off when Father Mark showed up. Everybody was thinking about the hospital and was uptight about it. Nobody was talking about it out loud.

By 9:30, he decided he may as well break the news to Kruger. Say good-bye to his deal. Nothing else had come to mind. Nothing else would. No way around it.

He retrieved the cell phone he'd been carrying in the athletic bag with the fifties and carried it into the backyard.

The red light was on. Kruger, trying to call him.

He drew in a slow breath and punched in the number on the phone's ID strip, last number first, the way Kruger had told him. The phone rang three times. Kruger didn't answer; a pager did. Joe said his name and hung up.

Thirty seconds later, Kruger was on the line.

"Your timing is nearly perfect, Mr. Walker", he said. His voice was muffled. "Anthony Junior is dying. The doctor's with him now, back in New York. He may be gone already, as we're talking; he's that close."

Joe closed his eyes. God, he hated this.

"I'm ready to have the plane fired up", Kruger said. "Pontiac Airport. We're not far from you, right in Troy, on Big Beaver. It's time you got going."

Joe said, "If you're that close to the house, you've seen the feds come up to see us, and you know we're in government custody here. They say now that it's about national defense or some crap. But they won't let us argue, and they won't let us out."

A pause. "What are you talking about?"

"I'm talking about, it's not my fault, but our deal is off. I'm sorry. That's the way it is, though." Joe sighed and shook his head. He'd never said good-bye to five million dollars before.

There was another pause. Joe decided that Kruger needed a few seconds to get used to the idea, so he didn't try to fill the void.

Finally, Kruger said, "That option is not acceptable, Mr. Walker." His voice was tight and hard as a wire.

"Well, I'm sorry for everybody all the way around," Joe answered, "including us. But it isn't a question of us having a lot of options, so let's not pretend it is. We can't get out. The deal's off."

"The boy may be dying, but your contract is not. You've taken our money on it."

"I'm talking federal marshals and the United States Department of Defense, Kruger. The deal is off. I'll get you your money back."

"Unless you're under arrest, which you're not, begging off is not on the table, Mr. Walker. Do you understand what I'm saying?"

The "do you understand" was spoken real low, Joe thought, the way you'd say a threat. But he felt like he'd taken enough crap for one day, so the question didn't rattle him. In fact, it gave him an excuse to stay mad, which is what he really wanted to do. "Argue with your congressman if you want, but it's out of my hands", he snapped. "I called to tell you something, not to ask you if you approved. We're all sorry, but the deal is off. Give me an address and I'll send you back your money. I don't have it in a bank. I can't wire it. I'll send back your phone, too. That's the end of it."

Five million dollars gone, he was thinking. Kirk's Kiss, only a million times worse, and now this flack coming back at him.

He pulled the phone away from his mouth and sucked in a deep breath, telling himself to settle down. He should have waited to call. He should have called this afternoon, when he'd be more calm.

He heard sounds in the house. All of them were getting ready to go to the hospital. Lifting the phone again, he inhaled and said, "Hey, I'm sorry, man, okay? I mean, I don't like it, either; you can tell that. You think I wouldn't come for five million dollars if we could get out of here? Or you think we wouldn't let you come in here if we could or if you'd have a prayer in the world to be near us with all this crap going on? So what else can I say? I'm sorry. My wife is sorry. Tell your boss we're sorry. But give me your address or forget your money. That's it."

There was silence. Then there was Kruger. "No address. And no breaking the contract."

"Really?" Joe said it, and then he snapped. He slapped the phone closed and slammed it hard down on the bench seat as he heard his own anger burst into a muffled shout at Lynn and Kruger and his life and at himself, himself most of all, and at every plan he'd ever made that was any good, and at how his plans were always, always, always screwed up by something or somebody else, and always at the last minute.

He stopped. He exhaled hard through pursed lips. He examined the phone to see if he'd cracked it. It didn't look cracked. Maybe busted inside, maybe not. He dropped the phone into the back pocket of his jeans and glanced at his watch. They'd be gathering to go to the hospital, maybe already set to leave.

One more time: the rest of the world getting ready to leave, and Joe Walker was going to have to scramble to catch up.

Nineteen

They pulled down the driveway at exactly 9:50 A.M., drove slowly through the faces and signs and bodies and shouts from the crowd one more time, this time in Bennington Reed's shining Lincoln sedan, with Reed at the wheel and Father Mark sitting beside him. C.J., Lynn, and Joe were huddled in the rear. They were ten minutes ahead of schedule.

Two state police cruisers joined them in the street, positioning themselves in front and behind the Lincoln. In back of the second cruiser but in front of the slew of media vans and private hangers-on that rushed to stay in close pursuit, U.S. Deputy Marshal Paul Curry and Captain Shuler hung tight in their gray Ford Taurus with government plates.

Reed was his buoyant self again, smiling, highly enthused, and impeccably dressed. The blue of his suit was so dark it was nearly black, his light-blue shirt splashed with the bright yellow shout of a wide silk tie, like a man expecting pictures to be taken.

The others were dressed much more casually, especially C.J. in his jeans and favorite Detroit Red Wings cap, fiery red, and Lynn in her usual jeans and a yellow, button-down oxford shirt, like a mother and son who couldn't care less what pictures were taken.

As they eased away and moved slowly down the crowded street, Lynn read the look of concern in C.J.'s eyes and made up her mind to keep the atmosphere in the car positive. But the crowd that could be so easily blurred at a distance was once again just five feet from her window. No more blur. One more time, just a suffocating line of individual pains and agonizing appeals, row after row of them.

She tried to look straight ahead, and to keep C.J. looking straight ahead, but a young mother with dark hair caught her attention by bursting from the right side of the road. She rushed toward the car with anguish in her eyes and a young girl held tight by the hand, the girl being pulled as the woman ran calling at Lynn and waving, a little, dark-haired girl with her mother's eyes, two or three years younger than C.J. and wearing a white dress, like a First Communion dress, of all things.

Lynn winced. She tried to look away but couldn't. She wondered if it was the woman's husband who had died. Or another child. Or maybe it was this little girl in her special dress who was not yet dead but was dying from cancer or some other terrible disease. And it was then, as the car kept moving and the woman and the girl in the white Communion dress faded into the back window, that the pain of who she was and what she was doing suddenly threatened to overpower Lynn.

It wasn't the pain of seeing a mother with her anguish. And it wasn't the little girl, looking so scared. It was Lynn's knowing with such terrible certainty that C.J. could very probably, in fact, heal them all, and do it in a single hour, no more. She knew that. But at the same time, something deep inside her remained absolutely convinced that in that one hour pause for healing, she would be throwing C.J. into such a free fall of demand-and-response that she would lose any and all control over whatever would happen to him next, and she would never get it back.

She swallowed hard and closed her eyes.

"We should have left before sunrise", she said. "We should have gone in the middle of the night."

In the cordoned-off area of St. Paul Hospital's north parking lot a crowd had already formed, spurred initially by news leaks from the hospital medical staff about C.J.'s coming, and most recently by the live coverage from the two news helicopters and string of vehicles that tracked the entourage from Royal Oak to Eastpointe, which used to be called East Detroit.

Hundreds of people pressed together behind the flimsy, yellow tape of the police barriers. They were framed by rows of local video camera operators and press photographers. A single police helicopter closed in to thump in tight and hungry circles immediately overhead, the area's various news copters being kept at a safe distance.

But this crowd, they all noticed, was different than the crowd in Royal Oak. This crowd was not grim from long vigils or frustrated from petitioning so long for attention without response. In fact, they rose up cheering at the vehicle's entrance. Many of them looked ecstatic, smiling and laughing on tiptoes. Some were hugging one another. Some were teary-eyed and waving and calling out at the same time, like citizens of an occupied nation welcoming liberation.

That's when it struck Lynn, and she was horrified. "My God", she said. "They think we're here to start healing all the people in there!"

Joe shifted to the edge of the seat and moved closer to his window, trying to measure whether what Lynn had said could possibly be true.

C.J., seeing Lynn's eyes and hearing the sound of her voice, looked alarmed and sat bolt upright to stare at his mother, his eyes wide and demanding to know what was happening and why was it bad.

But Lynn didn't notice him. She was watching people cheering. She was trying not to think about how much longer she could go on brushing so close to people and not unleash the firestorm by telling C.J. to start healing them now.

Father Mark was watching C.J., his expression heavy with concern.

Reed, wide-eyed, was still smiling. He even said, "Extraordinary", one time, but softly. Then he looked embarrassed and cleared his throat and sat back, silent but still smiling.

Their vehicle eased past two state police cruisers and two Eastpointe police cruisers and pulled to a stop next to a black Chrysler sedan. Cardinal Schaenner lowered his back window and nodded to them with a smile. Monsignor Tennett leaned forward from beside the Cardinal with a smile and a raised hand of his own.

The crowd surged. The yellow tape snapped and broke, and the police rushed to circle the vehicles, shouting at the crowd to stay back.

"We should have come in the middle of the night", Lynn said again. This time showing that she was angry.

Two patrolmen moved with their captain to her side window. Deputy Curry and Captain Shuler had joined the police standing watch next to the limo, their eyes locked on the crowd.

Lynn lowered her window to speak with the officers. The shouts of the people nearest the cars grew louder. "What now?" she said, nearly yelling.

A middle-aged state police lieutenant leaned down to the open window, close enough to be heard over the crowd, and said loudly, "You can see the doctors right at the door, ma'am." He waved a thick finger toward the building entrance, just thirty feet away. "You won't have any problems at all. They have everything worked out."

When Lynn nodded, the trooper swung open the car door. The Cardinal's car door swung open at the same time, and the Cardinal and Monsignor quickly climbed out to join them. It was another signal for the crowd to press closer and for the cheers to escalate, only by this time the cries were even more noticeable than cheers. Now room numbers were being shouted out, numbers pleaded in short cries, each one louder than the one before, each competing for the Lazarus Boy's attention, and then the names of specific people.

As Lynn and C.J. jogged the few feet to the hospital entrance they heard the names of individual patients ring out above everything else, individual names in individual rooms, real people who had faces and husbands and wives and kids and diseases, their names shouted all at once, louder and louder.

Lynn felt C.J. squeezing her hand hard. She squeezed his hand back and realized again, even in the middle of the chaos—especially in the middle of the chaos—how very small her son's hand was in hers.

Inside the hospital, no patients were in sight. No visitors. No reporters. Just the blues of police officers and the whites and pale greens of the curious doctors and nurses and aides and medical technicians who were pressed together in doorways or clustered in eerie silence behind medical stations and at the ends of adjacent hallways where they stood on tiptoes and watched the group move with the hospital's director of medical services from the hospital entrance to the staff elevators and then up to the fifth-floor conference room, where the morning's schedule would be explained.

Joe excused himself. He said he was going to the men's room and would be back in five minutes, but for them to go ahead. He'd catch up.

No one cared that he left, he thought, which made him mad. They paused as he left, but went ahead like it did not make any difference to them at all. He heard them start up again as he walked out the door.

In the hall, he headed to his right, toward the elevators. He tried to look like he knew where he was going. He smiled a lot, but only at the people who looked like they recognized him.

No reporters, he noticed; the cops and hospital security were keeping them outside.

At the end of the hall, a doctor stepped out of the elevator with his name and photo on a large, plastic-covered badge clipped to his chest and a legal-sized clipboard in his hand. He glanced at Joe, glanced away, then looked back again, with a quizzical expression on his face, like he wanted to ask Joe if he was the father of C.J. Walker, because he was pretty sure he'd seen his picture on TV.

Joe spoke first. "Doctor Peters," he said, reading the man's nametag, "I'm looking for Intensive Care. Can you help me out?"

The doctor nodded, his expression quietly satisfied, like he knew he'd been right. The boy was here, on this floor, and this was his father, for sure. "One down from this one, on four, right below us", he said.

His eyes had lit up as he spoke though. Something going on. Why did the father of the Lazarus Boy need ICU?

Joe thanked him and headed quickly for the stairway across the hall. No need for an elevator to go one floor. The doctor, he noticed, entered the stairwell behind him, staying back, but following him.

He could feel his heart picking up speed. He breathed deeply and tried to keep his cool.

Into the hall on four. Looking. ICU to the right, twenty yards: two big doors, no glass or windows in them, a big sign telling what was behind the doors, saying "Authorized Persons Only". A metal plate was on the wall to the right, just before the doors, the switch to open them.

He pushed it and entered.

The doctor was in the hall behind him. Not to stop him, he was sure of that. Just to watch.

Let him watch.

Down the hall toward the nurses' station. Rooms to the right. People all hooked up to tubes and wires. None with visitors. Who looked worst? Carlyle, 441; Mitchell, 442. He'd have to remember the name of wherever he stopped, get the name and room number, then call back in a half hour, see what happened.

The nurse was coming at him, ready to ask questions.

Sunderville: 444. He would remember that. A woman, puffy, no hair. Cancer. No visitors. Monitors beeping. Looked like hell.

The nurse said, "Can I help you, sir?" The doctor was behind him, closing in. His heart kicking against his ribs.

He entered the room, put his hand on the woman's arm, and said it once, right out loud: "Be well, Mrs. Sunderville."

The briefing in the conference room ranged from an initial verbal review of C.J.'s health history based on his medical records, which had been delivered the evening before from his pediatrician's office and from Fremont Hospital, to proposals for lengthier and more involved explorations, including an ultrasound, MRI, and a CAT scan.

The doctors looked at papers and at C.J. and smiled. Names of tests were exchanged. Times were discussed. More smiles from the doctors. It would, they assured Lynn, be simply done, start to finish.

Joe came back, looking sullen.

C.J. didn't know exactly what some of the tests were, especially the ones with initials instead of names, but after fifteen minutes of the doctors talking with him and his mom and dad, they said they were ready to begin.

He stood up when they did. He stood close to Lynn. He tried not to show weakness, but as he looked at his mom his eyes filled with fear and with questions, each one beginning with a silent "Why?"

Lynn knew the question was there. She wondered if she still had an answer.

For more than fifteen minutes, while an ultrasound was tracing pictures of C.J.'s organs, Joe sat in a chair turned to face the window of the waiting room, his feet grinding into the baseboard. The Cardinal; his two priests, Father Mark and Monsignor Tennett; and Bennington Reed sat huddled next to the door, none of them talking, like they were patients themselves, waiting for results.

He had called ICU—twice—asking if there had been any change in Mrs. Sunderville's condition.

They all knew who was calling. They all knew what had happened. They all knew what had not happened, and told him. They were sorry. They'd been hoping, too.

He'd call again, he thought, in an hour or two. But not every ten minutes.

Then he thought, no, he wouldn't call again. He felt like an idiot. Nothing had happened, and he knew it. C.J. had it all; nothing for him.

He replayed his earlier arguments with Lynn and Kruger, went over them in bits and pieces, wondered what he should have done differently, and, not knowing, got mad all over again—the whole nine yards, like his frustration was a drug or something.

Time to move on to other things, he told himself. Time to move on to the one thing he could control for certain. Get a plan, no matter what happened, to sell the C.J. story for a screaming fortune.

Through the window, he watched the police helicopter circle north of the hospital one more time, painted all blue and gray, and reviewed what he'd tell the tabloids and other news sources when they made their offers. He'd turn down the first ones, for sure. And he'd just tell them that he's C.J. Walker's father. He's the man who discovered the power, single-handed. He's the guy who took the kid to the hospital both times, all by himself, and then arranged the whole Turner deal at the MacInnes' funeral home. He's the one person who made all of this possible; that's who he was.

Whatever they came with, he deserved more. His story had to be worth a ton.

Following the ultrasounds, a gray-haired woman from the hospital Community Affairs Office who wore a dark-gray suit with an ID card identifying her as a nun arranged to have ice cream, soda, cookies, and coffee brought to the physicians' conference room.

They were all invited to take a ten-minute break before moving C.J. into the heart of the hospital's new Imaging Unit.

Lynn touched C.J.'s arm and said, simply, "You're doing fine."

He stopped sipping from his can of Pepsi and pulled lightly at his mom's sleeve, urging her to bend down so he could whisper very close to her ear. When she did, he said, "What are they going to do now?"

"It's the 'imaging' we talked about, like X-rays", she said in a whisper of her own. "They call it an MRI, but it's just an X-ray."

"There must be some difference, or they wouldn't call it something else."

"It's not exactly the same", Lynn admitted, laying her hand on his arm. "It's kind of like it, but it takes different pictures. There's really not a lot to it."

A pause. C.J. thinking. "Different pictures of what?"

"Of how great you look." She grinned and ran her fingers through his hair. "Only it's in color. It's just different."

Joe was grinning at her when she looked up, but it was a grin without warmth. It was a thin curve under cold eyes, meant to deliver a message. Something like, after that little bit of dancing, I can't wait to see how you break it to him that a bunch of people twice his size are going to make him lie down like he's dead himself inside a little tunnel, like the barrel of a cannon, and not let him move again for a good hour.

Twenty

The march through the still-crowded halls to the Imaging Unit on the seventh floor of the north wing was an eerie procession—everyone watching; no one speaking. Footsteps slapping lightly against light-gray vinyl; monitors beeping in the background, their impersonal language rising and then falling as the group passed by with C. J. staring straight ahead, no longer holding Lynn's hand.

Inside the MRI room, two doctors and two special techs offered to show C. J. the MRI Unit itself. Lynn asked the others, with an especially cool glance at Joe, to wait in the nearby waiting room.

They had already told Lynn that, if she preferred, they could sedate C. J. "Just enough to take the edge off." But she didn't prefer. Now they explained together that, either way, the procedure was easy. "You can even listen to music," the youngest doctor said to C. J. with a smile, "and we'll just take forty-five minutes or so. How's that?"

C. J. bit his lip, looking angry, saying nothing, staring at the long, smooth machine and at the deep, white tunnel built into it, which he knew was for him.

The older of the two doctors tried again to portray the test in its best light, this time going down on one knee, his hand lightly on C. J.'s left arm. "That's not much longer than a TV show, forty-five minutes. Then you're on your way."

C. J. shot a surprised and disturbed glance at the doctor and reached to grab Lynn's wrist and lead her to the other side of the room. He felt panic. He pulled her close and whispered into her ear with sharp determination, "I'm not going to lie in that thing, Mom! Don't put me in there; that's bullshit!"

Lynn pulled back, her eyebrows raised. She stared at him. He had grabbed at the word and used it awkwardly simply to show her how serious he was. She knew it, and she got it, down deep. She didn't argue with him. Instead, she turned to the doctors and said pleasantly, "You know what? C. J. and I are going to have to talk about this by ourselves for just a minute. Would you make sure the changing room is still empty for us? I think it might be best if we talk in there."

The young doctor, on the way back down and across the hall, whispered to her again that modest sedation wasn't out of the ordinary, and that C.J. would be fine. "I'm sure that's true", she said, still with a smile. "Thanks."

They entered the changing room. Lynn shut the door. They were alone, only lockers down the middle, lockers down the left end, benches to the right, and a second door leading to another hallway at the far end of the room, on the right.

Lynn sat down on one of the low, green, padded benches. She said, "Well, what are you feeling, hon?" She smiled a soft and sad smile.

"You told me I wouldn't have to do anything I didn't want to do, Mom", he said. He had tears in his eyes. His tone softened, and his words were lilting, closer now to an appeal than a demand. "Why do I have to do this when you promised?" He reached out to hold her forearms. Small fingers, not yet a young man's, still just a child's, hanging on tight, looking hurt. His voice small and soft and hurting, too, like his eyes. "Would *you* want to? Would you go in that thing, especially when you know there's nothing wrong with you? They can't make me do anything they want, can they?"

The question struck Lynn hard. His look struck her hard. His fear struck her hard, and her attempt at a smile faded.

C.J. said again, softer than before, his head tilting slightly to the left, now surprising his mother with even more tears: "You *promised*, Mom!"

Lynn lowered her eyes and stared at the floor. She thought about why she was letting her nine-year-old be poked and questioned and chased when he didn't want any part of it. Did she, really? She thought about it all over again, and she thought, too, about what Joe had said about the boy's already being owned by someone else. In custody, Joe had said; she and C.J. already in custody, and she was too stupid to realize it.

What am I making him go through all this for? she thought. Is it really for C.J.? Or is it really for them? "Oh God", she whispered. Her hand was over her eyes. Her head was bowed.

C.J. watched without asking what she was thinking.

Then she raised her head sharply, stared into her son's eyes, reached to hold him by his shoulders, and said in a hard and quiet voice, "Let's get out of here, C.J."

His eyes widened. "You mean out of the test with the white thing? Or do you mean, 'Let's get out of the hospital', like we're done and we can go now?"

"I mean this might have been a mistake. I thought it might show us some things that would be important, but I think I made a mistake, and I'm sorry. So I mean ... let's just walk away. You and me. Right now."

C.J. blinked. He started to speak and blinked again and said, "Just you and me?"

"Just keep up with me", she said. She leveled her gaze, making sure he was listening. "Keep up with me, honey, no matter what happens. And don't stop unless I do, no matter what anybody says to you. Is that a promise?"

C.J. gripped his lips tight and nodded. Then he took her outstretched hand and pulled her abruptly toward the door.

"Not that door", she said. She could feel her heart racing. "The other one, in the back of the room. It leads to a different hall."

They hustled past the lockers to the alternate door and, for just a moment, stood ready, Lynn's hand resting on the door's long, silver handle. She turned the handle quietly and opened the door just a half inch, listening and watching. No sound. No one there that she could see. Everyone gathered back down the hall and around the corner, waiting for C.J. to make his exit on his way back to MRI.

She nodded to him, and he nodded back, confirming their pact.

C.J. whispered, now with a nervous grin, "This is so cool", and with that, Lynn swung open the door, and they stepped out quickly and quietly to start down the hall toward the main body of the building, away from the Imaging Unit.

Twenty yards down the hall. No patients' rooms, not in this hall. And still no one in sight.

She felt exhilarated; scared but not scared, her heart pounding, the feel of C.J. close by her, squeezing her hand. She realized that she didn't have the slightest instinct to turn around and go back. Thirty yards. Lunch time, she thought, people breaking for lunch, not so many of them walking around just now.

They reached a new corridor and turned right. No shouts behind them. No one chasing them. But there were people in this corridor, and they were looking up, looking at her and C.J.

Lynn wasn't smiling anymore. Her breath was suddenly coming in urgent bursts.

Several staff members seemed to recognize them and stepped aside, startled and confused. One asked if they needed help, but Lynn forced a wooden smile, and they kept on going. Forty yards. Nearly out of the north wing. Nearly to the main, crossing corridor.

Suddenly there were voices behind them, calling from all the way back in the heart of the Imaging Unit, startled voices suddenly yelling that they were going the wrong way.

C.J. looked up at Lynn. He was still cool, still determined, not looking back, keeping his promise.

Lynn didn't look down. She put her hand behind his shoulder and urged him forward, whispering to him that they were going all the way.

They turned the corner into the next hall, again moving right, now back into what she believed must be the main body of the hospital. C.J. broke into a jog. Lynn was walking that fast.

A doctor moved in front of them and reached out his hand, wanting to slow them down. Then he recognized them. Before he could speak, they shoved past him, Lynn saying, "Bathroom? Up this hall?"

The doctor, startled, just stared. A nurse passing by looked alarmed and said, pointing, "There's a restroom back that other way, ma'am." Another nurse called out, "Can we help you?" and Lynn heard a different voice, a man's voice from farther behind them, say, "It's C.J. Walker, and something's wrong!"

She said, "Stay with me", to C.J. and broke into a slow jog. They rushed past carts of food and carts with monitors and patients walking with IVs. They ran because there were other voices now from much farther back, voices they had left in the main unit but that were now chasing them, just rounding the last corner and insisting that someone stop them, please! But no one did.

Both of them were running, Lynn starting to breathe harder and neither of them slowing down and neither of them looking back, and now, footsteps, still far behind them but slapping fast and hard, someone breaking into a run and someone shouting in anger, "Please, stop them!"

They were at a staircase. Lynn pulled C.J. through the door. They raced down the stairs as medical staff members moved into the doorway above them to cluster and gawk, watching them and asking again what was wrong, but blocking the way of Curry and Captain Shuler and the police and the others who had to wrestle their way through before they could lunge down the stairs in pursuit.

They burst through the doorway on the fifth floor and were racing to the center of the building and the elevators, now with a new cast of worried staff and startled patients looking on and asking loud questions. They were recognized. The cry went out. People reached for them and called after them, asking where they were going and what was wrong and what they could do to help, but no one dared to stop them. Several nurses grabbed phones to call security, afraid of the worst, whatever the worst might be. One young doctor jogged behind them, keeping up, offering help but not trying to stop them.

They kept running. Down the white hall, Lynn praying, "C'mon God. C'mon God . . ." Old habits. Old reactions.

The police and federal marshals burst through the door of the staircase far behind them. Hard shouts of hard pursuit rang down the antiseptic hall. The doctor that was running behind them stopped and wheeled to face their pursuers, startled at the violence in their voices.

Lynn saw that one of the staff elevator doors was about to close, the elevator heading down with just one orderly in it, alone with an empty stretcher. She breathed a quick, "Go!" and she and C.J. bolted through the door, letting it shut behind them.

Joe heard a voice cry out and bolted from his seat to elbow his way past the Cardinal and the others and charge first into the hallway. Somebody scared. Somebody shouting where no one should be shouting. Something bad happening to C.J.

In the hallway, people were walking too fast, and two policemen were hustling into the men's changing room where C.J. should have been, while others, police officers and medical staff alike, scrambled down the hallway that led away from them thirty feet to Joe's right, on the far side of the changing room.

He noticed an elderly nurse standing in the hall, rigid as a statue, back against the wall, hands at her side, her expression one of alarm. He shouted to her, "What the hell's happening?" But he didn't wait for an answer. He rushed into the changing room as four more shouts rang out from the hallway, almost simultaneously.

"Where are they going?" "The mother and the boy!" "What's she doing?" And from farther away, around the corner, "They're running out of the unit!"

In the changing room, Joe saw two doctors watching the policemen who had entered in front of him charge out the back door, into the far hallway. Neither of the doctors moved. They didn't even turn to look at Joe, who had stopped, frozen, thinking, understanding what was happening, the whole picture hitting him like a thunderclap, realizing that he was the only one among them who got it that Lynn was leaving the hospital. She was heading outside, trying to get away with C.J., something they didn't know yet, but he did.

She drove him crazy, the way she did things. She wouldn't sit down and plan it out with him. She would hold on and try to play by the book way too long, and then, when C.J. said just the right thing, or if he cried, or if somebody jerked him around and she didn't like it, she'd just say "the hell with this" and grab him and bolt, not even stopping to think.

But she was trying to get away, sure as anything. Just running, no place to go. And the place she'd be running to first, Joe felt sure, would be the farthest exit from where they'd come in.

Lynn gasped for breath and tried to smile at the startled orderly. She said, "Wrong elevator. Sorry. We're not staff." But the orderly wasn't paying attention. He was staring at C.J. blankly, wondering if it was really "him".

The floor lights blinked over the door. Four ... three ... Suddenly Lynn slammed her thumb into the button marked 2, catching it just in time. The car stopped. The door opened. She pulled at C.J.'s arm and they hustled into the hall. "They'll be going for the elevators down-stairs", she said. She started running down the hall to the right again, away from the north wing. "We'll go to the other end of the building and down the stairs."

They were jogging down a wide, carpeted hall past rows of office doors in a department marked "Hospital Administration". They went past a receptionist who didn't seem to recognize them and asked them to stop and picked up a phone when they didn't. They made it all the way down the hall and nearly to the staircase at the far end before two secretaries just back from lunch saw and recognized them. One of them yelped and cried, "Oh my God!" and pointed, but Lynn and C.J. had reached the stairs they needed and were already going through the door, charging toward the first floor and the south exit.

"Where do we go when we get downstairs?" C.J. cried out, his voice bouncing off the walls and ringing loudly up the staircase.

"I told you", Lynn said in short breaths. "Gonna take a walk. See what happens."

"Cripe, Mom!" C.J. laughed nervously and loudly, just once. Nothing more.

Main floor. "Okay!" Lynn said sharply. She reached her arm across C.J.'s chest to stop him; then she peered through the small, glass insert into the south lobby. They were just twenty feet from the outside exit. She could see people walking in and out as though nothing was going on. She couldn't see any police rushing to take up positions or marshals setting up exit blocks.

She turned and bent down to hold C.J.'s face in her hands, terrified that she'd hear the slam of a stairwell door just one or two floors above them and the tumble of feet overhead. She said, speaking very quickly, "Walk fast now, hon."

"Okay." He nodded hard.

"But don't run and don't look up at people."

"Okay."

"Just stare at the ground and keep walking, right beside me."

"Okay."

"Okay?"

He nodded one more time.

She took a deep breath and shoved the door open.

Joe took the stairs as fast as he could, hand on the rail, feet flying, jumping down the last three stairs at every level, trying to make sure of his directions, planning which way he had to turn once he got to the ground floor, wishing that when he hit the lobby he could break into a flat-out run but knowing he wouldn't be able to do that. Walk fast, he told himself. Walk fast and look natural. Look at his watch a lot. Look like a guy missing an operation on a relative, or an important phone call. Into the lobby. To the right, past the elevators, quickly. Police were in the lobby behind him, moving in the same direction, but when Joe glanced back he saw them stop at the elevators. They stopped and waited, radios squawking.

He called, "South lobby?" to an information aide at the counter forty yards past the elevators, not even stopping for her answer, just looking at her as he hurried by.

"Turn right in the main lobby and watch the signs", she said, pointing in the direction he was going.

Stepping up to a slow jog, looking at his watch, he was saying out loud, "Oh boy, look at that", as he rushed past three doctors in scrubs.

Into the main lobby. A policeman standing alone by the elevators. No, not a policeman; hospital security. Watching but not seeing. The police weren't there yet. The security guard looking at Joe. Joe looking at his watch again, ready to say, "Oh boy, look at the time", then figuring, skip it; not for a security guard. Listening to his heart hammer. Listening for shouts. Noticing, at the last second, two policemen, real ones now, coming in fast from outside like they knew what was going on.

He moved quickly through the lobby and down the south corridor, knowing Lynn and C.J. would be there, heading for that same exit. Knowing that for just a few seconds, maybe even for a few minutes if he really got lucky, they'd be there together, just him and them.

And then he saw her, all the way at the end of the corridor, breaking out of the staircase door bold as hell, heading for the exit, C.J. tight by her side.

Finally, he broke into a run.

The heavyset man in the dark-brown suit knew it was Joe as soon as he saw him moving across the lobby looking at his watch like he was scared, looking like he wanted to move faster but was holding back, looking around to see if he was being followed. He recognized him from the night he and Carl were there with Torrie Kruger in Joe's apartment. He and Carl no more than six feet away from him when the guy took Mr. Cross' money and gave Kruger the contract; the same one he told Kruger this morning that he was going to break. Cross' kid dying now, and just like that, the guy thinks he's breaking the contract.

The man jerked around to follow Joe, moving in an easy, rolling rhythm, like a bear, his phone already in his hand, his wide fingers already punching in numbers.

When he turned the corner into the south corridor he stopped and hunched his shoulders, turning around to muffle his voice as he spoke into the phone. "Kruger, the kid's father is heading for the south exit right now, walkin' fast and lookin' scared. He's alone, but cops just showed up in the lobby. Something's happening." He paused, checking Joe, his left hand still muzzling the phone. Then he raised his head and said, right out loud, "Get the car to the south exit! He's running!"

Three people were moving through the revolving door ten feet in front of Lynn, one coming in, two going out, but there were no police and no one who looked like they were hunting for them, although Lynn didn't dare look back up the corridor, back toward the center of the building where the elevators were being checked, and by now the stairwells, too.

Ten feet. Her heart racing. Her breath straining. C.J.'s hand hot in hers. Almost there.

Then a shout, sudden and shrill, from right beside them, not four feet away: "It's him!"

Every eye flicked to capture them.

She was two feet from the door. She let out a small sound and pulled hard on C.J., both of them rushing into the gap, Lynn pushing hard on the bar protecting the revolving door's glass.

"Mom!" C.J. cried.

Lynn didn't answer him.

They were outside.

A woman on the sidewalk was pointing at them, shouting the news to others.

The woman who had shouted first was hard on their heels, through the door behind them, and now reaching out to grab Lynn by the arm and shout, "Please!"

Lynn pulled away, muttering apologies.

"Please!" the woman said again, loudly, sounding desperate. "My father's in oncology on three!"

Lynn felt the panic rise in her chest, squeezing her breath, hammering as fast as her heartbeat. She glanced at the woman and said breathlessly, "I'm sorry", but she kept going, sliding C.J. along the building to the right. She said, "I'm sorry", again, even louder and then said it again, a third time, as she saw the crowd gathering, all looking, some running, many of them shouting.

The woman who was trying to tell Lynn about her father on the third floor reached again, sputtering and crying, to grab Lynn's arm.

"Mom!" C.J. tried to step between Lynn and the woman, trying to protect his mother, but she pulled him back to her side and tried to cut toward the road.

The woman's eyes were moving back and forth from Lynn to C.J., not sure where to settle, not sure whom to appeal to. "Please!" she said again, this time sharply and very loud. "It will just take you two minutes, for God's sake! He's dying!"

C.J. was watching Lynn's expression, frightened, waiting for a cue, not sure what to do.

Lynn said it loudly: "I'm sorry! Please let us get through!" But the crowd was louder than she was, and just as desperate, and had already closed around them in a tightening circle of eyes and hands and desperate appeals. "It's him!" "Oh my God!" "Please!" "The Pediatric Unit!" "It's the Lazarus Boy!" "My mother!" "My son!" "Oh, please, help me!"

C.J. was terrified. Lynn held him tighter and shouted again to let them by. Desperate hands were reaching out to grab her, insisting that attention be paid.

An old man with tears in his eyes pulled at C.J., but Lynn wheeled sideways and knocked the man's withered hand away, shouting, "No!"

C.J. heard the panic in his mother's voice and pressed even tighter into her side, and then he was shouting, too.

And Joe was shouting. All of a sudden, Joe was shouting, from very nearby, "Lynn! Lynn!"

"Joe!" She turned toward his voice and saw the people closest to her, on her left, including the old man who had reached to grab C.J., pulled suddenly backward and shoved to one side, and she saw Joe picking C.J. up and holding him chest to chest, and C.J. was shouting, "Dad! Get us out of here!"

Joe grabbed Lynn with his free hand and pulled her closer and shouted, jerking his head toward the road, "This way, Lynn! It's okay!" And then, shouting to the crowd as loudly and as threateningly as he could, he said, "The boy's sick himself! Now get out of our way, or I'll hurt you people, so help me God!"

Marshal Curry and Captain Shuler, as well as the state and the Eastpointe police, had been slow. They decided that something had frightened Lynn and C.J., and had rushed to follow them, and to cover the nearby elevators and stairwells, but they wasted several precious minutes before putting out an alert to close off the hospital exits, as well. As a result, when their radios crackled with alerts about a commotion involving the boy and his mother outside the south exit, they had most of the hospital to travel.

They did it running, radios in hand, as officers in cruisers with red and blue lights flashing and sirens wailing scrambled to circle the roadways outside the building and close in on the south wing.

A dusty, tan station wagon was moving slowly because of the crowd and the commotion, so when Joe jumped in front of it with C.J. in his arms, the old man at the wheel stopped abruptly. But he quickly rolled his window up as he saw Joe running around to reach for his door.

The door was locked.

"I'll give you twenty thousand dollars for your car!" Joe shouted, pulling at the driver's door one more time. "This is the Lazarus Boy, and I need your car!"

The old man, his eyes desperate and wide and suddenly on the verge of panic, protested by blowing his horn and trying to inch his way through the dozens of people that had suddenly rushed his car without his knowing why. But he didn't want to hit them. He stopped again, still blowing his horn in short bursts as he shot feeble glances at the crazy man who was now pressing even closer to his window and who was now threatening him, shouting, "He can kill you if you don't open this door! Do you realize that?"

C.J. looked up, freshly startled.

There were gasps from the crowd, and those closest to C.J. pulled back. But more people had run from the hospital and the parking lot to join them, and there was little room to move.

"Joe!" Lynn shouted. She saw C.J., tucked between them, now crying, gripping Joe's shirt. She pulled at Joe's arm. "Stop it!"

Suddenly there was another horn blaring, and a black Lincoln Continental bullied its way toward them, through the alarmed crowd to their right. Its aggressiveness gave rise to loud and angry shouts as jostled spectators protested being shoved aside. Some even slammed their hands into the Lincoln's doors and fenders, as if slapping the beast would grind it to a halt. But the Lincoln only veered over the curb on the left side of the roadway, causing even more people to shout and scatter, as it pulled even with the station wagon.

When the two doors on the passenger side of the Lincoln opened, a voice that Joe recognized shouted, "Let us through!" and Torrie Kruger was there, putting his arm around Lynn's shoulder and saying, "This way, Mrs. Walker. We can help. Into the car, please."

Lynn pulled away from him. C.J. did, too. Pressing even tighter against Joe, the boy looked up at his dad for a signal of how dangerous this new man would be.

But Joe shouted, "Yes!" He took Lynn's right arm with his free hand, and, with C.J. still clinging to his side, he rushed toward the open doors of the Lincoln. "Lynn, yes!" he said loudly, grinning. "I swear to God, it's okay now! Do it! Go back now, and they'll take him away from you for sure!"

Lynn moved slowly at first, but she watched Joe and heard "take him away from you", and she pushed to go faster.

The crowd was straining for a better look. The old man in the station wagon opened his window several safe inches and stared. Two men were inside the Lincoln, a driver plus a man in the back who had slid to the far side of the seat, giving Lynn, C.J., and Joe room to get in. The man in the back was heavyset, in a dark-brown suit. He gestured them in with a fat hand, calling, "It's okay, Mrs. Walker! We know Joe!"

A siren whooped from near the hospital, and Lynn turned, startled.

Suddenly there was a loud thumping overhead, a helicopter swooping in fast from the far side of the building.

Lynn whispered, "Oh God", and as she said it, the first police siren was joined by another, both wailing louder as the police cruisers started separating the crowd at the corner of the building, moving closer. A voice suddenly boomed from a speaker on one of the approaching cruisers: "Clear the way! Clear the way!"

Joe said, "Please, Lynn, they're coming!" and she lurched into the car, into the back seat, into the side of the man that she didn't even know but that Joe knew, with C.J. right behind her and Joe behind him.

The man who had approached her in the roadway jumped into the front passenger seat. The car was moving before his doors slammed, not down the road, but hard over the curb and into the crowd with its horn blaring as people screamed and cursed and scattered all over again. Then it veered west to tear two dark semicircles in the neatly manicured hospital lawn between the hospital's south wing and the cancer-care center. From there it powered its way to the far edge of the property and onto the roadway leading toward an eight-lane street that ran directly to the eastern edge of Detroit's busy downtown area.

Twenty-One

C.J. had twisted backward and was looking out the back window as the Lincoln lurched over the sidewalk to race wildly south toward the massive structures of the Covington Towers, twin, twenty-story office buildings joined in the middle by a parking garage built over the entrance drive and covered for fifty yards by a thick canopy.

It was, the driver knew, just sixty seconds away. At these speeds, less.

Two approaching cars slammed to a stop to avoid a collision. A white delivery van peeled sharply right, getting out of the Lincoln's way. C.J. squirmed sideways, now looking out the front window as the distance closed between them and the building up ahead.

Torrie Kruger was speaking on his phone, giving their location, making demands.

"Who are they, Joe?" Lynn demanded, panic in her voice.

Joe didn't answer. He was staring at Kruger, trying to make out what he was saying up front.

One of the men behind Lynn called out, "Chopper coming over the hospital!" But it was something they already knew; the thut-thut-thut was loud enough even at its present distance that they couldn't miss it.

Kruger shoved the phone at the driver and said, "Andretti." The driver took the phone and listened for just two seconds, then tossed the phone in Torrie's lap and swerved up and onto the empty sidewalk. He said, "Good to go, but it's a horse race!" They were approaching the Towers' parking garage.

The pounding of the helicopter softened as apartment buildings rose up behind them and on their right, forcing the chopper higher. But a second one was already coming over the hospital.

The car suddenly veered back into the roadway, slowed sharply, and took a hard left into the Towers' west pick-up parking area, where it veered left again and skidded to a stop under a long customer weather canopy. Lynn saw a dark-maroon van with no side windows parked under the canopy no more than fifteen yards away from them. Its doors flung open as Joe shouted to her, "They want to take him from you, Lynn! This is the best thing could've happened!"

Kruger was shouting, "Into the van! Fast!"

She hesitated to move with C.J. for a precious two seconds, but in that single moment, in the breadth of those few seconds, the recognition shot through her that maybe this was the best thing that could have happened: Cross owing C.J. for the life of his son!

And suddenly she moved, and she was fast. She grabbed what she realized could be the only chance she'd ever have again. She said a quick, "Hurry!" to C.J. and jumped out of the car with him, still holding his hand, and rushed him into the van that lurched away from the curb as soon as the door was pulled shut behind her and Kruger jumped into his front passenger seat and slammed his door behind him.

She was realizing, it isn't the money! It's what a father or mother is willing to do to keep their only child safe and still with them!

Cardinal Schaenner, with Father Mark, Monsignor Tennett, and Mr. Reed at his side, had watched two police cars and the federal marshals roar out of the north parking lot to join the chase after C.J. The crowd behind them was louder than ever, now calling questions to the police and clergy alike. Reporters badgered officers to give them inside information and to let them get nearer to the Cardinal and the others.

The sergeant monitoring calls in the nearest police cruiser confirmed to Monsignor Tennett that the lieutenant in charge would be along in a matter of seconds. The state police, he said, were still in charge of the operation, and the lieutenant would be personally in charge of the pursuit.

The Monsignor thanked the officer and reported what he'd said to the Cardinal, who announced his intention to wait there, at the door, for the lieutenant. "He's still in charge of the pursuit," Tennett said to the others, "but the FBI will be called in to help now. Anything involving a potential kidnapping across state lines or out of the country, and with us being just a few miles across the lake from Canada, they're called in automatically. If they don't establish a kidnapping, they'll just be there to help. And in this case, with the victim being C.J. Walker, I guarantee you, they're on their way already."

The Cardinal nodded his agreement but said nothing. They were just outside the glass door of the hospital. He fidgeted with his chin, glanced at his watch, looked again through the door to the lobby, which was bustling with staff and police, but no police lieutenant, and he began to pace. He said to Father Mark, who happened to be nearest to him at the time, "How long do you think they can avoid capture in broad daylight with helicopters overhead?"

Two members of the medical staff opened the door, nodded at the clergymen, looked at the crowd, said something to one another, suddenly smiling, and went back inside.

"They've probably got them already", the Monsignor said.

"I'm sure the boy will be okay", Reed added, although they knew he wasn't sure at all.

The Cardinal eyed the door again. Still no police lieutenant. His eyes, usually so full of cheerful welcome, had turned as dark as a Doberman's. "The question isn't, will they be caught?" he said. "It's, what will they do with them once they catch them? If it is a kidnapping, and I have to believe it is, will that hand the government the provocation it needs to take the boy into protective custody or whatever they'll call it immediately, this afternoon, with no more said about it—that's the question."

The idea made him feel physically ill. He stopped pacing and tried to collect his thoughts. When the lieutenant appeared, he would have to be ready.

He didn't know if C.J. had been kidnapped. He didn't know what he could do to get him back if he had been. All he knew was, when they found him, he had to be present. He had to be there, to try and preempt any government action. He had to be there, and he had to be ready to weigh in with whatever authority his position as pastor of the Roman Catholic Archdiocese of Detroit would bring to bear. If he did not do this one thing well, he realized, he might never see C.J. Walker face-to-face again.

With Father Mark standing beside him, and Monsignor Tennett and Bennington Reed and then the police and reporters and the crowd behind him, the Cardinal thought about the now-faint sounds of the distant helicopters. He considered that C.J. and Lynn were somewhere beneath that sound. He noticed the sirens sounding in the same distance, knowing that their wail was being heard by C.J. at the same time. He heard the bark of police radios from the cruisers nearby, and he continued to watch the hospital's exit. He did all of that, but most of all he prayed over and over again, in whispers and in anguished thoughts, that he not be allowed to lose so easily the most profound opportunity for bearing witness to the presence of God that would ever be placed in his care, ever, in all of his lifetime.

The stakes were that great to him. The situation that critical.

Suddenly the hospital doors banged open, and the lieutenant rushed out, followed by two other officers. He was a tall man in his early fifties. His barrel chest and broad shoulders were put on stage by his gold-buttoned and insignia dark-blue uniform. His hair, eyes, eyebrows, and

mustache were all thick and black, which gave him a hard and dangerous look, like a warrior. He glanced at the clergymen as he passed by
them but made no gesture of recognition. He was clearly heading for his
police cruiser, and he was clearly in a hurry.

Something had happened; the Cardinal knew it.

He signaled for Father Mark to stay with him and just as quickly
whispered to the Monsignor and Reed to go back to his residence in his
own car and wait for him there.

Monsignor Tennett nodded, but Reed flushed and said, "But I can
help. I know the police ..."

The Cardinal waved him off with a sharp "Not this time, Ben" and
hurried to match the determined strides of the uniformed man in charge,
with Father Mark hard on his heels.

Two more sirens wailed at the corner of the hospital.

The crowd pressed tighter to the barriers. The questions and other
appeals for attention rose like a single shout.

"Lieutenant," the Cardinal said loudly, already starting to breathe
hard, "I'm Cardinal Schaenner, and this is the boy's pastor."

The lieutenant turned and looked at him but didn't slow down and
didn't answer. The Cardinal heard an officer's radio squawk C.J.'s suspected location: Covington Towers. Units closing in.

His heart was racing. "If you need an intermediary of some kind, we
can offer valuable assistance", he said more loudly than before, walking
faster just to keep up. "You may be in a hostage situation, something
where negotiations might be critical. However, we can help."

At the words "hostage situation", the lieutenant eased his pace and
turned his head to show that he was listening.

"No one outside the boy's family knows him well," the Cardinal
continued, "but his pastor, here, knows him very well. Like no one else
you have. And believe me, no one is likely to have more influence on
his parents, and possibly on others that may be involved in this, than
myself, as a Cardinal representing not only the diocese but the Church."

The lieutenant was at his car door, his fingers wrapped around its
handle. His driving trooper was already jumping in the driver's side. He
said, "If we get into negotiations, you may be in harm's way."

"We're willing to do whatever might help", the Cardinal assured
him.

The lieutenant nodded firmly one time. "I appreciate the offer", he
said. He turned to a second trooper that had come up behind them.
"Take the Cardinal and Father, here, with you and Sergeant Davis", he
said, "and stay close. Don't take any chances, but stay close and have

them ready to intervene if we call on them." As he jumped in his cruiser and slammed the door, he barked, "Don't make me look for you a half a mile away."

The panel van carrying C.J. and his parents pulled away from the cover of Covington Towers and onto eight-lane Gratiot Boulevard heading toward I-94 just forty seconds before the first helicopter arrived and eighty seconds before the first police cruiser arrived.

Two new men sat like guards in thickly padded captain's chairs positioned at the two back corners of the customized interior, watching Joe, Lynn, and C.J., who sat together on the left side of the van, on one of the two equally well-padded bench seats along the van's two sides. The bench on the right side stayed empty. Two small lamps with shades provided soft light, which was helpful since there were no side windows. A wooden table with holes cut for glasses had been folded out from the console behind the driver's chair. The radio was on police band, turned down low. The driver was monitoring it, just in case.

Kruger turned in his seat and introduced himself by name as soon as they were dropping down into traffic on I-94 and while the sirens still sounded behind them, although now faintly and at a growing distance. He smiled and thanked Lynn for her willingness to come along. He even reached to shake Lynn's and C.J.'s hands. He didn't shake with Joe; he just nodded, his smile quick and wooden.

He didn't offer names for the other men, either, and they didn't offer any for themselves. Their expressions were professionally composed. They each had their hands clasped between slightly spread knees, like it was a position they'd been trained to assume.

So the others didn't matter, Lynn realized. Kruger was the one who mattered. She shifted in her seat to face him more directly, her right arm still around C.J.

The van swooped into a slow turn, and Lynn looked out the front windshield to see where they were. She saw an "I-75, 4 Miles" sign and guessed they'd take it to be heading north again, back in the direction of somewhere north of Royal Oak and their home.

Kruger kept talking, sounding cordial—lawyer-cordial. He repeated his expectation that any "misunderstandings" would be cleared up, and told Lynn that he was a personal attorney employed by Mr. Anthony Cross of Shandise, New York. He even presented her with his card. "Or did your husband tell you all this already?" he asked, without looking at Joe.

She took his card and slipped it into her jeans pocket unread. "I know about Mr. Cross", she said, "and his son's problem. He wrote a letter, which I saw. I know you're the contact for him. I know about a hundred thousand dollars, and an offer for what I understand is five million more if the boy is brought back to health. If there's something else that Joe didn't tell me, or if any of this isn't accurate, I expect you'll tell me now." Then, without pausing, she turned to C.J. and continued, "These men know a man named Mr. Cross whose son is dying, honey. Mr. Cross wants to pay us to say your prayer over him and make him better."

C.J. stared at her for a moment, but as he was about to speak Lynn raised her hand to check him. "We're just going to talk about it with these men, is all", she said.

C.J. nodded, "Okay."

Joe watched and listened, hands clasped between spread knees, just like the others, only he was leaning farther forward and looking more intense.

"You didn't mention the contract," Kruger said, "but you have the main elements. The only thing is," he added, his voice dropping slightly, "the situation has changed as of this morning."

Joe's eyebrows shot to attention. "How so, changed?"

Kruger said it flatly, no emotion. "Anthony Junior died this morning—10:10, eastern time."

There was silence. Lynn said a soft, "I'm sorry", and went silent again. She needed a moment to think, to assess how the boy's death would impact whatever might happen next. If nothing else, she thought, it will make Cross, and that means these men that he hired to bring her to New York, a little more desperate than before. No, not just a little more desperate, probably a lot more desperate. "Which means it's decision time", she said softly.

Kruger said, "It's time to honor the contract, yes."

"So tell me this", she said. "Without discounting how much he must be grieving, which I accept and I'm sorry for, is Mr. Cross in the business of kidnapping?"

Kruger didn't answer. He studied her. His eyes narrowed.

Joe shifted in his seat and said, "Easy, hon. Let's just talk. Misunderstandings, remember?"

She added, "Are you Torrie Kruger? These your friends?"

She noticed two of the men stir—hardly noticeable, but there. She wondered if Kruger ever squirmed, even a little.

He didn't seem to. He said, "All Mr. Cross wants is for your boy to save his boy. What is it about that that you find hard to understand? Or what part of this is hard for you to understand: the man offered you a whole lot of money in good faith, and even put a hundred thousand dollars extra into your hands, which you accepted ..."

"Which my ex-husband accepted."

"And it was cash", Kruger continued without missing a beat. "A hundred thousand delivered and received in good faith. You don't really blame Mr. Cross because Joe here was the first one to actually touch your money."

C.J. glanced at Joe, who remained silent.

Lynn closed her eyes slowly. No, she couldn't blame Cross.

Kruger's voice was rising. "And, understanding that there's a lot involved, Mr. Cross asks for and receives a signed contract, again, all in good faith. A contract signed, to the best of his knowledge, and ours, by you, as well as your ex. So what does he expect now? He expects delivery. Good faith. That's how simple it is, Mrs. Walker. So don't talk to us about kidnapping, please."

"You're telling me you want to take a nine-year-old across state lines against his will, and you don't want me to talk about kidnapping?"

Kruger glared at her. Slowly, he thrust out his finger, keeping it low, chest-high. "As of 10:10 this morning, Mrs. Walker, no is not an option."

Lynn let him glare for a long moment, then said, "Actually, I'm not sure I'm saying no." It was almost a whisper, like something confidential between her and Kruger.

Joe held his breath.

Kruger leaned back. He studied her again. He nodded and said, "That's good." His expression relaxed, and he said it a second time: "That's good."

"I only bring up kidnapping to give you a second reason why you should forget trying to put us on your plane."

"What?" Kruger leaned forward again, hands sliding into the approved position.

Lynn eased her arm from around C.J.'s back and leaned forward herself. She clasped her hands, too, staring at Kruger. She said, "The other reason is, we're not getting on your plane, period. We're not getting on your plane because planes can land anywhere. We get on your plane, and you can land us in Saudi Arabia or the Sudan or wherever you want to sell us, for all I know. I don't even know if there is a Cross, or a dead boy. I saw a letter. What is that? Do you really think I'm going to let you put my son on your plane?"

"That's not up to you", Kruger whispered coldly. "That's up to Mr. Cross. And you, Mrs. Walker, are going to live with it."

Lynn's jaw set under hard and narrowed eyes. She said it calmly, but louder than she'd spoken before: "It's not up to Mr. Cross. It's up to me and my son. Everything we do is up to me and C.J. And you, Mr. Kruger, are going to live with it."

Kruger shook his head slowly. His lips twisted in the beginnings of a smile. "That contract is going to be our protection against any 'kidnapping' bullshit", he said.

Lynn snapped, "Watch how you talk in front of my son."

He stared hard at her for a moment, then glanced as C.J. just as quickly came back to her. "What we're willing to bet", he said, "is that when you see you're not in Saudi Arabia or whatever, and you've got Mr. Cross handing you five million dollars—that is, if your son can really do what you say he can do—you'll be happy as a clam. You won't be running to the police then, lady." He smiled. "Which means, in about twenty minutes from now, you, and your boy, and Joe, here, if you want—doesn't make any difference to us—you're on a plane to New York."

There was a pause. Then Kruger let the smile slide from his face and said each word separately, as though it stood alone, with no connection in the same sentence. "No ... is ... not ... an ... option."

More silence. Lynn and Kruger, eyes locked. Joe watching. Not blinking.

And then, another voice. Quiet. Speaking slowly. C.J., saying: "Should I kill him, Mom?"

They turned and stared, all of them, Lynn included, their expressions frozen. No one spoke. The van began to slow down. The driver clicked off the radio and tilted his rearview mirror cautiously, trying to find C.J.'s face.

C.J. was on the bench seat next to Lynn, leaning all the way back against the van's side. His hands were in his lap, not moving. His chin was lowered almost to his chest. His nostrils were flared, his lips tight. His eyes were narrowed and staring at Kruger. He was not blinking. "I can touch somebody and say the words and they come alive", he said. "Or I can touch somebody and say other words and they die." He started to pull himself slowly forward on the seat. "Should I kill him, Mom?" he asked again. And then, even more quietly, "Should I kill them all?"

Lynn felt immobilized. She wanted to speak but had no idea what to say, so she stared like they were all staring, her expression frozen in uncertainty—her, Joe, Kruger, all of them, no one daring to move.

The van was in the right lane, moving very slowly now, ready to pull onto the shoulder.

A faint whisper came from the man closest to the rear, across the van from C.J., a softly breathed "What the hell?" Not strong words, though. Words breathed weakly and filled with worry.

C.J. slid to the edge of the seat, his eyes still holding on Kruger. He said very softly, "Do you want me to touch him, Mom?"

Kruger eased sideways in his seat. One inch. Two inches. No answer from Lynn. C.J.'s voice was just a whisper. "Do you want me to say, 'Be dead, Mr. Kruger'?" The van suddenly slowed onto the shoulder and came to a quick stop, the engine still running. The driver watched C.J. in the rearview mirror. Kruger had turned to watch him, too. His eyes stayed steady as he slowly unclipped his seat belt. Then he suddenly opened the door, jumped out, turned, grabbed the top of the door frame, and stared back with a furious glare to stare again at C.J.

"Whoa", Joe said to Kruger, one hand rising like a stop sign. "Think about it. If the Cross kid is already dead, he won't mind traveling, will he? I mean, you tell me. Cross must have access to another plane. You know he does. So why don't you just get us into a house somewhere and he can meet us there. We can do it today. What is he, an hour and a half away, a quick flight from New York? He doesn't need us there; he just wants his son back. You don't think he'll travel for an hour and half to have that happen? You want to jeopardize it with all this acting hard or whatever you're doing?"

They all stared at Kruger. Kruger was still staring at C.J.

He took in a breath, knocked softly twice on the roof of the car with the knuckles of his right hand, and said, turning to Lynn, "I'll make the call. That's all I can do."

He wandered away from the van, talking low.

Three minutes is all it took.

He came back, climbed back inside, turned around again, and said, "He'll come here. We've got a place farther north." Then he turned back to face the windshield and motion the driver to head out again, before he added, "You just better hope that the kid can actually pull this off."

Twenty-Two

"Listen up."

The twenty-four local, state, and federal law enforcement officers and agents gathered in the windowless briefing room of the Wayne County state police command post fell silent. Each had a folder containing critical notes and photographs. Each knew the seriousness of the afternoon's work. Most knew and respected the "briefing face" put on by Michigan state police lieutenant Phillip Beneman, the Bay City post commander and now director of Operation Red Cross, the C.J. Walker locate-and-rescue mission. All knew that six of the troopers were members of the state's Special Response Team (SRT). All knew that SRT did not gather loaded and ready to go unless the operation was highest priority and the commander expected the bell to be rung without wasting time.

It had been five hours since the Walker boy disappeared from the parking structure of Covington Towers, and the lieutenant was determined that it not be another five before the boy was safely back home. He studied the manila folder in his left hand and rubbed his black moustache with the first knuckle of his right thumb. Then he studied the group.

Six troopers in plain clothes immediately in front of him, in the middle of the room; two of them pilots for the helicopters that would be used for the operation. SRT to his left, all in a cluster. Two special agents from the FBI were toward the rear, in the middle, with a deputy U.S. marshal and an Air Force captain behind them. The Catholic cardinal and a priest sat next to them, on their right.

"I'm going to do a quick pass, starting at the top", he said, settling the group down. "You all know a lot about what's going on, but we have some new entries, and we're real close to moving out. So take notes, ask questions; let's get it right."

Folders flipped open. Pens were raised. Heads nodded.

In the back of the room, the Cardinal made a quick and muted sign of the cross.

The lieutenant spoke quickly and held relentless eye contact, moving his focus from officer to officer.

"This is being pursued as a kidnapping until proven otherwise", he said. "Given the significance of the boy involved, nine-year-old C.J. Walker, the 'Lazarus kid' everybody's talking about, this is a highest priority pursuit.

"The vehicle used to take the family away from the hospital showed no signs of forced entry or hot-wiring, so we have the stolen car question still up in the air. The owner has an office in the buildings where the car was dumped, insists he had no knowledge of its being used, but we'll stay on him. We'll find out."

A quick glance at his notes. "Importantly, the mom and son ran away on their own, apparently for reasons unknown, from a physical the kid was having. They were running looking scared, either running from these guys, or running from something else and these guys picked them up, we don't know. Don't know if it was planned or spur of the moment, either. But we've got nine witnesses saying that the mother, Mrs. Walker, Lynn Walker, and the kid, looked real scared. The same witnesses say, though, that she jumped into the car on her own, and that her husband was all for it. He even called one of the abductors by name: 'Torrie'.

"So, the father may have even arranged it. Joseph Walker. Divorced for a couple of years but still living close by the kid and the mom, and apparently still sees the boy pretty regularly."

A hand raised; it was one of the plainclothes troopers. "He got a record?"

The lieutenant shook his head. "Petty theft when he was fourteen. Shoplifting. Did community service. A speeding ticket since then and one DUI four years ago, but no serious bad guy stuff that we know of at this point."

He looked down, checking again, getting back on track.

"Torrie and his buddies had no time to wipe the vehicle down real good, so they left some prints. So far we've identified the owner's, we have the father's, we have the kid's, just going by size, now, and we have a Milton Kesner ..."

He looked at the FBI personnel and said to them with a grin, "Your ID system gets these things nailed down faster than God."

One of the agents smiled, nodding approval. The other just stared.

"We have prints of a Milton Kesner", the lieutenant continued. "Flint, Michigan. Contractor. No criminal record and confirmed to be in Denver this afternoon, and been there since Sunday. And then ...", he paused, taking a moment to leaf slowly to another page in his manila folder, "then we have Torrie."

He held up an 8 × 10, black-and-white glossy photo. "Torrie Kruger. The front seat passenger the father knew. The chatter between them at the time the mom and kid hopped in the card is still being reviewed with more of the witnesses. Make sure nothing else was said that makes a difference. But Mr. Kruger seems to be what TV calls 'an attorney for the mob'. And, like some others at the top of that heap, he's got just one client, and had one client for the last six years."

He held up a second glossy. "This shot's two years old, from when the guy's wife died. Mr. Anthony W. Cross. Shandise, New York."

"Cross was born somewhere in Italy sixty-nine years ago", he said. "Antonio Crossetti. Parents immigrated, but not with the wretched masses on Fire Island. Well set, well connected. Changed his name to Anthony Cross after his folks died. That was thirty years ago. Been dirty since way back. A family man, and dirty. Three times indicted but no convictions. No time served, ever. Had good lawyers, and hung onto one, I guess, in Torrie Kruger. So now he's just another rich New York retiree. Probably goes to church on Sunday and everybody smiles."

He turned his eyes to Father Mark and said, "So far, he's no one that Mrs. Walker would be likely to know too well herself; would you agree with that, Father?"

Father Mark said, "I wouldn't think so. No."

The lieutenant slipped Cross' photo back into his folder and placed the folder on the desk behind him. When he turned around again, he said, "Anthony Cross was married just once. And married late. Wife a lot younger than him. She gave him a son: Anthony Junior. And two years ago, she dies. Cancer. That's when the photo of him was taken. Then, not long after that, Anthony Junior, who's now fifteen, gets sick himself. At this point, today, he hasn't been in school for nearly a year. And the reason is, if you see where this is going ... the reason is that Anthony Cross Junior is on the verge of dying of leukemia himself. Maybe already dead."

No one stirred.

"Federal agents in New York have been on it for about an hour. They interviewed the boy's nurse in New York about thirty minutes ago. She says that at eight thirty this morning she left the kid's bedside, and the estate, at her usual time; but this time, against her will. She was told to leave, she says, and so she did. Cross' doctor was with the boy, she said, him and Mr. Cross, and it was Cross that told her she had to leave.

"The reason she didn't want to, she said, especially today, was because she felt sure the boy was dying. Any minute, she told the agents. Still, they make her leave. So when she gets home she calls the house. She was mad, she says. She loved the kid, too; she wanted to know what happened. Half a dozen times, she says, for half the day, she calls, gets no answer. But she was sure of it, she told the agents. The boy was real close to dying. And that, at eight thirty this morning."

He glanced at his watch, which read 3:55 P.M.

"I said when we started, we're real close to moving out. That's because agents in New York have confirmed that Cross took off from Davenport, New York, in a private, eight-passenger Learjet at fifteen-thirty hours this afternoon, same time as here. Three men boarded with him, identifications unknown, although we're pretty sure one is the boy's doctor, an oncologist named Conlin. Anthony Junior also boarded, or at least his body did, on a stretcher. His face, witnesses at the airport said, was not covered, but whether he was in fact dead at that time, they don't know. His body was immobile and on a stretcher—that's all they know, that's all we know."

Curry said it first: "Destination: C.J. Walker."

Cardinal Schaenner reached over and laid his palm on Father Mark's arm. He smiled a tired half smile. He kept looking straight ahead.

"Destination," the lieutenant said, "City Airport, Detroit. ETA: 0800 hours. Which means that in sixty-nine minutes from right now, a man named Anthony Cross is going to lead us to C.J. Walker."

Joe came up behind Lynn, walking quietly, noticing how her hands were tight around the railing that separated the raised section of the home's north living room from the lower section.

They'd been taken to a sprawling, contemporary home sixty yards from Lake St. Clair in the rolling hills area thirty to forty miles north of Detroit. It was a single-story structure with plenty of land on either side, all of it as trim as a golf course. It was a well-furnished house that seemed to have two of just about everything in two nearly identical wings, one north and one south. It had two comfortable reception areas, two sunken living rooms, two dining rooms, and even two powerful runabouts docked on the bay, and eight bedrooms in all, according to Kruger, four in each wing.

A long, pine deck ran the full length of the back of the house to a large, graveled parking area behind the south side of the home. The parking area began against a six-vehicle carport and swept around the south end of the house to the driveway out front. That, also according to Kruger, was so that guests could remain more or less anonymous, their cars, at least, hidden from the road.

C.J. and two of Kruger's men were watching a large-screen TV twenty feet in front of Lynn, C.J. sitting on a large upholstered pillow placed on the floor near the TV, Kruger's men on a white couch a few feet behind him. They were all watching a female cartoon superlady in a tight, red-and-gold suit jump over cartoon rooftops.

"What are you thinking?" Joe whispered to Lynn, touching her shoulder.

"That hospital push terrorized C.J.", she whispered after a moment's thought and without turning to face him. "You should have seen his eyes."

"That never should have happened, like I said", Joe whispered.

Lynn remained silent.

"But Cross is on the way", he said. "And what I gotta ask now …"

He stopped midsentence and motioned to her to move with him to the farthest corner of the room. She followed him to sit with him at an ornate, felt-covered card table where they were still able to keep an eye on C.J. and C.J. could still see them.

Once settled, Joe continued, still in a whisper, "What I want to know now, straight up, is whether you're thinking that with nobody following you, you can skip out of here and parlay Cross' code of honor, or his gratitude or whatever you want to call it, plus some of his money, of course, into going straight into hiding with C.J. But just you and C.J."

He waited. When she didn't answer, he said, "So is that your plan now or what? Or do you even have a plan?"

Whispering as quietly as Joe, she said, "I'll wait to see if Cross even has a son, first. Then we'll see if C.J. can still do anything. Then, if we do leave, it will be me and C.J., yeah."

He studied her without responding. He didn't look happy.

"That doesn't surprise you, does it?" she asked. "We're still kind of good friends, Joe, you and me. And I'm glad we are. And I'm fine with staying that way. I want to stay that way, and intend to stay that way. But you didn't think we'd turn into a 'couple' again just because there might be a lot of money on the table, did you?"

He shrugged. "It just isn't what I had in mind, is all. It isn't the way I saw it happening."

She said, "The money's not going to be able to make us an 'us' again, Joe. That's probably the last thing it could do. C'mon."

More silence. Then he said, "I love C.J. too, though."

"I know you do", Lynn told him. "And I'm really glad you do. But your loving him, or my loving him, for that matter, either way, that's not going to bring us back together again. Not like we'd be an 'Oh, look at the happy couple!' again."

Another pause without an answer from Joe, and just a stare, eyes narrowed—an "I need a few seconds to think" stare.

Lynn said, "I'm going to do everything I can to make sure that this is the last time he does this, so help me. And you know that. Day and night, that's what I'm going to try and do. And you wouldn't be able to take it if we were hiding together and he didn't use it. You'd hate it. You know you would. And you'd end up hating me for being the one standing in the way."

She gave him almost half a minute to respond. When he still remained silent, she added, "Besides, you'll have two and a half million dollars if we each take half, and you'll probably double that in a year's time and have a ball doing it. And nobody will be hunting you. Don't forget that. They won't care about you if C.J.'s not with you. So you'll be totally free. Really, have you thought it all the way out?"

He nodded, then said, "I'd have to see C.J. sometimes, though. You can't just disappear with him, and that's gonna be it."

"I wouldn't do that, to you or to C.J.", she said. "I'll have to give it some time, but if we do find a safe place, even in another country, Kruger could be a go-between. Just remember to act as smart as you really are. No mail, no phones, no eyes on you, no tracking chips snuck into your shoes. No traces. Kruger knows something about that kind of stuff, though, I'm sure. He'd better."

"I do, too", Joe added quickly.

She turned to look at C.J. again. Her eyes narrowed. She said, "He wants out as bad as I do, Joe. I know he does. So it's going to be all over with Cross' son. Live with it, starting now, because this will be it."

Joe gave it a few seconds; then he said, tilting his head and sounding melancholic, "So how about the killing thing with Kruger in the van. Can he really do that?"

Her answer came quickly. "He doesn't know. And he promised me he'd never find out."

"I wouldn't be surprised if he's tried it out, though", Joe said. "On a bug or something. Not on a person. But I wouldn't be surprised. On a bug or something."

"He said he didn't", Lynn said. "I believe him."

Joe thought about it. "Might not be bad if he could, though, you know? Like somebody tries to kidnap him or something. Might not be bad to find out soon, too, so you don't have to guess if you really need it."

She closed her eyes, tightened her lips, and shook her head slowly, all without bothering to turn in his direction.

Joe pursed his lips, nodded his head several times, and turned again to look at his son, and at the TV.

The superlady had thick armbands running up to her elbows, both of them with gold buttons and some switches in various colors. Joe wasn't sure what the buttons and all did, but he knew they gave her more power.

He thought, everybody wants more power.

Then he thought, no, just almost everybody.

The superlady was spinning a crook around like a top and throwing him down the street through a gang of other crooks.

Joe thought, bowling with bad guys.

He started to smile, but lost it quickly. Instead, he leaned very near to Lynn and said, "You can't ever let them find you, you know."

She shook her head. "I know. They won't find us, Joe."

"Even if you gotta dye your skin or something that far out. Honest to God."

"They won't find us."

"And they'll always be looking for you, you know that, right? With never any let up."

"They won't find us, Joe. I promise."

He nodded slowly and looked back at his son. A moment later, Lynn heard him whisper, quietly and bitterly, as though to no one in particular, "The government will find out if he can kill people. That's for damned sure."

Twenty-Three

Lynn and C.J. were sitting next to one another at the glass-topped table in the breezeway, by the open doors, saying nothing. Their untouched lemonades were pushed to the middle of the table. Saginaw Bay stretched out on the other side of the doorway in front of them, now under thick, white, fast-moving clouds. Joe was pacing behind them. Torrie Kruger was sitting in the living room, visible to them through the archway behind Joe. The other three men lounged on couches and easy chairs around him—the big man still in his brown suit, his red tie still in place, the other two in jeans and short sleeves, their sport coats having been tossed aside hours ago.

It was 6:40 P.M. Cross had landed on time and was on the way. They would get a call, Kruger had been told, when they got close. They had guessed about 6:50. They had end-of-day traffic to contend with.

No one spoke. Kruger moved the phone from the side table, near the front window, to the arm of his white easy chair.

Joe sat down at the glass-topped table across from Lynn and C.J. He checked his watch. He raised his eyes and looked at Lynn. He said to C.J., "You doin' okay?"

C.J. shrugged, then nodded.

Lynn slid her arm around his shoulders. They waited.

Lynn smiled at C.J. and withdrew her arm. She rested her chin on her fingertips, prayerlike.

Joe got up and paced again, this time drifting into the living room to look out the front door. He wondered what Cross would arrive in. Probably a limo, he thought. Then he thought, no, not a limo, not with a dead kid to transport.

He hoped it would not be an ambulance, drawing attention.

The phone went off like a shot, and Joe spun to face it.

Lynn, who was on her feet in the breezeway, reached instinctively for C.J., holding his shoulder, feeling her own heart pounding.

Everyone looked at Kruger, who let the phone ring twice before answering it with a quiet, "Kruger."

He listened. Three seconds passed; then he nodded and said, "Right", and hung up.

The other three men were on their feet, waiting, but Kruger didn't look at them. He looked at Lynn and C.J., who were now standing in the archway to the living room, and said, without standing up, "Three minutes down the road."

The two vehicles approached from the south, two dark-gray Chevy Suburbans turning slowly into the driveway, not seeming to be in a hurry.

An orange moving van lumbered past on the road not far from the house. The slogan on its side read "We make your life brand-new."

Lynn was watching from the two front windows, C.J. close at her side, Joe with his hands on the boy's shoulders, the four men flanking them like sentries. She thought of her nightmare—of the parents carrying their dead children to her and C.J., and of the horror of it when she dreamt it that way. She wondered if Cross could see her and C.J. standing in the window. She wondered why the sound of the tires crunching on the graveled driveway could be heard so plainly even from inside the house. She wondered what Cross was thinking, and if his heart was pounding, too.

"Let's go", Kruger said. He moved quickly across the living room to the breezeway, where he slid open the doors to the back deck and the parking area. Two of the other men slipped their sport coats back on and hurried past him to position themselves at the end of the back deck, near the corner of the house, where they could help usher the group in. Joe went out with them. Kruger glanced once at C.J., and walked quickly down the deck to join the others.

Only the big man in the brown suit stayed, standing behind Lynn and C.J. Like a sheepdog, he eased himself closer, silently pressing them through the open door where gravel was crunching and a man from New York and a boy that was dead were already turning the corner at the back of the house.

C.J. stopped on the deck, staring at the dark Suburbans.

The vehicles stopped, too. Their engines died.

Lynn put her hand on C.J.'s back. He didn't show that he noticed. He looked mesmerized.

She heard a muffled "Hello, Mr. Cross" from one of Kruger's men, who stepped forward to swing open the door of the first vehicle, and a soft "It's good to see you" from Kruger, who moved to the open door with his right hand extended in welcome.

With that, Mr. Anthony Cross stepped out, moving slowly.

He wore a dark-blue suit, double-breasted, and a light-blue shirt with a button-down collar. His silk tie was also blue, as dark as his suit. He was not a tall man, and he was now rounding slightly with age. His hair was gray and short, his round face deeply lined, his expression grave. Thick brows pressed over eyes that looked dark and very tired. He stood beside the vehicle as he shook Kruger's hand and the door was shut behind him, but his attention was already riveted on the boy who stood on the wooden deck thirty feet away, holding his mother's hand, studying him.

A quick series of metallic snaps sounded behind him and he turned. Two of the men he had traveled with were unloading Anthony Jr.'s body from the back of the converted Suburban. A middle-aged man with thick glasses hovered nearby, watching the stretcher, saying nothing. Three other men from the second Suburban joined them, and in a moment, the rolling stretcher was trembling slowly over the gravel to stop at Mr. Cross' side.

A white sheet had been pulled up to the boy's neck, his face left uncovered.

He appeared to Lynn, from her place on the deck, to be not much older than C.J.—he had been that sick. That sick, she thought, and that thin for a long time.

Mr. Cross eased forward, closer to the deck and to C.J. Walker, his hand still holding the resting place of his only son. His old man's eyes, suddenly soft and vulnerable, filled with tears.

C.J. moved, too. He began inching to the end of the deck, moving toward the old man in the blue suit and toward his dead boy, who was fifteen, he remembered, and whose name was Anthony.

To Lynn's surprise, the moment struck her as something very nearly sacred: the old man and the young boy easing toward one another, staring at one another, each measuring the other, each measuring the moment and finding it good.

C.J. walked alone to the edge of the deck and stopped. Then he looked back suddenly, urging Lynn with his eyes to please come with him, and she did, staying close behind but not touching him.

Mr. Cross, still staring at C.J., came forward the few steps that separated them. He extended his hand and said very quietly and very slowly, in a voice that was thick and low, "My name is Mr. Cross. My son has died."

Then, as C.J.'s fingers closed on his, a soft, new sound rose in Cross' throat, a soft cough, like a gasp, and tears began trailing down his face. His lips twisted in an attempt to hold them back.

Lynn's eyes showed tears, too, as she watched C.J. step off the deck and walk to the edge of the stretcher and the boy he didn't know, who was dead like Mrs. Klein had been dead, she and Mr. Turner.

Cross looked at Lynn and extended both hands. He said, still speaking very softly, "I'm so sorry for how all this has come about, Mrs. Walker..."

Lynn nodded slightly.

She was focused on Mr. Cross, and on C.J. and the fifteen-year-old on the stretcher, and on the magnitude of the moment, so she didn't focus on the sound, not at that point, but it was there, faint in the background but already somehow disturbing the grace of the moment, the first hints of a soft, repetitive thut thut thut thut.

She stopped, horrified. The sounds were not faint in the background anymore, but getting closer: Thut Thut Thut Thut.

Her mouth dropped open. She spun to face the house, wild-eyed. She looked at the sky over the lake, then over the yard, seeing nothing, turning again, over the cars and the house, and the others were suddenly turning, too, hearing it and looking up, starting to move, and then it was there, sliding right over the house and right over them, so dark and massive and violent that the ground shook with its presence: THUT THUT THUT THUT.

Lynn turned toward the stretcher, screaming, "C.J.!"

The yard to the south and the graveled driveway behind the Suburbans exploded with the sound of engines, all of them roaring under the pounding from the sky. Black vehicles tore around the bend in the road and up to the house on both sides. They ripped through the grass and over the flying gravel with sirens whooping, and there were men in flak gear and uniforms, all with guns, all jumping from vehicles and running, and all of them shouting, all at once, "Let me see your hands!" and "Against the house!" and "Do it now!" and "Show me your hands!"

Cross had grabbed his chest with one hand and the sheet covering the body of his son with the other. His eyes looked like he'd been cut down with gunfire. The man with glasses tried to pull him away but stopped, not knowing where to go. At the same time, Lynn grabbed C.J. by the arm and shouted, "Do it, C.J., now!" But he just looked at her, too terrified to move, and she had to shout it again. "Do it quick, C.J., before they take us!"

She felt the air from the THUT THUT THUT pulsing and pressing on her, now filled with dirt swirled hard from the ground against her face and arms and hands. She saw Curry running from the far corner of the house, a gun in his hand, and the man from the Air Force close behind him, both of them seeing her and running toward her and C.J.

But she saw C.J.'s hand, too. She saw it flick over and touch the boy's face, and she saw his lips move. She grabbed the lapel of the man with glasses who stood frozen next to Cross and jerked and shouted loud enough for both of them to hear, "Don't tell them he was dead! Everything depends on that! Say he was sick! Not dead!"

The mouth of the man with the glasses hung open.

Cross stared, paralyzed with terrible questions.

C.J. was cowering at the side of the stretcher, reaching for Lynn's hand, shouting, "Mom!"

A state trooper grabbed Lynn's arm and pulled as she saw another trooper reach to grab C.J., and she heard Joe's voice behind her shouting, "No one's done anything wrong!" Then she saw Cross being pulled away, and she knew that Curry would be all over C.J. in a heartbeat, so she twisted hard and lunged forward to grab Cross' face with both hands as they pushed the old man past her.

Her thumbs pressed hard into his cheeks, and her fingers wrapped hard over his ears and the side of his head to hold him still. She forced her mouth close to his left ear, and as she heard the trooper who had been holding her shout at her to release the man and move away, and as she felt the trooper's two hands close hard around her arms again from behind, she shouted in a desperate, muffled voice, tight against the old man's ear, "He's alive!"

Cardinal Schaenner found A.W. Cross in the living room, in the south end of the house. He was not in handcuffs, and he was not alone. Two state troopers stood inside the door, arms crossed, watching the old man pace in the far corner of the room slowly, like a dying bull. He was being detained, the police had told the Cardinal when he asked for permission to talk with the New Yorker privately, but only until his Detroit attorneys arrived, which they all knew would be soon.

The initial explosion of police force had lasted less than ten minutes, but the Cardinal could sense the shock of it still trembling in the air, even in this room, deep in the house.

Lynn, C.J., and Joe were waiting for him in the state police cruiser that would take them to the nearby Wayne County state police post for the necessary deposition. Deputy U.S. Marshal Curry and his companion from the Air Force would be there, they were told. At Lynn's request, Cardinal Schaenner could accompany them, too, although he would not be presently included in the deposition.

But first, the Cardinal had asked for just three minutes alone with Mr. Cross. First, the Cardinal had to know.

He realized as he entered the room that he was looking at a man cut loose from his moorings, a shocked and shaken soul, a person that the Cardinal would dearly have loved to spend long hours with and pray with and counsel and try to help. But not now.

He nodded to the troopers standing just inside the doorway, asking them with a gesture if they would leave the two men alone. Then he approached Cross slowly, inviting companionship with a smile and a simple extension of his hand.

The old man laid his large hand in the Cardinal's palm gently, then squeezed and held on tight. His expression was still edged with anger from his not being able to accompany his son when they rushed him to the hospital, but he also looked vulnerable and confused.

He whispered a coarse, "Padre." His eyes softened, and he smiled a joyless smile and bowed his head.

The Cardinal slid his long arm around the man's shoulder and eased him as far from the troopers as they could get, drawing him into the corner of the room, where the two looked like they might be brothers, huddled in prayer.

"I have an appeal to make of you," the Cardinal whispered, "an appeal for the truth, for me, and for the Church. And for the boy and his mother."

At the mention of the boy and his mother, Cross arched his eyebrows and raised his head. His chin quivered.

The Cardinal withdrew his arm from around the man's shoulder. He turned around to check on the troopers in the doorway with a quick glance, then eased a few inches to his left, placing the troopers squarely at his back. He narrowed his eyes and whispered in a clipped voice sharp with urgency, "I beg you for the truth. Was your son dead? Was he declared dead by a doctor? Clinically dead? Please!"

Cross blinked and returned the Cardinal's stare, his mouth open.

"Was Anthony dead?" the Cardinal said, louder and sounding even more desperate.

Cross tried to ease backward, but the Cardinal reached with both hands to grip the man's upper arms and stare even harder at the father of the fifteen-year-old boy, boring in, insisting on the truth.

There was a long moment of silence. Neither of them moved. Both searched the other's expression. Both found anguish there. Then Cross' chin wrinkled once again. His lips twisted. Tears rose again in his tired eyes, and when they broke over his eyelids and ran into the deep creases in his cheeks, he didn't try to stop them. His shoulders trembled. He nodded once. "Yes, Padre", he whispered, softly but firmly. "Anthony was dead."

It was an epiphany. It came to Lynn with such clarity that she held her breath as she thought of it, just to make sure she took it in before any of it got away.

It came to her after the police cruiser carrying her, C.J., Joe, and the Cardinal turned onto I-696 toward Detroit and Royal Oak, after they had denied at their disposition that they had been kidnapped and insisted that they knew nothing about any stolen car, after they told the questioning officers that they had no way to tell if the Cross boy was even sick, let alone dead, and after United States Deputy Marshal Curry and his Air Force colleague started following too closely behind their cruiser's rear bumper, apparently to remind Lynn and Joe of their mission to bring C.J. under the government's wing, whether his parents protested innocence in this latest affair or not.

It came to her after the raid had left her shattered by making her realize, even in those very few horrifying minutes of engines and guns and shouting and orders and arrests, that any hope she had about Cross being able to rescue her and C.J. had been destroyed. They would be taken back to her house now, she knew, where they would live like prisoners until God knows what happened, because nobody with Cross' underworld history in the headlines would have any possible chance of smuggling her and C.J. safely past federal agents or the Cardinal and his friends or half the reporters in southeastern Michigan or the crowd that would be circling her house by now.

And the crowd would be angry this time, she had realized that, too. The story line of the news already being aired would be that, while C.J. was not allowed by his parents to give anybody in the crowds of hurting people, who had been begging for his help just fifteen yards away from their front door, she and Joe had willingly bolted from the hospital to rush him out of the city in an obviously planned getaway so that C.J. could raise the son of a rich man from New York who has a long history of mob ties on the East Coast and elsewhere.

She had even wondered when the first rocks would come flying through their windows, and, with that, she'd felt physically ill. What would she be expected to do for C.J. then? But it was at that point that the whole picture cleared up for her. The epiphany poured out in a single moment's time as quickly as a light going on in the dark.

The Cardinal turned from his front passenger seat to say to her, "You know, with the impact this day is certain to have, I strongly suggest that you consider staying at St. Mark Seminary, where we can keep you safe until we get you away on a flight to Rome", at which point Joe leaned close to her ear and whispered, beginning even before the Cardinal had finished speaking, "Just don't forget who owes you now, Lynn, and how much he'll owe you, and always will owe you, even way down the road."

And that quickly, there it was. The open window. After all the ups and downs, their best way out. Not just out of Royal Oak, but out of Rome after the Cardinal had gotten them safely out of the country.

She said to the Cardinal, sounding totally calm, "Thanks, but we'll stay at home tonight. I want C.J. to know whose bed he's sleeping in. And I want to be home, too."

Then she sat back to think it through, starting with, how Cross, or "Crossetti", as she remembered Joe telling her the man's real name, still had family and deep roots and powerful connections in Italy. Influential connections, maybe even influential connections in the Vatican.

So yes, she would let the Cardinal fly them away from Curry and the government and the reporters and the crowds, because now he was the only person who could do it. And both he and she would want it done right away, before the surgery on Turner proved anything that would cause them even more chaos and attention, and before the media had made their lives a fresh kind of hell with their newly discovered "the Walker family's choice of a criminal connection" headlines.

They would leave for Rome as soon as possible, but she would refuse to let C.J. raise anyone else from the dead once she got there, whatever that would take. She had never promised otherwise. She hadn't agreed to a resurrection over there. Everything the Cardinal was envisioning was his own doing, his own imagination. And they couldn't force him to do it. And they couldn't force her to make him do it. So how long would it take without letting anyone else witness it before people started to disbelieve it, and even forget about it? Six months at the most? Especially with the news coverage drying up more every day?

She and C.J. would be safe there, and stay safely out of the news, and Cross could be there overnight, and would be if she needed him, she felt sure of it. So she would ask him to start planning now to get them out of Rome and into a new and more normalized life somewhere else. They could dye their hair at that point, get some added weight on C.J., wait while he stretched a little taller. He was at that age of quick-changing spurts of growth, so pretty soon he wouldn't be so easily recognizable after all. It would work, and it would be a heck of a lot easier for Cross to get them away from a church facility in Italy than it would be for him to get them through the nets that were being thrown over their house in Royal Oak.

The Cardinal interrupted her train of thought again, this time to say, "I'll look forward to our meeting tomorrow morning at your house, then, if eight o'clock is still good with you."

"Sure", she said. "Eight'll be fine."

She looked at Joe, who was staring stone-faced back at her. She squeezed C.J.'s hand again and leaned back smiling.

At last, she knew how it would end.

At eleven o'clock that evening, in front of the window of his darkened bedroom on the second floor of his home in Palmer Park, the Cardinal held the white lace curtain back with his left hand and watched a single, canoe-shaped cloud slip under the three-quarter moon, cover it briefly with the small rise in its tail end, and then slowly slip away from it, moving west to east. He watched the cloud for a few seconds more, and then he stared at the moon for a long time. But he wasn't thinking about the moon, or about the cloud. He was thinking of eternal things, things very possibly more significant than the moon or the planets or even deep space itself.

Then, with an air of determined resignation, he let the curtain fall back into place.

He would not sleep this night, he was sure, even though it was late, and he would probably not sleep for several nights to come, perhaps many.

The world had been changed for him. It had been changed in that single moment when he had first accepted beyond any doubt the oath given him by Anthony Cross that his son, Anthony, had indeed been dead, and that C.J. Walker had indeed been the one to call the boy back to life with a simple touch of his hand and a three-word prayer.

It was breathtaking. It was unspeakable. But it had happened.

History had been changed, and in a matter of another forty-eight hours, the enormity of that change would not only be evident to all of the world; it would be irreversible.

The plan that had come to his mind's eye was like the ringing of a thousand bells. History had been changed, and it would be changed again, he thought, but not in Rome. Right here, in his own diocese, before flight, before capture, before meddling, before fear or doubt or any power on earth could move to stop it. What he pictured would be in motion by five o'clock the next morning, and it would be an event so unthinkably shining, he was utterly certain, that it would have the power to virtually tear down cultures, to elevate kingdoms, to resurrect from the sleep of death not just persons but entire civilizations,

civilizations like our own that had grown so comfortable with deca-dence that people were existing now like painted fruits, dying from the inside out; civilizations that would, in the stark light of the single experience he had in mind, be so shocked that their disbeliefs and deni-als would be forced to rise up again, brand-new and faith-filled and God-centered and wonderful to behold!

He stood on the crest of the future, and it was glorious.

No, he would not sleep this night.

At last, he knew how it was going to end.

It was late, and dark, and quiet.

Lynn realized that she had been asleep and dreaming, and wondered if she still was, no longer dreaming in dark visions of the gray table at the police deposition melting and dying, or of troopers in uniforms shouting at C.J. to touch it and bring it back to life, but dreaming now of some-one knocking on the wall that was very close to her. And then knocking again. Three more knocks, quickly: rap rap rap.

She opened her eyes. Her heart was pounding with the alarm that comes from being awakened in the middle of the night and thinking that you've missed something incredibly important, or missed doing some-thing you should have done.

She sat up realizing that she was in C.J.'s room, that she had come upstairs with him as soon as they had given Nancy and Burr a run-down of the events of the day. She wondered, in a terrifying moment of half-consciousness, if the surgery had been completed early on Turner or if they had confirmed that the Cross boy had been dead and Curry was waiting in the hall even now, standing there and knock-ing softly with a half dozen other armed federal agents behind him and a grin on his face and a sheet of paper in his hand to make C.J.'s abduction legal.

She looked for C.J.'s clock and saw that it was only 11:10 P.M. She realized that she was still dressed, still in her jeans and wrinkled, yellow oxford shirt, and she stood up to grope her way quickly to the door and to whoever had filled the room with fresh fear by knocking once again, three more times, not too loudly but quickly, wanting attention.

It was Father Mark. He was alone in the glow of the night-light in the upstairs hallway, his clerical shirt open, his Roman collar gone. He looked like he hadn't slept for a week, but he didn't look frightened, not like federal agents were raiding.

"Cross is here", he whispered. "Joe said to tell you. Told me you were in here with C.J. He asked for you, Cross did."

She sighed and closed her eyes for a moment, regaining her composure. Then she stepped into the hall, easing the door shut behind her. "Who else is with him?"

"Three other men. They're in the kitchen with Joe."

"How'd they get him through the crowd outside?"

"Driver and bodyguard types. His men. And the crowd's a little thinner, this late."

They started down the stairs together, moving quietly, Lynn asking questions over her shoulder in whispers. "Is Joe with him now?"

"Joe's with the three guys. Nancy's asleep with Burr, if they can sleep. In your spare room."

She stopped near the bottom of the stairs as Cross came toward her from the other end of the hallway. He looked grave as he approached her.

"I'll talk with him alone", Lynn said.

Lynn's visit with A. W. Cross lasted nearly twenty minutes.

The aging man with a fifteen-year-old son who was alive again and who bore his father's name was still wearing his blue suit. His dark-blue tie was still in place, and his eyes were still moist, just as they had been the last time she saw him up close, near the stretcher at the house on Lake St. Clair.

They talked back and forth with her chair pulled up very close to his at the far corner of the otherwise empty living room.

At the end of their few minutes alone, Lynn led him and his men to the side door. The old man, whose eyes were nearly shut from weariness, paused and stood still for a long moment, just staring at her.

Maybe it was the strength of the appreciation they were both feeling, or a shared sense of relief, or maybe it was the fact that they had so unexpectedly come to share something beyond anything they had ever really be able to understand fully, Lynn really did not know. But it seemed like the thing to do. Without saying anything more to him, Lynn leaned forward and hugged him, and he accepted it and gently hugged her back.

She felt it was parental somehow, on both their parts, and she knew it was deeply felt.

Twenty-Four

Lynn was awakened early, just after 6:00 A.M. A roll of nearby thunder and the realization that a dark morning rain was splashing through her opened window forced her out of bed.

From her window, she saw that the crowd outside had been thinned by the night and the rain, but not as much as she might have hoped.

She stood at the window for several minutes, still half-asleep, mesmerized by what looked like several hundred statues, wet with rain; so many people were still huddled on the sidewalks, still standing sullenly on the tree lawns and along the edges of the street, still waiting for C. J.'s salvation.

She wondered if their persistence had anything to do with last night's news about Anthony Cross Jr. She wondered if they believed that if she saw their determination she would change her mind and bring them the boy and the healing they so desperately wanted. She wondered if any of them felt that if they just stayed and suffered a little bit more they might finally deserve it. She dressed quickly in her jeans and blue pullover sweater and went downstairs. There would be so much to do, so much to think about and plan and say good-bye to.

She found Joe in the living room, watching TV, the sound down very low. "I stayed on the couch", he said. "Mark left about twelve thirty last night, but the rain was starting by then, so I thought, what the hell."

He also knew the Cardinal was coming to see Lynn soon. Lynn had told him all about it. And he thought it was smart, he had told her that, along with telling her to "watch yourself".

She had said she understood, and she wouldn't take any unnecessary chances. She also reminded him that he was more paranoid than any other ten people she'd ever met, but that was okay. She'd watch out for things.

"I've got to start packing some things", she said.

"Schaenner can't have much to pack", Joe said. "Clothes all the same wherever he goes. A guy like that, if he loses his own stuff, he just wears some other priest's. Who's to know?" Then, noticing an editorial coming on the TV, he gestured and said, "This was shot last night. They don't like the Cross thing, I'll tell you that."

She turned to watch.

The Channel 2 news director, with Cross' grainy black-and-white photo in a mortise over his left shoulder and the words "Action News Editorial" across the bottom of the screen, looked like a man determined to right a wrong. He was saying, "In our view, it was a remarkable selection for the C.J. Walker family. With several hundred sick and dying average citizens begging for help less than thirty feet from their home in Royal Oak, they apparently agreed to a frantic getaway from St. Paul's Hospital in order to avoid the public eye as they gave a New York millionaire with a history that is reportedly mob associated open access to whatever powers C.J. Walker has to share. The exact price paid for his services, if we can assume a price was paid, is still unknown. But one can't help thinking, shades of 'The Godfather'. What *can* this family be thinking?"

Lynn muttered, "Well, we know what they're thinking about us, now."

Joe said, "He just wants to drum up viewers for his program."

Lynn stared solemnly at the screen for another five seconds, then said, still just above a whisper, "I'm not sure, though. I know it didn't happen that way. But I'm not sure ... that they don't have a right ..."

The Cardinal arrived with Monsignor Tennett at Lynn's home at 8:05. The mood of the crowd that witnessed their arrival had, in fact, begun to deteriorate. Already pounded by the hours and by the weather, weary with carrying the pain of their loved ones, frustrated by the lack of any meaningful response from C.J. or his family, and now embittered in varying degrees about the "escaping to help the mob" news stories, their underlying desperation was clearly growing into something darker and more active.

The Cardinal smiled and raised a hand in a small wave as he climbed out of the black sedan, but just a few in the crowd responded with a vocal greeting. Others in the stirring body were not as gracious. Some demanded on the verge of shouting that the Cardinal tell C.J. to come out and help them. Others asked him in shouts why C.J. was being saved for special people but not for them. One young man shouted, "I'll pay you! Can I get to see him now?" Those nearest the shouting man joined in with heckling of their own.

Disquieted but focused, he entered Lynn's house reverentially, the way he might enter a shrine. After offering quiet hellos and thanking Lynn for receiving him, he inquired about C.J. Lynn told him that her son was still sleeping.

Lynn noticed that he looked all keyed up—more than excited, almost driven, but working hard to hold his energy in. That's okay, she thought. I'm driven, too.

And she was. Facing the fact that she would very likely be leaving her home and possibly her country for the rest of her and C.J.'s lives, her nerves were already on a jagged edge. She was scared, and working to hold it in.

They both wanted to speak where they could be alone, so she offered him a coffee, which he declined, and led him to the same out-of-earshot corner she had invited Cross into the night before.

The Monsignor went to the kitchen with Joe.

Once alone with the Cardinal, Lynn left no room for small talk. "I'd like to leave for Rome as soon as possible", she said as they sat down to face one another. "Right away. We can be ready just a few hours after C.J. wakes up, which should be pretty soon. There's very little we'll need to take, and I've already packed clothes and some necessary personal things—family pictures and videos, that kind of thing. Probably the only things I really care about. Not much to be packed beyond that, but after yesterday it's important that we move on this, so we're ready."

"Yes", the Cardinal said. He stared at the back of his hand and then at the floor, thinking, before looking back at Lynn. "Yes", he said again.

She squirmed. Something going on.

"Let me suggest, though," he said softly, "that we wait until Friday. The morning of the operation on Mr. Turner. But early. Well before the surgery actually takes place. That would be good for you, wouldn't it? Give you more time to get ready, say farewells, all of that."

Lynn looked at him like he had just spoken in a foreign language. "What do you mean?" she asked. "Why wait?"

"It won't be a problem, Mrs. Walker. You don't have to worry about anything, I promise you. In fact, I can guarantee you that no one will interrupt the plans, if that's your concern."

She twisted in her chair, upset and showing it. "But why let it go for two more days?"

"It's ... a consideration", he said.

"Cardinal Schaenner," she said, "I'm sitting on the edge of a cliff, about to move my son out of the country on sixty minutes' notice into I don't even know exactly what. So please, just tell me what's going on."

"I'm sorry", he said. He leaned forward with his eyes on alert and suddenly narrowing. "Yes, there's a reason for Friday rather than today or tomorrow, that's true. But it's a reason, and I feel absolutely confident in saying this to you, that you'll be as enthused about as I am. That's my deepest prayer and my deepest expectation."

Lynn bit her lip. Her hands found and closed around the arms of her chair.

The Cardinal stared at her for a few silent seconds, then, speaking even more slowly than before, like an adult might speak to a child, he said, "What do you think would have happened to human history, Mrs. Walker, if Jesus had waited until today, this day and age, to come to earth and raise Lazarus from the dead?"

Her hands locked tighter. She whispered, "What are you talking about?"

"I'm saying ... what would the impact be if Jesus had raised Lazarus from the dead, not in front of a little, nameless group in ancient Israel, but here and now, today, in a live, televised broadcast over a global television hookup?"

Lynn was stunned. She felt like she was listening to him under water.

"What kind of impact", he continued, "do you think that would have on the course of people's faith and their ultimate behavior today, in the here and now, with instant and replayable sound and video from global television, and with computers in play, and the Internet, and tablets, and smartphones, and flash drives, and on and on and on ...?"

She whispered, "I can't believe you're saying this ..."

The Cardinal remained lit with his vision as he leaned even closer to say, "What I want to propose to you, Mrs. Walker, is no less that on this Thursday morning, at sunrise, some forty-five hours from now, the greatest single act of evangelization in the history of the world can take place in the sanctuary of Holy Trinity Cathedral, right here in Detroit. A public resurrection. Early in the morning. Sunrise. Well before the Galvin Turner operation. The public resurrection of a man officially certified by respected medical authorities to be not only dead but embalmed. An authentic resurrection from the dead that will be televised live to all the world. Imagine what that will mean, Mrs. Walker! The influence of it!"

"I can't believe you mean this", she said, still whispering but now fighting a growing panic.

"As much as it seems to argue with our human reason, Mrs. Walker," the Cardinal continued, "you and I know beyond doubt that Marion Klein was dead. Not only dead, but embalmed. We also know beyond doubt that Mr. Turner was dead and embalmed. The records are unassailable. The photos and video of his embalmment are unassailable. The witness of Father Mark to his condition, and the firsthand testimony of you and your husband and the funeral director and your son to the man's being raised from the dead, whole and healthy, is unassailable!"

He paused briefly, then said, "I do understand that if we arrange for a globally televised resurrection, there may be a chance that it would fail. It may have been a temporary gift to your son, a temporary power, for whatever God's reasoning may be. I've considered that. But the gift is real; we have no more doubt. And weighed against the gains of the whole world witnessing a proven, documented, uncontestable death followed by proven, documented, uncontestable resurrection from that death ... well, can we even imagine the impact of such a thing?"

Lynn's mind raced to imagine just that, and she had to fight to hold her composure. What he saw was a better world. What she saw was a firestorm, all out of any possible control and all pointed at C.J. for the rest of his life.

She struggled to breathe more deeply, to not let her expression show what she was feeling, to stay focused on what the Cardinal was saying, to think.

The Cardinal was saying, "Jesus sent out his disciples with instructions as to what their mission was. And what was their mission? Jesus said that in the power of God they were to go out and 'heal the sick' ... do you remember that? They were to 'heal the sick'. They were to 'cure lepers'. And they were to '*raise the dead*'!"

He quickly brought his palms together into a prayer attitude with his extended fingertips pressing into his chin. "Think hard about this, please", he said. "In just ten minutes' time—that's ten minutes, no more—in just that blink of time, what God has given your son the power to accomplish can reach and influence the beliefs, the behavior, and the entire lives of more than one hundred thousand times the number of people that saw and heard Jesus himself in all of his thirty-three years of life and ministry! *More than one hundred thousand times the number Jesus himself reached, in his whole human lifetime!* Why, it leaves me nearly breathless just to realize that this can actually happen, but it can! And the opportunity has actually been given to us, here and now! To you and to your son! Today!"

He paused to draw his lips tightly together for a moment and open his palms to her like wings. "So I'm only asking this of you. I'm asking you to give full and deliberate and prayerful consideration to this single question. What do you think, Mrs. Walker, that God is wanting to do for the world through you and through C.J. at this astonishing point in our history? *What is God wanting to do?*"

He stared at her and she stared at him, with neither of them moving. Nearly a full minute passed before Lynn shifted the focus. "You already have somebody who died picked out", she said. "Don't you? Planning it for that early on Thursday, this has already been all thought through, hasn't it?"

The Cardinal lowered his head for just a moment, then said, "A United States senator from Ohio has died. His death was largely lost in the news here in our area with all the Detroit coverage being of Anthony Cross and C.J. But it was U.S Senator Paul Thessler. You've heard of him, I imagine. He died at his home in Findlay last evening. A good man. He had a heart attack. He was ..."

Lynn interrupted him. "And his family actually told you they'd let this kind of thing happen?"

"They're faith-filled and devoted people. With my personal assurance verifying the authenticity of C.J.'s gift, yes, I'm convinced they will. They want him back. They'll take hold of this. If for no other reason that they won't choose to put his body in the ground and then spend the rest of their lives wondering what would have happened if they'd only said yes."

Lynn felt doors shutting and walls closing in. "The Pope? The Vatican? They'll actually let you do something like this? And at just the drop of a hat?"

"Questions will be asked", the Cardinal said calmly. "And I'll answer them." He then inhaled and exhaled quickly before adding, "Mrs. Walker, God and the Church have made me the bishop of this diocese. My first mission, as I know it to be, is not to try and figure out what it is that I can do for God. It's to try and recognize what God is wanting to do through me. And I am convinced soul-deep that I know what that is in this extraordinary case. I have two priests in Findlay as we speak, priests that know the Thesslers well, who are ready to approach the family within one minute of my leaving your home this morning. The senator's embalming will be witnessed by medical authorities from no less than the Cleveland Medical Center. The cathedral in Detroit is ready now. The senator's body will be transported without any problem or any great rush. The family and relatives will be transported and housed by the diocese. The media, for an event like this, will be in place in half that time, if need be. Security in and around the cathedral would be ready in half that time, as well."

"As for possible outside interference, the announcement of this event will guarantee against it. Marshals could be moving up your driveway to place your son under federal protection right now, for all we know.

But the moment we announce this plan, this time and place, believe me, they wouldn't dare to intrude. In fact, they'll want to be there themselves to see the proof of what happens."

Lynn was aware that her heart was pounding as she raised her biggest horror to the Cardinal. "How many people do you think will see this? You've thought about that, for sure."

He couldn't help smiling at the glory of the vision. He said, "There are seven billion people in the world today. Which would mean two to three billion, certainly, and probably a billion more than that by the time it's gone back and forth around the world for five or six days. In any case, the scope of the outreach will be more than spectacular. But for all of that, the event will be completely under control. Have no doubt about that. As with Mrs. Klein and Mr. Turner, we can count on more than ten minutes from the instant C.J. touches the body to the time anyone will have visual evidence that the senator's life really returned. But we'll have left by then. We'd leave immediately, in the first seconds of that interval."

They heard a sudden tumbling in the hall, and a laughing. It was C.J., rushing downstairs for breakfast with Burr.

Lynn felt physically sick. Five billion people watching C.J., seeing his face. She turned her head, but the Cardinal didn't skip a beat. "As soon as C.J. says his prayer, we'll move you, C.J., and Joe into the sacristy in back of the altar, then out through the cathedral's south basement door. You'll still be on church grounds, remember, and in my company, and under security that can't and won't be breached."

Lynn thought about a sparrow they had found caught in the house two years ago, how it flitted through the rooms so crazily, so scared and trapped, not knowing how it got into such a place and not knowing how to find a way out. They tried shooing it with pillowcases into the kitchen, and an open window, but it never made it. They found its body a few weeks later in the upstairs hall closet.

"On the south lawn of the cathedral, which is large and isolated and entirely fenced-in, there'll be a helicopter ready to go, one with our own pilot. I guarantee you that inside of ten minutes after C.J.'s prayer for the senator, and that means ten minutes at the most, you and your son will be crossing the border into Canada."

"I'd have to ask C.J.", she said meekly. "He may not do it."

"I doubt very much he'll deny you, Mrs. Walker", the Cardinal replied. "Not when you tell him how important it will be for so many, many people. Not when you promise him that you and his father will be with him every single second, without fail."

Her hands came together in her lap. She looked at them, not at the Cardinal. She knew that he was right. C. J. would do it if she asked him.

"That flight takes just five minutes. That's all it will be. You'll be safe in Canada that quickly. You understand that."

Barely a whisper, "I understand."

"And it will have all been arranged and cleared beforehand, start to finish, here to there and out again. From the Windsor Airport we'll fly you, still under the strictest security, on a private flight to Rome. No stopping. No interruptions. No complications."

This is the way it will always be, she thought. This is the way it's always going to be, and it's never going to end.

She heard him say, as if from a room in the distance, "Just the prayer, Mrs. Walker. And then you're out."

"I understand."

"It will be like a replanting of human consciousness. Like a restart to human culture. More than attitude shifting, it will be world-changing."

She stared at him in silence as her mind continued to flit through every room in the house, looking . . .

They were in the endgame. They both knew it.

After nearly five minutes, Lynn took another deep breath, let it out slowly, and said to the Cardinal, softly and without emotion, "It will make what happened to Marion Klein seem almost irrelevant, won't it?"

The Cardinal beamed victoriously.

He said, "It will make countless things in this world seem irrelevant!"

Twenty-Five

Within ten minutes, C.J. had agreed to raising one more man, this time at the cathedral in Detroit, his mother's request outweighing his revulsion at the thought of any more crowds pressing in on him. Within sixty minutes, the Cardinal received a phone call advising him that the family of Senator Paul Thessler had also agreed to the Cardinal's proposal. The Cleveland Medical Center was being contacted in order to secure the most authoritative medical confirmation of the senator's full embalming.

The Cardinal immediately instructed Monsignor Tennett to coordinate communications through the Diocesan Communications Office with the Apostolic Nunciature in Washington, D.C.; the diocese of Findlay, Ohio; and the rest of the archdiocese of Detroit, including, importantly, the rector of Holy Trinity Cathedral. He was also asked to oversee broadcast arrangements. Bennington Reed was assigned, breathless as a school boy, to work with federal, state, and local authorities to oversee security as well as transportation to the cathedral for C.J. and his family. He would also direct arrangements for the helicopter that would take them across the Detroit River to Canada and the necessary flight arrangements from Canada to Rome. Father Mark was asked to stay close to the family, keeping them focused, keeping them at ease, making sure they followed through on Lynn and C.J.'s promise to cooperate.

At 9:50 A.M., the Cardinal gave Lynn, Joe, Father Mark, and Nancy Gould, who had been invited by Lynn, a private briefing. C.J. stayed upstairs with Burr.

He began the briefing while pacing back and forth, his hands as animated as his words, his eyes shining with the stunning possibilities as he saw them.

They listened like statues.

"Senator Thessler's embalming", he announced, "will take place this afternoon at 4:30 P.M. in Findlay, Ohio, his home city. The embalming will be witnessed by a three-physician team that includes the chief medical officer of the Cleveland Medical Center." He paused, letting the name of the respected medical facility sink in, his face bright with satisfaction.

Joe was the only one taking notes, scribbling in a small pad he'd drawn from his back pocket.

"The senator will be prayed with by C.J. in the sanctuary of Detroit's Blessed Sacrament Cathedral at sunrise, which will be 5:42 A.M., on Friday, approximately forty-two hours from now."

The Cardinal smiled again, this time at C.J., who had just come downstairs and was staring back at him with his dark eyes narrowed and his hands pressed flat under his thighs. Then he continued, savoring the moment as much as the expectations. "It will be the most remarkable and blessed event that we're likely to experience in our entire lives, I promise you", he said. "And the early hour will not only let us move well before Mr. Galvin Turner's operation, but it will guarantee the most extensive audiences in Europe and other parts of the world, including Rome."

Lynn closed her eyes slowly.

The Cardinal's right hand opened and extended across his chest to his left, then swung slowly in a full arc to his right as he said, "Broadcast coverage will begin early. C.J. and his parents, the three of you, will be picked up by 4:30 A.M. and driven from here in the center of a high-security motorcade to the cathedral in Detroit."

He looked at Lynn for approval.

She nodded, then closed her eyes again.

"Your drivers will be state troopers, armed but plainclothes. State police, Royal Oak police, Detroit police, and Oakland County sheriff's deputies will all be involved either as escorts or in crowd and traffic control. It will go smoothly, I promise you."

"Aren't the federal guys in there somewhere?" Joe asked.

"Yes", the Cardinal said. "They'll be involved, too, and part of the motorcade." He waited to see if there were more questions. When there weren't, he added, "We'll have another briefing by the police well before any of us have to leave for the cathedral, and all the details will be covered, I'm sure."

Still no more questions or remarks, so he continued, "A single police helicopter will also accompany the motorcade, and news copters will be assigned to broadcast our progress, with all of the news services sharing the videos live, of course."

Mark was staring at Lynn. She didn't notice. She still had not opened her eyes.

"We'll all arrive at the Cathedral at no later than 5:00 A.M.," the Cardinal said, "a little more than a half hour before sunrise and the senator's resurrection."

Father Mark said, "You're going to have media coverage inside the cathedral, I take it."

"Of course. The object of the whole event is evangelization. We want the world to see and to believe. We want every major global news organization represented inside the cathedral, as well as in a string of locations outside—although," he raised his hand as a caution, "I'm sure that whatever is arranged will not detract from the sanctity of the event itself."

Lynn opened her eyes again. "And then, as soon as C.J. says the words ...?"

The Cardinal nodded. "As soon as C.J. says the words and touches the senator's body, we will extract you and your son from the sanctuary, along with Father Mark, Monsignor Tennett, and myself. We'll board the helicopter that will be in place on the south lawn—archdiocesan-contracted, with our own pilot and security—and take off immediately for Ontario, Canada, and then to Rome. No waiting, either at the cathedral or in Ontario."

Joe began to ask a question, but stopped. The "you and your son" had hit him hard. No surprise, but it had still hit him hard. He tilted his head slightly and listened for more.

Lynn's thoughts had slipped away to a sparrow, still flying through the house, still looking.

The plan for a live TV resurrection of a confirmed corpse at the Catholic cathedral in Detroit was first broadcast as a white-hot rumor over Detroit's WXYZ talk radio at 11:30 A.M. With no denials forthcoming, either from Senator Thessler's family in Ohio or from archdiocesan sources in Detroit, the speculation rocketed to national and international broadcast news and the Internet overnight.

By the time Bennington Reed accompanied the director of Archdiocesan Community Relations to his Wednesday afternoon news conference, where the facts were publicly confirmed, TV and radio programming and Net chat rooms were rocking with renewed resurrection speculations, and not a few questions still begging for answer, most of them beginning with "what if". "What if the boy healed everybody at the cathedral, as long as he was at it?" and "What if they set up something like a weekly World Life Lotto, with the winners getting somebody raised from the dead and the proceeds going to feed the poor?" and even the dreaded, "What if the boy's initials are a clue, and they were really backwards, so the boy is really the Second Coming of Jesus Christ?"

Spokesmen for religious institutions, including the Vatican, made quick plans to position themselves at a safe distance from what was already a rising controversy with as much disapproval as interest and approval, with some faith-based organizations appealing publicly for prayer and others denouncing any traffic with the dead as being recklessly unholy. The Catholic Detroit Chancery office and local parishes were inundated not only with questions but with requests for prime seating in the cathedral itself, some of the calls originating from the offices of respected business leaders, medical authorities, and political dignitaries. One rumor in the nation's capital suggested that the assistant surgeon general of the United States would be there. It was publically doubted, but, again, there were no denials.

The mayor of Detroit and governor of Michigan appealed publicly for media sources to resist a "Super Bowl-type buildup" that might create such a high level of resurrection fever that life and property in the cathedral area would be threatened. Even with so few hours of lead time, the mayor worried publicly that "we could see one man resurrected and kill three thousand people in the stampede to touch the boy's garment."

By 5:00 P.M., a local candlelight vigil was proposed by a group of Michigan's representatives of the World Council of Churches for the three hours leading up to sunrise at 5:42 A.M. on the morning of what most pop-media sources were already referring to as "Resurrection Day".

By 5:30 P.M., a hundred people had already taken up positions around Blessed Sacrament Cathedral, staking out territory, guarding food and drinks held in quickly packed coolers, working out cell-phone communications with family and friends regarding more substantial provisions, unrolling sleeping blankets to mark their territory overnight, making their cameras and video recorders ready. They were just the first of what city officials expected could become, by sunrise on Friday morning, a crowd of more than thirty thousand people, all pressing toward the corner of Boston Boulevard and Woodward Avenue on Detroit's north side before sunrise of the next day, all determined to catch at least one glimpse of the coming of God to earth.

By 6:00 P.M., Joe had not only confirmed a deal with CBS News, but he had pulled Lynn aside to give her the details. Why not? It was something anybody would feel high about. Given an authentic rising from the dead, he told her, they'd pay five million dollars in exchange for Joe's exclusive, live commentary from the sanctuary of the cathedral itself on Friday morning, as well as three more hours of exclusive video interviews at a later date.

"I'll give you a chunk of it if you need it", Joe told Lynn.

"I don't think we'll need it", she said.

"No," he said, "I don't think you will, either."

He didn't tell her that he had also guaranteed to provide never-before aired or published photos and videos of C.J., materials that would become the sole property of CBS News.

"Promise me one more time, though," he said, "that you get in touch with me as soon as you can, right? I know you have to wait awhile, but I get to see you two. So Cross arranges it, so no one knows where I'm meeting you, okay?"

She nodded.

She even let him hug her.

"It'll be okay", he whispered.

"I hope so", she said.

For his part, he could barely keep from cheering. The biggest event in two thousand years was about to happen, and he was right square in the middle of it—him and a ten-million-dollar pot of gold, all happening because he was the one who found out what C.J. could do and who was smart enough to deal with it. He'd see the miracle, he'd see them off to Rome, he'd see them again in some island paradise, with all of them richer by the millions.

After all these years, he thought, Kirk's Kiss was finally going to win in the mud.

The late afternoon air was warm and settled. There was no breeze, not even a sigh. A few thin strips of cloud were pasted tight across the tops of the trees in the sky to the west, unable to move. They glowed with pinks and purples like a fluorescent bandage.

Joe and C.J. were sitting at the picnic table, in the backyard, near the garage. It was a chance at some time together—a short visit between father and son, just the two of them, at Joe's invitation.

C.J. put his Red Wings cap on backward. His elbows were on his knees, his fists pressed into his cheeks.

They could hear the hum of the crowd in front of the house, past the garage, with a few individual voices calling out names and directions in short, unconnected spurts. An occasional siren whooped. The helicopter pulsed at a distance to the north. A second one thumped in the south, a quarter mile away.

Joe reached over to rub the boy's left shoulder; then he wrapped his fingers around it. "So how're you feeling about the cathedral, Ceej?" he asked, smiling. "And about the guy there? You feeling okay about it?"

C.J. nodded. He said, "Yeah", but at the same time he eased away from his dad's hand and stood up to move to the tabletop, his feet now resting on the bench seat.

Joe did the same, not hurrying and watching C.J. the whole time, now sitting even closer beside his son than before, their shoulders practically touching. He said softly, "You're feeling okay, though." It sounded like an order, quietly given. "You're feeling like you're sure you can do this again. It's still there and all that."

Another nod from C.J., this time with a quick study of his dad's expression. "I'm okay."

Joe licked his lower lip and nodded, "Okay."

"I know I can still do it. Is that what you mean?"

"Just how you feel about it."

"I'm okay."

Joe said, "It's the first time with that many people watching is all. That's why I'm asking."

C.J. squirmed. His heel, having nothing else interesting to do, began to bounce slowly against the outer edge of the bench seat. He said, "Can we go inside, Dad?"

"In just a minute, okay? I just wanted to talk with you for a minute. You and Mom go to Italy, you know it's gonna be a while before I see you again. She told you all that, right?"

C.J. nodded and nibbled at his lower lip.

Joe laid his hand on the boy's shoulder again. He forced a light smile. "You can still do it, though, for sure, huh?"

C.J. stared at him. "C'mon, Dad", he whispered.

"Yeah, well, it's just important to me. This one especially, is what I mean. I just want you to know that. We need this one to work for sure, you know? So, as long as you're okay ..."

C.J. didn't answer. His eyes grew dark. He eased away from Joe's hand with a shrug and slid six inches closer to the far end of the bench. His head was down, his eyes on the ground, his expression pained.

Joe inched toward him. "What's the matter?" he asked, trying to sound bright.

But C.J. wasn't looking bright. When he raised his head and turned to face his dad, his eyes were filled with tears. His chin quivered once, hard, and his lower lip twisted as he began to speak, and he spoke so quietly it was almost a whisper. He said, "Why are you just worried about if I can still do it and never about what people might want to do to me?"

Joe felt like he'd been struck in the face. The obvious pain in his son's sad eyes and voice and in his lips, making them tremble the way they did, tore at his heart, and he withdrew physically, his mouth and eyes wide with sudden hurt.

He blinked. He looked back at C.J. and then at the grass, and then at the house. He shifted his weight and leaned forward on the bench with his elbows settling on his knees and his hands folded together. "Jeez ...", he said softly, something he hadn't said since he was probably nine years old himself. But that was all he said, just "Jeez ...", and then he rose to his feet.

He was aware again of the crowd in front of the house, a lot of them looking from far away around the corner of the house at him and C.J. He was aware of someone yelling for somebody named Dale and of a horn honking and someone else calling "Mom" with a woman's voice. And he was aware again of C.J.'s eyes, still shining with moisture and questions. And in those few seconds of new closeness and new pain, with something inside him thrown back to old places and old and tender feelings, he knew exactly what was going to happen to C.J. at the cathedral.

He knew, not just what the Cardinal said was going to happen or what the Cardinal hoped was going to happen, but what the Cardinal believed was going to happen. And it was not what the man had said to Lynn and to C.J.

He turned, stunned, to stare at the house. He saw someone standing very still and watching from the screened-in back porch. He recognized Bennington Reed.

He heard himself whisper, "Oh my God!"

They met in Lynn's room, just the two of them, as the sun was setting outside and the house downstairs was strangely quiet, just Joe and Lynn.

His expression had alarmed her already because he had looked scared, something Lynn had never seen before: Joe, not cocky at all, not even trying to look like he had everything under control, his eyes wide, almost glassy, his head lowered, his voice clipped and urgent, saying to her in the kitchen, "I've got to talk with you now. Not in five minutes even. Right now. In your room. Not down here. Something you don't know yet. But you've got to."

The sun was behind trees and houses, and her room was getting dark, but Lynn didn't turn on the light. Maybe the less she could see the better. She moved, instead, to the wing-backed chair next to the dresser and sat down, defended by crossed arms.

Joe pulled up the chair from the dressing table and sat down facing her. He leaned forward.

"Tell me", Lynn said. She drew a deep breath and let it out slowly.

Joe stared at her in the low light for several seconds, neither of them moving; then he said it.

"C.J. may not be going to Rome, Lynn. He may be going over to the government. Schaenner's maybe going to let him go over."

Lynn was thunderstruck. She felt herself start to reel backward. She said, "What are you talking about?"

"Lynn, I'm trying to do some good here", Joe said quickly. "Please listen to me." He sat upright. He extended his hands in front of his chest as if he was trying to hold the world steady for just one more minute. He said, "Schaenner's one and only real goal is to get that resurrection to happen in front of global TV, not to get C.J. to Rome. That's what you have to start with. What counts to him is having that miracle happen on TV so those billion people he talked about can see that the power is real and all of a sudden believe in God. That's more important to him, Lynn, than what happens to you; it's more important than what happens to C.J.; it's more important than what happens to himself." His fists closed and pressed together tightly. He said, "Do you understand that?"

Lynn wanted to tell him to stop, to tell him to let her do this one thing and not have to think about it anymore or plan it anymore or be afraid about it anymore. But she didn't tell him anything. She sat frozen, picturing the Cardinal smiling at her in the living room and saying in his soft voice how much it will make so many things in the world today seem irrelevant.

Joe said, "The way he sees it, he's saving the world. He's not doing a bad thing. In his mind, it's him and God working this out with maybe billions of souls at stake. And both of them know, both him and God, that if Schaenner doesn't get this miracle to happen now, it won't really matter a lot whether C.J. ends up in Rome or with the government, because no one else is going to let it happen, ever again—not in Rome or anywhere else. He knows that. So they've cooked this thing up together, him and God; that's how he sees it: him and the Almighty, like a private pact between the two of them to sidestep everyone else and make sure that this thing happens for the good of the world."

"But why give C.J. over?" she whispered. "I just don't believe you."

"I'm not saying he wants it. He's not going to tie the kid up and deliver him in a bag. He's probably going to somehow try to get him away, just like he says. But what if he knows down deep that he's not going to make it, that's the point. Inside, what if he knows they're bound to take him. And instead of telling you what he knows, he's willing to go through with it anyway because he feels like the world has to have this miracle here in the cathedral at all costs."

He stared at her, noticing the darkness, not caring, leaning closer, watching her shake her head, knowing she was still not believing him.

"He'll have all the pieces there", he said, "all in order, the helicopter on the lawn and the whole shot. Maybe he's even kidded himself into thinking God will work another miracle, make half a million people go blind or something, break all the cameras so you and C.J. can get out of there in one piece. But down deep, I'll say it again, he's too smart not to realize that his plan to get you away probably can't work. And now you and I have to be that smart, too."

He stood over her, watching her face fading into the darkness. He bent down and laid his hands over hers, on the arms of the chair. His face was close to hers. His voice was low and intense. "The feds already know you're planning on getting away, Lynn. Think about it. They have to. They have to know about Canada; you can't just fly from one country to another without having flight plans and clearances and things." He suddenly squeezed hard on her hands and added in a loud whisper, "I think that that helicopter's being put there to help convince you to go *to* the cathedral, Lynn. It's not really there to help get you *away*."

She felt her mind racing and her heart racing and her breath racing, and she wanted to swing at Joe for making it happen. "But we'll be on church property", she whispered, refusing to give in. "I'm with a Cardinal, on church property."

"Lynn, we're talking about the U.S. government being an inch away from owning the one power on earth that's stronger than death. Having it right in their pocket. No one else having it. Real power, like nothing that ever was. You say 'church property'; they'll say 'national defense'. Those things they said at the house that day about dictators in the Middle East getting their hands on him—about cloning the power, maybe, about keeping all the key people alive, about bringing back whole armies by the hundreds and thousands at a time and all of that—they knew it could be true for them, too."

"They don't even know for sure that C.J. can do these things."

"They don't know that he *can't*, is the point. And they do know that he might. And they know the Cardinal, who's no dummy, already thinks he can. So they imagine, what would it do if they could find the key to it? To leverage out a country's power to make war, just for one example? This country or any country? And they can imagine that, I'll tell you, and they are imagining it. One of the greatest gifts to the human race ever. So do you really think, with all that at stake, they'll give a brass damn about one guy in a red beanie? You think they'll care if you cry and say, 'Oh, it's church property', like all of a sudden we're back in the Middle Ages?"

She stared at his darkened face. She pulled her hands slowly out from under his and laid them in her lap, one holding the other.

"I didn't even see it myself at first. But I kept thinking, since the Cardinal first started leaning on you back in his house, why did he want so bad to get C.J. over there to that hospital? Didn't that strike you as strange? I know I said okay to it, but I was thinking, there had to be a reason he wasn't telling us about, because all that pressure never really made sense. And then I realized, it was for him! He wanted to see it happen himself; somebody raised off their bed! They might have told him from Rome to shut C.J. down till they got him over there, but that way, he could say, 'Well, I told them not to let that happen', but he'd put you in a position where C.J. couldn't resist. He gets there, and the kid breaks the rules. He's a kid. You're a mom; you've got a big heart. The Cardinal heard what we all believed, but he wanted to see it for himself, because he was about to make the biggest decision of his life. Huge stuff. Huge stuff, Lynn. He was thinking about it even then, the miracle on TV. The Vatican maybe not even knowing about it, but if they did, him maybe even doing it when they didn't want him to, because God did, and because then he'd know! Huge stuff. Even then, the plan turning over in his head.

"I thought, my God, I must have been blind. I was thinking of all that money, I think; just like you say, I think about that and I go blind. But hell, Lynn, the feds, they see that going on at the cathedral, the man waking up in that coffin, they can put a gun in someone's pocket in the crowd if they have to. Say they had to grab C.J. for his own protection. They can have shots fired and say there's a militant loose; hold up some Christian-sounding nutcase, or a radical Muslim, whatever it takes. They'll create the excuse to take him, I promise you. This is a whole lot bigger than whatever was behind the worst thing you've ever heard of the government doing, guaranteed. At the very least, they'll have their own pilot on the helicopter. Or they'll be on the helicopter with you, and once you're off the ground, they'll make you fly to the Selfridge Base or something.

"You think they can't force that? You think they won't force that, even if they don't have their own pilot? Some fly-for-dollars pilot out there, got a wife and kids, doesn't want to go to jail or lose his license or get shot in the head; you think they won't threaten the end of life as he knows it and make him fly you someplace different than Canada, or at least keep you there on the ground at the cathedral till they see if the man from Ohio twitches his little finger? And when he does that …"

He paused. He sighed. He said, "That's the way our son's world is going to end, Lynn. A man from Ohio is going to twitch his little finger."

The room was so dark that Joe could barely see her lips, parted now, and still. She was listening without moving. Her eyes were fixed on the space in front of her, seeing nothing.

"The Cardinal will probably be really sorry when it happens, after the miracle", Joe said, speaking more softly than before. "He'll ask God to protect you or whatever, and he'll ask God to forgive him if he's doing the wrong thing and all that. But he doesn't really believe he is. Because billions, of souls are worth whatever happens. And that, for this man, is the bottom line."

Lynn waited through a long silence; then she pushed herself to her feet and walked unevenly to the window, feeling her way, feeling shaky.

He followed her, the room now simply showing dark shapes. "And you know what the worst thing is?" he said. "The worst thing is, those billions of people aren't going to all of a sudden believe in God, anyway, even if they do see what C.J. does. The Cardinal believes that because he wants so bad to see it happen that way, everybody rushing to get closer to God and all. But he's wrong. All those people … they won't believe in God. They'll believe in C.J. Walker."

She continued staring out the window. The crowds, now with flashlights lit, and lanterns. So many people. So many cameras and police and so much craziness.

"Two weeks ago," she said, her voice barely above a whisper, "C.J. was playing soccer in our backyard. Kicking the ball into the side of the garage. I told him to stop because he was making mud circles on the paint." She stopped. Five seconds went by. "That's what I was worried about two weeks ago. Mud circles on the garage."

She fell silent and the silence stretched. Without turning around, she said to him, "What was it for, then, Joe? I mean, C.J. having this, if it isn't for the cathedral? At least I want there to be a good reason why it was him."

Joe stood close to her. "Just because it's the biggest thing any of us has ever seen doesn't mean it couldn't have been happening for just one or two people", he said. "Maybe it's mostly for C.J. or Marion. Could be mostly for her. Turner, or Cross' kid. How can we tell? Maybe it was really for Cross himself, or for one of the cancer ladies at Fremont."

She thought about it. "Maybe it was a mistake", she whispered. "Or maybe I'm the mistake, even being mixed up in it."

He put his hand on her shoulder. He said, "Maybe it was for you, babe. Or for you and C.J. both."

She smiled softly in the dark. She couldn't help it. Joe being philosophical. But more than nice talk was going on with him; she could sense it. Somehow, Joe was trying to think about C.J., really trying to help. Maybe not even thinking it through, but trying to put C.J. ahead of himself, and to make it real, to make C.J. even more important than his CBS deal. Maybe make her more important than that, too.

She couldn't be certain it was happening that way, and she wouldn't trust that it would last, whatever it was. But she sensed that it was real, at least for the moment, and she was grateful.

"Maybe it was for you, Joe", she whispered.

He removed his hand from her shoulder. They were both silent for several seconds, both of them moving past the moment.

He said, "We haven't got a lot of time, babe. What do you want me to do?"

Another long pause. She said, finally, "Can you help me get in touch with Cross again. I mean, without anybody else knowing about it?"

"I have a cell phone from him", he said. "You should have one, too. But I have it here. He had his guys set it up, so it should be as confidential as possible. But they're watching you too close to let you go with him, you know?"

She said, "I know", paused for nearly five seconds, and said it again, softer than before. "I know."

Twenty-Six

The sun rose on Thursday, Lynn noticed, at 5:42, the same time it would rise in twenty-four hours, give or take a matter of a few seconds. She was lying on her side in her bed, a light sheet over her legs, her hands folded over her waist. Just the way it would to signal, what had the Cardinal called it? ... the greatest single act of evangelization in the history of the modern world?

She turned onto her back, moving slowly. Her stomach was in a knot. She decided she would not try to eat that day.

A minute dragged by. She turned again onto her side.

She noticed the curtains moving slightly in front of her open windows and thought of the lightness of the breeze, and she thought about how lightly C.J. used to breathe in his sleep, especially when he was just a baby. She thought, there is nothing in the world as soft as the way C.J. used to breathe in his sleep when he was just a baby.

She was aware of car engines murmuring in the street outside—engines and low voices, the light just beginning to take over the morning, the crowd just coming to life.

Twenty-four hours, exactly.

She wondered if C.J. was still sleeping, he and Burr, together in his room. The arrangement had been one more attempt to pretend that something in his world was still normal.

The curtain stirred again. She realized that this would be the last time she would ever see that curtain stirring from her own bed at sunrise, in her own home on Westlane Avenue.

This would be the day of last times, she thought. It would be her day of one last time.

She felt slightly sick, but she knew it was nerves rather than a virus. If it was a virus, she thought, she could have C.J. cure it.

She wondered if he could do the same for runaway nerves. She decided not to find out.

She rolled to her left again and looked at the clock; it was 5:46. Now less than twenty-four hours.

She came downstairs at 6:50 A.M. wearing an Eastern Michigan University sweatshirt that hung low over her jeans and an expression that signaled a woman feeling both wary and exhausted.

Joe, who had stayed overnight, was sitting quietly on the couch in the living room, a cold coffee in his hand, staring at the window. "Really busy out there", he remarked.

She crossed over to the window and peered out.

The police were already prowling across her lawn, even gathering on the front walk, in front of her porch, half a dozen of them on the walk alone, and other people moving around inside the barricade tapes with radios and earphones and serious expressions. People where they shouldn't be, talking low, keeping secrets in front of the house and around the south corner, by the driveway.

They would be at her door soon, she was certain: police and other officials, the U.S. deputy marshal, various church people, all of them intruding again and again from now until it happened; coming to make plans, to give orders, to enforce securities, to confirm details, to channel her and C.J. without any deviation into exactly the right place at exactly the right time: Blessed Sacrament Cathedral, sunrise, the following morning.

To her surprise, though, it wasn't the police who knocked on her front door first, at 7:00 A.M. It was Bennington Reed.

The Cardinal's associate stood on the porch like a curtain, his bulk blocking her view of the officers standing behind him. He was smiling and, as always, it seemed, impeccably dressed, today in a rich, light-brown suit and paisley tie. He looked so excited when Lynn opened the door that it struck her that this man, standing there so expansive and so well groomed and so buoyant, was the absolute antithesis of everything she was feeling.

He grinned and greeted her with, "Good morning, Mrs. Walker! And how is C.J. today?"

Lynn stepped aside to let him in and had just started to tell him that C.J. was still sleeping, when he cut her off with a quick "He's well?" Then he raised his chin sharply and laughed a loud "Haw!" and said with his next breath, again, before she could answer, "But how could he not be well? If he's sick, he just tells himself to get well!" His eyebrows shot up and his eyes widened in mock surprise as he added, "Am I right?" Then he laughed again and glanced past her at Joe, still on the couch, for his approval.

Joe stared at Reed but didn't smile and didn't rise to greet him. He sat there with his head cocked slightly to the right, just watching, his eyes narrowed, like he was trying to decide something important.

Lynn left the door open as Reed moved by her, her hand still on the knob. She said, "I know it's a big day, but is there some specific reason you came over, Mr. Reed? And so early?"

Reed looked as though he hadn't heard the question. He said, "They'll look at tomorrow morning as we now look at the signing of the Magna Carta, do you realize that? Or the Declaration of Independence. But even that's an understatement, isn't it?"

Lynn let the door click closed.

Reed took a single step toward the living room, his smile insisting that Joe smile back at him. But Joe continued to study him. No smile. No words of welcome.

"Please. What can we do for you?" Lynn asked.

Reed turned to face her very slowly, the way a ship turns. "I'm sorry", he said softly, his smile fading. "I know it's early, but I wanted to put your mind at ease about security, in case you had any concerns in that direction. I've been put in charge of security coordination, you know."

Lynn shook her head, saying, "I'm not worried about it. I'm sure it will be whatever we need it to be. And we appreciate anything you're doing along those lines."

"We're doing more than enough", Reed said. "And it's already in place, that's why I came, to assure you of that. 'A net of protection', one of the officers called it, but that isn't accurate, and I told him so. Because a net has holes, I said, and what we have around that boy doesn't."

He stopped and started to smile again, this time in approval of his own analogy. Then his face settled again into a much more serious expression. He took a step closer to Lynn, his wide back squarely to Joe, and said in a confidential tone of voice, "I want you to be rest assured, Mrs. Walker. That's all. I know full well what this event means to the world, and I want to give you my solemn word that we have so much security wrapped around you and your son, now and from this moment on, that you won't even need the angels of God to protect you."

Father Mark arrived at 11:00 A.M. He had barely gotten through the side door when Lynn asked him in a subdued voice if the two of them could talk privately.

She led him into the backyard. They didn't sit down. They stood close and spoke in whispers next to the garage, on the far side of the picnic table.

"I appreciate the support you promised us, Mark", Lynn told him. "I want you to know that, okay?"

Mark nodded and smiled lightly. He said, "I haven't been able to do much, though, have I?" Then he added, "You know that I was surprised you agreed to all this, don't you? The way you felt about everything; it just caught me off guard."

She stared at the lawn, then looked back toward the house. "As they say, it seemed like a good idea at the time."

Mark studied her, studied the look in her eyes, especially. "How does it seem now, Lynn?" he asked quietly. "What's going on now, today?"

She glanced around one more time, first left, then right, then she eased herself sideways, putting her back to the house. She reached out with her hand, closing the two-foot gap between them. Her fingertips touched his arm just above the wrist. She said, "You told me you'd be on our side no matter what we decided we had to do."

He took a deep breath. He nodded. Then he asked it again, more quietly and more urgently than before: "What's going on, Lynn?"

"No matter what we decide to do", she said. She bit her lower lip, thinking, then said, "That's all there is, Mark. I'm sorry."

Joe, more than the others, was drawn to watching the buildup at the cathedral on TV as the day dragged on. He watched it before and after Royal Oak's director of police, John Ball, came with half a dozen other officers to reiterate what the Cardinal had told them about the makeup and timing of their 4:35 A.M. motorcade to the cathedral. He watched it while the others nibbled at food or drink, or huddled in quiet conversations in distant corners of the house, Lynn with Nancy, especially, the two of them acting as though they were trying to make up for the lost time to come. He watched it as the police came and went with their questions and cautions and instructions and with radios that squawked with static and distant voices. He watched it through the afternoon and into the early evening. He watched it with the remote control in his hand, clicking from one channel to the next.

It was Ruth Cosgrove who owned his attention now, the original holder of the C.J. Walker secret, her blond hair tied back straight and flat, her expression somber and thrilled and flushed with secrets and satisfaction all at the same time. She was at the cathedral and dressed in a deep red suit that made her stand out like a flare against the gray stone of the cathedral's walls.

"Detroit's Holy Trinity Cathedral is a magnificent structure", she assured her viewers. She was a woman who clearly recognized and enjoyed her element, a reporter covering not only the biggest story of her life but a story that she, herself, had broken and loved to continue reporting, especially now, when it was flying headlong into deep and uncharted territory. "It is a thirteen-hundred-capacity house of worship, completed in 1939, and the central house of worship for the Roman Catholic Archdiocese of Detroit."

The camera covering her began to swing, following her lead. Her right hand held her mike close, her left pointed along the lines of the structure and over the already gathering congregation. She held it out like a female Jesus calming troubled waters. "These great, gothic arches tower over forty-two rows of richly carved mahogany pews, and all of this under extraordinary, eighteen-foot stained glass windows, twenty-four of them, windows which, in less than twelve hours, will light up in the rising sun of a new Friday morning to glow with brightly colored depictions of Jesus, and Mary, and the hand of God, over there, and all along there, a sweeping ridge of clouds and angels and so many saints!" Close-up. Her voice suddenly hushed. She turned again, dramatically, this time, with a generous sweep of her free hand, the camera still following her lead. "And right there", she said, "at what we're informed will be in just a few hours from now, between three and three thirty in the morning, just ten feet in front of that marbled altar, in the space between those two high candles, the embalmed remains of the popular Republican senator from Ohio, Senator Paul Thessler, will be placed to wait for young C.J. Walker."

A pause. The camera holding. Then moving in slowly to a close-up of the space between the candles.

Joe leaned forward, mesmerized. Lynn's friend Nancy Gould was behind him, in the kitchen doorway. She whispered, "God help us."

Another close-up of Ruth. Her voice still hushed. "The senator's family will arrive here at the same time, of course: his wife of thirty-seven years, Eleanor; his daughters, twenty-four-year-old Katlin and twenty-two-year-old Caroline; and his son, Brian Paul, a sophomore at Ohio State University."

The camera cut away from Ruth and swept slowly across the empty front pew. It found a small, white "Reserved" sign hung from the pew's carved end, facing the center aisle. It stopped for a close-up of the sign, then pulled back. Ruth walked into camera view, her hand gesturing to the sign. "They'll watch from here", she said, "from this front pew, as nine-year-old Christopher Joseph Walker attempts to do the impossible, and bring their husband and father back home to them again, alive and well."

Joe got to his feet, still staring at the screen—picturing the family, picturing them staring at the body in the space between the candles, picturing them watching the man who was dead, and wondering, and hoping.

The camera looked past the pews to the banks of cameras along the north side of the cathedral. It moved to the balcony. More cameras. Cameras and mikes and other announcers already murmuring to listeners and viewers all over the world.

"This place of solemn worship", Ruth continued, "has been transformed, as you can see, into a theater bristling with the technologies of communication."

Joe tried to spot CNN but couldn't. No matter.

"Network. Cable. Private communication services. And up there, in the balcony, all of that: international sources. You can see their announcers broadcasting already, many of them to places where it's already sunrise."

The camera moved back down, now to the other side of the church. More cameras. More people busy with wires and mikes. And other people, too: men in uniforms and men in suits, watching carefully, some wired and talking into headsets, others with two-way radios. "You can see the police and other officials", Ruth said. "Security is extraordinary, not only here, but outside, where we'll take you in a moment. State police. Detroit police. Wayne County sheriff's patrols, out in the streets. And these men you see in civilian clothes? Many of them are federal law enforcement officers: U.S. deputy marshals and special agents of the FBI, among others. Again, an extraordinary presence for an extraordinary event."

The camera was back on Ruth, who confirmed her new camera direction by saying, "Let's take you outside now. The sun hasn't quite set, and we'll still be able to see the crowd. It's just astonishing."

Joe sat down again. He was staring at her suit. He was remembering it from religion classes in his Catholic grade school, how red robes in church always had a special meaning. They always wore red for the blood of martyrs.

Lynn was in her favorite place in all the world. She was in C.J.'s bed with just the night-light on and her son lying warmly at her side in the dim light and the blessed quiet.

She had closed her eyes, and, very tentatively, was trying to appreciate what might be the last sense of peace and quiet she'd enjoy for a long time.

She tried one more time to ask God if a gift as unthinkable as C.J.'s power could be returned, but gave it up. She'd asked it enough already, so what was the use? The pressure of what she was about to try to do began to press in again, like it wanted to steal her breath, and she inhaled a deep breath and held it for a few seconds before letting it out.

C.J., still awake, looked up at her and whispered, "Are you okay, Mom?"

"I'm fine, honey. Are you okay?"

"I guess so. You're going to be with me all day tomorrow, right?"

"Absolutely positively for sure", she said. "And not just for tomorrow. Absolutely positively, honey."

She took his hand. He nestled closer, squirmed a few times, very slightly, and soon fell asleep.

Lynn stayed with him. Her favorite place.

She found herself thinking about all the things they were going to leave behind in Royal Oak, things she never expected to see again. She thought of baby things still in boxes in the back room where her antique bench was. She thought about mud circles on the garage and picnics with a six-month-old on the green blanket in the backyard, in the summers gone by. But she also realized that, for all she would miss, there really wasn't much that she could and would like to take with her. The only really important things were the photos and videos on the shelf in her bedroom closet. Everything else could be replaced easily, but not the images of the best parts of her life.

Then she thought about the day that waited for her. Crouching and waiting for her, she found herself picturing it. Crouching in the cathedral, waiting for her. With that, the pressures of the next day's plans started to feel tangible to her again, started to press out the good memories and steal her breath.

C.J. squirmed and squeezed her hand in his sleep.

She pulled him close.

By midnight, at the cathedral, six deputy U.S. marshals had already taken up positions in three teams. They covered the church's main and side doors, including the door leading out of the sacristy to the south lawn. Each was armed. Each had a radio and a headset. Each understood the critical nature of his assignment.

There would be no mistakes.

Inside, state and local police nervously eyed the capacity crowd that was still moving in to fill all three aisles and jostle into dark, wooden pews that were already humming with quiet conversation. The heavy federal presence made the veterans of the force even more apprehensive than they might have been otherwise.

By 2:00 A.M., in the center of the sanctuary, ten feet in front of the main altar, the soft light of candles already glowed from two tall, gold-leafed stands, as the harsh lights of television cameras lining the outer walls were being tested.

By 3:00, the casket holding the body of the senator from Ohio had been put into place near the main altar. His family members, frightened and desperately uncertain, along with selected local and federal political figures, hovered nearby, trying their best to support one another in this excruciatingly tense time in their lives.

All they could do now was wait.

Behind the casket, on the north side of the sanctuary, a discreet, seven-member choir was already gathering while an instrumental ensemble to their right side began to softly play Bach's *Sleepers Awake*.

By 4:00, other invited guests of honor were safely moved into their reserved seating, including Mrs. Welz and Mrs. Koyievski, who were still healthy after their own healings from cancer at Fremont Hospital, plus select parishioners from St. Veronica's Church and the school staff. Behind them, a pressing crowd of hundreds more, many of them practically shivering with a palpable sense of anticipation, pushed through the now-opened doors and raced, some of them running, to find seats where they could easily see the casket.

Something extraordinary was about to happen, they were sure. It was in the air. Something beyond anything they could have ever imagined was possible.

Outside the building, the crowd was already swelling well past the hundreds. They pressed toward the church entrances from every side, ebbing and flowing in the streets and now over the parking lots and nearby lawns. Half a dozen hymns could be heard from patches among the crowd at the same time. Dozens of people claiming to know God well mounted their boxes or coolers and preached loudly to their nearest captive clusters, two of them with bullhorns. Police with loudspeakers reminded the crowd at three-minute intervals to remain orderly and stay behind the barricades. Sirens whooped intermittently, and spotlights swooped in scrambled patterns, helping to maintain order, if not calm, and to keep a two-lane path on Woodward Avenue from the cathedral to the Davison Expressway clear for the boy who was going to change everyone's life forever.

Nearer to the cathedral doors, on both the front and south side of the church, teams of mobile announcers and camera operators and paparazzi pushed for favored positions, then found even more favorable positions and pushed again. Camera lights and hand mikes were everywhere. Reporters had their pick of middle-of-the-night interviews from people who had come for a piece of history and a piece of eternity on this extraordinary morning in Detroit. Overhead, two commercial blimps, which had been commissioned to hover a quarter mile south of the cathedral, broadcast it all to a watching world from a vantage point that one of their announcers suggested was "just a little bit closer to heaven".

On the darkened south lawn of the cathedral, in what had been the only motionless spot on the grounds, five federal agents approached the archdiocesan helicopter, which had been resting silently, like a great insect, its hard body black with white markings, its thin wings long and slightly bent and very still, waiting.

They abruptly opened the helicopter door. IDs were shown. A few words exchanged, quietly but sharply. The pilot was ushered out and led away. He was complaining, but not loudly. Two private security guards that had been hired to stand guard against vandals, but not against agents of the federal government, rushed inside to whisper in alarm to the rector of the cathedral, or to someone, at least to one of the ushers near the doors, what was happening.

In the meantime, a new pilot settled silently into the cockpit of the helicopter. A second federal officer climbed into the passenger seat directly behind the pilot.

The doors were closed.

Thirty seconds later, the great insect was resting again in the once again motionless spot on the great cathedral's grounds.

Twenty-Seven

Lynn and C.J. said good-bye to Nancy and Burr upstairs, in Lynn's bed-room—Lynn and Nancy with a hug and tears, C.J. and Burr with a handshake and a few smacks on the arms. When they came down, ready to leave for the cathedral, they were each carrying just one bag, an ath-letic bag for C.J. filled with music, electronic games, and clothing, and an overnight bag for Lynn that contained some clothing, some grooming items, and not much more. Their good-bye would be virtually complete.

The archdiocese's black Chrysler sedan, there to pick them up, had been pulled up to the side door. The plainclothes trooper who was to be Lynn and C.J.'s driver carried their bags to the trunk.

Circles of protection formed, protecting them as they moved sol-emnly from the safety of the house to their respective vehicles. A larger crowd than any of them had expected, made up of people who wanted to see the Lazarus Boy but didn't want to fight the thousands they knew were already ringing the cathedral, pressed tight against the flimsy tape barricades and called to C.J. in loud shouts and lilting appeals.

Candles were lit and lifted everywhere.

The crowd roared as Joe, Lynn, and C.J. hustled across the few feet from their side door and into the back seat of their waiting car. C.J.'s Red Wing cap was pulled down tightly, nearly to his eyes—a young boy in hiding. Lynn's arm was wrapped tight around his shoulder.

Shutting the door behind him, Joe peered out his window, his face tight, watching the faces in the crowd and the candles flickering in the breeze, and listening to the song that was beginning to rise and spread, replacing the shouts with a prayer. It was "Amazing Grace".

The Cardinal and Father Mark were in the sedan right behind C.J.'s; Father Mark gave the Cardinal plenty of room to himself in the backseat by riding up front with the driver.

Monsignor Tennett and Bennington Reed, he knew, had been at the cathedral all night, making sure the many arrangements would all be airtight and ready for them.

The Royal Oak officers assigned to usher the vehicles away from the house on foot scattered for their assigned positions and vehicles. Two stayed at the side door of the house, three more in the driveway, six more across the front of the house, their flashlights sweeping left and right like laser swords.

Curry started his engine. Captain Shuler was silent beside him. Their car was already in place in front of the house, ready to fall in immediately behind the Walkers.

The two lead police cruisers eased twenty yards down the street, making room for the two Chryslers to back out of the driveway.

"The Lord has promised good to me ..." swelled from the crowd over the vehicles, and candles rose higher as C.J.'s vehicle eased backward down the driveway. The police guards focused the beams of their flashlights on the Lincoln's back window, illuminating Joe, Lynn, and C.J.'s cap, which is all they could see.

The crowd pressed tighter, straining for one last glimpse, and a number of people sank to their knees.

As their car started to back down the driveway, Lynn suddenly lurched forward and shouted, "Wait!"

The trooper hit the brakes and turned to face her, startled.

She was already leaning across C.J.'s lap, reaching for the door on Joe's side. "Open the door!" she told him sharply, and then, to the driver, "Tell them just a minute. Tell them I'm sorry, but I didn't bring my family albums and videos, and I won't go without them."

Joe said, "For God's sake, Lynn!" but he swung the door open and stepped out of the car at the same time.

The two officers posted at the side of the house rushed to Joe's side, looking alarmed. Three other officers rushed up the driveway.

The driver was on his radio, his voice crisp and hard, saying, "Request officers back to the house. We've got a routine—repeat, routine—delay. The mother's going back to retrieve something. I say again: this is routine."

Joe jogged to unlock and open the side door, his free hand raised, signaling for calm. He said loudly to the approaching officers, "Give 'em one minute! Just getting one thing", and ducked inside the house.

C.J.'s red hat shined like a flame in the beams of the police flashlights as he rushed to follow his father and mother back into the house with the two officers originally posted at the side door close at his heels.

The crowd of onlookers surged forward, frightened by what might be going wrong. Some of them started asking loudly what was happening, then shouting among themselves what was happening, then crying out that something bad was happening to C.J. as their candles fell to the ground and the yellow tape strained and broke in front of them.

Curry was out of his car. He raced across the street and over the sidewalk to the lawn, thundering at the onlookers to get back and waving his arms. But his shouting and angry gestures just drove fears to a sudden fevered pitch, leaving his voice drowned out by a new surge of shouting from the crowd.

Suddenly a large man and woman stormed in front of the U.S. deputy. They were heading for the house just five feet in front of Curry. They were shouting for C.J. to come out and "please, just let us touch you!"

Curry reached for the man's shoulder, demanding that he stop, but the man wheeled suddenly to grab Curry by the arm with a strong hand and spin him around backward, shouting, "Please! Please!"

The man's wife was screaming, too, along with half a dozen other people who rushed forward from the edge of the crowd.

Captain Shuler and four Royal Oak officers collapsed on the man holding Curry, three of the officers drawing their weapons, one of them shouting the announcement of the man's arrest, along with a shouted recitation of his rights.

But the man's wife wasn't held in check. She jumped at Captain Shuler, swinging her fists against the side of his head and screaming short, furious bursts about police brutality.

A panic overtook many of the other spectators. Some of them screamed at the police to stop. A few shouted warnings about guns being drawn, one shouting, "Oh my God! They're gonna shoot us!" A few rushed forward to help their friends, cursing at the top of their voices.

The two policemen who had entered the house behind the Walkers were already about to mount the stairs in pursuit of Lynn and C.J. on the second floor behind, their weapons drawn in reaction to the shouting outside, when Joe stepped in front of them and held up his hand like a stop sign. He even reached past one officer's gun to press his palm hard against the man's chest. His tone was tight but forcibly calm, his face an intentional smile. "Give them a break, please", he said. "They'll be right down." And then, "Please! The last thing we want to have is a panic here."

The officers hesitated. They were young and uncertain, assigned to maintain order, nothing more.

Lynn shouted from upstairs, "We got 'em! We're all set!"

Their footsteps thumped in a rush down the stairs.

Outside, the man who had attacked Curry was facedown on the lawn and being handcuffed. His wife was on her knees beside him, held by two officers who were placing cuffs on her, as well, when three other women suddenly broke through the police line to march toward the deputies and the officers closest to the house. They stopped without touching the officers but were shouting at them, "Leave them alone!" "Stop this!" "What are you doing?" The police from the street were still on the lawn, holding people back, a few threatening with shouts and raised flashlights.

Joe moved away from the bottom of the stairs to make room, easing the officers back toward the kitchen. The officers hesitated for a second but then pushed past Joe to assure the mother and the boy's safety.

Lynn and C.J. were already getting into the car again by the time the two officers came out the door. Joe, just behind them, slammed the side door and followed them to the car, calling calmly as he got in, "Allllll right! Got everything she needs now. Sorry about that, but thanks a lot." Then, more quietly, to the driver, "Let's get out of here! C'mon! Let's move it!"

Curry had moved out of the now-settled group on the lawn just in time to see Joe and the others pile back into the Chrysler and the two officers in control quickly shut the sedan's back door and resume their places up front, ready to go. The engine revved. Two more women from the crowd suddenly rushed forward, trying to reach the vehicle's side. Police collapsed to restrain them as Curry raced forward shouting, "Let's go, officers! Get them on the road!"

He reached the Chysler's side as it lunged backward toward the street, and for just a moment he jogged beside it with his hand on the door, trying to peer inside, trying to make sure in the very few seconds available that the bag they were all hunched over and emptying onto their laps really did contain photo cases and home videos.

It did.

He broke from the sedan and raced to join his partner, who was already back behind the wheel of their own car with the engine running. "The guy got dirt all over my suit", he complained as he jumped into the car and slammed the door behind him. "Lucky he didn't get himself shot."

Captain Shuler grinned.

Sirens whooped under flashing reds and blues, and they pulled away.

Curry eased into a deep and determined silence. In just over fifteen minutes, he was thinking, they'd all reach the cathedral, where another and much larger crowd and the body of a dead U.S. senator from Findlay, Ohio, would be waiting for them.

"From here on out," he muttered, more to himself than to his partner, "the good guys better know what they're doing."

At 5:06, thirty-six minutes before sunrise, the motorcade pulled onto Detroit's Woodward Avenue and began crawling through a canyon of onlookers south toward the great, gray, already visible tower of the city's Blessed Sacrament Cathedral.

Cheers surged through the crowd, the largest the cathedral area had ever witnessed. Shouts and praises and pleas for help were heard. Personal cameras flashed. Spotlights converged. Video cameras swung into fresh positions. Reporters and photographers pressed forward.

The police led the way to the cathedral's northside door and pulled aside. The two Chrysler sedans eased to a stop. As the door to the first sedan opened, C.J.'s name rose from the crowd like a wave, everyone wanting a look in the predawn haze, even the policemen maintaining the barrier.

But their look was brief. Five seconds was all it took for Joe to lead the way in a dash up the seven concrete stairs and through the thick, wooden door of the cathedral. The Cardinal and the others jumped out of the second sedan and moved as quickly as they could to follow.

The long and eager reception line that began just inside the door snaked sixty feet down the side aisle of the cathedral sanctuary. Largely on the strength of the event's endorsement by the Cardinal himself, the line included the associate nuncio of the Roman Catholic Apostolic Nunciature, the Church's embassy in Washington, D.C.; four Catholic auxiliary bishops from the Detroit archdiocese; the mayor of Detroit; five members of the Detroit city council; representatives of the Michigan governor's office and the Michigan state Senate and House in Lansing; as well as key representatives of the Michigan Jewish Federation, the Michigan Council of Islam, the National Council of Churches, the Pentecostal Assembly Board for the tri-state area, and a long list of other local and out-of-state spiritual, political, business, and community leaders.

The cheers of the crowd outside seemed to surge through the walls, and, within seconds, the people pressed inside the building were also standing and applauding. Then, the congregation, as if suddenly aware again with a single mind of the sanctuary and of the dead and of the sacredness of this time and this place, fell into a hush again, leaving people to jostle silently for a better view as the choir began to sing softly, *"Amazing grace, how sweet the sound . . ."*

Camera lights flooded the reception area while the muted voices of announcers rose in the background. Then the question was heard for the first time, a question from right behind the reception line, very near the side door, in a voice a little louder than a whisper: "But where's C.J. Walker?"

Joe turned to the Cardinal, who had rushed in behind them, and spoke quickly, introducing the Cardinal to Lynn's good friend, Nancy Gould, who looked trim and formal and very much like Lynn in the dark-blue suit that was identical to the suit Lynn had worn at the house. Then he introduced C.J.'s best friend, Brendan, whose nickname was "Burr", and who was dressed in a dark-blue suit and red tie and was holding a Detroit Red Wing cap in his left hand—a boy who not only looked terrified, but, as the Cardinal and those nearest to him realized, looked very much like C.J. Walker.

A voice behind Joe demanded for all of them, "But where's C.J. Walker?"

Police and U.S. deputies' radios crackled to life.

The Cardinal looked confused and suddenly very much frightened.

Bennington Reed was the first to shout it: "But where is the boy, Christopher Walker?" There was a clear panic in his voice.

Security personnel rushed to seal the doors. Police outside rushed to the parked sedans.

Nancy and Burr eased backward. Father Mark pushed into the crowd to offer them at least a small measure of support and protection.

Eyes strained. Onlookers pressed forward. The question was asked again and again, more and more loudly, now moving like a current through the congregation, which had already passed from puzzlement to alarm.

Nancy and Burr were squeezing up the side aisle beside Father Mark to the pews filled with other parishioners from St. Veronica's parish, who moved to let them in.

Someone had Joe by the arm. It was the Cardinal. He looked like he was in a clinical state of shock.

So much at stake. Holy God! Chaos.

Joe pulled away hard, without speaking, and pushed as quickly as he could through the pressing crowd toward the two steps at the center of the sanctuary and the hand mike on the portable podium that had been readied for Auxiliary Bishop Thompson, who was going to introduce the solemn prayers preceding the resurrection event. He grabbed the mike and shouted into it, "I have an announcement to make!" But the mike wasn't yet turned on.

He flipped it over and fumbled to click on the two switches. He wished his heart wasn't pounding so hard, and then he shouted again, this time in an amplified voice broadcast to the whole world, "I have an announcement to make!"

Cardinal Schaenner took three shuffling steps toward the high-back, red-cushioned chair that had been reserved for him in the sanctuary, then he stopped. He reached for the arm of Monsignor Tennett and held on. He was staring at Joe, dazed and terrorized by the unthinkable disaster unfolding like the apocalypse before his eyes.

From the pews, again and again, and now from the dead man's horrified family: "But where's C.J. Walker?"

Joe, his voice shaking as he reached to pull a letter from his back pocket, said loudly, "Please let me have your attention! I have a letter to read!"

Bennington Reed had moved to the center aisle, his eyes raging with shock and anger, knowing now exactly what had happened and certain that he knew how, certain that the treasonous switch was all tied to the criminal Mr. Anthony Cross—all those people on the lawn screaming and causing so much confusion, and the new blue suits delivered to Lynn and C.J. being duplicated in the same delivery for the Gould woman and her damnable son, with them looking so much like Lynn and C.J., with their hair even cut differently now, and the woman's hair colored lighter to make her resemblance to Lynn even more striking. He was not only certain of the treason, but he was certain that both Father Cleary, a priest, for heaven's sake, and C.J.'s own father were behind it. And, in fact, he was also certain that Joe had probably orchestrated it—Joe Walker, with his sneaky mind so hard at work to make money, now arranging to let a criminal steal away the world's most important child in two thousand years.

He felt suddenly overcome by the sacrilege of it all, by the outrage he was witnessing, by the breaking of the holy covenant, by the depth and darkness of the loss being announced in this holy place to all of humanity by this treacherous snake of a father.

His eyes glistened. He struggled for breath. He worked to keep from screaming.

Joe had the open letter in his left hand. He began to read it as loudly as he could. "This is a letter from C.J.'s mother, Mrs. Lynn Walker. It reads: 'I want to express my deepest grief and compassion for the family of Senator Thessler, and to give my heartfelt apologies not only to them but to Cardinal Schaenner, whom I respect very much, and to everyone who is watching and waiting all over the world.'"

He glanced up quickly and nervously. Cardinal Schaenner. Reed. Father Mark. The police. All the priests. All the dignitaries. All the people. All of them gaping, still unbelieving. But not for long; he knew that.

"'There will not be another resurrection involving my son, C.J. Walker'", he read. He wished his voice wasn't shaking.

"'C.J. and I thank God for the gift given to our friend Marion Klein, to Mr. Galvin Turner, to Anthony Cross Jr., and to Mrs. Welz and Mrs.

Koyievski. But we believe that true gifts are given without demands. We believe this because we believe in the goodness of the Giver, who has given me my first responsibility of loving C.J., and of protecting him from being used or manipulated in whatever way I can.

"'I believe with all my heart that this is what I am now doing. I believe that I have no choice but to do it in this way, and that no other way is open to me. I am trying, in the best way I know how, to protect my son from what other people would make him do and make him become simply to pursue their own interests and their own visions, however well intentioned they might seem.

"'With that in mind, C.J. and I have gone. We will not be back. And if God is willing to let us get away safely and to live without interference, anonymously, in some other place, we ask everyone who hears this letter to please be willing to do the same.'"

Joe paused; then he read Lynn's last words. "'We ask that God bless you. And we ask you, if you would, to pray for us, as we will be praying for you.'" He looked up. He pressed the microphone even closer to his lips. He said, "This letter is signed by both of them: Mrs. Lynn Walker and Christopher Walker."

He lowered the letter. He lowered the mike.

He knew that the silence that still gripped the stunned congregation would shatter in a matter of seconds, and he knew that its shattering would be terrible. He sought out some other place to look, somewhere other than right into their eyes. He noticed the saints and the angels in the windows above him, noticed them already beginning to lighten, and he realized that it was almost sunrise and that Lynn and C.J. and Cross and his friends had gained enough time to get away safely, and he was glad. More than glad, he felt proud standing tall in the face of so much shock and outrage. He had actually done something heroic. He had come through for his son and for Lynn like a champion, and he knew it.

He also knew something of the price that he had paid for their freedom. But he didn't know all of it.

As he lowered his eyes he heard the crowd begin to murmur like a single, living thing, and then he saw Reed's hand rising to point at him. Something in it. What the hell? He froze, holding his breath, watching Reed cry out his name, not "Joe" but "Mr. Walker!" Then Reed's hand jumped once, twice, three times, quickly.

The first bullet shattered Joe's rib and drove through his right lung directly next to his sternum, sending his arms flying and the mike clattering to the floor in front of him. The second splintered the tip of Joe's jawbone and snapped his head sharply backward just before his body hit the marble floor fifteen feet in front of the still-dead body of Senator Paul Thessler from Findlay, Ohio.

Screams. Dreadful screams and echoes of screams, but no one moved.

Reed dropped the gun and rushed forward, his arms straight up, surrender-like, his voice shouting out that he had no gun, he had no gun, as police and federal marshals plunged toward him from the side aisles. He reached Joe's body and saw his face, not being able to avoid it, and suddenly he was crying as he saw the blood already pooling under Joe's jaw and saw the blood spattered in tiny droplets across Joe's face and saw the blood dusting his black hair like a deadly red powder, and saw his eyes, Joe's eyes, still opened wide and staring at him, disbelieving.

He choked hard and reached down, grabbing the handheld mike from the floor just as the officers and onlookers fell on him, all at once. But he was powerful, and now he was driven. He buckled into a crouch, his back to the congregation, refusing to go down and refusing to be pulled upright, protecting the mike, and then he began shouting into it. "There is no murder where there is no one dead! There is no murder where there is no intent to kill!"

The congregation was screaming and breaking into the aisles, some surging away from the horror, some surging toward it, wanting to help. The senator's wife and daughters in the first pew were standing with their faces covered, making sounds, no words.

Nine men tried to reach and pull at Reed's body. One threw an arm-lock around his neck, but he couldn't pull him upright. Reed's shout rose to a scream into the still-open mike. "Don't you see? Christopher Walker will not come back to bring back the senator from Ohio! Don't you understand? He doesn't love the senator from Ohio! But he *will* come back to bring back his own father!"

There was a sudden break in the intensity, and the men stopped trying so hard to wrestle him to the ground, an uncertain pulse, something instinctive holding them back for just a second because of what the man had just shouted into the mike.

Reed was crying so hard he was gasping for breath. "Christopher!" he wailed into the mike. "I know you can hear what's happened! Wherever they've taken you, I know that you and your mother are listening! Oh, please, son, please, come back! Hurry, C.J.! Your daddy needs you!" Then he reared back his head and screamed one more time, in terrible and genuine pain, like an animal dying, "Oh Christopher, come quickly! Your daddy is dying!"

Twenty-Eight

C.J. cried, "Mom!" and grabbed Lynn's arm. Pulling it hard he screamed again: "Mom!"

There were banging and loud voices cursing and yelling over the van's radio as Reed's microphone fell to the marble floor of the cathedral sanctuary and the guards and police wrestled him into submission. Then an announcer was shouting frantic descriptions of the shooting of C.J.'s father to his millions of radio listeners, including Lynn and C.J. and Mr. Cross and his son, Anthony Jr., who was still pale and dressed warmly but awake and alert, and Torrie Kruger, and the square-shouldered driver of the burgundy Chevy van that was carrying them south on I-75 toward Ohio, but that now lurched sharply into the far-right lane and began to slow down.

A.W. Cross had wheeled around from the middle seat to look at Lynn, who was sitting in shock next to C.J. in the far rear. Torrie Kruger turned to look at Cross, waiting for directions and hearing none. No one was speaking but C.J., who was still screaming through sudden tears, angry and disbelieving and shrill. He pulled again at Lynn's arm as hard as he could, jerking her sideways.

"Mom! He shot Dad!"

Lynn heard C.J. screaming as though he was very far away. She felt him pulling at her arm and heard him screaming, and she leaned forward, searching uncertainly for Mr. Cross, hoping in a daze that she might find Joe instead, that she might come out of all this, wake up from the madness . . .

The announcer was trying to describe the chaos surging around the man who had just shot and apparently killed the father of C.J. Walker when Lynn suddenly looked up sharply, now crying hard, and shouted, "Turn it off!"

The newsman's voice disappeared in a click, and Mr. Cross' voice took its place. "Mrs. Walker?" he said. Nothing more.

Lynn was staring at C.J., now holding him by the wrists, tight, unmoving, saying nothing as C.J. twisted and shouted at her in a hysterical pitch, again and again, "Go back! Go back! I can save him, Mom! Go back!"

It was monstrous to her, to have to go back now, when C.J. was free from them, and knowing that if he went back now he'd be taken by them. Not just taken, but they'd see him save Joe and he would never be able to escape again. It couldn't be real, but she knew that it was. She felt like she could hardly breathe.

"Mom! What are you doing? We have to go back!"

Cross spoke. "You're going back, Mrs. Walker?" Hard words spoken softly.

She felt undone. She felt like she was going to faint, but refused to give in to it.

She started to cry, hard, and closed her eyes when she said it. "We have to go back."

C.J. stopped screaming. Mr. Cross put his hand on Lynn's arm and squeezed her lightly. She heard Kruger calling 911, saying, "C.J. Walker is in a burgundy Chevy van, Michigan plate 485-YVJ. I'm calling from that van. We're pulling off southbound I-75 at Sibley Road and will be heading north on I-75 from Sibley in thirty seconds. We're requesting an immediate police escort to Blessed Sacrament Cathedral."

Lynn had not yet opened her eyes.

Joe recognized Father Mark; his face was very close.

The priest had his arm under Joe's head, holding it up and cradling it in his lap as he kneeled in the blood on the hard marble floor and bent down closer to Joe, his soft words speaking encouragement.

Joe heard other voices, too, and then he felt hands tearing open his shirt and knew it must be the medical support team that had been stationed at the back of the church to take care of the senator from Ohio, just in case—the senator who would not need them now.

Pain began to vibrate like a bell thick in his chest, hurting so terribly, all of a sudden; and then his chin, and jaw, and in fact, the whole bottom half of it; and then his whole head, like he'd caught on fire, but he couldn't move his arms to put it out.

He started to cry. He tried to stay conscious and concentrate on what was happening, and he started to cry. He realized he'd been shot, but he didn't remember falling. He remembered Reed shouting his name. Was it really Reed that shot him?

Past the face of Father Mark and beyond the faces of the medical team he could see the stained glass windows of the cathedral glowing now with vivid angels and saints in blues and reds and yellows and greens, some with crowns, some standing over demons that cowered at their feet, trying to hide, others on clouds, victorious and rising.

He tried to stare at them and not at the faces around him, but he was so afraid. And it was so hard to breathe. And it hurt so bad.

Then other people were there, their voices sounding farther away from Joe than their faces, their hands pressing against him where the fire was calming down now, and he began to say to himself over and over, "This has really happened. This has really happened. This has really happened." And he started to cry harder, thinking about C.J. And he thought, I don't want to die.

He wanted to scream it, to them or to God or to everyone everywhere. This wasn't right! What the hell is this? He didn't want to be the one that had to stay dead!

The first police cruiser pulled alongside the van as it swept down from the entrance ramp to I-75 North and headed back toward Detroit and the cathedral, just minutes away. The driver of the van nodded at the cruiser. The officers demanded to see the boy.

C.J. peered out and stared, looking terrified, trying not to cry. The officer covered the boy's face with the beam of his flashlight and waved the van on.

Two cruisers pulled ahead, two more dropped back to ride behind, lights flashing, sirens wailing. Others sped even farther ahead to join cruisers that were now dropping down from distant cross streets to clear any potential roadblocks. News helicopters roared south to pick up the early-morning caravan with long lenses and chattering on-board announcers. The camera of the commercial blimp was able to find them first because the early-morning light had improved.

It was nearly sunrise.

Joe was secured to the stretcher. His heart was racing but beating softly. He saw that Mark was very close again, and he fought to stay focused, to not pass out. He heard the medical staff's final directions. They were going to move him out as fast as they could.

But other noises were sounding, too, noises from the crowd. All of a sudden people in the cathedral were calling out things that he could not make out, and he heard radios, too. He wondered where Reed was, and he wondered how far C.J. had gotten, and he strained to find the saints and the angels again, and then he heard sirens, and Mark was shouting, "C.J. is coming back, Joe. He's on his way back. He's almost here!"

The stretcher had stopped moving. Joe struggled to take in what was happening. He wondered, flashing in and out of the thought in a heartbeat, what that would be like, to die and then not be dead anymore because of C.J., like Marion. She knew.

But C.J. was coming back! And Joe thought, No! No! No!

In a wave of clarity he suddenly experienced a terrible wave of grief as deep as his soul. C.J. was going to be taken away by them, after all. C.J. was going to come and be taken and held and used and never let go. And it was not a senator from Ohio that was springing the trap on him; it was Joe himself!

The roar surged skyward and rippled west and north as the crowd on the south side of the cathedral heard the sirens and now saw the lights of the approaching police cars and finally saw the van that they knew carried the boy that was stronger than death. Another three minutes more, and he would be with them again, maybe less.

C.J. Walker. He was coming!

The sirens sounded loudly through the cathedral's open doors at the same time that the roaring cheers sounded from the crowd outside. The congregation inside had turned like one living thing to face the doors. A few of them joined in the cheers from outside. Some called out short prayers of thanksgiving, others whispered them. Some cried. All of them were standing, watching, holding their breath.

One man in the medical crew argued that they had to leave with Joe now; another, on the radio with Henry Ford Hospital, argued for "less than a minute" and began pressing tape on Joe's face to better hold the padding in place against his jaw.

Joe urged Mark closer. His struggled to move. "Tell C.J. to keep going", he whispered. "Please. Tell him to stay away."

"He's here, Joe", Mark said, confused.

"Oh God."

"He's right outside."

"Help me to do this, Mark."

Mark nestled his forehead against Joe's. His eyes filled with tears.

Joe stared past him at the stained glass angels and saints shining in the sunrise. "Tell God not to let me come back", he whispered faintly. "No matter what C.J. does, let me stay there."

He closed his eyes and let go at the same time someone in the open door of the cathedral shouted, "He's here! C.J.'s here!"

The crowd pressed to stand even higher on the kneelers and move even more tightly into the aisles; everyone straining, the senator's family included, pressed around the dead man's casket, standing on tip-toes.

It was miracle time.

"Dad!" C.J. had jerked free of Lynn and was racing up the main aisle, crying. Lynn was rushing to stay with him, pushing back at people who pressed too close, trying hard to be at C.J.'s side when he first saw his dad up close, but she wasn't fast enough.

There was absolute silence now. Everyone was quiet except C.J., who shouted, "Daddy!" He stopped abruptly at the first pew, his mouth hanging open, his eyes on the stretcher, and on his father, and on the priest, whom he knew, standing next to his dad and looking like he was crying, too.

He saw his father's mouth open and his jaw padded with bloody ban-daging. He saw his shirt open, and more bloodied bandaging. And he saw his jaw. And he saw blood. And he saw his dad's arms, lying limp, and his hands, and his lips. And he saw his eyes closed. He reached out for his mother's hands and started crying harder as Lynn went to her knees and held him close. The force of the terrible sight had undone him. He shuddered and shook his head and wailed softly in the shelter of his mother's arm, his breath coming in quick, high-pitched gasps.

Lynn held her breath, her mouth hanging open. Joe was dead, and she had no idea what was coming next.

Monsignor Tennett approached to cover Joe to the neck with a white vestment from the sacristy. Another priest helped him spread it out. Mark faded back to the side, his eyes on Lynn and C.J.

There wasn't a sound in the church.

Lynn leaned her head against C.J. and said breathlessly, "Oh C.J. You're going to be okay, honey. You're going to be okay."

But C.J. had seen the blood, and now he saw the new, white vest-ment growing small, dark circles of red, as well. And he felt the press of the crowds and saw the people staring and the lights bright, with the air thick and heavy, and with everyone watching on TV, and even all the kids from school watching. He suddenly felt the room spinning and fading away, and he knew that he was going to faint, which he had done once before when they thought he had scarlet fever. But he didn't want to faint. He willed himself not to faint, not now, and not to be sick. He forced himself not to faint or be sick but to stand up straight and swallow the sounds of his own crying, because his dad was dead and he had to help him.

He was the only one who could.

Lynn was staring at Joe, trembling under the weight of everything having gone so wrong. She looked to the side and saw the family of the man from Ohio in the first pew to her right, the wife staring back at her, looking terrified and utterly spent. The dead man's two daughters each had an arm around their mother, trying hard to protect her from any more pain. Lynn moved her gaze to the left and saw the Cardinal standing in front of a tall, red chair in the sanctuary. She saw him struck with fear himself, and not moving, with Monsignor Tennett at his side once again. She saw the police and the cameras and the people who had come to put on robes and sing in the choir.

Everyone was staring back at her, and staring at C.J., and waiting.

And then she saw Bennington Reed, who was still inside the north exit in his dark silk suit with his hands cuffed behind him, now surrounded by police who wanted to see for themselves, almost as badly as Reed himself wanted to see, whether there was going be a charge of murder or not.

For a brief and terrible second, their eyes met: Reed's desperate and eager, pleading for Lynn and her son to save him, hers dark and fiercely unforgiving.

And then, moving suddenly, C.J. pulled away from her grip and moved forward.

Lynn forced her legs to move with her son. Her hand found his shoulder again. They walked slowly, inching closer together.

C.J. stood staring down at Joe for a long moment, saying nothing, not moving. Lynn knelt down. It just seemed like what she should do. But her hand never left C.J.'s arm.

Every camera was broadcasting, but every news announcer was silent. Every person in the congregation was silent. Most of the crowd outside was silent.

C.J. braced himself, anxious to have the miracle done. He shivered, then reached out with his right hand. He let his fingertips settle on his father's right shoulder. He whispered it. "Be well, Dad."

Lynn held her breath. Those closest to the mother and her son inched forward. They all waited.

Four minutes passed. Then five. Then six.

Suddenly a loud cry from near the north door broke the air above the sanctuary. Reed, who was being pulled toward the door by six officers, was crying out for more time. He was crying out again that the power was real. He was crying tears and screaming, "I would never kill Joe Walker, or kill anyone else, ever! For the love of God! What do you think I am?"

In a sudden, ferocious lunge he tried to break free and gain one more look at Joe, whose body still hadn't moved. He screamed again for the man to please wake up, and swore it would still happen—swore it, begged it, demanded it. Then the door to the church closed behind him, and Bennington Reed was gone.

Four more minutes passed.

C.J. slowly inched next to Joe again. Lynn let him go. He moved his fingers first to Joe's shoulder, and then, after a very slight hesitation, let them settle lightly on his cheek, where the skin still felt warm. He said the words again, a little louder than before. "Be well, Dad."

Lynn stiffened. He never said the words a second time.

Ten minutes, eleven minutes, twelve minutes . . .

The Cardinal saw and understood and staggered backward. One step. Two steps. He felt his chair meet his legs and he let his legs cave in until he was sitting. His right hand rose slowly to his chest, his left arm hung limp over the armrest.

The senator's wife choked with a short cry of her own and tried to get up to leave the pew. She looked frightened and confused and fiercely angry. Her children begged her to wait. How did they know how long it should take? It had just been a few minutes.

She agreed to sit down again, too much in pain to argue, but she began to cry harder, and her crying murmured throughout the pews, where the rustle of initial alarm was already changing into hard questions whispered behind cupped hands.

Lynn realized what had happened, and she wanted time. She wanted to be able to talk with C.J. about what she had realized, and she wanted to do it before the crowd and the clergy and the media stole the moment away. She wanted to tell him what Joe had done for him. She wanted to rush him away and be alone with him and remind him that in Cross' van, when they could have gotten away, C.J. chose to come back to this place that he was most afraid of because he wanted, even more than he wanted to be okay himself, to help his dad. She wanted to try and explain it to him now, before they had to leave, that that's what his dad had done for him—to explain that sometimes really loving somebody else meant you had to choose not to survive yourself, because you loved them even more than you loved yourself. She wanted to try and explain that C.J. and his dad loved each other that much, and it was the most wonderful love in the world. She wanted to remind him that dead people didn't really die, and that the love that he had for his dad, and the love his dad had for him, was so strong it would never go away.

But she had no time.

Monsignor Tennett had pushed forward to ask her the question they all wanted to ask. He said, "Is it not going to happen?" He tried to sound strong and stable, but he sounded frightened because he was.

C.J. pressed into her side, and Lynn shook her head so slightly that the priest barely noticed the motion. But he understood her words. She whispered, "We're sorry."

The air exploded behind them. There was a single, sharp cry; first one, and then others. Confused and grieving expressions and short, agonized prayers rose in a muted chorus.

Mark stepped forward. His arm went around C.J.

The senator's wife stood, suddenly shaking. She shouted out loud to the Cardinal, who was still crumbled in his red chair, far back in the sanctuary, about how terrible this was for her and her family and everyone. Nearly hysterical, she fought off her children's attempts to quiet her. How terrible that her poor husband's body had been subjected to this. How terrible this hoax was. How terrible this memory would be for all of them, for all of their lives. Then, moaning under the sudden recognition of crushing public mortification, she pushed her way frantically out of the front pew as seven horrified Chancery representatives closed in to huddle around her, trying frantically not only to keep up with her but to comfort and quiet her down.

Nancy Gould elbowed through the crowd to join Lynn and C.J. Burr was pressed tight to her side.

In the pews and in the aisles, some cried with disappointment; some slunk backward, feeling sorry and embarrassed for everyone, including themselves; some explained through thin and humorless smiles that they knew all along, of course, that it could not possibly be true; some simply ached with sympathy for the boy and his mother and for the wife and family of the senator from Ohio, and even for the Church, and for the Cardinal himself.

The word "hoax" passed from pew to pew like a weapon.

In the sanctuary, the Cardinal sat bending forward in the chair reserved for his presence; he was a man devastated. He did not move. He just continued to stare silently in the direction of the spot on which Joe died, his expression pressed blank by the weight of so much that he had hoped for, so utterly destroyed.

Deputy U.S. Marshal Paul Curry stood grimly against the north wall of the sanctuary, his eyes half-closed, his expression drained. His radio was crackling with words he could ignore, and he did ignore them. It had been real and he knew it. And now it was gone. And he knew that, too.

Ruth Cosgrove and the nearly two dozen other reporters relaying the events over the air had the most difficult job. They were passing along the news that no one was coming back to life in this place. Not the senator. Not even the Lazarus Boy's own father.

It was a dreadful announcement to have to make. It meant that the approaching death of themselves, and the death of every one of their listeners and every one of their viewers, was going to be irrevocable after all.

C.J. Walker would not be there to save them.

Mark approached. When Lynn was ready to move back from the body, he wanted to be there for her and C.J. both. She hesitated. She knew that when she moved, it would be her last good-bye. She would not go to a wake service. She would not go to a funeral Mass. She would not face more TV cameras and lights and crowds and questions. She would not see Joe's face again in her lifetime, not after this moment, and neither would C.J.

C.J. knew it, too. He looked at his father. He touched him, and even whispered the words one more time, but he knew the power was gone. He started crying again, silently. And, again, Lynn pulled him close.

The medical crew and police moved up, now standing ready, but without insistence.

Nevertheless, the message was clear. Science was back in charge.

Twenty-Nine

They walked behind the slowly moving stretcher toward the front door—a long walk through deepening silence. The crowd that had spilled from the pews opened to let them pass, then closed behind them again like the sea.

Lynn turned very slightly toward Mark, who had stayed by her side in so many ways. "What will they do?" she asked in a sad whisper. "I mean, to you?"

"Nothing", he said quietly. "I was a good priest today. Better than I have been in a long time. I'll be fine, I promise."

She said, "I'm sorry."

He shook his head. He said, "For twenty years, I've doubted I'd ever see a miracle. Today I got to hold one in my own hands."

She leaned forward and hugged him lightly. Then she found his hand, and, without another word, she squeezed her thank you and her good-bye.

And in that moment, and with that gesture, as she said good-bye to Mark and turned to watch Joe's body gliding down the aisle in front of her and she saw the pews and so many familiar faces easing out of her sight on both sides, it struck her how very much she was saying good-bye to, in so many ways.

She was saying good-bye to the unpredictable love of the husband who had once owned her heart, and who had so unexpectedly given everything up for the son he really did come to love even more than himself. She was saying good-bye to all her dearest friends. She was saying good-bye to her home and to all the places and sights and sounds that had been hers for all of her life, because she would never come back again—not now. She and C.J. would leave with Mr. Cross and they would find a new home and a new life far away from this place where even the power of life over death could be twisted into something deadly by people with visions of their own.

More than all of that, she realized that she was saying good-bye to the nine-year-old boy that had once been hers, but who would never be a little boy again. Because from this moment on, she knew, C.J. would be changed. He would never again be the same as he was when she asked him to go to Mrs. Klein's funeral with her, so very long ago.

And he would still wonder, for all of his life; she knew that, too. Even if this was really the end of it, even if God was satisfied that none of us was ready for this Final Power and no one ever appeared again to shake the dead loose from their sleep with a word and a touch, even if no one appeared to remind C.J. that it once had been him, even then, every time C.J. stepped on an ant or slapped a mosquito, he would wonder. Every time he saw a friend die, for all of his life, he would wonder. And when she died herself, whenever that would be, he would do more than wonder. At that time, she knew, he would try again.

In fact, she thought, she would wonder, too, every day of her life.

She would wonder how right she had been to fight against the power that her son had not asked for and that neither of them could understand. And she would wonder what might have been.

They were near the door. She reached out and held the stretcher and said, "Wait. Please."

They did.

Familiar words and phrases echoed like whispers in her mind as she bent to say her last good-bye, and they lingered: words like "Resurrection Day" and "raising Lazarus" and "humanity's rising to become something divine".

She hovered close to Joe, and with a sudden conviction beyond words it struck her that it had happened after all. It had. A real Rising that not even death could reclaim again, as it would certainly come back to someday reclaim Marion Klein and Galvin Turner and young Anthony Cross. Another small part of humanity had really become divine.

She closed her eyes and held them closed tightly for a long moment, saying good-bye to Joe; then she opened them slowly to look again through fresh tears at her once-closest friend and at what he had chosen to become for his son and for her. She brushed Joe's black hair with her fingertips. She touched his cheek one last time, bent to kiss him lightly on the eyes, and said good-bye beneath the shining Jesus and the soaring angels and the multicolored saints that celebrated high above her in that time and in that place, and in every time and in every place, with all the highest angels of our nature, the gift of our rising from the dead.

The crowd outside pressed closer, ready for C.J.'s exit. The heavy pulse of the police helicopter sounded overhead. The voices of reporters and photographers rose and fell as they raised their microphones and cameras and surged forward, banks of them.

Cardinal Schaenner was suddenly there, touching Lynn's arm, his face like a death mask. His eyes were clouded with a grief all his own, but he asked no questions and he made no demands. "We still have the helicopter ready", he said softly. "Our helicopter, our pilots. I don't think you can take your son through that crowd."

She stared at him.

He said, "There's room for Mr. Cross and his son, too. And Father Mark. The Crosses are in the back of the church." He was looking with anguish at Joe but he continued speaking to her, still very softly. "Father Mark can have you taken to St. Mark Seminary if you like", he said. "The grounds are secure, so you'll at least be able to make plans there. And stay there for as long as it takes. And leave whenever you want. And I'll be in contact to see if there's anything more I can do."

They were both silent for a long moment; then he raised his eyes to look at her again, his lips pressed together in a thin line. He shook his head slowly, withdrew his touch from her arm, and said it again. "I'm so sorry. We all are."

As the helicopter rose over the cathedral, Lynn and C.J. watched the people in the streets below working themselves toward the vehicles that would snake them ever so slowly back to the way their lives and their deaths had always been.

They had said good-bye to the Cardinal and to the small cluster of friends who had come from their church and who had pressed forward to hug and cry with them as they left, and to Nancy and Burr, who had been such good friends through it all, and whom they could only stay in touch with now from a distance.

Lynn's arm was around C.J., who was next to the window, and who, despite his mother's soft words on the way out of the church, still looked devastated by his failure. But it was not a time for more words. Not yet. It was a time for things much deeper than words.

Mark sat across from C.J., next to Mr. Cross. Anthony Jr., who had also tried to encourage C.J. on the way to the helicopter, and to befriend him, sat on the other side of his father.

Lynn leaned past C.J. to look out the window as the helicopter continued to rise. All those people, she thought. So many people. And so many of them watching the helicopter as it circled higher, and still reaching up to point after them, as though they were holding up needs to C.J. that had not been met and would never go away.

She stared over the edge of the city to the east, where the sun was already large and clear of the horizon; then she looked again at the cathedral and its towers and whispered in a nearly silent breath, "Thank you, Joe."

Only C.J. heard her. He turned to face her, wondering.

She took his cheeks in her hands and kissed him on the eyes and on his forehead. It would take time, she knew, but it would come. Someday he would look back on Joe and on this day and on this place, and he would understand how much he had been loved here, and still was.

She breathed, "I love you, C.J.", and slowly eased her face away from his.

He turned from her, also very slowly, and leaned to his right to look outside. His forehead was resting on the window.

Then she heard him whisper it. To himself, to the people in the streets below, maybe even to his dad, who had gone way beyond the waiting place, she heard C.J. whisper, "We don't really die. That's the gift."

She pressed her lips softly against her son's warm hair.

The helicopter banked and headed toward the east, where, over new horizons not far away, the sun was always rising.